1

# 24

Rosalind M. Miller

4

## Dedication

This book is wholeheartedly dedicated to my 3 most favourite people.
My Parents and my Husband.

To George & Audrey Miller.

I would dearly have loved for you both to have been here….to share in my joy.
I hope that I have made you very proud.

I love and miss you both incredibly so - every day….
……with all of my heart.

"Your baby did it..!!"


To my Husband – Jonny.

Without you,
I would be a leaf in the wind.

You calm my soul…..you are my song, my dance, my
sleep, my whole world….
…..and I could never be without you.

Always, Forever, and Beyond.
Thank you darling, for your continued support….. I couldn't have done it without you.
…..and thank you for all of your Love…..

….I Love You….

"....a story that engages your imagination like no other.
Beautifully written; both heart-rending and heart lifting.
....Unforgettable....

Ghost Reader

"....A page turner that takes you on a magical journey, and presses
the button of every emotion in its reader.
It stretches your imagination to believe beyond
what you thought possible....
....and leaves you wanting, and needing another adventure....
.....with the fantastical character, of Mary..."

*Speech & Drama Teacher*

"....INCREDIBLE.... is the word I need to describe this magical
fantasy novel. A true page turner; full of love, greed, mystical
escapism; and with the most
intricate detail, that won't allow you to put the book down...!!..."

*NHS Nurse*

"...Very well written, and completely engrossing.
A fantasy - with wonderfully placed hints of humour; and with meticulous attention to
detail.
This book will definitely leave you wanting more...!"

*Housewife & Accounts Administrator*

"...I could not put this book down....
If you like a cliff hanger, page turner, mythical fantasy fiction,
AND....a time travelling novel....
...this book is for you...!!!

F.C. Jones – Business Owner

"...a story, wonderfully told...
Captivating and intriguing..."

Ghost Reader

## The Chapters                                          Page No:

# Character Pronunciation List

| | |
|---|---|
| Endor Dornc Le Fey | En-daw Dawn Le Fey |
| Agnes Sagen Le Fey | Ag–n's Say–gn Le Fey |
| | |
| Eldon Donel Le Fey | El–d'n Donn'l Le Fey |
| | |
| Ooshiya-Lion | Oosh – eea - Lion |
| Magnus Gunsam Le Fey | Mag-n's Gun-sam Le Fey |
| Bridget Begdirt Bishop | Brid-jit Beg-durt Bishop |
| Rubec Bruce Le Fey | Roo-Bek Bruce Le Fey |
| | |
| Therian Rathnie Le Fey | The-Ree-'n Rath-ni Le Fey |
| Celeste Selcete Fallswood | Sell-est Sell-ket Fallswood |
| Samuel Elmaus Le Fey | Sam–yu-ell El–may-uss Le Fey |
| Abigail Gilibaa Osbourne | Abbi-gale Gil-i-bar Osbourne |
| | |
| Sorcier Resoric Le Fey | Sore-see-air Rez-oric Le Fey |
| Omega Mogea Gata | A'meega Mog –aya Gay-ta |
| Kairos Soriak Gata | Ky-Ross Saw-Rye-Ak Gay-ta |
| | |
| Cubre the Cat | Koo-Bray |
| Beruc the Dragon | Bare-Ruke |
| Tufri the Fruit Bat | Tuff-ri |
| Luci the Firefly | Loo-si |
| The Oreads | The Orry-ads |
| The Satyrs | The Sat-ears |
| Mr Bercu | Mr Bur-koo |
| Taurus Saturu Fallswood | Taw-Russ Sat-Oo-Roo Fallswood |
| Uber-C the Fox | Oo-bur-see |
| Edward Drewad Le Fey | Edward Droo–ad Le Fey |
| | |
| Viktor Rivkot Bishop | Vik-ta Rivcot Bishop |
| Sailen Alenis Cripp | Say-l'n Allennis Cripp |

Vagust Tusgav Bishop — Va-gust Tuss-gav Bishop
Moroi Romio Bishop — Mor-oy Rom-yo Bishop

Fiedric Rifecid Fallswood — Feed-rik Riff-a-sid Fallswood
Yggdrasil Skau Borson — Igg–dra-sil Skow Borson
Orlane Noelra Fallswood — Or-lane No-ell-ra Fallswood

Dreegar & Ivan — Dree-gar & I-v'n

Strigoi Grisoti Bishop — Strig-oy Griz-otti Bishop
Daciana Caandia Lycan — Dassi-arna Carn-dia Lie-can
Tohrdin Indroth Bishop — Tor-din In-droth Bishop
Madrig Gridam Bishop — Mad-rig Grid-am Bishop
Dorthian Riantohd Cripp — Door-thean Ree-an-tod Cripp
Demelza Lazmede Tempest — D'melza Laz-meed Tempest
Veikr Keriv Cripp — Vike-a Keriv Cripp

# 24

## FORWARD

*

In the garden, and around where 'Tree Stump Corner' is; lends itself to being – well…..quite an unusual, but an exceptionally practical, but more importantly - a very magical and busy place to live – but with much intrigue and deception…..

I wanted to call it that because it does remind me very, very much of a small garden I used to have many years ago……

Anyway, Tree Stump Corner is tucked away at the very top right hand corner of a large country garden. The garden in question; and what happened there……….well, I'll leave that for now, and let's get on with the story…..

# Chapter 1

# **The Happening**

<u>Monday 1<sup>st</sup> August 1864</u>

The day in question, had been an exceptionally hot one, given that it was the height of the summer, and there hadn't been a cloud in the sky - all day. It had also been a very peaceful and quiet day across the meadow and down by the stream, in this old Yorkshire village - apart from the Farmers, who were endlessly and tirelessly working the fields.

As the sun, mercilessly continued to beat down upon the exhausted meadow, the ground became conspicuously harder, due to the lack of rain, and the air was very still. It had also been a very notably dry year so far; the main drought period being from mid-April, right up to present; and the hot August sun, certainly wasn't taking any prisoners.

The local Farmers, who tended to all the surrounding fields, which went far beyond the meadow, and across from the stream; had found it extremely difficult and labour intensive, trying to pull their horses across the dry land, to plough all the fields. All they wanted was a bit of rain, as it would certainly help the summer crop of corn.

What no one expected that very night; was one of the biggest freak rain storms for many years…...

At exactly 11pm that night, a slight breeze had picked up across the meadow, which gently blew through the trees, causing the trees to make a rustling sound, as their dry leaves upon the branches, swept backwards and forwards.

Down on the ground, a gentle wind began to whip up the arid land all around the fields and across the meadow.
As it grew in strength, it swiftly picked up and swirled the dry earth, around and around in small circles, which, after a few moments, caused quite a fierce dust storm, making visibility, if anyone was to have been out in it – extremely

difficult, as it would most certainly have blinded them, and steered a weary traveller completely off track – especially in the dark.

Here and there – large droplets of rain had started to pitter-patter. A few moments later, the drops of rain came down a little faster and faster. Within seconds, it was raining so hard; that the noise coming from the ground bore resemblance to that of a quick succession of beating drums. Steam rose from the ground, as the cool rain penetrated the warm, dry soil; but the wind had suddenly turned quite fierce, and was now billowing and churning. The rain - was now torrential, and the mass of water soon soaked the parched land, and puddles began to appear, as the deluge created mudslides which were moving at a fast pace.

The biggest flash of lightening tore across the meadow, lighting the fields up for a split second.

The horses and the cattle in the various barns and out buildings were nervously moving around, as the storm reached its peak. The thunder and lightning together, crashed again and again, like they were fighting one another, and chasing each other across the sky!

The storm raged on for only a matter of minutes, but caused much devastation to the land and the out buildings around the fields, and especially near the meadow.

What was once, only a few minutes before, a tiny stream; had now quickly grown into a racing flood. The quickened and afraid pace of the swollen stream, now brussened with leaves, twigs, branches and mud; was hurtling wildly, as if running away from the storm itself. The swell had brought the torrent up to the banks, and it was now seeping out onto the land.

Most of the fences had snapped and broken with the wind…..and lain strewn and forlorn.

The farmers woke early the next morning to complete and utter havoc. The storm had caused much devastation, and they were horrified at the sight that met their eyes. They spent most of their precious time, trying to fix the broken fences, herding the cattle and horses, and nailing down the roofs of the barns. It took quite some time to get things back to some kind of working order; and although there had been much destruction, they were in fact, very grateful for the rain, as this made the ground perfect for sewing.

What no one was aware of - was that during the night; a certain 'something' had taken place amidst the storm – 'something' that no one saw, or even heard. In fact, the storm was an integral part and an immeasurable cover, for what had REALLY taken place that night.....

It was called 'The Happening'.......

# Chapter 2

# **The Summer of 1993**

When Mary and James moved into number 24 Copley Lane Meadow, they couldn't quite believe their luck, as this was going to be their very first REAL home together. They had been searching for an old cottage in the countryside for quite some time, but now suddenly, this one had come up for sale.

Mary's love for the outdoors, and her thoughts of a cottage in the suburbs with a large country garden, had been her dream for a very long time – and now it was beginning to come true.

James had been working for the Government for a few years, and had quite an important job in the city centre; but the hustle and bustle of daily life, and living in an apartment in the city, along with the noise of the daily traffic, were becoming too much for Mary. She was finding it more and more difficult to concentrate on her work. She liked the freedom of working from home, at her arts and crafts business, but she was distracted with the continuous sound of car horns beeping, and the rumbling noise from the big lorries, and the buses droning on and on outside. Shutting the balcony doors was the only way to block out the sound – so she felt trapped.

More and more she longed for the peacefulness of the countryside, and all the smells and sounds that she had vague memories of as a child. Mary had discussed with James, from the start of their relationship that she eventually wanted to move back to the countryside. James hadn't been too keen on the idea, as he liked working close to home, but this had caused quite a few arguments between them both. Mary would storm off and bang the door, and James would be left with his hands in the air.

James worked as a Field Agent, and his job was very important - and top secret, which he never spoke of. Sometimes, he would have to fly to another country at a moment's notice – which left Mary sat in the apartment in the city, sometimes for a month at a time. The apartment they lived in was quite swanky, and really spacious. It was also very well equipped, and they had everything they needed....but she still felt trapped.

Mary had made the apartment very homely, and had filled it with lots of her favourite things – which were very reminiscent of her family home as a child. Lots of artefacts were dotted about the apartment, that had come from her Mother's side of the family, like an old fashioned biscuit tin which once belonged to Mary's Grandmother's, that Mary would keep lots of different coloured buttons in, like her Mum used to do. She didn't own anything at all from her Father's side of the family – she didn't know anything about them really.

Apart from the balcony to the front of the apartment, there was also a rear veranda. It was only small, but it was a little quieter than at the front, and Mary could just fit a small bistro set, comprising of two wrought iron chairs, and a little round table. She had managed to plant out a couple of big green ferns, and lots of ivy trailing over the veranda, which just gave her a sense of peace. She would often sit out on the veranda at the back, and take a glass of wine with her.

One particular day, while Mary was trying to work; the constant noise from the outside was just getting more and more on her nerves. What with people chattering and laughing, and shouting across the road to one another, and car doors slamming, plus the continuous noise from the traffic, had got Mary feeling so exasperated, plus the smell of the fumes - she just completely lost her temper, and in her frustration, she banged both her fists down hard on the table and shouted.

"I just can't bloody work like this anymore, or even LIVE like this..!! I can't even THINK straight..!! That's it – I can't take this anymore..!!"

She got up – angrily, from her chair, strode over to the bedroom, flung open the door, and banged the door so hard behind her, that a few of the bottles on her vanity unit fell over. She threw herself on the bed, and just sobbed and sobbed.

James had come home a little earlier that day, and had just walked in, as Mary had banged the bedroom door. He rushed in.

"Mary, what the hell's going on....?!! What's happened..?! Are you alright...and what are you crying for...?!!" He sat down on the edge of the bed, and tried to turn Mary over - worried that something had happened.

Mary lifted her head up from the pillow, and with an angry face and clenched teeth, she shouted.
"I am SICK of living here James….. I HATE it, and I'm not living here a moment longer than I have to…. I've had ENOUGH…!!"

She sat upright, and turned to face him.
"I'm telling you now, I can't do this any longer..!!"

James took his hand away, put his head down and sighed.

"MARY, we've been through this before…. I can't 'just leave'. I have a job here…!"

Her face, red, and mascara running down her cheeks, she got closer to James' face and said.

"Well YOU can stay here then, I'M leaving as soon as I can…!!"

She got up from the bed quickly, brushed past him in anger, and stormed off down the hall to the bathroom, and banged the door behind her. Presently James heard the taps running, and knew that Mary would feel better after a bath – she always did.

James walked slowly into the room, and sat down on the edge of the sofa, and with his elbows on his knees; he buried his face in his hands, and heaved a rather large sigh. After a few moments, he recovered himself, and run his hands through his thick mop of dark hair, and sat back in the sofa – pondering. He looked up and around at the apartment, and then dropped his head and looked at the floor. He went over the heated argument that they'd just had, which was very much like the previous heated arguments they'd had – about the same thing. He knew how much Mary wanted to go back and live in a cottage in the country; but he just didn't have that kind of money, well not yet anyway. They were desperately trying to save, but they didn't quite have enough.
He then sighed again, pushed himself up from the sofa, and walked slowly over to the kitchen whilst slackening his tie, and opening the top button on his shirt.
He opened the fridge door, took the half full bottle of white wine out, that was on the inside of the door, and reached for a glass from the cupboard. He poured a good measure out into the glass, and took a good gulp.

"Can you pour me a glass..?" Mary said quietly from behind him.

He turned around, and Mary was stood there in her pyjamas and dressing gown. She hadn't even been in the bath, but had just been sat on the edge of it, crying. As soon as they locked eyes, Mary's filled up, as the corners of her mouth went down, and more tears spilled over and down her cheeks. He put the glass down on the work top.

"Come here, come on…" he said gently – and gave her a hug.
Mary sobbed.

"I HAVE money James, you know I do..!" she cried.

"No, that's YOUR money Mary; I'm not using that. That's yours, from the sale of your Mum's house. You can spend that on whatever you like, it's MY job to look after YOU. I want to provide for you..!"

"James….." Mary answered as she drew back from him, holding both his arms. "This is 1993, not the 1960's. We do this together, even if it means that I pay for a deposit, and you give me it back when we have enough saved. I really just can't bear living here anymore…! It's like….. I don't know, just lately, I've had a really strong urge to return to the countryside. It's completely wearing me down…!" She then began crying again.

James put his arm around her shoulder.

"Come on, come and sit down. You're worrying me; I haven't seen you like this before"

He walked her over to the sofa, and sat her down. Mary was really, really upset, and James looked at her, quite concerned.

"Mary, what's going on…? It's not like you…. Has something happened..?"
He cupped both his hands on her face, and lifted her head up to look at him, as he wiped her tears away with his thumbs, and looked at her sad face.

"Mary – look at me….. What's going on…??"

Mary brought her sad eyes up to his gaze, and James looked at her searchingly, and said.

"You know that as soon as I start earning more money, we can take things further. You know that I'm working towards this promotion at work; and once I get that - (fingers crossed), it will mean an increase in my salary, more responsibilities, status within the organisation, plus benefits, so....what more can I do...?!"

Mary's eyes filled up again, and she turned away.

"James - there's nothing 'wrong' as such; and I don't know why, but all I know is that I just HAVE to, well, I WANT to.....to go back to.....to.....well, just 'go home'..."

She thought for a few moments, then stood up, straightened her dressing gown, and carried on speaking – this time, a little bolder, as she stood above James and looked him straight in the eyes, and spoke directly to him.

"Look, like I've just said James – and this is what's going to happen, ok..?. I'm going to use the money from the sale of Mum's house, and put a deposit on a cottage – when I find one that I like; and you just give me it straight back when you have it. That way, we don't have to wait and wait..... I just can't live here anymore, I've literally had enough and it's really starting to wear me down, and I feel really oppressed – I HAVE to get out...!" Mary began wringing her hands. James watched her.

Yes, Mary had a strong temper, and she wouldn't take any crap from anyone; she wasn't a pushover either, and knew what she wanted, but she was also quite laid back. This was Mary – not quite being the Mary that he knew......

Only a few days after their conversation, James' continuous hard work at his high profile job, had finally paid off, when he received the promotion he had been waiting for, which was very welcome news indeed, and not expected so soon.

When James delivered the news of his promotion to Mary, one particular Tuesday evening, her hands clasped to her face, as she searched his, with wide eyes; and exclaimed.
"Does this mean what I think it means..?!"

James gave her the biggest grin as he hugged her. He knew how much this would mean to her.
Mary gasped.

"Are we REALLY going to move to the countryside..?!" James nodded his head.

"Make sure you find one with a big garden, I know how much you love being outdoors". He smiled as Mary grabbed him the around his neck.

"Oh my God, that's made me so happy. I am so, so excited!! Thank you James – I do love you soooooo much!"

"Anything to make you happy….Now, can you stop strangling me, and go look for us a cottage!" Mary ran off to find the local paper, turned round and blew him a kiss.

James smiled as he watched her; he knew how important it was to her; and she came bouncing back through into the room, and went over to sit at the table.

"Mary – come and sit down for a minute" he said. "I want to talk to you". Mary came straight over to the sofa where James was sat.

"What about…??" She asked.

"Come and sit here a minute" he said, as he patted the space on the sofa beside him.

"Ooh - how much can we spend..??" she suddenly asked, as she looked at James as she put her hand on his shoulder.
He opened his mouth to speak….but didn't manage to say anything, as Mary was now thinking about moving.

"......Ooh I wonder where it will be...!! Oh yeah – and we've got all the paint to buy, and I'll have to start thinking about what different colours I'm going to paint each of the rooms. Oh shit, we need new furniture...!! .....well – just everything...!!"

At this point, she had stood back up, and slowly began to walk away from James as she was completely lost in her thoughts. As she looked around, Mary's faraway gaze suddenly came back around to James, who was still sat there, trying to speak, but Mary was so excited, she wasn't paying any attention.

"Mary...... Mary... Listen" He stretched out his hands and managed to take Marys hands in his. As he caught her attention, he said.

"Are you going to be ok with this..??"

"What do you mean?" She asked, smiling, as she sat down on the edge of the sofa next to him.
James looked down at the floor briefly, then back up at her.
"I...I just don't want it to bring back any bad memories, or......make you ill again – that's all"
Mary suddenly focused on James and took his hands in hers this time, as she looked at him lovingly, with her head on one side.

"James...."......she sighed. "That was a long time ago – and I was only a child" She answered.

"I know Mary......but – that was the reason why your Mother wanted you both to move away - away from it all; and leave the countryside, and go and live in the city......to start a new life and forget about it all"

"Yeah that's right – and you know that; and I understand what you're saying James, but it's all in the past now, and I'm not sure that I'll ever really remember anything about that......that day"

Mary paused as she looked down at the floor.

"My memories are really blurry now anyway" She looked back up at James, who was looking a little worried.

"Besides, Mum and Dad aren't here anymore, and I have to live my own life now. Being back in the countryside has always been a yearning for me – you know that. It's just that I don't remember much, so how can it affect me??"

Mary's eyes glazed over as she looked towards the balcony doors, which were shut.

"I just feel so 'closed in' here – it will be really good for me – well, good for both of us"

She looked back at him, and reassuringly squeezed his hands.

"I know" he said. "I just don't want you to have any flashbacks of any bad memories - that's all. I mean – moving back to the country may just trigger something off……."

Mary looked at his worried face.

"That was THEN – it was 1976..!!  I'm not a child anymore – I'm a big girl now" She said smiling.
"I REALLY want this James – more than anything!"

He looked at her happy face, and gave her a big kiss on her cheek. He half smiled back and said.

"I know – you're right. I just want to make you happy, and you can have anything you want, but you DO know that with this promotion, it does mean I will be away from home a little more often, and I just don't want you to be on your own too much"

Mary got up from the sofa, and smiled as she ruffled the top of his head as she walked away towards the kitchen. Then with a cheeky look on her face, she said.

"Unless you buy me a dog, a cat, and some guinea pigs to keep me company…..??" She darted as James threw a cushion at her as he laughed, shaking his head at the same time. It missed and hit the wall. She popped her head from around the kitchen door.

"I'll be fine, I promise. I'll be in my element..! I was brought up in the country don't forget. There'll be plenty to keep me occupied – believe me...!!  I mean – what could possibly go wrong...?!"

# Chapter 3

## **<u>Changes…..and the Fir Tree.</u>**

So, for the next few weeks, James and Mary would take the car out at the weekend; or if James had an odd free day in the week, they would drive around the villages where Mary used to live as a child.

Passing fields and meadows with the windows down, and the breeze blowing through her hair; and watching the cattle grazing, and the Combined Harvester working the fields, gave her a strong sense of 'belonging'. She closed her eyes momentarily, and she felt relaxed.

Mary had known that she had felt quite 'different' these past few weeks. Since they had been coming back a few times, to drive around the villages, Mary couldn't really explain it if she wanted to, but it was like a familiar feeling, like seeing an old friend……but there was something else that she couldn't explain.

James had asked her one evening whilst they were sat in their apartment.

"You look different Mary" He'd said.

"How so..?" she asked.

He smiled at her and said. "I don't know – it's weird, it's like you've become bolder, and you seem more confident, and more assertive"

"What like – you mean more bossy than I normally am….?!" Mary asked - laughing.

"Well you've always been bloody bossy, so there's no change there!!" James answered, and then a smile appeared on his face.

It was true, Mary had felt different, and certainly appeared different. She felt a sense of 'knowing' and she had felt wiser, stronger and happier....strangely; but there was something else that Mary couldn't quite put her finger on, and it plagued her. Sometimes she would wake up in the night, thinking that she had heard lots of faint whispering, and someone calling her name; or the wind blowing, or even raining, but when she looked out of the window, it was a still, dark night outside, apart from the odd car or taxi.

"You look really happy" said James one particular Saturday afternoon while they were enjoying a cold drink sat outside a country pub.

"I am" she sighed..... "For the first time in a long, long time" She answered smiling, as she rested her elbows on the table and supported her head with closed hands.

"No....episodes, dreams or nightmares...?? James asked rather sketchily, through gritted teeth.

"I'm fine – honestly" lied Mary, as she clasped his hands. "Stop worrying".

They had been out that morning looking around the estate agents again in all the villages, and driving up and down lanes; just looking all the time. All the agents had Marys number, just in case anything came up for sale, but James had felt quite worried, as he knew that cottages didn't come up for sale that often - they were quite rare. He was concerned for Mary – he just didn't want her to get disappointed, after getting her hopes up so much.

Just at that moment, Mary heard a rustling sound coming from some nearby bushes, close to where they were sat. She stole a quick glance, and then stared for a few seconds. She was sure she had just heard voices.

"What's up?" asked James.

"Did you hear that??" Mary answered.

"Hear what ...?" James looked at her searchingly.

"I thought I heard……." She trailed off. "Nothing" She quickly answered. "It was nothing – it must have been a bird rustling about in the bushes…..Anyway, have we decided what we're having for lunch yet…??. Shall we have another drink first, and then order....?"

James got up to go inside the pub. Mary turned slowly again and glanced towards the bushes where the noises had come from. What was it she had heard…?? She then averted her eyes to the scenery around her. It was so quiet and peaceful. She closed her eyes as she tilted her head back slightly, and took a long deep breath in. The sun was on her face, the birds were tweeting, and the faint clinking of glasses could be heard coming from inside the pub…….just perfect. Just as Mary brought her head back up, a bee suddenly swerved past her rather quickly, which made Mary jump, as it nearly caught her nose.
Mary watched it, as it flew off towards the pub, just as James brought out two more drinks.


"I can't believe we haven't seen anything remotely what we're looking for" Said Mary, wishing she could just conjure up the perfect cottage.
"We've driven through nearly every village, and there's nothing"

"Don't worry – something will come up, you'll see. It always does" Said James

A breeze suddenly arose, and lifted Mary's straw from her drink, which consequently fell onto the floor. She bent down to pick it up from under the table; and as she did, a piece of newspaper that had blown from over near the bushes, blew onto her straw. She picked up the piece of old newspaper, and the straw underneath, and went over to put them in the bin. She suddenly stopped, as she looked down at the newspaper page.

"J a m e s…." She said slowly.

"What…?" he asked, as he turned around.

Mary walked slowly over to him, whilst looking down at the newspaper.

"Look!" she said, and pointed to an advertisement. She pushed her sunglasses up onto her head, and could just make out the print.
She gave the paper to James to read.

**'Cottage for Sale'**. It read, in bold letters.

"I think I know where that is!" A very excited Mary exclaimed.

"Eh..?? How….. Do you remember it..?" he said looking up at her.

"Copley Lane Meadow….yeah…I remember" She looked away from the newspaper briefly, as if something had just come back to her.

"Do you know this place.??" James asked her.

"I….I don't really know if I do or I don't now….." Mary was searching her brain. Did she know this cottage and where it was, and was it a distant memory..??
Hurriedly, Mary said… "I think it's because we've been driving around so many times, it just seems familiar"

James looked back down at the advert, but Mary looked away for a brief moment gazing around her, and wondering why she felt a little strange.

She quickly brought her thoughts back to the cottage for sale.
They both read the advertisement, and stared at a faded photograph of the prettiest cottage they had seen yet.

"It looks like it could do with a bit of work" James said, a little worryingly.

"Yes, but that's perfect James. I can do most things myself through the week, and you can help out at weekends..!! It's the perfect project… Oh please say yes..!!" Mary said eagerly.

"Well let's hope it hasn't been sold yet…..and Mary - PLEASE don't get your hopes up too soon, I don't want you to be disappointed"

Mary didn't answer; she was dreamily staring at the photograph.

Mary rang first thing, the very next morning. It was a private sale, and the older gentleman on the other end of the phone was very helpful indeed.

An arrangement was made to view the cottage the day after, which was a Monday morning at 11am. James took some time from work, which he was able to do so, now that he had his promotion under his belt.

They arrived on time, and the instructions were to pick the key up from under an old plant pot at the front door. As they got to the front gate, they both stood and stared. Mary gasped.

"It's just exactly as I had pictured it in my mind, I can't believe it. Just look at it…..it's just gorgeous….!!"

It was indeed exactly what they had been looking for. A large rambling cottage that had a thatched roof, quite a big garden to the front, but there was an even bigger garden to the back, which seemed to stretch on and on.
This lovely, old pretty cottage sat all on its own, right on the far edge of a sleepy village with lots of surrounding meadows and fields. They knew they had looked around that particular village before, but strangely enough, had never seen this cottage, but as soon as they looked around it, they fell in love with it. It had 4 bedrooms, an attic, a large dining kitchen, and a huge living room. There were lots of cupboards, and nooks and crannies, and two quaint chimney pots. It was just so charming.

The cottage had been empty for some time, which meant that Mary and James had an awful lot of work to do, but they had to sell their apartment in the city first, which left Mary feeling a little worried; but James had another surprise for her. He told her that his employers had offered to buy the apartment from them, as it would be a good base for meetings, or for potential business people to stay over, when they had overseas visitors. Plus, they offered James a little more than the asking price, as they saw it as a good investment. So, with that, and James' promotion, it meant that they could spend more money doing the cottage up. It just couldn't have gone any better.

Soon enough, they were packing their belongings into boxes and bags.
They left a lot of the furniture behind, so that the apartment could be used pretty much straight away, which gave Mary some time to go shopping..! So, she spent her time visiting lots of antique shops and fairs, as Marys love of vintage furniture and artefacts was another of her passions. She would rather buy something that was once pre-loved, and give it a second chance of

ownership, rather than buying something brand new, which just didn't have anything nice or authentic about it.


Soon enough, they were dusting everything down, cleaning and scrubbing, painting and decorating, and filling their home with all the lovely old furniture that Mary had collected.

It really was such a beautiful old cottage; and had so much character; and the location couldn't have been any better. The cottage was right next door to a very large rambling meadow that went back as far as the eye could see. It had a big old wooden front door, which was a faded shade of periwinkle blue. The paint was coming off, which had obviously worn with time. It had a big old door knocker on the front, and a little wooden porch that had lots of ivy, and cream coloured roses, which climbed up the side of the trellis, and right over the top to meet the roses on the other side. The garden at the front was quite big, with lots of over-grown shrubs in the corner, and hedging that went all around the front of the house.....but around the back - was an even bigger garden...!! It was huge, quite long and winding, and right at the back was an old stone wall, with the meadow beyond.

Mary and James both looked out of the kitchen window at the back of the cottage, over-looking the huge garden.

"My God..!" exclaimed Mary. "This garden needs a lot of work doing... It's so over-grown...!!..... BUT, hard work doesn't bother me, and do you know what...? I really can't wait to get started, and I've already got visions in my head of what it's going to look like!!" she said, already plotting it out in her head.

"I can't believe how sad it looks though. I just don't understand why there are no flowers or trees anywhere. It looks so un-loved and unhappy, how strange"


James looked out over the garden; and smiled. He put his arm around her shoulder and said to her encouragingly. "Do you know what I know..?" He looked down at her, and she shook her head.

"I know you so well Mary, and I know that you will put your heart and soul into this garden, and I can't wait to see what you do with it" and he gave her a big hug as he kissed the top of her head.

Mary didn't waste any time at all, and got to work very quickly, and went out and bought all the necessary tools she needed to begin restoring it. Nobody had bothered with it for such a long time, and it was so over-grown.
She was right though, it did look very sad. There were no flowers, so there were no bees or butterflies, or birds.

Mary worked really hard over the summer, although sometimes, the weather took a turn for the worse, and the rain would come lashing down, or it would be really windy – strange for the time of the year, but Mary was undeterred.

James would be waiting with a towel and a hot cup of tea when she came in drenched and tired. She continued to work hard throughout the summer and the autumn, and into the winter.

It wasn't all plain sailing though, as Mary found out. There were times when she was exhausted, and she ached from head to foot from all the digging. James helped at the weekend with carrying the heavy loads, like bags of soil, big branches, and bags and bags of nettles, and old shrubs. Most of the weekends were spent doing nothing else but the garden, and through the week, when James was at work, Mary would be doing stuff in and around the cottage, and then back out into the garden again. She was so tired, and would be in bed early most nights not long after tea, and James would tell her to have a day off. Then they would argue as tempers would flare, but Mary just wanted it all finishing. James just couldn't understand the rush to get it all done.

Springtime came at last, and eventually Mary had finished..!! She had planted lots of bulbs, seeds, and plants, and bought several tall trees, and fruit trees, so come late summer, she would have an abundance of pears and apples. James had built a nice big shed in the top left hand corner of the garden for all their gardening tools and plant pots; and next to that was a big old greenhouse that they had uncovered when they tore all the old bushes away. They also found a wooden table and chairs that had been left in the shed. Mary cleaned it all up and stained it all in a rich oak colour, all ready for the summertime.

Now that it was all finished, you could see the extent of the back garden, and how large it was. The big new lawn stretched all the way right to the top of the garden, where the wall was, that ran along the whole of the back garden. Down either side of the garden, James had fought his way through the over-grown hedging, and trimmed it all back, to find a beautiful old stone wall that ran the full length of the garden, from the front of the house to the back. Mary had created a little strawberry patch and also a vegetable patch next to the greenhouse, so they could grow their own fruit and veg.

The last thing Mary did, was create a little winding pathway and steps, and filled the pathway with stones. She had found an old bird box in the rubble when she was clearing the garden, so she dusted it down, and painted it green, and nailed it to the side of the shed.
All of Mary's hard work had most definitely paid off.
As she looked out over her garden, there was just one thing that made her feel strangely sad. Up at the top right hand corner of the garden, was an old sad looking fir tree that she had found when she was clearing out all the old bracken and over-grown bushes away. It had obviously once been very tall and green, and stood proud in the garden; but now it was very old and brown, and it really needed to be chopped down.

So, Mary asked James if he would dig the fir tree up, then it could be chopped into logs and they could use it for firewood for their big open fire.
 So James went to get his spade and a saw from the garden shed, and Mary followed him up the garden path. James put his gardening gloves on, and picked up the spade.

"Wait…!!" said Mary quickly.

"Why what's wrong..?!" asked James, leaning on the spade.

"I can't let you do it…!!"

"Why, what do you mean??" he asked.

"I can't let you dig it up…….I don't know why, but there's just something about it, and …I…I …I don't know what it is" she said, staring at it, as she turned her head to one side and then the other.
"I feel like it belongs in this garden, and it HAS to stay. I can't bear to dig it up!!"

James gave Mary an exasperated look, whilst putting the spade down, and pointing at the tree, he said.

"…but Mary, look at it – it's bloody dead…! It's going to spoil the look of the garden anyway. It needs to come up…!"

James proceeded, and picked up the saw this time.

"Stop..!" She cried.

James turned around quickly, and took a long look at Mary.

"What's got into you – what's going on..?!" he asked.

At that brief moment, Mary thought she could hear faraway whispering sounds. James continued looking at Mary for what seemed to be a few moments.

She carried on looking at the tree, and then said suddenly.

"We don't have to get rid of it completely. If we just chop it down to a smaller size, like a stump, and maybe just leave a couple of the small branches - you never know, it might just grow again, and if it doesn't, then it will always be a part of this garden". She said smiling.

James, still giving Mary a worried look, shook his head, and did just that, and chopped it down to a nice little stump.

Just at that moment, a slight breeze had picked up, and then suddenly changed direction, and got a little stronger, which whipped a few leaves and light twigs up off the ground, and the trees in the meadow beyond the wall suddenly swayed and rustled. The leaves and twigs swirled around and around in the air, which was very strange, as it had been such a sunny peaceful morning. Then they all came fluttering down, and rested on the ground, as if nothing had happened……

James looked around him for a few seconds.

"What the hell was that…?!" he said, as he looked at Mary. Mary shrugged her shoulders, but had secretly felt something a little strange herself. James proceeded to chop the rest of the tree up into logs and put them into the shed for the winter.

Mary tidied up around the tree stump, and made a little feature of it, by planting some little white Daisies around the base of the stump. She even used an old dark blue teapot she had found on the ground, under all the over-grown weeds, and used it as a plant pot. She filled it with different coloured pansies, and placed it just under the lower branches of the tree stump. She also planted some lavender bushes in and around the tiny steps she had made, which filled the air with a fragrant aroma, every time there was a gentle breeze.
She looked at the corner of the garden for a few moments, and then said to James.

"Awww – it looks so cute. It looks kind of higgledy-piggledy doesn't it..?" she said laughing.

James shook his head.

"What's that supposed to mean…are you taking the mickey out of me...?!" She asked, as she shot him a quizzical look.

James looked a little shocked at Mary's tempestuous stare.

"I'm only shaking my head because that's just so typical of you to say something sweet. I'm not taking the mickey". James realised that Mary was probably really tetchy from being over-tired.

"What I'm trying to say……is that I'm really proud of you – you've worked really hard love" said James. "Albeit with a few tears and tantrums on the way….." and gave Mary a knowing look. Mary looked back at him indignantly.

"What do you mean by that…?! Yeah, I know I haven't been the best person to live with these past few months, but I've just been too tired to sometimes to get ready and go out for a few drinks, or go to the pictures on a weekend; and I'm sorry about that, but I just wanted to get it all finished. You didn't have to be so sarcastic..!"

"I'm joking – stop been so uptight. Come on…" James put his arm around Mary's shoulder.

"Honestly, it's absolutely beautiful Mary - everything. You've literally thought of everything, but you need to rest now, and put your feet up. Tell you what….I can see us having some great summers out here, with barbeques and drinks; and can you imagine what it's going to be like in the winter, with all that snow..?! Come on, I'm starving, what we having for dinner…?" and they slowly walked down the garden, and back to the house.

Suddenly, a host of tiny voices had just made the biggest, loudest cheer….

# Chapter 4

## **<u>Returning Home</u>**

Mary, at that point, stopped and turned around and looked back towards the tree stump.

"What's up now….?!" James asked, as Mary was looking over her shoulder.

"Can you hear that..?" she said.

"Hear what?"

All of a sudden the cheering and excited chattering had ceased.

"Do you think she heard us..?" said one voice.

"Ssh….." said another.

"Everyone keep quiet...!!" A rather authoritative hushed voice said.

Mary looked puzzled.

"I don't know – sounds mad, but I thought I heard……… 'something'…."
Mary said the word 'something' in a quiet voice; that gave her a strange feeling.

"The only mad thing around here is YOU…!!" James said; and started laughing as he saw Mary's face change. He made a quick getaway down the path, then turned around and started trotting backwards whilst still laughing, as Mary quickened her pace.

"Right, just you wait James Thompson..!! YOU can make the dinner, AND wash up afterwards for that…!"

Mary ran down the path after him, until they were both out of sight and inside the cottage. Once the door was shut……. laughter could be heard coming from inside the kitchen.

"Can we come out now..?"

"Do you think that she REALLY heard us..?"

"I think she did, did you see her turn around..?"

"No, she can't have done, how could she hear us…?!"

Lots of voices had indeed begun to talk, all at the same time.

"I really can't believe we're here - at last…." said Patsy, as she stared around the garden, and then started fluttering about madly in the sunshine.
Patsy was a Butterfly, who right at this moment was indeed, flapping around rather excitedly, and nearly going dizzy with elation…!!
"I've never seen so many gorgeous flowers; and this garden is just heavenly!!" she shouted as she hovered above the clump of white daisies, and then again, fluttered around and around; and in her excitement, bumped into Henry, the Bumble Bee.

"Patsy, calm down! If you keep on twirling around like that, you're heading straight for that tree..!!" said Henry.

"Oh I know, but how long have we waited to come back here…. sorry Henry, I'm just so happy…!!

"Well, I have to agree with you, and I can honestly say Patsy, it has indeed been too long - but you are quite right – Mary and James have indeed brought this garden back to life…!!" said Henry, as he looked towards the back of the cottage, where he caught sight of Mary and James in the kitchen, chattering away.

Henry had been around for quite some time, and was a very wise Bee. He had remembered the old garden from many, many years ago. It had once been quite a lovely place to live…..until a spell had been cast over the whole garden……..by a Witch. A Witch, who had quickly banished all living creatures to the meadow beyond the wall; and in her haste in doing so, she had accidently given them all extended lives. Everything in the garden then went into a long, long slumber, for many years; and over time, the garden became so overgrown, it became completely unrecognisable. The cottage remained empty, no one moved in, all the animals had gone, and the garden was left unkempt….until now…..

After the Witch - Endor Le Fey was her name, had cast her spell, and banished them all; they became really quite worried and frightened. They had all felt very safe living in the garden; but now living out in the open meadow for years, had made them feel very insecure, and it wasn't quite the same anymore. The meadow was beautiful, but it was huge, and very open.

One day not so long ago, when Henry had been flying about on business, he had heard a lot of noise coming from the garden of number 24 Copley Lane Meadow, and up until this point, no one could enter the garden or the cottage, because of the spell that had been cast by Endor Le Fey. It was completely impossible..!!
Henry, all of a sudden, had found himself flying right over the wall and over into the garden!! That's when he first saw Mary, to his complete surprise, happily digging away. He was so shocked at what he saw, he couldn't believe his eyes, and nearly skidded in mid-air, as he turned right around and hurriedly flew back to the meadow to tell all the others!!

That was nearly a year ago, and now, here they all were once again, back in the safety of the garden……

Henry could still hear Patsy, flapping about and chattering excitedly with her friend in the background, as he recalled his Father telling him, many, many years before, when Henry was a only a young Bee; about the day in question. A day that his Father had remembered very well indeed – about the spell that had been cast, and now Henry was left curiously wondering; as he saw Mary and James happily chatting in their kitchen…..

How had the spell been lifted on the cottage??

What had Mary and James done, and who WERE they…??
Had the spell run out..?? If it had, that could mean trouble……

Henry intended to find out…… but his attention was taken back quickly, to all the cheering and laughing that was still going on around the tree stump.

It had been quite a bit of a job to rally everybody together so quickly that day, and tell them that he had seen a young woman digging, in the back garden of the cottage. He couldn't wait to see the looks on their faces, as he knew that this news would make them very curious, but equally happy, to know that someone had moved into the old cottage, but more so – how and why……?
They couldn't wait, but wait they had to do, until Mary had completely finished the garden.

Henry had done an inventory of everyone who wanted to come back and live in the garden, so that he had an idea of how many there were going to be. He was very efficient, and liked to run a tight ship – plus, everyone trusted Henry.

The day eventually came, and one by one, they had all hurried across the meadow with their bags and sacks; and some were pushing old match boxes, and empty acorn shells, filled with all their belongings.

When they eventually arrived at the stone wall at the back of the cottage, they didn't waste any time. Some climbed up and over the wall, others flew over, and other smaller creatures had found really tiny cracks in the old stone, and got in that way.

Wilbur, the Dragonfly however, had a slight problem. One of his wings had never really worked properly, due to an accident that he had quite some years before; so he always did funny little hops and jumps, as he couldn't quite make it into 'flight'. He couldn't squeeze through the tiny cracks, and he certainly couldn't fly over the wall, but before he could think whether he could climb it or not, Henry and Patsy had picked him up, one arm under each of his, and flew him right over the top of the wall!!

"Oh no……no, no, no, no…!!" he cried out. He had never flown so high before, and not for many years either.

"Don't look down Wilbur!!" shouted Patsy. Too late – he already had.

"Don't worry, we're nearly there!!" shouted Henry. Then a few seconds later, he was coming down to a safe landing on the other side of the garden wall.

"You can open your eyes now Wilbur. Look – we're here!!" Patsy said excitedly.

All of a sudden, everyone at that moment; had stopped – open mouthed, and not saying a word, at the wonderful sight that met their eyes. Every single one of them just looked around the garden in complete amazement. They saw plants, fruit trees, big shrubs, a new shed and a big greenhouse. There was a fine looking table and chairs. They saw little walls and pathways, and hundreds of beautiful flowers. After living in the meadow for so long, this was just like being in paradise.
It was the most beautiful sight, and the happiest day!!

"Mum, Mum, can we go and play, please...Mum, MUUUUM...??!!" shouted Jack. Jack was the youngest of Nancy the Ladybird's two children.
Nancy, like everyone else, was still looking round.

"MUM!!" Jack was still hopping up and down.

"Jack, be quiet for just one minute!!" she told him sternly. "We'll have to ask your Father and a few of the others first, to have a look around to make sure that it's safe, and THEN you can go and play"

Everyone thought that this was a good idea, but of course the younger ones thought otherwise, so as you can imagine, there were lots of moans and groans from all of the children, who wanted nothing more than to go and play, and explore the new garden!

# Chapter 5

# <u>**The Meeting**</u>

Everyone seemed to settle in very quickly, in and around different places in the garden. All the animals made their way around, and soon found their favourite places to dwell, and built nice cosy homes. They felt very safe indeed, and of course, it felt great to be back. Patsy and Henry were able to fly around the whole of the garden to do daily patrols. Wilbur the Dragonfly really did wish he could join Patsy and Henry up in the air, but as his wing didn't work properly, he made himself very useful by being as helpful as he could on the ground. All the children would pretend to help, but they would end up hiding behind the huge plant pots and stones, and jumping out and scaring the wits out of any passer-by.

Henry, on the other hand, was still curious to know who the new residents were, and how the spell had 'apparently' been lifted on the cottage and the garden. If the spell HAD been lifted – how..?

Did this mean that everyone could possibly be in danger again...? Henry was indeed quite worried, but Mary and James seemed to be a lovely young couple, as he had seen them many times now, so there was nothing to feel suspicious about, but he just couldn't quite put his finger on what was making him scratch his head.
He would sometimes fly down to the kitchen window, and settle on the windowsill and have a nosy inside the house, but everything just seemed normal - as far as HE could see.

As he was flying back up to the top of the garden one day, he decided it was time to have a meeting, so he sent Patsy and Wilbur to go around the garden and tell everyone to meet him at the tree stump, which they had now affectionately named Tree Stump Corner, at 12 noon. Everyone turned up, wondering what was going on.

Henry cleared his throat, as he stood on the tree stump so everyone could see him.

"Ahem….. Good afternoon everyone. Thank you all for being on time. I just want to say at this moment, please do not worry, there is nothing untoward, I just felt that as we are all now settling in rather nicely into our lovely new home, it would be good to have a meeting to see how everyone is getting along. I think it would be a good idea to talk about any matters of urgency, any problems, any ideas etc. etc. As you know, Patsy, myself and Wilbur are doing daily patrols of the garden, and I think we can all agree that seeing as this is a fresh start for all of us; we certainly don't want to lose what we have here. Mary and James seem to be good people, and it's up to us to keep this garden ship shape, and a safe place for us to live, and for our children too. So, does anyone have anything they would like to say??"

There was a bit of muttering between a certain few. Then a Caterpillar said.

"But Henry, how do we know if we ARE going to be safe here, as you say..?? Yes, it was quite bleak and open out over in the meadow there, but how do we know…??"

A few of them agreed with this, and looked at Henry.

"Well….." Henry began, and then Nancy, the Ladybird slowly put her hand up. She was rather timid and quite nervous, but so kind and very helpful

"Yes Nancy" said Henry, quite relieved, as he didn't really have the answer to the Caterpillar's question.

"Well…well…first of all Henry, thank you for holding a meeting, I think it really is a good idea" she said.

"Here, here" a few of them muttered.

"I WOULD like to make a couple of suggestions though" she said, looking around.
Erm…firstly, as the summer nights are so lovely and long at the moment, and we are all enjoying the late summer evenings, I know that the dark nights will soon be upon us before too long, and I would like to see a patrol of the garden on an evening. I have two young children as you know, Jack and Timmy, and

they like playing out, as all of our children do, but just before dusk, I think it would be a good idea if someone could volunteer to do this. I would certainly feel safer." She looked around at everyone, a little nervously, hoping for a good reaction.

There was some muttering going on as Nancy waited, but everyone seemed to be nodding in agreement with this suggestion.

"Yes Nancy, a very good idea, I agree" said Henry. "Does anyone want to volunteer?? If not, I will put some names in a hat, and draw one out"

"I vil do zis!!" said a voice, boldly, from the back of the crowd. Henry was straining to see who spoke.

"Ah, Lars, there you are my good fellow" said Henry.

Lars was a Beetle, from Germany. His English was quite good, and he was very polite, but sometimes a little difficult to understand.

Lars came striding forward, rather sturdily, wearing a smart black jacket with gold buttons, and tall, knee high shiny black boots. He stopped abruptly, and did a funny little salute and clicked his heels together.

"I have my bicycle, so I can ride around zis garden on an evening. Zis I vill do" he said in his funny accent, and did a little bow, and then clicked his heels together again. Some of the children giggled – they thought Lars was very funny, because he rode a bright orange rickety bicycle all the time, but what was even funnier, was that Lars wore big round black glasses, because he couldn't see very well, but his eyes looked HUGE. He was quite funny looking, in the nicest way of course.

"Thank you Lars" said Henry. Everyone clapped.

"I can help too" said a lovely sweet voice. Bonny the Spider was Patsy's best friend. "I can scurry up the wall at the back of the garden here, and patrol along the top every evening, if that's any help..?" she said looking round at everyone.

Henry looked at her and said "Bonny, thank you, that is a very good idea, but I can't let you do that alone, I think you need someone with you. It can be quite dark up there, so I am going to suggest that Elma does this with you. Elma, are you there??" said Henry looking round.

Elma was a Daddy Long Legs. He was an extremely helpful and kind spider, and always made everyone laugh, as he was exceptionally funny. He was most definitely the right man for the job, BUT he did have a tendency to be very clumsy.

"Here I am!!" he shouted, as he ran forward, rather awkwardly on his long legs; but because his legs were so long, everyone moved out of the way very quickly, and gave him a wide birth. He came to a swift halt, causing a small dust cloud, which set everyone coughing, and nearly fell over doing so.

"Great…..ahem, ahem… that settles that then. Ahem!!" coughed Henry, punching his chest with his fist, but also, looking rather pleased.

"Let's start tonight, there's no time like the present!!... AHEM.!!"

So, Lars the Beetle, and Bonny and Elma all had new jobs, which they started that very evening; although there were a few teething problems to begin with as they settled into their new roles.

Bonny and Elma climbed up the stone wall at the end of the garden with ease that night. They had decided that when they got to the top of the wall, they would start off, in the middle, back to back. Then slowly walk away from each other, so that one would walk to one end of the wall, and the other would walk to the other end of the wall. Then, when they each turned around, they would walk back, and meet in the middle. So they did this to begin with, but when they met in the middle, they couldn't pass each other, as Elma's legs were too long for Bonny to pass, and she didn't want to run underneath them, just in case Elma toppled off. So, they decided that it would be better, and much, much safer if they both walked together, one behind the other, and patrol that way.

Lars, on the other hand, took his role very seriously. He had cleaned and polished his orange bike, and cleaned the lights on the front and back, until they were gleaming. Then he retrieved a wooden box, which he kept under his bed, and inside, folded carefully in an old cotton handkerchief, he pulled out a very fine shiny looking whistle. This had belonged to his Grandfather Kafer, who had used it during the war. Lars was very proud of this – it was his most treasured possession. He polished it until he could see his face in it. He then tied some string to it, and hung it around his neck. He polished his boots once more, got on his bicycle, and cycled off down the path.

The children however, thought this was very funny that Lars was taking his 'role' very seriously, and scared him many times, jumping out from behind the rocks and stones….poor Lars.

One early evening, they frightened the wits out of Lars that much, he shouted in his native tongue.

"Meine Gute!!" as he skidded to a halt, which in turn made him fall from his bike, and onto his bottom. That's when he laughed as he saw the children giggling from behind the flowerbeds.

"Ahh children, you are very funny, yes..?!". He said, but unfortunately his big black round glasses had fallen off and onto the grass!! His eyes were so tiny without them. Poor Lars, he did look funny as he sat there trying to feel about on the grass for his glasses, and 'patting' the ground, until eventually he picked them up, popped them back on, and rode off down the path on his bike.

# Chapter 6

# **The Visitor**

One evening, after his usual patrol, Lars was cycling back along the path away from Tree Stump Corner. It had been raining that day, and the last glimmer of sunlight was shining on the wet path, which was lighting up the way back. Suddenly, Lars noticed something shining on the path in front of him.
It was a long silvery thread. He slowed his bike down, and followed the silvery thread-like residue, until he came across something in front him on the path. He slowed down a little more as he got closer. He wasn't at all sure what it could be, but as he got nearer, he craned his head forward, then his big eyes widened, as he made out the shape, of a snail. He braked really hard, skidded on the wet path, and nearly fell off his bike!!

"Sssss snail!!" he shouted at the top of his voice. He then remembered the whistle around his neck; fumbled quickly for it, and blew it really hard..."Peeeeeep!! The snail quickly went into its shell, and sat still, not moving. Within seconds, Henry and Patsy were there.

"What is it Lars??" asked Patsy, as she fluttered down. Lars was pointing at the snail.
Henry flew over to the snail, and knocked on the snails shell.

"Hello??" shouted Henry; then put his head on one side, expecting to hear a reply.

"Is there anyone in there?? You must come out at once, you're trespassing!!" said Henry, rather firmly.

The snail slowly poked its head out from under its shell. In a slow drawling voice, the snail answered.

"Trespassing...?? I most certainly am not!!"

Patsy, Lars and Henry all looked at each other.

"Excuse me, Mr Snail" said Patsy gently, as she stepped forward. "….but you ARE trespassing. We all know everyone who lives in this garden, but we have never seen YOU before"

Lars tapped the snails shell. "Vot is your name, and Vot is your business here?!"

The snail quickly put his head back into his shell.

"Lars!!" cried Patsy "That's no way to treat a visitor!!" and she turned to the snail.
"Erm, Mr Snail, please would you mind telling us who you are??" Patsy asked, in a much gentler voice, as she stole an angry look at Lars.

The snail slowly poked his head out from under his shell again; looked at all three of them in turn, and said in his slow voice, but rather heavily.

"My name - is Jeremy Snail." He sighed.
"I have come such a long way on the pathway today, past the meadow. I am looking for somewhere to live for me and my wife and our little son. The recent rain we have had has flooded our home, so my wife is looking after our son while I try and find us all somewhere new. It has taken me all day, and I am so very tired; so I wasn't trespassing at all, I just got a little bit lost I'm afraid. If you would kindly point me in the right direction, I'll be on my way – and I'm very sorry to have disturbed you"

"Oh no…." said Patsy. "That's terrible, isn't it Henry?!" as she looked over at a very concerned Henry, who was scratching his head. Henry stepped forward.

"Erm… look Mr Snail, I…I mean, Jeremy" he said. "It's really unfortunate that you have lost your home due to the rain, and I'm very sad to hear that. I just feel a little concerned for your wife and son, and the fact that you now don't have a home to go back to. So if you wouldn't mind just giving me and my colleagues a few moments, as we need to discuss what should be done here"

Jeremy nodded in agreement, and put his head back in his shell.

Henry, Lars and Patsy walked a few steps away, and began talking in low voices about what they should do. After some discussion, eventually, they all agreed that they should help Jeremy and his family. They also agreed that there was plenty of room in the garden, and they would try and help him find a spot that he liked. It was also discussed that Henry and Patsy would 'fly' Jeremy back to his family to tell them the good news, and then they would bring them back this very evening one by one. Not forgetting the fact that Jeremy being a snail, was very, very slow, so it would have taken him days to get there and back again!!

Henry told Jeremy the good news, and he was delighted and very grateful. Henry and Patsy then picked Jeremy up between them, and flew him out of the garden, over the wall and across the meadow, to the spot where he had left his wife and son. Jeremy introduced his wife Jemima, and their son Ben, who were both very surprised at what they were hearing..! Patsy explained everything to Jemima, as it would have taken Jeremy such a long time to tell her, and time was getting on.

"We have to get back to the garden before the sun sets" urged Henry.

So they flew Jemima and Ben back across the meadow, and eventually over the garden wall. Jemima had kept her head firmly in her shell, but Ben thought this was very exciting, as he had never been off the ground before. He peeped out from under his shell, and squealed with delight as he looked down at the ground, which seemed so tiny and faraway.

After Patsy and Henry had been back to the meadow to bring Jeremy back, the sun was just setting behind the trees across the meadow. Jemima had already found a perfect spot behind two plant pots, which were very close to the hedging, and just in front of the big stone wall, just at the side of some nice growing moss.

"I am very grateful to you – well WE are very grateful, and thank you so much" said Jeremy.

 Patsy smiled and said. "Get some sleep, and tomorrow, we'll introduce you to everyone"

Jeremy waved goodbye and went to join Jemima, who had just put Ben to bed. He had fallen off to sleep very quickly with all the excitement, and was already dreaming of flying.

# Chapter 7

# <u>Henry gets a shock…!!</u>

One morning, a few days after Mary had finished all her work in the back garden, she decided to make a start on the garden at the front of the cottage. As she went to pick up the morning mail, she noticed that some of the envelopes were covered in dirt. She brushed it off, and idly put the mail on the kitchen table, pulled on her wellington boots, grabbed her gardening gloves, and went outside into the front garden. She pulled on her gloves; then with her hands on her hips, she looked around the front garden slowly.

"Oh bloody hell, where do I even begin?!" She mumbled to herself. "Come on Mary, standing here won't get the baby bathed" She smiled, as she recited one of her Mothers many sayings – which all made perfect sense to Mary now, but didn't mean a thing to her when she was a child.

Her mind drifted away as she started to think about her Mother, and tears welled up in her eyes, as she wished that her Mother was here – and her Father of course; she missed them both so much. She knew they would be so proud of her, buying a beautiful big cottage in the countryside.

She made a pile of wood with lots of bits of broken branches, so that James could light a fire. The bigger pieces could go into the shed to be stored, and then at least they would have plenty of wood in time for the winter.

As Mary was deep in her thoughts, and digging away, she suddenly felt a little chilly, and uneasy. The warm morning sun was still out, so there was no need for her to feel the cold so sudden.
Then - she 'felt' like someone was watching her. She stopped digging, stood up straight, and turned around to look behind her.
An old lady, quite small in height and slightly stooped, and wearing a green scarf tied under her chin, was stood at Mary's gate – staring straight at Mary.

"Oh hello……Good Morning" said Mary brightly, and put a hand up to wave. She was about to turn around and carry on digging, but the old lady stared at Mary, as if she was looking straight through her. Mary looked back at her, and the old lady was scowling!! Then, all of a sudden, the old lady's scowl turned into a smile.

"Hello my dear" replied the old lady, sweetly.
"I didn't know that someone new had moved into this old cottage….. I've, I've been away for quite a while. Imagine my surprise!" She said, still smiling. She was looking at Mary as if she was trying to figure something out.
"My name….." said the old woman…."…is Old Mother Sage. Well, that's what everyone in the village calls me, because I grow lots of herbs, and I wear a green scarf"
Still smiling, she said.
"I shall bring you some my dear, if you would like…?"

Mary pulled off her gardening gloves, and put them in her pocket as she walked towards the old woman to greet her. Then Mary put out her hand to shake the old woman's hand, which she had already outstretched to Mary. The woman took hold of Mary's hand as if to shake it, but instead, clasped both of her hands fully, around Mary's right hand – then leaned forward a little, and looked very searchingly into Mary's eyes. The old woman had quite a big ugly scar that went from the top of her left ear, and across her cheek, and then it went all the way down to just under her chin.

As Old Mother Sage continued to stare at Mary, a sudden strange feeling, like a huge rush of air breezed right through her. This made Mary take a sharp intake of breath, but she quickly recovered and said.

"Oh…..well, I'm very pleased to meet you – Old Mother Sage" she said, expecting the old woman to then let go of her hand. Instead, she looked down at Mary's hand, and turned it over and over, looking very closely at it. The old woman stooped further forward, taking a much closer look now at Mary's hand, and she was muttering, in what seemed like another language.

She was looking at Mary's palm…!! At that moment, Mary felt another strange and sudden 'rush-like' feeling; this time it was like a sharp lightning bolt that passed right through her, making her cough, which Mary then quickly brought the back of her left hand up to her mouth to try and stifle it.

Then Mary asked very quickly… "Sorry, but what was that you just said..?!"

The old woman quickly looked up at Mary with narrowed eyes.
"Why, I was just saying my dear, what delicate pretty hands you have, and they're all dirty. You must be very, very busy"

Mary suddenly withdrew her hand quickly from the old woman's grasp, and wiped it on her jumper and said hurriedly "Oh I'm so sorry, my hands are really dirty, even with these gloves on..!!" Mary felt quite uncomfortable, and a little confused; and she felt the hairs on the back of her neck stand up, but she didn't know why.

"Oh that's alright child" replied Old Mother Sage, with a wide grin. Then the old woman looked a little confused, and stared around her. "By the way, if you don't mind me asking – what year is it dear..? I get so forgetful these days".

"What 'year'…??!" Mary repeated. "Well it's….it's 1994…" Mary answered, thinking that the old woman's memory must be REALLY bad if she didn't know what year it was. How strange…..

"Oh….is it really…?? Well, well, well…" She answered, as if surprised. Then hurriedly said "Yes, yes, of course it is – silly me, what was I thinking, you must think me quite mad..!"

Mary began stepping backwards.
"Anyway, I… I really must get on with this garden, I've got such a lot to do, but it's really nice to meet you…Bye!!

Mary raised her hand to wave, turned back around and began to walk quickly back to the pile of wood, pulling her gloves on, and feeling a little strange.

The old woman still stood at the gate.
"You didn't tell me YOUR name dear!!" Old Mother Sage shouted over.

"Oh, it's Mary!! She shouted back, over her shoulder.

"Mary WHAT…??!! The old woman shouted the last word, so nastily - her voice had suddenly changed.

Alarmed at her angry tone, Mary quickly turned around, and saw that the old woman was scowling once again, through narrowed eyes. Mary was just about to open her mouth to speak, when a big bumble bee flew right in front of Mary's face. Mary was startled, and shrieked. She let the spade drop, which she had just picked up, and began wafting her arms about, but the bee did not fly away, and seemed to be angrily buzzing around her. She didn't want to hurt the bee, but didn't want to get stung either, so thought that a quick escape into the house would be better. Mary ran towards the front door, flung it open and quickly shut it behind her, hoping to leave the bee outside – along with that strange old woman.

Once inside, Mary kicked off her boots, pulled her gloves off, and threw them on the floor. She then tiptoed quietly over to the kitchen window, and slowly peered from behind the curtain. Oddly, Old Mother Sage was still there with her gnarled looking hand on the gate, looking around the garden, as if she was looking for something. She was mainly looking over to the corner of the garden, where there was a secluded bit, but it was still very over-grown. Mary quickly pulled her head back away from the curtain; she didn't want Old Mother Sage to see her peeping. She then - very slowly looked again, and as if by magic, the old woman had disappeared!!

"Oh!!" It startled Mary that she had gone so quickly. Clutching her chest she said out loud.
 "Where on earth did she go, and so quickly…? What a bloody strange woman…! Blimey, I think I need a cup of tea after that..!!"

She made her way over to the sink, washed her hands, and dried them, and all the while, shaking her head, as she thought about the strange encounter and conversation with the old woman. She got herself a nice big cup from the cupboard, filled the kettle and put it on the stove, and lit it. She kept glancing out of the window, as if she expected the old woman to re-appear.

What Mary didn't know, was that Henry the Bee; was sat on the kitchen windowsill, also peeping outside to the front garden.

He had been outside, and had been watching the whole thing. He had seen Mary digging in the garden because he had been closely watching from the side of the cottage, and then he saw 'Old Mother Sage' suddenly appear at the garden gate. He squinted in the morning sun to try and get a clearer look at the old woman. He then heard the conversation that had started between them both. Just at that point when Mary had opened her mouth to tell the old woman her surname, Henry had flown straight to Mary to distract her from telling the old woman anymore.

You see, Henry had made a shocking discovery, that very morning.......

Earlier on, before Mary had come out into the garden, Henry had been waiting for the Postman.
As you know, Henry has been wondering who Mary and James were, and he had been quite puzzled as to how they had suddenly been able to buy the cottage, when it had been stood empty for so long. There were lots of unanswered questions, so Henry decided to play Detective, and try and find out as much as he could for himself.

He had been waiting on the wall down by the side of the cottage - and he had a plan.

When Henry heard the Postman whistling a merry tune as he was walking down the lane, Henry was ready. The Postman unlatched the gate and walked into the garden with some mail. Henry flew out at once, straight over to the Postman, and headed straight for the Postman's hands. He buzzed about angrily in front of the startled man, until he dropped all the letters he was carrying. Henry quickly took his chance, and flew down to the envelopes on the ground, before the Postman had the chance to pick them back up. Henry had just enough time to read the address on the letter, and who it was addressed to......The envelope he was looking at, was all the information he needed.

It read 'To Miss Mary Le Fey'........

# Chapter  8

## <u>Who is she…?</u>

Henry immediately flew away from the Postman, who was left picking up the mail, and feeling slightly bemused, before posting it through the letterbox. He then left the cottage, and resumed whistling his merry tune, as he closed the gate behind him. Henry then flew over to the front doorstep, and sat down rather heavily. 'Mary Le Fey' He kept saying the name over and over, again and again to himself.

You see, Mary's surname just happened to be the same surname as the Witch, who had cast the spell over the garden and the cottage, all those years ago…!! The Witch's name was Endor Le Fey, and now he had just found out that Mary had the same surname….. who WAS Mary Le Fey...??!!

This was no coincidence….

That surname was a very unusual surname indeed…..he had to think about this for a while, and so he sat there for a bit, whilst pondering, before flying around to the back garden. He needed to speak with Patsy.

Without a fuss, he quietly called Patsy over.

Henry then began to explain to her, what was on his mind. He told her that he had wondered who Mary was from the moment he had first seen her that day, when she was digging in the garden. He had thought about nothing else since Mary and James had moved in. How had they been able to buy the cottage and just move in..? Had the spell been lifted, if so – how, why even…? He had to find out who they were..!!. Telling Patsy his concerns was the only thing to do at this moment. She was very fair and honest, so he knew that he could trust her not to say anything to anyone else.

Patsy wasn't born at the time to remember the spell that Endor Le Fey had cast, but she had heard about it from her parents. She was very keen to help Henry in any way she could; so when Henry told her how he had just found out that Mary's surname was also Le Fey, from the letters the Postman had dropped, Patsy couldn't believe it.

"Oh Henry.....what does it all mean then - what are we going to do…??!"

Henry told her that he was going to have to keep a closer eye on Mary, and find out as much information as he could about her. He didn't want any danger to come to any of the residents in the garden, IF Mary was indeed, a direct relative of the witches……so he needed to find out.

If anyone was to ask of Henry's whereabouts that day, then Patsy was to tell everyone that Henry was patrolling the front garden for a while. Patsy agreed.

Henry had then made his way back to the front garden, and had landed on the side wall again, watching Mary, who was now out in the garden digging away; when all of a sudden, he saw the old woman appear at the gate.
Henry stared at the old woman for a few moments, wondering who it was……
Then, he very slowly realised, and he couldn't quite believe his eyes…!!

He had been listening to the conversation between Mary and the old woman, and watching very closely, when he suddenly realised that the old woman wasn't telling the truth, when he heard her say to Mary that her name, was Old Mother Sage.

As Henry had been staring at the old woman, he suddenly felt a little strange, and then a slow realisation came over him, and something which his Father had told him many, many years before…… suddenly became very clear in his mind. It then occurred to Henry who she REALLY was.

She was much older; but there was no mistaking who was stood at Mary's front gate.
Her REAL name, was Agnes Le Fey……and she was the sister…of Endor Le Fey…!!

Agnes Le Fey had not been round these parts for many years, so why, all of a sudden was she back…??!

Agnes and her sister Endor had fallen out a long, long time ago. Henry had vaguely remembered it, but it was his Father who had told him the whole story; but because he was only young at the time, he didn't understand.......but the whole story, all came back to him...... right at that very moment...

Agnes was an evil nasty Witch who wanted something that wasn't hers, and Endor wouldn't give it to her. So apparently, there was a mighty fight between the two Witches. Endor had no choice but to cast a spell over the cottage and the gardens.....to prevent Agnes from getting in. She did this.......to protect it all; which put the garden into a slumber. The spell was cast to keep it safe; that's why all the animals were banished to the meadow, to protect them all, and keep them from any harm, just in case the spell was broken and Agnes could somehow enter the gardens and the cottage; take what wasn't hers, and maybe kill whatever was in her way...!!

Henry was very bewildered and shocked to see Agnes Le Fey at Mary's gate post; and why was she lying about her name...? Now that Henry had found out what Mary's surname was from the mail which the Postman had dropped earlier, he realised that she MUST be a descendent of the sisters, but how was that possible..??!

Henry seized his moment, just in time before Mary had the chance to tell the old woman what her surname was. If Mary had told her, then Agnes Le Fey would have known straight away that she was related to her, and god knows what would have happened. The reason he flew over to Mary, was to distract her – and it worked..!!

# Chapter 9

## **<u>The Relative, The Friend & The Longest Day</u>**

After Mary's strange 'meeting' with Old Mother Sage at the garden gate, she sat down at the kitchen table with her cup of tea, wondering about the conversation that she had just had, and how very odd she thought Old Mother Sage was. She didn't like the way that the old woman had scowled at her - at all. In fact, Mary had a very, very uneasy feeling about her….She felt uneasy when the old woman started mumbling as she had taken her hand. No, Mary didn't like it one bit….what a strange woman…!!

Mary sat, sipping her tea, and feeling oddly tired.

Henry was still sat on the kitchen windowsill, catching his breath from what had just happened, and the realisation of the whole event from the past. He had hurriedly followed Mary into the house without her knowing, and he too had been staring out of the window from behind the curtains, at the old woman at the gate. He couldn't quite believe that he had just got to Mary in time, and stopped her from revealing her identity…!!

"Dear, dear me" he muttered wearily to himself, as he sat back on the windowsill, shaking his head, and mopping his brow with his handkerchief.
"That was close – I honestly can't believe what I have just witnessed out there. I need to get back to Patsy to tell her what's happened straight away".

"WHO'S THERE….?!!" Mary suddenly shouted loudly, and stood up quickly from her chair.
Henry jumped up and looked around. Had Mary heard something? Had the old Witch come back? He looked out of the window, but there was no one there. He was looking around desperately, but couldn't see anyone, so he peered out of the window again, to see if Agnes had returned.

"I'm going to ask you, one more time. Who are you, and who is Patsy..??!!
I heard you!" shouted Mary.

Henry - startled – quickly turned back around, and kept looking from left to right. Was Patsy here..??

Then, Henry's eyes widened, as he slowly turned towards Mary…… Could Mary HEAR him...??!!
Surely not, but how…how could she hear him, it wasn't possible...?!

He decided to cough into his hand. "Ahem…."

"I said, who's there…??!!" Mary repeated. Henry realised that she COULD hear him.

He quickly thought about it. The only thing he could think of doing, was to talk to her…!!
He didn't have a clue what to say though, but plucked up courage and just said.

"H….H.. ..Hello, can you hear me??" he stuttered, and then put a clenched fist into his mouth. He was half hid behind the curtain, with wide staring eyes. It was the only thing that he could think of saying.

"Y…Yes, I CAN hear you……but who are YOU, and where are you..?!" Mary shouted. She was very frightened, he could see that. She slowly reached for the sweeping brush that was just leaning against the wall.

Oh no, not the sweeping brush…!!
Then Henry realised how frightened she really was...

"P…P….Please, please don't be alarmed, and don't be afraid, and don't hurt me either…. I'm over here - on the windowsill" said Henry, trying to sound calm, although he was very, very nervous. Then thinking what an idiot he was. What if she tried to swat him with the brush?!

"Where…?! I can't see anyone…!!" Mary had walked cautiously over to the window, with the sweeping brush in her hands, and was searching around wildly; although she didn't really know who or what she was expecting to see.

 "I'm going to ask you ONE….MORE….TIME - where are you, and WHO are you?? If you don't come out, I'm going to call the Police!!" Mary shouted.

"I'm here, I'm here…!!" shouted Henry, as he slowly emerged with his hands in the air, feeling like a fugitive…

"I'm not going to harm you. In fact, I'm probably more frightened than you are…!!" Henry replied, and started waving his hanky frantically at Mary.

Mary looked down to where the voice was coming from. Henry was still trying to wave at her, quite madly now.

All of a sudden, Mary gasped, and put her hand to her mouth as she slowly bent her head down to take a closer look at a Bee - waving a handkerchief, from her kitchen window sill……

"What in the name of……..really….??" she started to speak, as she staggered backwards, one hand now across her chest, and the other still firmly holding onto the broom.

"Is that YOU talking…??" she managed to say.

Henry nodded.

"Erm, yes, it is me talking….and…and…I…I do talk – quite a lot as it happens…..well, every day anyway…..." He answered back, rather awkwardly, but his voice didn't sound quite right, because he realised that he was just as shocked and nervous as Mary, but more shocked that she could hear HIM…!!

He quickly managed to say "How can you hear me..?? I don't understand"

"How can you even TALK…?!!" Mary answered, now slowly walking towards Henry. She bent down to take a closer look at him, with the brush still in her hand.

Henry's eyes were shiftily looking at the broom.

"I would feel SO much better right now, if you could put that brush down….please..??" Henry said in a rather high voice.

"Oh no…!! What's happening to me…?!....this isn't right, I'm going mad. I'm actually going quite mad!!" she wailed, as she held onto the back of the chair with one hand.

"Please can you put the brush down..?" said Henry looking decidedly worried.

"Mary, I, I, I know this is difficult for you, so please try and stay calm. My name is Henry" said Henry, pointing to his chest and trying to reassure her.
Mary was looking straight at Henry, and feeling a little dazed. Then, surprisingly she said.

"It's not the fact that you are a Bee, who is talking to me, and I should be so afraid that I think I might be going mad. I've always known that I'm a 'little' different"

She was now talking out loud to herself, as she slowly walked away from the windowsill, and then around the table. She put the brush back against the wall, (which made Henry feel suddenly better) and then began wringing her hands.

".....so I suppose it comes as no surprise really" she carried on.

Then she suddenly stopped, and slowly walked back to the windowsill, her head bowed low to take another closer look at Henry.

"…and this is happening – right??"

Henry nodded – lots of times.
"Ok – well I'm not afraid" she said. Henry was relieved.
 "….but please tell me I'm not dreaming though"

"You're not dreaming, and yes, you ARE talking to me, and yes I AM a Bee, and I'm sat on your windowsill, and you're not going mad, and as a matter of fact, after what has just happened outside, I feel quite faint!!" said Henry. He suddenly felt a little light-headed after all the excitement, and sat back against the windowsill, and wiped the back of his hand against his forehead.

"Was that YOU buzzing around my head outside just now??" quizzed Mary.

"Yes, it was. I was trying to protect you" he said, whilst mopping his brow, but with his hanky this time.

"Protect me… from what exactly..??" Mary asked.

"From telling that awful woman your surname…!" replied Henry, who had now sat upright.

Mary looked at Henry surprisingly and said.

"Do you KNOW her….and why would you want to protect me??" she asked

"Yes, unfortunately I DO know her. Well, I knew OF her. I remember her from a very long time ago, and she's a bad Witch" replied Henry.

"A 'what'….. A WITCH…..did you say… a WITCH..???!...But there's no such thing…!!!"

Henry nodded solemnly. Mary clasped both of her hands to her mouth.

"No, no, no……this isn't right. I actually am going mad aren't I..?? I mean, talking bees and Witches in the same sentence. No, I'm not accepting that. None of this is right. A 'witch'..?? Is there really such a thing..??. This just can't be happening – not again..!!......... WHAT…???….why did I say that, what do I mean by 'not again' ". Mary exclaimed, as she started to walk around the kitchen with her hands in the air, and feeling suddenly puzzled.

"Mary, what did you mean when you just said '....this can't be happening - not again…' What do you mean by that.."?

"Mmm..?? What…??.....D...d…did I say that..?? Oh yes I did didn't I..??" Mary asked. She was looking very confused.

"Maybe I've been out in the sun too long, or maybe I'm just over-tired. Yes, that's what it is. I should probably take some tablets and go have a little sleep or something. I'll wake up, and it will all have been a dream……right…?!!"

She looked over at Henry, and he shook his head.

"Mary…… I DID say a Witch" said Henry…." and, like I said, she's a really bad one; and…….."

Henry looked at her and grimaced.

"….and what…??! Mary quizzed, "What is it…..does it get worse…??!"

"Well, there's a possibility…….that….that she's your 'relative'…." He grinned – rather awkwardly as he said the word 'relative' in a high pitched voice.

"She's my WHAT…?!!...What do you mean, she's my relative…?! Well that's a lie - because I don't have any living relatives..??!!" She gestured with both her hands in the air and looked at Henry triumphantly.

Henry realised that Mary didn't have any idea WHO Agnes Le Fey was; and then saying that she had no relatives…? This was getting confusing….

"Oh….. I feel really, really strange, I just don't understand what's going on..!!" Mary said, as she held the back of the chair.
"How do you know my name anyway…??" Mary asked suddenly, realising that the talking Bee knew who she was.

"Mary, I think you should sit down, and drink that tea. There is a lot to tell you" said Henry, suddenly feeling the urgency to tell Mary who he believed she was related to.

Mary was feeling a little bit shocked – not only had she had a strange meeting with an old woman who was really a Witch, she THEN had a conversation with a Bee, who then proceeded to tell her that she might be related to the Witch….!! It was all far too much for her to take in, so she sat down at the table and put her head in her hands for a few moments. Henry flew down to the table, and waited.
Mary seemed to be talking to herself for a few moments.

She looked up, and saw the kindly bee, who was now smiling at her. She felt a strange sense of familiarity, and didn't seem as shocked or afraid.

"Drink your tea Mary" he urged kindly.

Mary sipped on her tea, which she now held with both hands, and started to calm down.

Henry asked Mary where she was from, so Mary told him about moving from the countryside with her Mother to the city, and then meeting James, and living

in the city centre in a large apartment, and then how she came about buying the cottage. Henry was bemused.
Then she turned the conversation back to the old woman outside at the gate.

"When the old woman took my hands out there, I felt something REALLY strange surge through me, like something had breezed right the way through my soul, and now I'm feeling so odd, but at the same time – a sense of belonging. I know that doesn't sound right, but that's all I can explain right now. I feel really sleepy" Mary put her cup down.

"Did she say anything to you..??" Henry asked.

Mary told Henry that the old woman had looked at her hands instead of greeting her with a handshake; and that she began to turn Mary's hands over and over in hers and started to mutter words that Mary couldn't understand, and it seemed like she was reading her palm.

"She's not to be trusted" Henry said. "At any cost, do not engage in any conversation with that woman again..!"

"I don't know why, but I really don't feel that shocked that I'm having a conversation with you Henry, and it's really nice to meet you". Mary put out her index finger, and they 'shook hands'.

 Henry smiled.
"I'm very pleased to meet you too Mary".

Mary yawned., and then picked her tea back up.

"I am so, so tired….but whatever it is you have to tell me Henry, tell me now. I really don't know what is going on, but something very, very odd has just happened, and now this is all making me feel really strange all of a sudden"

 Mary put her cup of tea down, rather clumsily, and spilled some of the contents onto the table. She brought her hand up to her head, and touched her forehead, and it seemed as though she was trying to remember something……something from her past.

"Mary…??" said Henry gently. "Are you alright..?"

Mary didn't look so good.

"I feel….I feel…really, really…. ti……" Mary's head flopped onto the table.

"Mary….MARY!!

# The Story of Jenny Malone

## *Chapter 9a.*

## *1976*

"*Mum, can we take a picnic to Fallswood Hill today....pleeeease..?*" *pleaded Mary, as she jumped up and down.*
"*Please say yes Mum!*".... *and clasped her hands together and looked up at her Mother with hopeful eyes.*

*Mrs Le Fey ignored her daughters' plea, and turned to Jenny – Mary's best friend.*

"*Jenny, have you asked your Mother if you can go with Mary to Fallswood Hill..?*" *Mrs Le Fey said, giving Jenny a quizzical look.*

"*Y...Y..Yes Mrs Le Fey, she said it would be alright*" *Jenny answered a little nervously, as she shot Mary a quick look.*
*Mary looked quickly at Jenny, gave her a broad smile, then she looked back at her Mother.*

"So can we go Mum...pleeease..??"

"Well, I suppose so, but please, just try and be careful. You know I'm not too keen on you going up there."
Sarah Le Fey wiped her hands on her apron, as she went into the kitchen to prepare some sandwiches for Mary and Jenny.

As she got the un-cut white loaf out from the bread bin in the pantry, Sarah Le Fey muttered under her breath....

"Makes me feel really nervy that place".

She cut some nice thick slices and began buttering them.
She got the picnic basket out from the bottom of the kitchen cupboard, and carried on preparing the picnic.

"See, I told you it would be ok" Mary whispered to Jenny, nudging her as she smiled.

"Yeah, but I never asked my Mum if I could go to Fallswood Hill with you..!" Jenny answered, looking a bit worried, and thinking that she was going to get into sooo much trouble when her Mother really DID find out.

"Well, don't tell her then!" said Mary cheekily, and slipped her arm into her best friends.

"Here you are you two; there are cheese sandwiches here, and an apple each, and a chocolate biscuit; Oh, and a little bottle of milk to share"

"Thanks Mum!" Mary took the picnic basket eagerly, and both girls turned round to go.

"Be careful you two – and don't be late!!" Sarah shouted after the two excited girls; who were now halfway down the garden path.

"Bye Mum..!"
"Bye Mrs Le Fey.!"

Sarah then shouted after them.

"The picnic blanket is at the bottom of the basket – don't leave it..!!" She was wringing her hands on the front of her apron again.

Sarah watched until they were both out of sight. She had always felt a little afraid, and had always been worried about Mary.
Since Sarah had lost her Husband only a few years ago, when Mary was only young, She had tried to manage, and bring Mary up the best way she could on her own, but it had been very, very difficult at times

without her husband, and of course, Mary was without her Father.

Mary was an unsettled child for some time after her Fathers' death, so Sarah had tried to keep her close to her, following her husband's wishes, and to try and not let her out of her sight; but she had to let Mary be a child and have friends.

She couldn't tame her wild natured daughter though, no matter how much she tried.

Mary was bold, lively, outspoken, vivacious and unafraid, and had a short temper, but also had a lovely, kind sweet way about her, and a good heart. Sarah knew she was a strong little girl.....but there was always something very special about Mary; and very different.......

# Chapter 9b.

## 1976.

## Talking to the animals...??

Fallswood Hill was on the edge of Fallswood Woods, which was about a mile away; and it was a fair walk, but it was a warm sunny day. It was the summer school holidays, and the girls chatted and laughed along the way.

The road out of the village was quite pretty with fields full of wheat, oats and barley, and all along the hedgerows grew wild cowslip. There were lots of beautiful gardens bursting with colour, and most of the gardens had apple and pear trees growing in them. Mary always loved peering over the hedges and the garden gates on her tip toes, at all the well-kept gardens in the village, and always wishing that one day, she would have her very own.

"Jenny, one day when I have my own house, I will have lots of apple and pear trees in my garden, and you can come round and help me pick some at harvest

festival time, and we can make lots of puddings and pies..!"
Mary loved the smell of the fresh country air, and all the associated noises of rural living, like the tractors on the lanes, the cows in the fields, and all the insects buzzing around.

"I just love the countryside Jenny, don't you..?"
She closed her eyes, tilted back her head, took a deep breath in, and flung her arms out wide. One of her arms skimmed across the top of the hedgerow, and she suddenly felt something on her fingers. She stopped, opened her eyes, and looked on the top of the hedge, just in time to see a Dragonfly fall over the other side.

"What's up Mary, what is it..?" Jenny asked, as she too peered over the top of the hedge.

As they both looked over, they saw the Dragonfly on the ground. Mary must have caught the Dragonfly with the back of her hand when she had flung her arms out, as one of its wings looked damaged.
The Dragonfly was making its way along the ground, and doing a funny little hop, then a jump as it tried to fly, but couldn't get itself off the ground.

"Oh Jenny, that poor Dragonfly…. I think I've just knocked its wing…..!! Oh I hope it's going to be alright…! It seems to be ok though…….Oh you are…? Are you sure……?! Is there anything I can do to help you....?? ......Oh, ok then - only if you're sure. I'm so sorry, I didn't mean it; it was an accident...Take care...!! Phew....thought I'd nearly killed it then!"

Jenny, very slowly, turned to Mary, and was staring at her as if she didn't want to ask, but really DID want to know, and said .....

"...how do you know the Dragonfly is alright.....??"

Mary looked a little awkward, but said brightly.

"Erm.....well....because he told me...!" she said with a strange smile on her face.

"The Dragonfly told you that....?? Oh....ok....right....I see...o...o...ok"

Jenny smiled awkwardly, and quickly looked sideways at Mary, and back to where the Dragonfly was, who had now gone, and then back at Mary.

"Oh look..!!" said Mary, suddenly nudging Jenny, and changing the subject, "There's Ken!"

Ken, the Grocer was at the doorway of his grocer's store, standing very tall in his smart dark blue coat. His hair was always tidy, with a side parting, and it was very neatly combed and slicked back. He waved at the two girls.

"Hello Mary, Hello Jenny" He called.

The girls waved back.

"Hello Ken – where's Bruce today..?" Mary shouted.

"Oh, he'll be somewhere; probably one of the neighbours' houses. You know what he's like. Anywhere where he can get a little tit bit of food, Bruce will be there!" Ken shouted back, smiling.

"Well he was at my house all last night, till quite late, but when I got up this morning, he'd gone". Mary shouted back.

Bruce was Ken's dog; a lovable little Staffordshire Bull Terrier, with lots of black and brown dapples of colour. He was everybody's 'friend', and everyone loved him, and all the children played with Bruce. Mary and Jenny – more than most of the other kids, spent a lot of time with Bruce. He was very loyal, playful and always seemed so protective.

"Making the most of the school holidays I see?" Ken nodded to the picnic basket.

"We're going to Fallswood Hill Ken, for a picnic!" Jenny shouted back.

"Ah well, if you're going up there then, you might need some of these"

He gestured with a pointed finger, as he quickly walked back into the shop and emerged with a small punnet of strawberries. He swiftly walked over the road to them, and winked as he gave them to Mary, who put them in the basket.

"Thank you Ken..!!" Both girls looked at each other...wow - strawberries...!!

"Take care mind" he shouted back, and waved as he went back into the shop.

The girls giggled at each other, and locked arms as they walked along the lane, towards Fallswood Hill, singing a song that they had sung many, many times before when they played out. It was a hand clapping song called 'Miss Mary Mack'

"Miss Mary Mack, Mack, Mack, all dressed in black, black, black, with silver buttons, buttons, buttons, all down her back, back, back..........."

The song went on and on, and they sung it over, and over again, whilst they walked and skipped further and further along the lane, until the song faded away, and the girls became two small dots in the distance.....
What a great picnic they were going to have...!!

Mary, and Jenny Malone had been best friends since the very first day at Primary School. Jenny was the quieter one of the two, and Mary was the chatterbox. Jenny warmed to Mary instantly, as she somehow felt protected by her friend. Mary had stuck up for Jenny on many an occasion, as she would get teased for her wavy auburn hair and her freckles. The boys at school would shout 'Moany Malone' or 'Freckles'

Mary would shout back at them and tell them to 'shut up'

Then they would make weird noises through their hands...

"Woooo......ooooooh"

"Who are you, Jenny's Mother...can't she stick up for herself..??!" They would tease.

"I said SHUT UP..!" Mary would shout.

"It's alright Mary, ignore them, they're not worth it" Jenny pleaded; but Mary would get really angry. She would run at the offenders, until they scattered; laughing.....

"Weirdo Le Fey, weirdo Le Fey...!!" They shouted.

Mary wasn't too bothered that they called her 'weirdo Le Fey', she didn't really care. She wasn't frightened of anyone, and could stand her ground. She had always been strong-willed, unafraid, different, and maybe even a bit 'strange'......

Well actually - Mary WAS quite special; in the fact that............ she could talk to animals.......!!

She didn't know that she could, until she heard a Robin in the garden one summer, when she was quite young; not that long after her Father had passed away.

She had been sat on the blanket in the back garden on the grass, and the Robin fluttered down to a small tree not too far away from her. She had looked up and quite nonchalantly said.

"Good Morning Mr Robin, and how are you today..?" while she was idly playing with her dolly.

"Good Morning to you too Mary" the Robin answered.

Mary – shocked - dropped her dolly and covered her mouth with both of her hands, as she stared at the bird in the tree.
The Robin didn't say anything, but flew down a little closer to Mary. She wasn't frightened, and took her hands away from her mouth, then slowly whispered.

"Can you talk..?"

"Why, yes of course I can talk" He had answered back.

"How do you know my name..?" Mary had asked.

"....because I have been a visitor to your garden for some time now, and I have watched you play, and heard your Mother calling your name" He answered. Mary was delighted, and so, struck up a conversation with the Robin, and chatted with him for quite a while. He told her his name was Mr. Bercu, to which little Mary had giggled, and said.

"Mr Bercu...?? That's a funny name for a Robin, where did you get it from?!"

The Robin laughed and told her that his surname had come from his Father, just like Mary's had come from HER Father.
Mary liked it all the same, and chatted away with Mr Bercu; until her Mother came out of the house to check on her daughter, and asked her who she was talking to.

"I'm just talking to my dolly Mummy"

Sarah Le Fey smiled nervously, whilst looking around the garden, and went back into the house, wringing her hands on her apron.

So, from that day, Mary would have many conversations with Mr Bercu, and any other passing creature. She didn't really think anything of it, being so young; but as she grew a little older, she knew and realised that no one else could actually hear any creature or animal talk at all, and to admit that, would most certainly have caused some concerns; so she kept the 'secret' to herself.

She did once, however, ask her Mother if she herself could hear animals talking, or if she had ever spoken to one.

Her Mother had shot Mary such a look.

"Don't you EVER say anything like that again; that's a stupid question to ask....!!"

Mary was quite shocked at her Mothers reaction, and had looked at her, really puzzled. She had never seen her Mother get so angry like that before.

"But you talk to the Budgie, and so do I" Mary had answered.

"Yes...yes...but that's....'different'...!" her Mother snapped, looking awkwardly at her.

"Why is it different..?" Mary asked.

"It's different...because......because.....WE taught the Budgie to talk, so it just repeats what we say....!"
An exasperated Sarah Le Fey said, who was trying really hard to discourage a conversation that she found difficult, and didn't want to have.
".....besides, I don't want you to ever ask that question again – to anyone – EVER!! Do you understand me..?!"
Mary's Mother was quite angry.

"You're never to say to anybody that you can hear animals talking, do you hear me...?! They'll think you've gone bloody mad Mary; and I'm not having gossip like that around the village.....so keep that secret to yourself!!"

"Ok – I won't" Mary had said, rather sorrowfully, putting her head down as she had walked away, whilst looking down at her shoes. Why had her Mother got so angry...?

That was the only conversation that Mary had with her Mother about the subject, and like her Mother asked - she never spoke of it again....

Mary didn't know why she could talk to animals and hear them talking back to her – she just could.
Sarah Le fey had a bit of a task on her hands with Mary. She didn't know if her daughter's defiant wild ways, her strength, and her very stubborn streak were the result of losing her Father at such a young age; or

whether it was just Mary's personality – either way, she was definitely a handful, but was never a bad child.

Strangely enough, she just knew that her daughter would always be able to take care of herself.

Mary had only the faintest memories of her Father, who was a very tall man, with striking good looks, perfect white teeth, and a big smile, who would pick her up, and hold her close, and whisper in her ear, until little Mary giggled.

She never really knew what happened to her Father. When Mary had asked her Mother…..

"Mummy……when is Daddy coming back…..??"…as a young child, her Mother would just say that her Daddy had got really ill and had to go away to a place to get better. That was all Sarah was able to tell her…… but he just never came home….

Mary had only one photograph of her Father, that she kept with her - all the time, and when she felt a little sad, she would take it out of her pocket, and stare at it, until the image was imprinted on her brain. She somehow drew strength from her Fathers photograph, and she could hear him, somewhere in the back of her mind saying.

"Never, ever be frightened Mary, you have more friends than you know. You will always be strong, and I will always be with you"

So, as Mary grew up, she never spoke to her Mother again about her 'secret' - or anyone else for that matter - until she met and befriended Jenny Malone.

She would tell Jenny that she could often hear animals' conversations, but wasn't frightened, and sometimes joined in! She found it quite comforting, and quite funny at times; but Jenny wasn't to breathe a word to anyone.
Jenny had agreed. She liked her friend Mary - a lot, even though she thought that Mary was indeed a little odd from time to time; but she knew that it just added to her character.

Mary was indeed, her very 'special' friend.

# Chapter 9c.

## 1976

# The Picnic, The Woods & The Argument

The girls finally arrived at Fallswood Hill that particular Thursday morning, around 11:30am. It was going to be quite a hot day, as the sun was already blazing down out of the forget-me-not blue sky. It was 1976, and the sun had been shining every day for the last few weeks now. One of the hottest summers – so the papers had said.

They found a spot on Fallswood Hill, looking down towards a huge stretch of grass at the bottom. There was a football pitch, and tall white goal posts opposite each other; and children often played football there. People would walk their dogs around the edge of the football field, and sometimes they would stand and watch. There was a small road at one side of the football pitch, which eventually led down the hill to the canal at the bottom. On the other side, was Fallswood Woods.

Mary got the blanket out, and laid it on the grass; then put the picnic basket at the top of the blanket, and the two girls laid out in the sunshine with their eyes closed.

They told jokes; they tickled each other until they were crying with laughter. They sung the 'Miss Mary Mack' song, and then did 'roly polys' down the hill, 'till they were covered with dry bits of grass, which was stuck to their dresses, and their white socks, and also stuck in their hair. Jenny even managed to get a piece stuck between her teeth..!!

"Urgh" Jenny said, as she tried pulling it out.

"You look like a farmer..!" Mary laughed as she pointed at Jenny.

Jenny then started making noises like a cow, as she put her two index fingers at either side of her head, bent her head forward, and ran at Mary. They laughed and laughed.

After they had eaten their cheese sandwiches, and chocolate biscuit, Mary said.

"Let's go into the woods Jenny..!"
Jenny wasn't too sure.

"Oh come on, don't be a scaredy-cat – I'll race you!"

With that, both girls ran down the hill at top speed, with their arms high in the air, until they tried to slow down, and it was more like a reverse flapping motion they did, as they come to a sharp 'stop' as they both grabbed a tree trunk and halted, right at the woods' edge.

"Woah..!! I didn't think I was going to stop then!" said Mary breathlessly.
"Come on Jenny, let's do a bit of exploring!" Mary said in a hushed voice, as she beckoned Jenny into the woods.

"I don't really want to, and I don't think we should Mary" Said Jenny, a little worried. "It looks a bit dark"

"Why not...?? We won't go too far in, come on, it'll be fun!"

Mary got hold of Jenny's hand before she could say anything else, and the next minute, they had left the glorious sunshine, and were now walking through shafts of sunlight between tall dark green trees. The dry twigs cracked underneath their shoes.

"Where are we going Mary, please don't go too far in, please. Let's turn back..?!"

"Oh Jenny, why can't you just have a bit of fun..?!!"

Just at that moment, they both stopped as they heard some other footsteps, and twigs snapping underfoot.

"Well, well, well. Look who it is. If it isn't 'Moany Malone' and 'Weirdo Le Fey'..." It was the boys from the playground at school.

A slight breeze had built up, and was making the leaves rustle high above in the trees.

Jenny looked up.

"Mary, let's just go...!" Said Jenny.

"Why – I'm not scared..?!" Mary looked angrily at Jenny; then looked back at the three boys who were now standing right in front of them.

"Scared..?? Oh - you will be scared" Said John Bracken. He liked to be known as JB. He was the ring leader, and loved nothing more than to make people frightened of him, by doing anything he could to provoke them, or tease them; but Mary wasn't budging.

"Mary...!!" Jenny shouted.

JB looked across at Jenny, and back at Mary.

"Looks like your friend wants to leave now - you WEIRDO" he said, as he looked her up and down. "Why don't you just do as you're told, and run along??" JB said sarcastically, and pushed Mary.

Jenny felt an uneasy feeling around her.

Mary had staggered back a few steps, as the other two boys stood behind JB, laughing. Mary straightened herself up, and took a few steps closer, squaring up to her perpetrator.

Surprised at Mary's stance, he said.

"Oooh...so you wanna be brave Le Fey..??"
JB turned around to his mates, smiled and nodded at them, to get some positive reaction - which of course he did.
As he turned back round to face Mary, Mary gave him the biggest shove - and JB fell back and onto the ground.

Jenny gasped, and put her hands to her mouth, as she started walking slowly backwards. So did the other two boys, who both looked at each other, in horror.
JB hurriedly got up off the ground; brushing his pants down as he did so. His face had turned red with anger (and a little embarrassment).

Mary was smiling.

"You're gonna be REALLY sorry you did that…!!" He said through gritted teeth. He was really angry.

Mary, on the other hand, didn't care one bit.

"Oh yeah..??! She answered, putting her hands on her hips as she stepped forward another step, until there were only inches between them.

The wind had suddenly picked up at that moment, and the branches started swaying above them. Mary was feeling more confident and stronger, and started laughing in JB's face.

Jenny looked up, and around her – she was very frightened, and had started to back off even more.

"Mary, I want to go home..!!" Jenny was wailing now as she stood behind a tree.

"Jenny – shut up..!!" Mary snapped, whilst still staring at JB.

"Please – I just want to go home!!"

JB looked at Jenny, and then at Mary.

"Looks like your little lap dog doesn't want to play with you anymore Le Fey…aw diddums…"

Mary was getting angrier, because Jenny was now crying. The other two boys were leering in the background, and JB wasn't about to step down.

"Jenny, just SHUT UP CRYING!!" Mary was clenching her teeth.

All the time, JB was prodding Mary, until she kept staggering back, but Mary was distracted by Jenny who was now sobbing.

"I just want to go home – now!!"
JB looked swiftly over his shoulder at his two mates and said.

"...'Ere, you two. Don't just stand there - shut 'Moany Malone' up, while I deal with THIS one!!" and glared at Mary.

"Don't you DARE touch her!" Mary shouted over J.B's head.

The sudden wind had now begun to swirl around, which raised up lots of small twigs, leaves and acorn shell from the ground, and they began dancing and spiralling round and round the children. This distracted JB and his two mates; who were now looking around at the swirling leaves, and then looking back at each other, with a slight fear on their faces. They had never seen anything like this before.......

Without another thought, both of the boys turned on their heels, ran straight through the swirling leaves, and out of the woods.

JB stood alone - now feeling extremely uneasy.

"Not feeling too well JB?? – I see you're on your own - now that your 'friends' have run away?!" Mary prodded JB with every word she spoke, as JB began to stagger backwards.
She was getting angrier and angrier, but more confident in her approach. The wind was now blowing her hair, and Mary's grey/green eyes were open wide. Her chin dipped as she glared at JB.

For the first time, he felt really scared.

Jenny was crying.
"Mary…..Mary – please, I want to go home…. Now…!! Pleeeease Mary. I'm frightened, and the wind is scaring me!!" She howled.

In that split second, Mary turned her head around to face Jenny. Her eyes were open wide and she glared at her friend, as the wind picked up her hair, and made it dance wildly.

"Well if you want to go – then why don't you just GO...!!! In fact just get lost and take the flippin' wind with you...!!!" She shouted at the top of her voice.

She turned back to JB, and everything suddenly went into slow motion. Her eyes seemed to bore right through his soul.....

The look on JB's face was one of sheer horror.

In this fearful slow motion, he turned around, and fled. He stumbled as he ran, and took one last look over his shoulder, to see Mary Le Fey – stood there; still with the same dark haunting look on her face – staring at him, as the leaves swirled around her. He just ran and ran - out of the forest as fast as his legs would carry him.....

Mary, in her haze, slowly turned back to where Jenny was – but Jenny - had disappeared......

# Chapter 9d

## 1976

# *The Disappearance*

On that hot sunny day, Thursday 12$^{th}$ August, 1976, the Police had found a 12 year old girl, Mary Le Fey, unconscious on a picnic blanket. The picnic basket was open, and on its side. The sandwiches had gone, and the bottle of milk had spilt over in the basket. The strawberries were tipped over, and two apples had rolled out and were found a little way down the hill.

There was a dog sat very close beside Mary when the Police had found her; he wouldn't leave her side, and he was gently licking her face. It was Ken the Grocer's dog, Bruce. She began mumbling and moved her head from side to side; then she slowly started to come round.

"Bruce....?"

Mary's memory was completely wiped of any information from that day. The trauma of the whole episode had made her unable to give the Police any details, and she was placed in a hospital for a few weeks. She was completely bewildered and couldn't remember anything at all about the incident. The last thing she remembered was running down the hill with Jenny.

Jenny Malone had disappeared – and was never found again.......

There was nothing more the Police or the Investigating Officers could do, and over time, search parties were eventually called off. Jenny's family never came to terms with it, and moved away from the area some years later.

The two boys that ran from the woods were questioned, and they had no memory either. They didn't even remember seeing Mary and Jenny that day. The last thing they remember, they stated, was walking through the woods with JB.

JB unfortunately lost his voice, for some strange reason, and the last thing he remembers was walking through the woods near to where Jenny disappeared, with his two friends.

In fact, everybody that was at Fallswood Hill that day, at the football field, and in and around the woods, were questioned, and nobody saw, or heard anything. Everybody said it was a lovely, peaceful and hot sunny day – although a few people that were questioned, had said that the weather suddenly changed, and became really windy, which was strange, because it just came and went within a few minutes, but other than that, just a lovely, sunny, normal day at Fallswood Hill.

One or two witnesses say they recall seeing Mary and Jenny playing on the picnic blanket, but that's about all.

Nothing untoward happened on that lovely hot sunny day; except a young girl, Jenny Malone, had gone missing, and no one could help or answer any questions as to why or where she had gone...

Mary stayed in hospital for a while; and then she was transferred to a quiet house in the countryside, where she convalesced, rested and played.

She eventually stopped having dreams of Jenny, calling her name over and over again. In fact, her memories of Jenny, slowly and strangely began to fade completely.

Mary slowly regained her strength, and the Doctors were pleased with her progress, enough to eventually let her go home. Her memories of that fateful day.........never came back. Events of her past, a lot of her childhood, and her 'secret' of been able to converse with animals, faded away......completely......

All she knew; was that she had been out having fun with her best friend Jenny on Fallswood Hill, and when she woke up with Bruce by her side, Jenny had just........ disappeared.

As Mary had no memories of that day, she had asked her Mum many times if it was her fault, and her Mother reassured her that it wasn't her fault at all, and that she was never to think like that again......ever....

# Chapter 9e

# <u>Sarah & James.</u>

The shock and the horror of a child going missing that day in the woods, caused so much distress and anguish to poor Sarah Le Fey, that she was afraid to leave the house. Her daughter, Mary, had been involved in a terrible incident of some sort, that no one could explain, and the poor parents of Jenny Malone wanted answers, but no one could give them any.

The Police, the on-going investigation, the Journalists from the newspapers, and people's reactions were just too much for Sarah to bear. A young girl had gone missing – her daughter, Mary's best friend.....

Sarah Le Fey had found this hard to cope with. She had always been a very nervous woman, timid and very private. The stress of that day eventually took its toll on her. She began to live like a recluse, never going anywhere or speaking to anyone – and sadly, she was never quite the same again.

Eventually, Sarah Le Fey and her daughter moved away from the country and moved to the city, to free themselves from the heavy burden of the whole sad affair. Plus, the reaction from people in and around the village, who were constantly staring and whispering also added to Sarah's depression and misery.

Mary grew up, left school, and went to an art college. She went out, had fun, and lived a normal life.

Her Mother however, didn't really recover fully from the events of that day, and her health declined.

Sarah Le Fey sadly passed away when Mary was only 20.

On Sarah's deathbed, Mary was holding her Mother's hand, and sobbing.

"Don't cry Mary – be strong, like you always are". Sarah said weakly.

"...but I need you" Mary sobbed.

A gentle breeze picked up outside.

"Stay calm Mary...." Sarah touched her daughter's face.
"You are more like your Father than you will ever know"

Mary was looking into her Mother's eyes.

"I wish he was here...why did he have to go....when we needed him..?!"
She felt angry, sad and confused.

"Mary, one day you will know EVERYTHING, and know who you REALLY are. It will come to you in time. You are so different and special. My beautiful strong Mary.... I'm just so sorry I wasn't enough for you...."

"Mum, what do you mean - don't say that..? You have been EVERYTHING to me - always there for me..!"

Sarah's hand slipped from her daughter's face.
"Mum...?...Mum..?" Mary saw her Mothers eyes close.

"Let me sleep Mary"

"I'm not leaving you, I'm staying right here" Mary whispered.
"I love you so much Mum"
Sarah managed a weak smile, and gave Mary's hand a gentle squeeze.

Mary watched her Mother for a few moments, just taking in everything that she loved about her. She had been a very striking looking woman when she was younger. Dark brown hair, such a loving smile and dimples at the side of her cheeks. She realised why her Father had fallen in love with her.

As she continued to hold her Mother's hand, and stroke her hair, Sarah's colour began to drain from her face.

"Mum..?" She whispered.

Sarah began mumbling.

"I believe you.....I believe you..."......over, and over again.

"Mum.....what do you mean... 'I believe you?'..."

"Your....your....s...secret..."

Mary didn't know what her Mother meant by that, but she squeezed her hand to let her know that she had heard her.
Then she heard her faintly say......
"Find your Father......the...the...s....stairs..." Her voice trailed off into a silent whisper.....

Mary couldn't understand what she meant.

The stresses of raising Mary on her own, everything that had happened that fateful day, and having to move away to the city to start a new life, had taken their toll on Sarah Le Fey.....

The funeral was a small affair, not many people attended. Mary noticed one or two people who she didn't recognise, as they were dressed all in black, and were at the very back of the church on the second to last row. Mary thanked the few that were there, as they had filed out of the church, but the other people from the back of the church, had gone. Maybe they were from the village from years ago, or some of her Mum's old friends.

At her Mother's funeral, Mary met James Thompson. He was one of the Pall Bearers, who carried her Mothers coffin. He was studying at University, and he had needed a part time job.
Mary chatted with him briefly after the funeral, thanking him, along with the other Pall Bearers.

A few weeks later, Mary was out shopping at the supermarket, and bumped into James Thompson – literally.
They had both been absent-mindedly not looking where they were going, and after James bent down to retrieve the loaf of bread that Mary had dropped, saying 'so sorry' as his eyes met hers, they both said an awkward 'oh hi'. They chatted for a while, and James asked her how she had been, and then he suddenly plucked up the courage, and said to her that if she needed a chat anytime, maybe they could meet at a cafe...?

James was a very attractive young man; dark short hair, big blue, kind eyes, and a lovely smile.

Mary agreed and they met up at the local café, and ended up chatting for hours. They arranged to meet again, the week after; this time at the local pub, and enjoyed a few drinks together. They just talked and talked, and laughed. They arranged to meet the week after that, and then kept having coffees, drinks, then having meals out.

Before long, they were talking about moving in together – and they did just that.

They were a perfect match; it was as if they were meant to be together.

Mary still had the house that was hers and her Mothers, so James eventually moved in.

They lived in the house for two years, until James landed his dream job. Mary sold the house and they ended up living in the middle of the city, close to James' work place, in a luxury apartment.

Mary had told James that she had been involved in some kind of incident in the woods. It was only snippets of information, as Mary didn't have much memory of it. She wanted him to know from the start, just in case he had heard anything from anyone, or seen the papers at the time.

She explained to him that now and then, she would dream of someone called Jenny, and that she would be calling her name. The next day, she would feel tired and a bit dizzy, and had sometimes found it really hard to leave the house. The Doctors couldn't find any way to bring her memories back, and said to her Mother that one day, it may all just return. She told him that sometimes she would just cry and cry, but didn't know why; but the awful truth was, she just didn't have any memories. They had all faded so much.

James was very sympathetic towards Mary, and explained that it was probably the shock that had made her forget.

She also told James about her Father, and Mother. James felt very protective towards her, as she had lost both her parents at such a young age. He comforted her, and Mary felt so protected and loved by him. He was just the perfect man for Mary. He was kind and funny, and made her laugh. He was very tolerant of her quick temper, and her outbursts of frustration, but he loved and understood all of her quirky, funny ways, and came to accept her and love her, for who she was.

She had told James that the only thing that she would wish for, would be to remember more of her past, and why was it so vague…?…but she couldn't.

*(She also didn't have any idea that she could talk to animals. That part of her past had left her memory, many years before.*
*The only person who knew about that - was Jenny Malone..........)*

# Chapter 10

## **<u>Realisations</u>**

In the distance, Mary could hear a man's voice calling her name, and felt a cool breeze on her face. The voice got louder and louder – and she slowly opened her eyes.

"Mary, Mary…..are you ok…?!" Henry was sat on the kitchen table wafting an envelope across her face.

"Oh thank goodness..!!" Henry sighed, when he saw signs of Mary waking up. He then sat down himself, rather wearily; feeling quite exhausted, and began wafting his own face with the envelope.

"You were out cold for quite a bit then – I was starting to panic Mary..!! Are you alright..?!"

 Mary brought her head up from the table, and looked at Henry. Rather dazed and unsure of what was going on, she stared at the Bee, who was clearly in a bit of shock, but he was now, as she noticed, looking quite relieved. She stood up very slowly, pushed her chair back, and staggered to the kitchen sink and poured herself a long cold glass of water from the tap – and drank the whole glass. She came back to the table, and sat back down, rubbing the side of her head. Henry was watching her closely.

"Mary – what's just happened..?" Henry asked, now rather concerned.
"Just take your time, it's alright". He assured her gently. He realised that she may have sustained a bit of concussion when she had passed out. What if she didn't remember anything…??

As Henry kept on looking at Mary for a sign – anything; he could slowly see the colour coming back to her face. She put her elbows on the table, and her head in her hands, covering her face. Then she took her hands away slowly, and looked at Henry and said.

"I remember….. I remember. It's all coming back to me...!."

Henry felt relieved.

"Oh thank goodness….!! For a minute there, I had visions of having to dodge that sweeping brush again, as you might not have remembered who I was….!! So…… just to reassure me, you remember the old Witch at the gate, and me flying over to you, and coming into the house – yes…??"

"Well yes, I do now…."

"Good…" Henry said. "Now, we must get……."

 Mary butted in.

"No Henry, you…you don't understand – I'm starting to remember EVERYTHING……. I mean from my past...!!"

He realised that Mary was talking about something else.

"What exactly do you mean…??" he asked slowly. "….everything about what…??"

"It's all coming back to me. My life…..my….my whole life. 'That' day; the house I lived in with my parents, my school……and my, my friend……..JENNY…!"

Mary's eyes filled up, and she started crying. It was all too much. All of her past, which had been completely missing, was slowly coming back, and she was finding it all very difficult to process, like she had just re-lived it all again, but it was new to her. All those years of who she was as a child; and what had happened on that day in Fallswood Woods. Her long stay in hospital……everything…but most of all, her best friend Jenny Malone.

Henry was most concerned to see Mary upset, and knew something traumatic had happened.

"I always knew…" she said  "….don't ask me how, but I always knew that one day, at some point in the future, something strange would happen. I was only a little girl"

Mary had started recalling her past… "I remember the picnic I went on; I remember Ken the Grocer, Bruce, his little dog..!" Mary's eyes were welling up. "We had cheese sandwiches, and a chocolate biscuit. We played – it was such a hot day. We ran down to the hill to the woods….we went into the woods. Why would I remember that now, I didn't know back then!!" Mary's eyes were widening.

Henry was very quiet, and trying to take everything in that Mary was saying.

"John Bracken….JB. It was him…!! I got REALLY angry, because he was making fun of me, and I remember the weather suddenly changing. It got really windy, and the leaves on the ground came up and were swirling round and round….!" Mary's hands were now either side of her face.
"Jenny…!! Jenny – my friend..!" Mary had got up quickly, and was now walking around the kitchen, as her memory got better and better.

"I got angry with Jenny – because……because she was…… crying..!"

Mary started sobbing, and had to sit back down at the table, her head in her hands again.

 "All of it…….!! It's my fault….I know now – it was ME..!!.......... Then we had to move away…!"

Henry quickly shot a glance out of the back kitchen window; the sky had suddenly gone grey, as if it was going to pour with rain.

"Mary…… I want to help you, I really do, but I just don't understand. Why would you suddenly remember something from your past, which you're saying you weren't already aware of…?"

She turned to Henry, and began to explain everything to him; it all just rolled off her tongue. Henry could hardly believe what he was hearing. He had to sit back down, with his back against the sugar bowl, with his mouth slightly open……… He had suddenly realised something.

"Mary – I vaguely remember the story – my Father told me that it was all in the papers at the time!! So that was YOU…??!!"

Mary nodded.

Henry got up and walked round and round the table, with his hands behind his back. Mary was wandering around the kitchen; they were both deep in thought.

"I have to tell James..!!...but he's not coming back home for some time yet, he's working away"

"No Mary – no, not yet..!!" Henry urged her.

As all her memories came flooding back, she was gaining more and more clarity. She recalled little snippets of memories of her parents. She remembered conversations she had with her Mother, and one conversation in particular, when her Mum had got really angry with her one day, because Mary had asked her if she could talk to animals, and she had got so cross with her, and told her never to repeat that again, or speak of it, EVER…………..

Then, just as she was thinking about that conversation, she remembered, with shock - that she had always – as a child, been able to talk to animals, and have conversations with them…and she had completely forgotten about that….until now…!! …..and there was Henry sat listening, and they were having a conversation - TOGETHER..??!!

Yes…..she could! Of course she could – she's always been able to..!!!
Why had she forgotten for all of these years..?! …and why now could she remember…..all of a sudden??

"Mary, if you have always been able to converse with animals, I wonder if you just naturally have 'a gift'…??"

Henry had a million questions, but didn't know where to start.

"It's so strange" Henry said whilst walking on the table cloth in circles.

" I mean, it was more than enough finding out that you had the same blinkin' surname as that awful woman……...calling herself 'Old Mother Sage'….bah…."

Then all of a sudden, Henry stopped in his tracks, and slowly looked over at Mary.

He had just realised something, as Mary had started talking again, half listening to Henry….

"…..My Mother used to say to me all the time 'you're just like old Auntie Doe'. I don't know who she was talking about, I haven't got a clue; I suppose it was an old distant Aunt of mine, but she must have been the same, a bit strange…."

Mary carried on talking, but Henry wasn't listening, he was now thinking about what she had just said.

"Mary…." Henry said, as he tried to get her attention; but Mary was still chattering away, about how she first remembered talking to a Robin in the back garden.

"Mr Bercu….!!" She shouted out loud. "That was his name…!!"

"Who..?" Henry asked.

"The Robin I used to talk to in my back garden when I was a little girl…!!"

She then recalled the time she had gone for a walk in the field at the back of her house, and whilst walking past a field of horses, she had stopped to stroke one at the fence, when Mary had suddenly sneezed, and the Horse had said 'Bless You'.!!

"Mary..!!" shouted Henry again. He had been pacing up and down the table, but Mary was now talking about something else….!

"…..and THEN there was another time, yes, it's all coming back to me now. When I was playing in the garden with my dollies….I was with Jenny…." Tears welled up in Mary's eyes again as she spoke her friend's name.

"We were sat down on the grass, and I was almost sure that I had heard a conversation between two worms. I told Jenny, and she started laughing at me, just laughing and laughing, and telling me how silly I was. I got really angry with her, and I shouted at her to stop….but she just kept laughing. Oh god….. I remember then, that the wind started blowing, and the branches in the trees started swaying… Jenny got scared, and so did I…!!"

Mary was completely re-living a scene that was so clear to her.

"Jenny shouted at me to stop being angry at her. She was pleading with me. I looked at her little pretty freckly face, and thought she was about to cry, and that made me feel really sad, so I stopped. Then she held me tightly, and tried to calm me down. I said I was sorry; and when I stopped, the leaves dropped silently to the floor, and the wind died down….. She KNEW…!! Jenny knew….!! That day in the woods, when she told me to stop; and that she wanted to go home……SHE WAS TRYING TO CALM ME DOWN..!! She KNEW…!! She was trying to stop me from getting angry, so the wind would die down……… but I didn't stop. I was so angry at JB for laughing at me….and, it's all my fault…!!"

"MARY…!!" shouted Henry, even louder this time.

Mary suddenly stopped talking, as she had realised that Henry was shouting.

Mary…..who……is…..Auntie……Doe..??" he asked, very slowly. He wasn't being unkind to Mary, but he could see that she was getting really upset, and he needed her to focus.

"Who….??" She queried, forgetting what she had just said.

"You just said that your Mum said that you were just like your old Auntie Doe….Who is Auntie Doe…??!"

"Erm….I...err…. Auntie Doe…?? I really don't know, like I said, I think she must have been an old Aunt on Mum's side maybe. Why..?" Mary was feeling really dazed. So much had just happened.

"Mary, look at me……!" Mary sat down and looked at Henry. "Listen to me carefully. Do you know who this house belonged to? Have you ANY idea…??" asked Henry, as he looked at Mary directly, already thinking he knew the answer.

"Well no I don't, how would I…?" She answered. "Why - does it matter..?"

"Well, let me tell you who this house belonged to" Henry slowly said.

"Her name……was Endor……..Endor…… Le Fey.

Mary's tear stained face stared at Henry, and repeated what Henry had said, but almost in a whisper.

"Endor Le Fey….???" Her eyes looked around searchingly, and then widened, as she was now feeling a little scared, now realising that someone else had the same name as her too.

"Henry, I told you before, I don't have any relatives!"

Henry looked at Mary and raised his eyebrows, knowingly.

"Mary…….. Endor Le Fey lived in this cottage, and is the sister of that old woman who was outside not twenty minutes ago, pretending to be someone else!!"

"What…??!!….I…..I don't understand ANY of this…..what do you mean..??!" She asked Henry.

"It means……" said Henry "You're going to have to tell me as much as you can. This is all getting stranger by the minute…!"

# Chapter 11

# <u>**What a Day…!!**</u>

Mary carried on telling Henry everything else about her past that she could now remember, (Henry had said that it was very important that she didn't miss anything out)…..

Meanwhile, in the garden, all was well.

After Jeremy the Snail and his wife and son had moved in, everybody welcomed them with open arms. The meeting was held the very next day to introduce Jeremy to everyone else. They all listened while Jeremy began to tell them how he had wandered into the garden by mistake, and that he was nearly run over by a German Beetle…!! This got everybody laughing. Although he spoke very, very slowly, he really was quite funny. Lars the Beetle felt very proud of himself that he had 'found' Jeremy and had sounded the alarm by blowing his whistle. He came up to Jeremy and saluted him.

"I vud like to introduce myself properly to you. I am Lars" he said as he bowed his head. "I am very pleased to meet viz you. Please forgive, I did not vish to startle you in any vay last night, I voz just doing my very important job of patrolling zis garden".

Jeremy thanked Lars, as he saluted once more, bowed his head, and strode off, puffing his chest.

"Does anyone have anything they wish to add to today's meeting whilst we are all here..??" asked Patsy. She was taking the meeting as Henry had asked her to.

"Where's Henry..?" asked Wilbur the Dragonfly, as he hopped up to the front.

"Oh, he has been spending some time patrolling the front of the garden, because Mary has started digging it all up, so he is just making sure that everything is ok" answered Patsy.
"Any other business..??" she asked hurriedly. She didn't want any more questions about Henry's whereabouts.

"Yes Patsy, me" Nancy the Ladybird stuck up her hand.

"Yes Nancy, what is it..?? Patsy asked.

"Well, I have been thinking lately that seeing as we are all now settling in very nicely, it would be a good idea if we started thinking about the children, and their schooling. I could take daily lessons over
by the greenhouse, plus I have my guitar, so we could have some singing lessons too. It will keep the children occupied as well"
Nancy looked around at everyone.

"Nancy I think that's a wonderful idea, and how very kind of you" said Patsy
"I'm sure you will have some volunteers to help"


"I'll help" shouted Bonny the Spider.

"Me too!!....." Elma the Daddy Long Legs shouted over from the back. He didn't bother coming up to the front this time, as everyone would probably have had to run out of the way of his very long legs.

A few more volunteers put their names forward.
"That's settled that then. !" said Patsy, smiling.

Everybody went back to their homes and families, and the children played out in the sunshine. Patsy looked over to the house, wondering how Henry had been getting on with Mary.

She fluttered over to the house, and settled on the kitchen window at the back. She looked through the window to see if she could see anything. She could just make out Mary sat at the kitchen table, but couldn't see Henry. Just at that moment, she heard someone shouting her name.

"Patsy….!!" She looked around, and she saw that Wilbur the Dragonfly, was hopping down the long garden path. She immediately flew over towards him, as she didn't want Wilbur to know what she was doing.

"I'm here Wilbur..!" she shouted back. She finally reached him, and asked him what the matter was.

"Well It's of no great urgency Patsy, it's just that I wanted to have a word with Henry about something, which is why I asked you where he was at the meeting"

"Well is there anything I can help you with as I'm not sure how long Henry will be..??" she answered.
"You look a little troubled Wilbur" He did look a little down, and she put a comforting arm around him.
"Come and take a walk with me Wilbur"

So they walked up the path, away from the cottage. Patsy really wished Henry was here.

"Well, the thing is..." he said …"…I've been getting a little bit upset, especially since we came to the garden"

"Oh whatever for Wilbur, are you not happy here..?!" said Patsy. She looked worried.

"Oh no, quite the opposite, I'm VERY happy here!" he answered. "….it's just that, since we have moved here, and everyone is volunteering to help out, I feel like I've not being very helpful. As you know Patsy, one of my wings doesn't work very well at all since my accident, and although I can get about, hopping here and there, it's just not the same. I just wish there was something I could do"
He did look quite upset. Oh dear, Patsy REALLY needed Henry right now.

"Look Wilbur, please don't worry. I will have a word with Henry, I'm sure he won't be too long" she said very calmly. "…I'm sure there's something we can do to help you. In the meantime, why don't you go see Nancy, I'm sure she will need some help with the little ones"

Wilbur agreed, and thanked Patsy as he hopped away up the garden path.

Oh dear, where WAS Henry…??
The moment she had that very thought, she looked up, and she saw Henry, flying from around the corner of the cottage.

"Henry…!!" Patsy shouted, as she waved. Henry saw her, and flew over.

"What's the matter..??" he asked, looking rather concerned.

Patsy told Henry about poor Wilbur.

"Oh dear me, the poor fellow" said Henry. "…..we will have to try and come up with something to help him, but in the meantime, we have more urgent things to attend to…!!"


They sat down on the grass just at the side of the path, and Henry then told Patsy about seeing the old woman at the gate, realising who she was, and then what he had to do to stop Mary telling the old woman her surname…..!!

"Henry, I can't believe this is happening…!! Agnes Le Fey…?!!.. I've heard stories of her, and I thought she had disappeared many, many years ago..!! I knew that her sister Endor lived in this cottage for quite some time. Wasn't there a fight or something between the two sisters, and that's why we ended up in the meadow..?? I only know what my parents told me, so I don't know how true that was, but that was just a story that I'd heard. Then the bad sister, Agnes, must have disappeared…. Are you quite sure that it was her you saw at the gate….??"

"I couldn't mistake that awful face Patsy, even though she did look much older; and I noticed she had a very nasty scar down her face. Definitely her, but why has she come back…?? It's funny that she should turn up not long after Mary moves in…..mmmmmm…" Henry was very intrigued.

"What are we going to do Henry…..I'm scared..?!!"

What indeed was Agnes Le Fey doing back in the village after all these years..??

Did it have something to do with Mary and James buying the cottage…possibly…?
This was turning out to be more than your average day..!!


Henry then began to tell Patsy about the conversation he had with Mary in the house, until Patsy butted in.

"Wait a minute - you had a 'conversation' - with MARY…??!!….. You mean she HEARD you…??!!" gasped Patsy.

"Oh yes, I forgot to tell you about that" he answered rather nonchalantly.
"Yes she heard me alright…..!!

An awful lot seemed to have happened in such a short space of time.

"How Henry…..how is that possible, I don't understand…?!!"

He then quickly explained to Patsy about his conversation with Mary, and how it came about.

"Do you think she's a Witch too…?!" Patsy asked in a hushed voice. "I mean if she can hear you and have a conversation with you, she must be…!!"

It did seem very coincidental that not long after Mary and James buy the cottage, Agnes Le Fey turns up after been gone for many, many years; the spell has been lifted on the garden, and then Henry finds out that Mary's surname is the same as the Witches..!! Henry thought for a bit and said.

"I'm not sure Patsy. She can't be – surely. Mary doesn't seem to know anything about any of it! She's completely in the dark and quite upset. I don't think she is a Witch; but then again, is she, and doesn't even know it …!!"

Patsy could not believe what she was hearing. She didn't quite know what to say next.
They sat in silence for a few moments. Henry was deep in thought. He then looked at Patsy.

"I have a plan" He said. Patsy was quite relieved to say the least.

# Chapter 12

## **Henry tells a Tale.**

They both flew over to a secluded part of the garden, so they could at least talk in private without anyone thinking anything suspicious.

Patsy lowered her head and asked in a hushed tone. "What's the plan Henry..?"

"Well......what we need to do is find out who Mary's Auntie Doe is - as she could be someone who lives around here, or maybe someone knows her. We also need to keep an eye on Agnes Le Fey. I don't want her poking her nose in anywhere, or asking Mary anymore questions. This is becoming stranger and stranger, and we need to find out as much as we can."

"Ok, and what about Mary..?"

"Well, we need to go back and see her, as we need her help too" answered Henry.

"WE..??" questioned Patsy.

"Well yes, I think we may as well introduce you both to each other, and there's no time like the present..!"

With that, Henry took off, and looked over his shoulder as he was flying away.

"Come on.!"

Patsy flew after Henry, feeling really nervous all of a sudden.

They flew around to the front of the cottage where the kitchen window was. One of the windows was open slightly, so they both squeezed through the little gap. Patsy had to fold her wings flat behind her, so she could get in. Mary was still sat at the kitchen table, deep in thought. Henry and Patsy were on the windowsill, but Patsy hid behind the curtain, just enough to peep.

"Mary..!" Henry shouted.

Mary jumped, as if she had just woken up from a long sleep.

"Hello..?" she said.

"Mary, its Henry" he answered.

Mary walked over to the windowsill.

"Oh hi Henry….I've been trying to get my head around all of this, and it's driving me mad!"

"Well, that's why I've come back – to talk to you; and I thought we could do with another pair of ears, so I've brought someone with me. I've brought Patsy."

"Who's Patsy..?" Mary said, looking around. She couldn't see anyone.

"She's right here…. Patsy, come out, it's ok" Henry said to a very nervous butterfly, who was still peeping from around the curtain.

Patsy came out very slowly, and looked up at Mary, her eyes growing bigger. She had never been so close to a human before.

"Oh wow, a Butterfly..! Hello Patsy, It's lovely to meet you…..and you're so pretty!" Mary exclaimed. Patsy was indeed a very pretty Butterfly.

"H…H….Hello….. Mary, it's really nice to meet you" said Patsy, very timidly.

"Well what a day I'm having..!" Mary said.
Henry felt uneasy by the window, and suggested that they go sit at the table. He just didn't trust the fact that Agnes Le Fey could walk by at any minute.

"Mary, we have a lot to do; and a lot to talk about" said Henry.

"So I've brought Patsy with me, as we work as a team together, and run the garden, along with everyone else's help of course, but we make the final decisions, and help each other out"

"You do…?!" Mary was shocked to hear this.
"There's more of you…?....and you 'run the garden'..?!!"

Henry and Patsy both nodded.

"Of course we do" Henry answered, and then said

"Right Mary, I'm going to tell you as much as I know, like you asked me to. It's a lot to take in, but you must listen carefully" said Henry, and he sat on the kitchen table with Patsy by his side.


Henry then began to relay the story to Mary, which his Father had told HIM; about how the garden was once pre-loved many, many years ago, and how it used to be full of flowers, trees, strawberry patches, and apple trees, just like it was now - and it was owned by Endor Le Fey, who lived there and tended to the gardens. She was a Witch, but a good Witch, and so lovely and pretty and such a kind lady. She had an older sister – Agnes Le Fey, who was evil, nothing like Endor.
Agnes was angry because she was the oldest, and believed that she should live at the cottage and not Endor. She wanted the cottage all to herself, and would stop at nothing to get it.

At this point Mary was hanging on to every word that Henry was saying. Then she said.

"I've just realised something Henry. If your Father told you this story many, many years ago, when you were only young, how come you're still alive..??!"

"Well I'll come to that….." he said.

Henry then told Mary that there was something else about the cottage, which was a deep, deep secret, and maybe there was only Endor that knew what it really was; but whatever it was - she wouldn't tell Agnes.

So Endor could never let Agnes enter the garden and the cottage. If she did, then something really bad would happen. Agnes was evil enough to never be trusted.

"I can't believe I'm hearing this - what the hell has happened here..?!" Mary butted in.

Henry then said.

"Well, for some reason, as the story goes, Agnes was forbidden to ever enter the garden and the cottage......and why...??.... nobody really knows.... So over time, naturally, Agnes's jealousy and hatred for her sister grew stronger and stronger, but it all began to wear poor Endor out.

"One day, they had a huge argument - Endor had no choice but to cast a very strong spell to stop Agnes from entering. In fact it took a lot of spells to keep her from stepping through that gate" said Henry.
"....but in doing so, just to keep the cottage and the garden safe, the spells she cast included all of us in the garden. We were all banished to the meadow, to keep us safe of course – so my Father told me, although I do remember vaguely. But in doing so, the spells gave us all long lives, like that of humans. At the same time that happened, apparently, Endor AND Agnes just simply 'vanished'…That's the story that has been passed down over the years anyway. How much of it is true – I don't know, or how the story might have changed over the years, again, I've no idea - that's all I know"

Mary was completely shocked to hear all of this – as was Patsy.

"Where did they go, and what happened to them…??!" quizzed Mary.

"No one knows" said Henry sadly. "Like I said, I was only young when my Father – Horatio Bee, told me. You see, I come from a family of Bees that have tended to this garden for many, many years" Henry proudly said, puffing his chest out.

"All I know is that they both just vanished without a trace, and the spells that were cast over the whole cottage and the garden, forbade Agnes to ever step foot in it again; but what was strange, was the fact that Agnes had disappeared at the same time too – until now, so where did she go, and why; and did Endor 'really' have to cast all those spells to keep her out if she had simply vanished at the same time..?? A very odd story, but it's a complete mystery. Unfortunately all the plants and trees died along with the memory, and as the years went by, and the garden wasn't being tended to anymore; and because no birds or bees could enter the garden, the flowers just gave up, and withered away. Not one single person, or any living creature could ever come into the garden, because of the spells.......until the day that I found myself flying right over the top of the garden wall, and that's when I saw you Mary for the first time, digging in the garden. So you can imagine how very shocked I was to see you..!!"

Mary interrupted.

"I can't understand why they both just disappeared. It doesn't make sense, especially if Agnes was so hell bent on trying to get into this cottage. Did both of them just become......invisible, disintegrate, melt..? Oh I don't know – whatever it is that Witches do…?!"

"Nobody knows Mary….. Anyway, that all happened many, many years ago. The cottage never went up for sale, and over the years, people who lived in and around the village just got used to it being empty; and because it was at the very end of the lane away from the village anyway, it went a little un-noticed"

"When I first saw you that day Mary, tending to the garden, I never realised at the time why you were even there – I was just so shocked to see you - well 'someone'. Plus the fact that I could just fly straight over the wall as well..! Since then, I have wondered how the spells have suddenly been lifted….. BUT……I think I'm slowly starting to realise now….. "

"How – why..??" Mary asked. She still looked a little confused, as her mind hurriedly tried to work this out.

Henry suddenly stared straight ahead.

"What is it Henry..?" asked Patsy, who had been intently listening to the whole story, not knowing all the details.
Scratching his head, he stood still – thinking.

"Well I've just thought of something..!"

Patsy and Mary moved in a little closer to hear what Henry was about to say.

"As we now know – Mary - is related to Endor and Agnes Le Fey – 'somehow' - as the surname is the same. Correct..?"

Both Mary and Patsy nodded.

"So....what if Endor and Agnes didn't have any children.....what is Mary's connection; in fact; HOW is Mary connected, more to the point..?!"

Henry looked straight at Mary.

"Who is your Father, and your Grandfather..?!"

# Chapter 13

## <u>Wilbur's New Wing.</u>

Mary looked at Henry with a blank gaze, and said.

"Well…erm….my Mother was called Sarah, and my Father was called Eldon"

"Eldon..?" Henry repeated. "That's a strange name"

"Is it..?" Mary enquired. "I've never really thought about it before. I don't have that many memories of my Dad very much – unfortunately. He died when I was 6"

"What about your Grandfather..?" Henry asked.

"Well to be honest Henry, I don't have any family. All I Know is that my Mothers parents emigrated not long after Mum and Dad married, so I've actually never met them; and I think Dad was an only child, and his parents died when he was a baby" Mary shrugged her shoulders.

"Mmmmmm…" Henry was in deep thought, when all of a sudden Patsy shrieked…

"Henry, we have to get back…!!  Wilbur's wing…!!"

Henry clasped his chest. "Hells bells Patsy, you frightened the life out of me..!!"
"Yes we had better make tracks; you're right, poor Wilbur; I had actually forgotten about him..!! They'll all be wondering where we are too"

"What is it - is there something I can help you with..??" Mary asked.

So Patsy told Mary about Wilbur the Dragonfly, and about his problem with one of his wings not working properly, and that he was feeling very fed up as he couldn't help Henry and Patsy as much as he wanted to.

"Erm….well I'm quite good with a needle and thread, and I'm sure I've got something in my sewing box. You'll have to bring him here though"

"Patsy, you go and find Wilbur and bring him here" Henry said.

"Henry, I think YOU should go and find him, as you will have to tell him about Mary, and I think that would be better coming from you" said Patsy. She didn't really want to be the one to have to tell Wilbur.

"Ah yes, I see what you mean" said Henry. "I won't be too long then" and with that, he flew out of the window.

Henry found Wilbur up at the top of the garden, near to the greenhouse, along with Nancy and Bonny, who were helping the children with singing lessons. Henry heard a very deep baritone voice – it was Wilbur singing..! Henry called him over.

"Not a bad singing voice you have there my friend" Henry said whilst giving Wilbur a pat on his back.

"I actually love singing – thanks; my Dad used to sing all the time, and got me involved with The DQ"

"What's The DQ..?" Henry asked.

"Oh it was The Dragonflies Quartet. It WAS going to be called The BBCW's, which was Billy, Bob, Charlie (my Dad) and of course me - Wilbur – but we didn't get much interest… Anyway Henry what can I do for you..?"

"Patsy told me about your concern about wanting to help and the problem with your wing. Come and take a walk with me, I want you to meet someone"
Mary was still feeling rather shocked to hear that she was possibly a direct relative of the Ley Fey sisters. So too was Patsy, who was sat on the kitchen table looking rather dumb-struck

"Tell me…." Said Mary "…how do you like living in my garden..?"

"What can I say, it's just wonderful..!" Patsy said, smiling suddenly. "I've always lived in the meadow you see – I was born there. Not like Henry and some of the others, who remember the garden from years ago. I've never lived anywhere else, but living here feels great - and so safe"

"Well that makes me smile…… My god, what a day this is turning out to be..!! Oh I must find some thread and a needle..!"

Mary suddenly got up and went to the old welsh dresser in her kitchen, and brought out an old sewing basket.

"My Mum made me this many years ago" she said, looking at it with a smile on her face. It was my very first sewing basket. I keep everything in here. Now then, let me see what I have"

She put the basket on the kitchen table, and Patsy leant over to see.
Mary found some invisible thread, and a small piece of gossamer. It was very fine indeed; you could hardly see it..!!
Then she walked over to the fireplace, and picked up a box of matches that she used to light the fire with, and picked out two matches. She took a small sharp knife from the kitchen drawer and sat back at the table, and cut the pink end of the match off, and then proceeded to slice the matches lengthways, so thinly, that she ended up with lots of very tiny thin pieces of wood. Patsy was mesmerised.

"I suppose I had better wait until Henry comes back with Wilbur, so I can see how big his wings actually are. I've never made anything so tiny before" said Mary.

At that moment, Henry had arrived back with a very shaky looking Wilbur. Henry didn't want to raise suspicion and 'fly' Wilbur to Mary's kitchen, and they couldn't run, so they took a stroll, which was enough time for Henry to tell Wilbur about Mary.

Wilbur was very nervous to say the least.

"Mary, this is Wilbur". Henry introduced the Dragonfly to Mary as soon as they came through the gap in the front window. Wilbur politely, but very nervously, stretched out his hand to shake Marys, which Mary gave him her first finger to shake.

"Oh what a gentleman..! I'm very pleased to meet y......." she suddenly stopped...and took a long hard look at Wilbur.

"I, I, I…" stuttered Wilbur.

"I think he's trying to say that he's very pleased to meet you too Mary" Henry cut in. Wilbur nodded – lots of times, in agreement.

"We can talk later, there's no time to waste" Henry said quickly.
"Mary, can you fix his wing..?"

As Mary continued to stare at Wilbur, he became more nervous, and didn't know where to look.
After a few moments, Mary finally said

"It's you - isn't it..??" Mary asked Wilbur.

"Wh....Wh…Who m…m…me?" He answered pointing to his own chest and looking then at Patsy and Henry, as if they might know something.

"Yes…it is….it's YOU..!!" Mary burst out. Wilbur was looking slightly worried and really needed some help here.

"Mary – do you KNOW Wilbur…?" Henry asked.

Mary was still staring at the Dragonfly, who was now feeling decidedly uncomfortable.

"Yes – I do..!! It was about......." Mary quickly did some sums in her head. "..17 years ago; it was the summer of 1976, and I was walking down the lane on my way to Fallswood Hill with my best friend Jenny, and I outstretched my arm, and I knocked you over….It was you wasn't it. Do you remember….?!"

Wilbur now had his eyes, and his mouth wide open. He had slowly turned to Mary, as she was talking.

"Y…Y..Yes… I DO remember that happening. Yes….Th….th….that was me! It was a very, VERY hot summer, and most of the ponds had dried up, so I was trying to stay in the shade between the hedging, and then before I knew what was happening – I was on the floor…!!"

Henry and Patsy looked at each other, bewildered, and then back at Mary and Wilbur.

"Well I am so, so sorry….. I really am; I hope I didn't hurt you Wilbur. God, I'm stunned - I can't believe that was you. If my memory hadn't come back, I would never have known who you were; and how strange our paths have crossed again..!"

Mary smiled as she picked up Wilbur's wing, which was just hanging to the side, and asked him if it hurt. Wilbur just kept staring open-mouthed at Mary, and shook his head, saying nothing.

"Yes, I can fix it. I'll fasten your broken wing to the new one I'm going to make you, and then I'll try and attach both your wings together, so when you flap your 'good' wing, it should make the new one move….well let's hope so anyway – fingers crossed" Mary said as she started to thread the needle.

Mary quickly got to work. While she was busy, Henry took Patsy to one side, and they sat on the edge of the table.

"What are we going to do Henry..?!" whispered Patsy, with her hand on her head.

"Let's think straight Patsy. We need to find out who Marys Father was, and his Father before him, and his Father before him probably..!!"

"Why..?"" answered Patsy.

"Well we could actually do with some information from old ancestry records. That way, it will tell us, who lived here many years ago, and what year, and even possibly names and dates etc. Once we have found that out, it will give us some insight into the line of family that lived here before, and what they did for work, just everything about them really. Then we will know for sure who Mary's relatives really were"

"Where do we get information like that from..??" Patsy asked.

"Mary will have to ask for the information from the records department – wherever that is. Maybe the local council or something – I don't know, I'll ask her"

They walked back over to the other side of the table, and Mary was just fitting the most tiniest, but beautiful of wings to Wilbur's own wing.

"There" Mary said proudly "How's that..?"

Wilbur looked at his wing, and moved his good one gently up and down. The other one moved at the same time – it was working..!!

"Do it again Wilbur..!!" shouted Patsy.

Wilbur did it again, but this time, he flapped his wing a little stronger, and again, the other one moved at the same time, and before he knew it, he was two foot above the kitchen table....and he continued to rise.

"OH NO....!!" he shouted, as he looked down. The kitchen table suddenly looked much smaller as he flew up into the air.

"Turn, Wilbur, turn..!!" shouted Henry.
Wilbur turned to the left, just before nearly hitting a shelf. He flapped his wings even more and flew a little higher, and nearly hit the ceiling.

"Wilbur, are you ok up there..?!" Henry shouted, through his hands.

Wilbur looked down.

"Yes, yes, I'm, I'm FLYING..!!"

As he shouted, he looked down at the others, who seemed so far away now. He hadn't been that high up for such a long, long time. He suddenly started to panic a bit – his good wing wasn't very strong anymore due to not using it much, and his flapping was all over the place.

"Wilbur – look out…!!" Patsy shouted, as she pointed to the back wall of the kitchen.

It was too late. Wilbur hit the back corner of the wall, close to the cellar steps, tumbled in the air as he fell, and Mary jumped up to grab him with a tea towel, but she just missed him, and he landed on an old earthenware pot that was on the back kitchen windowsill, which thankfully saved his fall, but sadly, the pot fell to the floor and smashed..!!

"Wilbur, Wilbur, are you alright..?!" shouted Patsy.

She flew over at once. Wilbur was sat up straight on the back windowsill, rubbing his head.
Mary too, went over to see poor Wilbur.

"I'm ok, I think" He answered…then realising what he had just done, he said "I can fly – I can fly…!!"…and suddenly forgot about his fall.

Henry, on the other hand, was on the floor next to the broken earthenware pot.

"Mary……..where did you get this pot from..?? Henry asked, who was now standing over the smashed pot on the floor.

"Oh, it was here when we moved in." Mary answered, over her shoulder.

She was making sure Wilbur hadn't damaged the wing she had just repaired…..or himself for that matter.

"I just thought it was too lovely to throw away, and it's so old, so I thought I would keep it on the windowsill. I could never open it though to see if there was anything inside it."

"Oh I'm really sorry about the pot…." Said a very 'sorry looking' Wilbur. After all, it was his fault that the pot had smashed.

"Well Mary" said Henry. " I would be congratulating Wilbur. It looks like we may have found something of great importance..!"

Chapter 14

## A Great Find

Henry was standing over, what looked like a piece of parchment paper that had been rolled up inside the old earthenware pot – but it had unravelled as the pot had smashed to the ground. Henry could just make out the words *'Last Will & Testament'*

Mary picked up the parchment and took it over to the table. She slowly opened it up fully and laid it out. The writing was a little faded with age, and the pen script was very fancy, but just manageable enough to read.

Mary read the wording out loud:

*The Last Will & Testament of: Mr Magnus Gunsam Le Fey.*

*I, Magnus Gunsam Le Fey hereby bequeath my home, the said property – namely;*

No: 24, Copley Lane Meadow, of Old Bram-Leia Village, Moorside, in the Vale of Yorkshire, to my Son, namely Mr. Samuel Elmaus Le Fey.

Upon my death, or where I may become ill of mind, or am too frail to keep up my responsibilities, he shall be the sole owner of the afore-mentioned property, and take good care and responsibility of the said property, along with the gardens and the land. He shall do this with much conviction and strength, of which is bestowed upon him.

In the unfortunate event of his death, or if he becomes ill of mind, or is too frail to keep up the responsibilities, then he – (namely Mr Samuel

Elmaus Le Fey), must pass this property down his family line, to his next child of his choosing; who shall be of strong stature, kind of heart, and merry of nature.

If my son bears no children, he must pass this pre-ordained task of ownership down the family line. This is my wish – as I hereby state, with the power that is bestowed upon me, that I am of sound mind and body to make this statement forthwith. The said property must be solely looked after, and cared for by way of the same manner by his youngest sister, my youngest child, Miss Endor Dorne Le Fey.


As my dearest wife Mrs Bridget Begdirt Le Fey (nee Bishop) has now passed away,

*I hereby make this claim, as the sole and rightful owner of the afore-mentioned property, and as a true descendent of the Le Fey dynasty.*

*Under no circumstances, should this said property fall into the hands of my eldest child, my daughter, namely Miss Agnes Sagen Le Fey, as in my wisdom and judgement, she is ill of mind, and the responsibility would be a too far greater task for her, and this would carry serious consequential risk to the cottage, and the family.*

*If anything should befall whereas my youngest daughter Miss Endor Dorne Le Fey, becomes ill of mind, too frail to keep up the responsibilities, or due to her unfortunate death, then the property must be passed down her family line to her next child of her choosing. If she bears no child, then she will* most certainly be required to make arrangements of sorts for this property to be kept safe, with the greatest responsibility, until a time comes whereby she chooses wisely, the next member of the Le Fey family who can respectfully, whole-heartedly and in the manner be entrusted to them; take sole ownership of this property, and continue to safely manage it, and all that comes with it, with the same instructions.

The law of the Power of Attorney has been given, by my request, to my son Mr Samuel Elmaeus Le Fey, and also to my daughter Miss Endor Dorne Le Fey. They both have been entrusted with all of my belongings, all of *my finances, and my health and care, until my death, and with regards to the said property.*

*These are my words, and this is my declaration.*

*Signed: Mr Magnus Gunsam Le Fey.*

*Dated: This 11th day of April, in the year of our Lord 1936.*

After everyone had listened to Mary reading the Will out loud, they all looked at each other, waiting for someone to say something. Wilbur obviously wasn't quite sure what was going on, but just fell in line, and did the same.

"Mary….." Henry said gently.
"Are you ok..?"

Mary didn't answer straight away. She was obviously dumfounded and shocked at what she had just read. Then she said.

"I can't believe what I've just read out…..So…..who do you think this gentleman is here….this Magnus….?? Obviously we all have the same surname. It's obvious he's a direct relative of mine. He might even be my…..I don't know….like a Great Uncle, or something…..who knows..??" She looked at Henry quizzically, who agreed.

"Yes, we need to find out; because this information which has just come to light, is completely fascinating, and very, VERY interesting. We have to think about it carefully. So……… today, we found out that you have the same surname as Agnes and Endor; and now we have just found out from this Will, that Magnus is their Father…..BUT that he also had a son – Samuel – which was their Brother; so there were three of them Agnes, Endor and Samuel"

"I wonder what happened to Samuel" said Mary.

"…..but wait a minute…." Mary hesitated whilst going through the Will again. "…it says here, that if Magnus's son Samuel wasn't able to take charge of this property; or upon his death, and then it says…..and I quote…… *'…..he must pass this property, down his family line, to his next child of his choosing…'*…….. Then it skips on to say *'….If my son bears no children, he must pass this pre-ordained task of ownership down the family line….'* ….and then it says that he wishes his youngest daughter Endor to take charge of the cottage… Well now we know that Endor DID take charge of this cottage…..because she lived here…!!...but WHY…when Samuel was his first choice…??!"

"Mary, what are you getting at…??" Henry questioned.

"…because, Endor living here, and taking charge of the cottage means that something MUST have happened to Samuel…Otherwise, why would she take over the cottage and not him. Something's not right……!!!"

Henry pondered…..

"…..maybe he died then, OR one of the other things that Magnus listed happened to him; like he became too frail, or unable to take charge…..or - ill of mind…… because they were the only stipulations in the Will, so it has to be one of those reasons"

"…OR…" Mary said…. "He didn't have any children to pass it down to – and THAT'S why Endor ended up living here…?"

"Good point…" Henry answered.

"It's such a mystery isn't it…??" she said.   "Also, what was it that was so important about this cottage that it HAD to be 'looked after'…?? ……I don't understand…… I need to make a cup of tea…"

Mary got up and made herself a drink. She came back to the table with her tea. "Any more thoughts..??"

Wilbur said.

"I actually think you need more information about your Father's side of the family, as obviously him being a Le Fey, that's where to start – you need to go back in time"

"Thanks Wilbur, but I don't know anything about my Dad's family - at all. I was telling Henry today. All I know is that my Dad was an only child; and his parents died when he was a baby….that's it"

Wilbur looked at the Will and read it again. He looked up at Mary and then at the other two.

"What is it Wilbur…?" Henry asked stepping forward.

"Erm…..correct me if I'm wrong. SO…..let's just assume then that this Samuel died – and that's why the cottage was left to his sister Endor, yeah…?? What if Samuel DID have a child; and the child was only a baby when he died….?? That child COULD have been your Dad Mary……"

"Oh my god….!!." Mary stared directly at Henry and Patsy, with her hands covering her mouth. They looked as stunned as she did.

Henry turned to Wilbur, and patted him on his back.

"I think you've nailed it Wilbur….I think that's EXACTLY what's happened..!!....So, Samuel HAS to be your Father's Father….it makes complete sense..!! So, it looks like you may have found the first bit of the mystery of who your relatives are, and you've just found your Grandfather Mary!"

Mary was completely astounded.

"Wilbur – thank you – it's logical, given that my Fathers Father died when he was a baby… So…..just assuming that's the case then – I wonder what happened to Samuel for him to die so young; and what about his wife – my Grandmother, whoever she was. Was she left widowed, or did she die at the same time – leaving my Dad orphaned…?? Oh this is so sad and so intriguing at the same time. No wonder Dad never spoke of it, well he wouldn't have done – I was just a child. He probably didn't remember his parents anyway really – but Mum never told me either….!"

Mary kept looking at the old script in her hands, as if someone had just given her a rare piece of jewellery. She slowly stroked her fingers over the old ink pen script.

 "Mr Magnus Gunsam Le Fey – wow, that's such a wonderful name isn't it..?" Mary said, rather proudly.

Henry had been deep in thought, when he suddenly said.

"…..So, it looks like Agnes wasn't allowed to take over this cottage, because her Father had written that quite clearly in this Will. No wonder she was jealous, and fought with Endor. I wonder why she wasn't allowed to take over the family home – after all, it looks like she was the eldest..?? Do you think she's done something bad..?? He'd written in this Will that he believed that she was 'ill of mind'.
I wonder what he meant by that……??"

Patsy suddenly spoke up. "Well…she must have done something pretty bad to be written out of the family Will – crikey! Do you think Agnes knows who you are Mary…?" and turned to look at Mary

"I certainly hope not..! No, she can't do because she asked me my surname at the gate. Thank God Henry got to me just in time…!! Hang on a minute though….she must know that only a Le Fey can take over this cottage, that's probably why she was quizzing me, and looking at my hands to see if she could read them…!!"

Henry realised that this was becoming quite a situation, and it could potentially be really bad.
Mary yawned – it had been a really long, long day; and quite emotional on every level.

Henry looked out of the back kitchen window.

"Mary, it's getting very late, we have to go. The sun has almost gone. Patsy, Wilbur, tomorrow I am going to call a meeting. Today has been one of the longest days I've ever known"

They both nodded.

"Say nothing to no one for the time being"

Henry turned to Mary.

"Are you going to be alright..?" Mary looked up from the parchment, which she had been continuously staring at.

"Well, James is working away isn't he..??....but I'll be alright, honestly, don't worry. I think I need some time on my own now…… I never in my wildest dreams thought that when I woke up this morning, that I was going to have a day like this – ever…..and I've got a lot to get my head around, and such a lot to process. This information is both wonderful, and completely new to me, but also, very worrying at the same time. Thank you so much for all of your help. I'm so glad you're here – I somehow feel at 'home'….. I think I'm going to make some hot chocolate, and have an early night tonight, I'm so, so tired"

Henry, Patsy and Wilbur flew out of the kitchen window at the back, and landed on the ground.

"Let's walk back" Henry said.

There was so much to say, but none of them could really say anything. What a long day!

"Oh no, I'd better hurry - I have to meet Elma at the back wall for the night patrol, he'll be waiting!" Patsy suddenly remembered.

"I thought that Bonny was the one helping Elma patrol the wall" Henry quizzed.

"She was initially, but she has now volunteered to help Nancy with the children, and I thought it would be a bit too much for her to do both, so I said that I would do it. Anyway, see you in the morning" Patsy fluttered away rather quickly.

Wilbur and Henry waved, and carried on walking.

"How strange that you encountered Mary all those years ago Wilbur" Henry said smiling.

"Yeah, that's so strange". Wilbur said. "I wouldn't have recognised her, as she was only a little girl back then, but as soon as she recognised me today, I could see straight away, and remembered.
She was kind. I remember her asking me if I was ok, and did I need some help, but I was just so shocked that she was talking to me, I just said I was alright and hopped away" He smiled as he recalled.
"I remember her friend peeping over the hedge, but she didn't hear our conversation. That was obvious"

"Ah that would have been Mary's friend Jenny. She was telling me about her today. That poor girl went missing. Now that IS a mystery where she went......and Mary was with her at the time. Mmmmmm...... How very, very strange indeed" Henry was pondering.

Suddenly they heard a noise and saw a light on the pathway in front of them.

"Stop..!! Who goes zere..?!" It was Lars – on his bicycle.

# Chapter 15

## **<u>Shadows and Revelations</u>**

Henry couldn't sleep that night. The events of the previous day were playing over and over in his mind, and he was trying to make some sense of it all. He eventually got up, but it was still very dark. He made himself a cup of honey tea and looked out of his window. The moon was still out, but it was faint as eerie wisps of cloud slowly floated past it. He looked over towards the back wall at the end of the garden, and wondered how Patsy and Elma were getting along on their night patrol.

He sat at his table with his honey tea, and was trying to unravel all of the mystery so far.

He got out some paper and a pen. He just had to make some simple notes to help him clarify a lot of unanswered questions. He wrote down the following…

1. Endor & Agnes are sisters.
2. They had a brother called Samuel, and their Father was called Magnus.
3. Why didn't the cottage go to Samuel..?
4. Why was the cottage looked after by Endor. Did something happen to Samuel..?
5. Why was Agnes not allowed to own the cottage, or even go in it?
6. Why did Endor and Agnes vanish..?? Where did they vanish to.....and why has Agnes come back..?
7. 7. How and why was the spell broken over the cottage to allow Mary to move in..?

8. Why all of a sudden, has Mary regained all of her memories..?
9. What was the secret of the cottage..?
10. Why didn't Mary know of her past, and that she was a descendant of a family of witches..?

Henry put his pen down, and read the questions over and over again. It still didn't make much sense to him, even after writing it all down.
He looked out over towards the back of the cottage. He was wondering about the Will that they had accidently found, and all the information contained in it. Poor Mary….

He saw a faint light come on in the kitchen.

"What's that I wonder..?" he thought to himself.

He flew out across the garden, which was very still, dark and quiet; and made his way over to the back kitchen window of the cottage. He landed on the windowsill.
He could just make out Mary sat at the kitchen table. What was she doing..?

The light he saw was a candle that Mary had just lit. She couldn't sleep either. She had tried to, but like Henry, everything was going around in her head; and because she had now remembered everything from her past - she was thinking about her Father.

As she sat with her hands around her mug of hot chocolate, gently blowing at the steam swirling from her cup, she smiled as she remembered the late summer nights, when she was a child……

Her Mother would put her to bed, but as the nights were still quite light, Mary could never get to sleep straight away. Her Mother would bring Cubre the Cat into Mary's room, and let him sleep there. His soft purring would send Mary off to sleep. He would lie down and curl up at Mary's feet, but more often than not, Cubre had walked up the bed, and was usually asleep on the pillow, right next to Mary. He was her Father's Cat, and he followed her Father everywhere, but he also never left Mary's side.

Later on when it got dusk outside, Mary's Father would come and wake her up. He would whisper to her…

"Mary, wake up. Come and take a look at the stars, and listen to the bats in the garden"

Mary woke up straight away. Her Father loved the night sky, and he would wrap her up in her dressing gown and slippers. Sometimes they would take a cup of warm milk and jam sandwiches with them, and they would go outside and sit on the back step, and he would point out all the stars to her. Then he would say.

"Ssh – listen. Can you hear them..??"

"Hear what Daddy..?" Mary would whisper, not hearing anything.

"The bats….....listen, hear they come!"

Mary still couldn't hear anything; but then a few moments later, she jumped as something quickly fluttered close by overhead.

"There, did you see that one..?" he whispered. "Look, here come some more"

Sure enough, a few more bats darted by very quickly. You had to be quick to see them. Mary never knew how her Father could hear those bats long before they came into view; as she now knew that bats have a very high pitched frequency; but her Father's hearing was impeccable.

"Always trust the bats Mary; they will lead you where you need to be" he would say to her.

She loved those times. Her Father would pick Cubre up, and they would all go outside together. He would sit Cubre on his knee, and the tabby cat would lovingly rub his face on her Father's jumper, whilst looking up at him. He would make little tiny happy 'meow' noises all the time.

"He's talking to you Daddy, isn't he?" Mary would say.

Her Father would look down at Mary for a moment – smile and then say.

"Yes Mary, he is"

Mary once asked her Father why he had called the Cat Cubre, and what it meant. He told her it was Spanish, and it meant 'cover' or 'coat'.

Cubre was so loyal, and even went on walks with them in and around where they used to live. He never strayed, and never got lost, he was always with them. Mary's Father had a very special way with all kinds of animals, insects, birds etc; and Mary knew that they all probably just wanted to be around him – they just all seemed to love him.

While they sat on the back step, Mary held her warm milk and said.

"Should we go and wake Mummy up, and let her come outside too..? I will share my jam sandwich with her Daddy"

"No, let her sleep Mary – your Mother needs her rest; this is our secret anyway" He would say, then gave her a wink, and touched the side of his nose with his finger. Mary knew what that meant.

"Ok Daddy" Mary whispered, and touched the side of her nose, and tried to wink back, but ended up blinking both her eyes.

Then they would cuddle up outside on the step, and munch on their jam sandwiches, and sip their warm sweet milk whilst looking up at the stars, and Cubre watching the bats darting by.

Mary loved her parents; but her Mother always seemed very sad, quiet and nervous, like she was always looking over her shoulder. She would often hear her crying, and when Mary would ask her what was wrong, she would just say that she had a bad headache.

After her Father had passed away, and the years that followed, Mary would often hear her Mother talking out loud, but in a whisper, on an evening, mostly at dusk, when Mary's Mother didn't even know that she was listening.

She would ask her Mother the next day who she had been talking to, and Sarah would simply reply that she had been silently saying her prayers.

Mary had always been brought up to say The Lord's Prayer every night before bed. She would kneel at the side of her bed, and after reciting The Lord's Prayer, she would then ask God to look after everyone she loved. Then she would hop into bed, and snuggled down, cuddling her favourite teddy bear, and a hot water bottle if it was a particularly cold night.

Her Father, on the other hand (from what she could remember), seemed very pre-occupied and distant sometimes, but Mary knew in her heart of hearts; that her parents loved each other very much, and they loved her so much too.

Sat at the kitchen table in the glow of the candle light, Mary was thinking about so many things. She slowly started to understand why her Mother was the way she was. Now Mary was older – and at 29, and not a child anymore, it became perfectly clear. Her Mother obviously knew of Mary's 'special' way about her, and why she tried to supress this in Mary, by telling her not to ever tell anyone that she could hear animals talking. Mary felt sad that she couldn't talk to her Mother anymore, and tell her that she now understood.

Mary's mind wandered back to the past again, as she stared at the candle flickering softly.

Christmas was always great fun, and very traditional. The tree would go up a week before Christmas Day, and Mary's parents and Mary would decorate the tree with all the old fashioned baubles, some of which were very old, and had been passed down through the years. Lots of silver and coloured tinsel would be wound around the tree branches; then Mary's Father would place the lights carefully, starting from the bottom of the tree, and then slowly going round and round until he got to the top. Because he was so tall, he could reach right to the top, without having to stand on a buffet! The lights were all different colours, and they had little flower heads, so when at last they were turned on, all the little coloured flowers would individually twinkle. Mary would watch them for hours. She loved Christmas time. It was always fun putting up the paper garlands from one side of the room to the other. They would cross in the middle of the ceiling, and Mary's Mother would stand on the buffet, while her Father held her still, while she would try and stick them all together at the same place in the middle of the ceiling with sellotape, so they would drape. It was all just so magical.

While Mary's Mother made all the Christmas dinner, her Father would make a huge Plum Pudding; and it was Mary's favourite thing to look forward to, because her Father would hide sixpences inside the pudding. Sarah Le Fey always told her daughter to eat carefully as she didn't want her to choke or swallow one of the sixpences! Then she would say a few passing words to her husband for putting too many in the pudding. It was so tasty though, and always with lots and lots of hot, creamy custard. One year, Mary ended up with three sixpences..!!

Mary was looking down at the Will on the kitchen table, but not really able to make much sense of it just now, she was still slowly coming to terms with everything.

She suddenly felt very uneasy, but didn't know why.

Henry had been watching Mary a while, when he thought he saw some movement, through the kitchen window that he was looking through, and right over to the other kitchen window, to the front garden. It was like dark shadows moving.

"What on earth is that?"" He thought to himself.
He flew from around the back of the cottage, down the side, and then stopped on the side wall.
He could see dark movements coming from outside of the garden. It was on the path, like someone or something was trying to get through the hedge..!

Henry needed to get a closer look, so he carefully and slowly flew towards the hedge, taking great care. That's when he heard muttering and mumbling of strange words. He landed on the gate post at the front of the cottage, and to his surprise, Old Mother Sage – Agnes Le Fey, was trying to get through the hedge…!!

Agnes couldn't get through, because the spell was still not allowing her to get in, but he could hear her muttering and cursing. Why did she want to get in so desperately, and at this hour of the night..? He had to try and distract her, so he quickly flew to the other side of the gate post and into the hedge, and started rustling in the hedge, which made a noise. In the stillness of the summer night, Agnes Le Fey suddenly stopped what she was doing, and then whispered in an angry tone.

"Who's there..?!!"

Henry rustled the hedging again.
Agnes didn't say anything, and it all went quiet. Henry couldn't see properly through the hedging, so just sat still for a few moments.
Suddenly, a large stick pierced right through the hedging, and stopped inches from where Henry was hiding…!

Suddenly, Agnes spoke in a frightening voice.

*"Presence of the night, who hides in the darkness……..My time is nigh. Tell the one who dwells in my house that they are no longer welcome. The darkness is coming, along with shadows that walk alone. Too long I have been away, and I have returned to claim what is rightfully mine…!!"*

In his fright, Henry quickly shot out, and escaped, just as the Witch's stick furiously poked through the hedge once again. He had got away just in time.
Once he was out of danger, he peeped from around the corner of the cottage, breathing heavily. He could see the silhouette of her frame, but she was facing the field opposite, and not looking at the cottage, then all of a sudden, Agnes Le Fey had disappeared.

The faint light from the early morning sky was just coming up over the meadow now, and the garden didn't look so dark. Henry flew round the back of the cottage to the back kitchen window, and looked through. Mary was still sat at the kitchen table. Henry squeezed through the tiny gap that had been left open, and got in.

"Mary" He half whispered.

Mary jumped slightly and turned around.

"It's me, Henry"…and he flew straight in.

"Oh hi Henry, are you ok..?"

Henry looked at Mary's tired face, and said.
"I couldn't sleep, and I'm guessing you couldn't either..??"

"No" she answered wearily. "I just can't stop thinking about everything"

"Me too; but at the moment, we have a problem – a huge problem"

"What is it..?!" Mary asked.

Henry told her how he had woken up, and about the questions he had written down, which he wanted to discuss with her, and then seeing the candle being lit.

When he got to the part about Agnes Le Fey being at the front gate, Mary shot over to the window.

"She's not there Mary; she just disappeared after I had distracted her"

"My god, that awful woman will stop at nothing to try and get into this garden..!" Mary exclaimed.

"Whatever it is about this cottage, she needs it badly Henry, that's all I can say!"

Henry looked at her then said.

"She said something out loud, which was quite sinister to hear, so I'll repeat it to you. She said.

"Presence of the night, who hides in the darkness......My time is nigh. Tell the one who dwells in my house, that they are no longer welcome. The darkness is coming, along with shadows that walk alone. Too long I have been away, and I have returned to claim what is rightfully mine...!"

"Oh she did, did she...?! Well this isn't her house anymore, it's MINE, and there's no way she's getting in...!"

"We need to start searching this cottage from top to bottom Mary. There HAS to be SOMETHING in here that she so desperately wants. The thing is I have no idea how long the spell will last. I don't even know when it was cast..!! It could run out at any time, and that will be the end of all of us..... We need some help!!"

Mary got up from the table and began walking round the kitchen with her arms folded, and was in deep thought. Then she stopped, and walked back to the table and pointed to the Will.

"Henry....this old Will & Testament here, has obviously been in this house all this time...yeah..? So then surely, other letters and certificates etc might be here too. If the spell was cast to 'protect' the cottage from Old Mother 'what's her face' from getting in, then everything else that is to do with this house has got to be in here as well..!!"

Henry looked at Mary and then he realised something.

"We need to take a closer look at this Will..!" He turned to the Will on the table, and opened it up.

"What did you want to see?" She asked Henry.

Henry read it out slowly to himself, then said
"There, look Mary, it's that bit at the end…" Henry read it out loud.

"The Law of The Power of Attorney has been given, by my request, to my son, Mr Samuel Elmaus Le Fey, and also to my daughter, Miss Endor Dorne Le Fey. They both have been entrusted with all of my belongings, all of my finances, and additionally, all of my health and care matters; until my death, and with regards to the said property"

"So they were both entrusted with everything to do with this cottage; plus Magnus's health and finances, and also his belongings – absolutely everything…! So whatever it is - it all HAS to be here….surely...?!"

They both looked around as if they were just suddenly going to find something.

Henry then looked back at the Will, and read it again to himself, whilst Mary put the kettle on, this time to make some tea.

Suddenly, Henry made such an exclamation, that Mary nearly dropped the cup she was carrying.

"Mary, come here and look at this…!"

Mary quickly put the kettle on the stove, came over and looked down at the Will.

"There, read that bit…!!" Henry said excitedly, pointing to a certain part.

Mary read where he was pointing.

## *"Miss Endor Dorne Le Fey"*

"Yes, what of it..?" Mary asked as she looked at Henry.

"Read it again" he said.

Mary looked back at the document, and read it out loud again.

## *"Miss Endor Dorne Le Fey"*

"What do you see..??" Henry asked.

"A name..??" Mary answered (a little sarcastically, as she raised her eyes towards the ceiling).

"Whose name..??" Henry asked.

"Well, if we are correct in what we are assuming, then it's my…my…erm…(she quickly worked out the family history)….well - that will be my Great Auntie's name – yeah..?"

"YES…!! Your Great Auntie……who …??" Henry quizzed her.

"My Great Auntie Endor..?" Mary replied; feeling a bit frustrated now.

"YES..!" Henry shouted again.

"I don't know where you're going with this Henry..!"

"Mary, who in the family, did your Mother say that you were like….?"

"Well she used to say that I reminded her of an old aunt of mine called Auntie Doe – I think…yes that's right – Auntie Doe….."

Henry didn't say anything, but kept looking at Mary, hoping she would work out what he was trying to show her, as he was making 'circles' with his hands as if he was trying to rush her along.

Mary took a few moments, and then gasped. She was wildly thinking.

"Henry – is that HER… Is that Auntie Doe..?!!"

"Who else could it be..?!! She's your Great Auntie for a start, and her name is Endor, so what if it got shortened to Doe…?? It's very possible…!!" Henry said, with his arms in the air.

"Henry!!" She gasped. "That means my Mother knew her…!! She did - she knew her! She MUST have done; otherwise why would she say that I was a reminder of her. She knew all along…! Why didn't my Mother - OR my Father ever tell me any of this..?! The fact that I was related to a family of Witches – and they KNEW...!!"

"Well I can understand why really" Henry said.

"Why....?!!" Mary exclaimed.

"They didn't tell you Mary, because……..they wanted to PROTECT you..!! They probably wanted to bring you up as normal as they could, but secretly knowing that you were 'special', and the added fact that, as you now know - you can talk to animals, and hear them – they KNEW that!!  When you said that you always thought that you were 'special' - you were right; and it makes perfect sense! Your parents just maybe wanted you to live a normal life, because they KNEW..!!"

"I just don't understand why though, if that's the case. Maybe it's just me not thinking straight." Mary said, looking completely bewildered. Henry felt so sorry for her.

"Henry......obviously we now know that Endor and Agnes are Witches....soooooo, their Brother, my Grandfather Samuel, must have been one....or a Wizard or a Warlock, or bloody something..! Oh I don't know Henry....!!" She raised her arms up and then quickly down again, as if she had desperately run out of things to say.

"Henry, for me to be able to understand in more detail what's going on here, and to be able to work any of this out, I need a family tree, or maybe there's a book of previous ancestors somewhere...that's what we need! That way, I will be able to see who married who, and where they lived etc.... I just need some HELP...!!"

"Yes!" Henry said. "Absolutely, and if we are right in what we're thinking here, then like I've just said – there's surely got to be more evidence in this house!"

As Henry continued to stare at the parchment for a few moments, Mary was looking around, and wondering where to start first with hunting for some kind of evidence; Henry slowly began to realise something.

"M a r y...." Henry said slowly. "I've just noticed something else, which is really odd; look here at the sisters' names. Their middle names are actually their first names...?!"

"Eh...??! What do you mean? Let me have a look" Mary looked down at the names straight away.

Mary read out both their names.

"Oh god you're right - Agnes's middle name is Sagen, and the letters A, G, N, E, S, make the name - S A G E N. I bet that's why she calls herself Old Mother 'Sage'…!"

"….and yes, it's the same with Endor's too. E, N, D, O, R,  makes her middle name Dorne. D, O, R, N, E. That's probably why she was affectionately called 'Auntie Doe' ..?"

Mary was really intrigued at what Henry had found out. Why would the sisters' first names be re-arranged to make their middle name…??

"I really have to go Mary. Go through this Will with a fine tooth comb, and find out as much as you can. I must get back to the garden, there's a lot to sort out, and I wasn't there much yesterday, and I could do with a couple of hours sleep if I can. Start searching around this house for anything of importance. Try and find some family history; and DO NOT speak to that woman if you see her. She's getting too close, and now she's hanging about in the dark as well… She must be desperate..!!"

# Chapter 15a

# __The 7__

Somewhere high above the clouds, in a place faraway, 7 beings sat around a huge oval table.

The table had thick, pure gold ornate legs, and the top was made of thousands of the most beautiful coloured crystals, which had been carefully mined, and polished to the highest degree.

The 7 were of different shapes, sizes and colour.

**Number 1 of the 7** - was female. She had long, waist length straight silver hair, which was slicked back away from her face, and had almost see-through porcelain skin. There were two black painted vertical lines which started at the top of her eyebrows, and stopped at her chin. She wore a high necked dark emerald green long fitted dress, which was made of thick course material. The dress had a thick green train which was studded with hundreds of diamonds and emeralds. Her eyes were black and motionless. She was over 8 feet tall.

**Number 2 of the 7** - was a Dryad. Her ethereal presence was calming, as she sat on the edge of her high gilt chair. Growing from her head were hundreds of small twisted branches which were covered with dark green leaves. Her tall but very slender frame was half wooden with growing moss covering her body. She was elegantly draped in a fine pale green mesh that resembled thousands of cobwebs, and covered in early morning dew. Around her waist she wore a belt made from twisted branches and lots of fine spun golden thread, which entwined, and then fell to the floor. Her long fingernails were wooden, and gold rings adorned each one of her fingers. Her face was perfectly sculptured, and her smoky hazel eyes were surrounded by long moss green lashes.

**Number 3 of the 7** – a tall mysterious regal looking man; was sat next to the pale motionless woman. He looked dark and quite sullen, and his head was bent slightly forward. He was wearing a large hooded black cloak, which covered his eyes; and all that could be seen, was a long thick bearded plait with gold rings and feathers tied to the end. He had well groomed long facial hair, and he was wearing a magnificent gilded jacket of royal blue with golden buttons and gold tasselled epaulettes, which were just visible under the long black cloak. He had large round hands, almost like paws, and was wearing black leather gloves. Behind him, and very neatly folded - were a huge pair of black leathery looking wings. He shifted about in his seat; then stole a look across the table to the Dryad.

**Number 4 of the 7** - was a Fairy, who was sat across from the mysterious looking man. She was dressed in a lilac and silver glittery dress, which stopped just above her knees, with black cycling shorts underneath, and on her feet, she had big black leather ankle boots. She had pale silver wings, and lilac hair, which was piled on top of her head in a messy bun. She sat on the edge of the huge oval table with her legs crossed, and blowing bubbles from some pink bubble gum she was chewing – as she bent over staring at her reflections in the crystal table.

**Number 5 of the 7** - was sat at one end of the table. A strange looking alien, with a very long elongated neck, pale cream skin, a small round head, almond-shaped dark blue eyes, and almost no other features. The alien had 4 arms, resting on the table, and was wearing a grey and gold robe, with a high necked collar.

**Number 6 of the 7** - was stood up, with both her hands on the table - opposite the alien. An Enchantress; who was beautiful, with pale cherry coloured cheeks, rose pink lips, violet eyes, and dark wavy waist length hair; and wearing a mauve and black tightly fitted long dress.

**Number 7 of the 7 -** was sat next to the Enchantress – a male, who had a white frozen face, a pale blue nose, and pale blue hair, which was frozen and hanging in icicles. He had the biggest black eye sockets, and from his forehead, a huge white stalactite grew up to a point. From the inside of this mouth, an ice blue beard grew outwards, and then down to a point. His long flowing dress and gown were also ice blue, and hung with icicles.

Suddenly a beam of celestial light, shone down brightly onto the table, which made all the coloured crystals shine; and wisps of white clouds swirled around the 7….. Through the clouds, there slowly appeared……lots of contrasting shaped clocks, which presented themselves to the 7. The clocks floated in mid-air, and were all different styles of clocks, and all telling different times, on different days, and in different years. Some were going fast, and some slow.

The 7 looked down into the crystal table for a few moments, and then looked up at each other in turn.

"Send Oohshiya-lion" said one. "Time is running out..!"

Five of them nodded in agreement……

# Chapter 15b

# <u>**What time is it…?**</u>

After Henry had left Mary, and as the morning had broken, Mary walked to the back kitchen window and looked out over the huge garden, and wondered who had lived there before her. She turned, and looked around her kitchen, and was trying to imagine her ancestors being in the cottage, and how they went about their day; what it was like, and what type of clothing they would have worn. Maybe the women would be cooking and baking on an old stove, and smoke would be swirling from the chimney pot. Maybe there had been a washing line in the garden where they would have hung their washing out. She smiled to herself, suddenly feeling a part of something, a place where she 'belonged'.

She wanted to find out as much as she possibly could, about her ancestors, but where to begin..??

As she sat back down in the light of the candle, the sun was just coming up over in the far corner of the meadow beyond the wall, which indicated to Mary that it was probably about 05:45am. She always liked playing the 'time game' when she was a little girl, and used to love to guess the time, and always got it correct - within a few minutes anyway. She then looked over at the clock on the wall to see if she could still correctly time it, and the time was 05:50am. She felt quite satisfied that she was only five minutes out, and smiled to herself…. Mary was pretty accurate with the sunrise and sunset. Why…? She didn't know, but she had always been able to tell the time with the sun.

As Mary laid her head down on her folded arms on the table, she thought about her Mother. She felt tired, confused, and somehow different, but enlightened at the same time. She wondered how much her Mother knew, and how she wished she could speak to her.

"Oh Mum, I do miss you" she whispered, but with a heavy sigh.

The sound of the birds distracted her, as they could now be heard singing their 'dawn chorus', which is why she couldn't hear, at first – a faint whispering.

Mary lifted her head slowly from the table, and turned her head slightly, as if it would enable her to hear much better.

As the bright morning sunlight had brilliantly shone through the back window; the shaft of light rested on the cellar door. She turned around, and there it was again. She could definitely hear faint whispering. As she looked over towards the cellar door, she knew that the whispering sounds were coming from there. She rose slowly from her chair at the kitchen table and cautiously made her way towards the cellar.

As she got to the door, she carefully and slowly put her ear to listen. The whispering was now much louder. She then stood back away from it, took a deep breath in, and muttered… "Come on Mary, don't be frightened" It was as if she was hearing her Fathers voice telling her not to be afraid.

She unlocked the cellar door with the big old rusty key that was always in the lock. As she turned it, the lock made a big clunk sound, and the cellar door slowly swung open, with a small creaking sound.

Mary had been in the cellar a few times before. It was quite a big space down there, and not damp at all, it was very dry……but this time, she was a little more cautious. She turned the light on which was just at the left hand side on the wall, and the whole of the downstairs lit up. Mary carefully made her way down the steep stairs, step by step, bending her head slightly as she did so.

Her hand felt the side of the wall on the right, as she made her way down. Apart from feeling the rough, cold stone, she felt something strange, like a warm tingling feeling in her fingers. She stopped and put her ear to the right side of the wall. She could definitely hear faraway voices now.

She got to the bottom of the steps, and the wall which was facing her; was the front of the cottage, and then the room opened up to the left. The right hand side, where Mary had touched the wall, stopped at the bottom. There was only a left turn into the downstairs cellar room, so why did Mary feel like she wanted to go right..? There was nothing there – just a wall. She felt compelled.

She touched the wall again on the right side, but this time, with both her hands, and she suddenly felt a force drawing her to it. The force was so strong that Mary couldn't prize her hands away from it, like it was sucking her in…!

Her hands were eventually released, which made her stagger back a little. Shocked, she stepped back into the room of the cellar, but as she walked further away from the bottom of the steps, the voices became more distant. She looked around. Everything was where it was the last time she had been down there. There were just a few odd bits, like paint brushes, tins of paint, a sweeping brush, and a couple of old towels and cloths etc. Mary looked around slowly, and saw the old chute where the coal would have been delivered many years ago at the front of the cottage.

The coal would then have been shovelled into a bucket by whoever lived there at the time, and then taken back up the cellar steps and into the kitchen, and put by the side of the fire.

Something caught her eye, as she looked back over her shoulder, to the bottom of the steps, where the wall was. There was now a glimmer of light, shining and dancing around the stones, which made all the cement between the stones glow a faint crimson colour.

Mary gasped.

She walked tentatively over to the dancing light, but the light began to fade.......but the voices became louder. What was happening..? She was eager to find out what was behind the stones, but she knew that it was just the outside wall of her cottage, and there was nothing there, just tonnes of earth.

Her hands came up again to feel the old stones, and this time the stones felt very warm to her touch...?? She felt like she wanted to go beyond the stone wall – but that obviously didn't make any sense to her.

As she kept both her hands there, the whispering became louder. She put her left ear to the wall, which then made her look back up the cellar steps. The door had closed, but Mary hadn't closed it behind her when she came down into the cellar. She felt a little frightened, when suddenly; she heard a familiar voice coming from behind the wall. She pressed her ear even harder against the warm stones, and there it was – her Mother's voice....!! It was faint, but it was definitely her Mother.

"Find your Father – the...the....s...stairs....I believe you....your....s...secret"
.......over and over she said the exact same words that Mary had heard on her Mother's death bed.

Mary sobbed uncontrollably. "Mum, is that you…?! I can hear you, I can hear you…!!  I don't know what to do, and I don't know what's going on; and what do you mean 'the stairs'..?!"

Then Mary looked at where she was standing. She was standing at the bottom of the cellar steps. Quickly Mary shouted

"Tell me more Mum..! I'm here. Don't go, please don't go…!!
The repeated words of her Mother began to slowly fade away, until Mary could hear no more.

The wall became cold, and the glow between each of the stones became weaker, until it slowly disappeared. Mary brought her head away from the wall, turned around, and lent heavily against it, with the back of her head tilted upwards, and she cried and cried, until she could cry no more.
Suddenly, she jumped, as someone was knocking at the front door. Who could be knocking at this early hour..? She ran up the cellar steps, switched the light off quickly, and made her way to the front door. She opened it – and there was the Postman.

"Oh…m…morning" Mary stuttered rather bewilderingly. "You're early..!"

"Morning..!" The Postman answered brightly. "I've got a package for you, although I don't quite know how it's made it here. Anyway here you are" and handed her a small box.

The sun was dazzling her eyes, as it was so bright and very warm. Mary shielded her eyes from the bright sun, and said.

"Wow, this is going to be a hot day..!! It's already really warm, even at this time of the morning..!" She said, as she took the package from the Postman.

The Postman looked at her up and down, as she stood there in her pyjamas and dressing gown, and dazzled by the sun, he said, laughing slightly.

"Slept in did we..?"

She was just about to say that she hadn't even really been to bed, but the Postman had about turned and was heading for the gate.

"Er....thank you" Was all she could say, as she watched him shut the gate behind him, and looked over at her, and nodded his head smiling; then walked off down the lane, whistling.

Mary looked down at the small package, and that's when she noticed the beautiful hand writing. She walked back in whilst still staring down at the package. It had been hand-written in ink, and in such a flourished style.

*To: Miss Mary M. Le Fey*
*No: 24 Copley Lane Meadow,*
*Bram-leia Village.*
*Moorside*

That's all it said, nothing else, no post code.

Mary took the package to the kitchen table, sat down and began opening the package carefully and slowly. Whatever it was, it was wrapped very well in lots of wool. She removed the wool, to find a smallish old tatty looking wooden box....??

She pushed the rusty old clasp to one side, and opened the box - with much trepidation, to reveal – an old key..??

"A key…?" Mary said out loud.

The key was quite large, and very ornate. As she picked it out of the box, and held it in her hand, a sudden rush of air blew across her face from nowhere, which made her jump, and sit back in the chair, which nearly made her drop the key.

"What the hell was that…?!"

She looked down at the key as she turned it over and over in her fingers, and realised that it was made of wood. It had strange markings on it, which she couldn't make out, but it was intrinsically beautiful all the same.

"What's this for, and who the hell has sent me a bloody key…?" Mary said quietly.

There was nothing else with it, and no note. Mary decided she needed a strong cup of coffee and some breakfast, and got up from the table, and happened to glance up at the clock on the wall, thinking that at least she had all day to herself to work out the mystery of the key, and do as Henry had suggested, and start looking around the cottage for anything she could find that might be of help to her.

Mary had it in her head that the time would be about 06:20am.

She stopped abruptly, as she stared up at the clock on the wall. The time…….was 11am……..Mary had been in the cellar for 5 hours…….

# Chapter 15c

# **<u>Beyond the Wall</u>**

The previous night, after Patsy, Wilbur and Henry had been trying to help Mary fathom out the contents of the Will; and after Wilbur accidently knocked the pot over, Patsy had flown off quickly, as she had remembered that she had the night patrol of the wall to do with Elma.  She only just made it in time.

"Ah there you are Patsy, I was beginning to wonder where you were!" Elma said.

Elma the Daddy Long Legs was idly waiting for Patsy at the foot of the wall, so they could do their nightly patrol. He had been sitting on the grass just looking around the garden.

"Sorry Elma" Patsy was out of breath.

"Are you ok?" Elma asked as he looked at her.

"Oh, yeah, yeah, I'm ok - sorry Elma, just had a bit of a busy day that's all" she answered quickly; and then said, changing the subject.
"Anyway, it's a nice evening…" She didn't want Elma to know where she had been….or the fact that she had actually had a conversation with Mary.

She wondered how on earth Henry was going to chair the meeting the next day…and how was he going to tell everyone in the garden about Mary?

"Well if you ask me, it looks like it's gunna rain" Elma said gloomily, as he slowly turned around whilst looking up towards the dusky sky. "Come on Patsy" he said, as he started to climb the wall.

He was up there in no time; being a Daddy Long Legs did have its advantages. Patsy fluttered up gracefully and settled on the top of the wall. Elma instructed Patsy that it was better if they patrolled the wall together, as him and Bonny had done. Doing it that way, they would stay together, and it would be safer. So they started in the middle, and began their patrol along the top of the wall.

Patsy walked behind Elma, although she had to tell him to slow down a bit because he took such big strides; but then he did look funny trying to take smaller steps. It was much better when they got to the end, and they turned around. This time Elma followed Patsy.

"I know there's something going on Patsy" Elma suddenly said. "You and Henry have been at the front of the cottage for quite some time now over the last couple of days"

Patsy carried on walking, not quite knowing what to say.

"I'm right aren't I?" Elma quizzed.

"Look Elma, I'm not going to lie to you, but I can't tell you either" Patsy answered – glad that she was walking in front of him, and also that now it was getting dark - he couldn't see her face.

As Patsy looked to her right over the meadow, which was now in darkness, she suddenly slowed down, which in turn, caused Elma to bump into her.

Elma exclaimed. "What have you stopped for..?!"

"Ssh" she silenced him, as they both stopped, and she put her finger to her lips, and then pointed and whispered.

"Look – over there. Do you see that?"

Elma looked over towards the blackness, not expecting to see anything, but he did; he saw SOMEthing.

"What is it?"" He answered.

What they were both looking at, they couldn't quite make out, but after a few moments, Patsy whispered back.

"It's a light, but it looks like it's moving backwards and forwards very slowly. How can that be?"

"That's because…" Elma replied. "Someone's carrying it!"

It was quite far away, as the meadow went on and on, so the light was small and faint. All of a sudden, it vanished.

They both gasped together.

"It's gone Elma! What do you think it was?!"

"It could have been a Farmer maybe?" Elma answered, shrugging his shoulders.

"A farmer..?! Out at this time of night?! I don't think so" Patsy said worryingly.

"Why not..? He could be looking for a lost sheep or something"

"I need to tell Henry" She wanted Henry to know.

"What – NOW…?!" Elma asked. "He'll be in bed. Tell him first thing in the morning, there's no point worrying him about it now. It looks like the light seems to have gone out now anyway. It might not have been anything really, like I said, maybe a Farmer"

Elma was right; she would inform Henry first thing in the morning. It had been a long day, and she was probably over-thinking.

"You look really tired Patsy, go and get some rest" Elma said gently.

"No, I'll be fine Elma, honestly" She lied. She was indeed, very tired.

"I insist - now go; there's only a few hours until dawn breaks. Go get some sleep Patsy, I'll be fine"
Patsy didn't need telling twice. She flew down to the garden, found her little dwelling that she had made to look so pretty. It was under a Wisteria bush, which had lots of pale green leaves; and just under it, were some stones and small rocks, and Patsy had made her home there. She settled down to sleep at once.

She can't have been asleep that long, for the next moment, Elma was whispering loudly.

"Patsy…Patsy….wake up!"

"What is it, what's happened?!" Patsy whispered back, getting up really quickly.

Quick!!" Elma was beckoning her, as she pulled the leaves back.

She came out of her tiny home, and Elma was stood there looking quite shaken.

"Quick, we must go, there's someone trying to climb the wall!"

"Climb the WALL..?!!" She repeated.

They dashed off silently. When they reached the foot of the wall, Elma whispered.

"Wait until I've climbed up, then you follow" and put his thumb up.

Patsy nodded. Elma scrambled very quickly and quietly up the wall. To say he was a bit clumsy, he moved like lightening. He beckoned Patsy up.

On the top of the wall, they crouched down as low as they could, and slid on their bellies to look down and over the wall onto the darkness below.
Without speaking, Elma pointed downwards to the bottom of the wall on the other side. Patsy could hear some slight murmuring, and a scraping noise, and a small dark figure moving slowly about.
Who could it be??
Patsy tapped Elma on the shoulder, and encouraged him to follow her. They walked across the top of the wall to the other end. The sun was just starting to come up on the horizon.

"Elma, what are we going to do?? We need to distract whoever that is, away from the wall!!" Patsy said in a hushed whisper.

"Well whoever it is, they obviously can't get up. They've been there the whole time"

"Well the sun is about to come up, so if we stay long enough, we'll be able to see who it is. Let's go back and see if they're still there" she whispered.

They ran silently across the top of the wall, back to the spot where they were before. As they got there, Elma slipped on some moss, and did a somersault in the air. As he was falling, he just managed to grab hold of some of the moss, but he was slipping!
Some of the bits of dust and stones fell over the wall, as Elma scrambled, and they fell down onto the other side. Whoever was down there, soon knew there was somebody above them, as they were suddenly covered in a light dusting of gravel. Elma's wide frightened eyes looked up desperately at Patsy.

A cold harsh whisper snarled.

"Who's there, who is it?!"

Just as the voice said those words, the sun came up over the meadow, and Patsy screamed as Elma was slipping. She grabbed both his hands, and with all the strength she had, she pulled him up and over onto the top of the wall. Patsy fell back, out of breath, and heaved a sigh of relief. They turned back around on their hands and knees and peered swiftly over the wall; but whoever was there – had now vanished.

"Elma, are you alright?!" Patsy was looking at a very grey looking Elma.

"I…I….just need to sit here a minute. Who WAS that down there anyway?!" Elma said, as he looked up at Patsy. They were both really quite scared, and shaken.

"I've no idea" she said, looking around as if she was expecting something else to happen.

"This is bad Elma – really bad; and I don't like it..! What on earth's going on…?!"

# Chapter 16

# <u>Bread, Wheat Beer, and Name Calling</u>

Henry had managed to get a couple of hours sleep that night, and he hoped that Mary had too. He was thinking about how to conduct the meeting whilst drinking his morning cup of honey tea. He decided to have a quick look round the front of the cottage, just to check around the garden. Everything seemed quiet and looked ok. He then flew round to the back and headed straight over to Lars, the Beetle's house, and knocked on the door.

Henry could hear a clatter of boots, and then the door opened.

"Ah Guten Morgen Henry!" greeted Lars, very cheerfully.

"Err yes – er…..Guten Morgen too – er… to you, Lars" Henry answered in a slightly awkward way.

"Ah your German is very good Henry, yes..!" He said smiling.

"How can I be of serveez to you..? Please, come in"

Henry walked into Lars' very neat little home, and everything was spick and span, as Henry would have expected it to be. Lars gestured to a small stool and Henry sat, and opened his mouth to speak…..but Lars interrupted.

"You vont a vheat beer Henry, I have very good vheat beer yah..?"…and winked at Henry.

"A what…..what's a 'veet' beer..??"

Lars laughed heartily at Henry's pronunciation, but then stopped laughing as he realised that HIS pronunciation was wrong..!!

"Ah my apologies to you Henry, look here…. this is vheat beer" Lars pointed to several slim brown bottles on the shelf. It said on the labels 'Wheat Beer'

"Good Lord no..!" Henry exclaimed, still tasting his honey tea.

"We Germans like our vheat beer, are you sure..?? I have very good strong coffee, yah..? You look very tired my friend – you look like you could do viz a big cup!" Lars was indeed, very kind natured, but wheat beer…at this time??

"No, no – but thank you so much Lars, I don't vont a…….I mean 'want' a wheat beer, I actually need you to do something for me"

"Ahh of course my friend, vot can I do for you?!"…and slapped Henry on his shoulder, and nearly knocked him off his stool.

"Lars, would you pay a visit to everyone around the garden, and tell them all that I would like to hold a meeting today at 12:30pm sharp..? It's very important that everyone turns up. Can I leave that with you..?" Henry said, as he scraped the stool away as he got up to leave.

"Of course Henry; of course I vil do zis; and anything else you are vonting, please, please ask"

As usual, Lars clicked his heels together, and bowed his head.

Henry thanked Lars, and made his way up the garden to Tree Stump Corner. It was very peaceful around there, and Henry sat down on a stone next to a small display of very colourful Dahlia's.

He was worried. He had brought everyone here from the meadow, and now that they had all built their homes, and were all settling in nicely and feeling safe, something really bad could happen, and he wasn't quite sure what to do. He sat there a while, pondering on everything, when Patsy flew over.

"Did you sleep much?" She asked him.

"No, not really…… You?"

"No not much at all really, but I have something to tell you Henry"

"So have I" Henry answered back. "You first"

Patsy told Henry about the patrol on the top of the wall in the early hours, and what both her and Elma saw and heard.

"Oh no, who on earth could that be..?!!.....Henry said, looking worried.
"….so, the faint light in the distance disappeared, then not long after that, there was somebody at the foot of the wall…?!" Patsy nodded.

Henry then told Patsy about Agnes Le Fey being at the front of the cottage, and trying to get through the hedge.
They both sat and looked at each other. What were they going to do…??

After a few moments, Henry said.

"Well, at least we're all still protected with Endor's spell – THAT, we do know. I'm calling a meeting today at 12:30 and I'm going to have to tell everyone what's going on, and about Mary of course. Patsy, would you go check on Mary for me. Take Wilbur with you if you want. I'm going to have a look over the wall and around the back towards the meadow"

"Be careful Henry" Patsy said. Poor Henry; she knew that he somehow felt responsible.

The children were playing out, in and around the garden, and jumping from one stone to another, and giggling from behind plant pots and flower beds, and playing 'Tig'. Nancy the Ladybird was shouting them over to the greenhouse for lessons, and Bonny the spider was shouting them all too; she looked over and waved at Patsy who was walking down the garden path with Wilbur. Patsy waved back.

Patsy and Wilbur squeezed through the window of the cottage, which was slightly open.

Mary was in the kitchen, and there was a wonderful smell of freshly baked bread. Mary's strange loss of 5 hours that morning was still playing on her mind, so she had decided to do some baking. Keeping busy at the moment was making things easier to cope with.

"Mary…!" Patsy shouted.

Mary came over to the window, wiping her hands on her apron.

"Oh Patsy, I thought I heard something. Oh, and Wilbur too. How's the wing.?"

"Well it's taking a bit of getting used to, but thank you once again" Wilbur was indeed very grateful.

"Well I actually think I 'owe' YOU really, so I'd say we're about even now" Mary said smiling.

"How did you sleep Mary?" Patsy asked. "Henry told me about Agnes being outside last night".

"She WAS...??!" Wilbur turned to look at Patsy, horrified.

"Yes, and that's not all. When Elma and I were patrolling the wall last night..."

"Patrolling the wall...?? Mary butted in.

"Yes, Elma and I patrol the wall every night together"

"Really.....why...?? Mary was astounded at this.

"Well we just like to keep a look out really, and it just makes us all feel safe....but I'm glad we were there because of what we saw and heard!"

Patsy then told Mary and Wilbur what they had seen and heard last night from over the wall.

"....and there's no one there this morning..??" questioned Mary. She was quite concerned on hearing this.

"Well Henry is out there now....." Patsy had no sooner said those words, and Mary had ripped off her apron......and was out of the door before either of them could say anything to her.

Henry was flying about over the other side of the wall, and looking around when he saw Mary striding around from the side pathway; he flew down to her.

"Mary, what's wrong....?!"

"Patsy has just told me about someone lurking about out here last night. I'm just not having it. This has to stop!!"

Someone had indeed been around at the back of the wall last night, as Mary noticed the grass looked a little disturbed and it was flat where someone had obviously been. She looked around some more, but couldn't see anything else.

"If it's that awful old Witch, she can think again…!" Mary was really angry.

Suddenly the skies turned grey, and a few dark clouds had appeared from nowhere.

"Who does she think she is anyway…?!! Well she's not getting in this garden or this house - EVER – let her try....!!!" She was now shouting, as her anger rose.

"Mary, please - calm down..!" Henry raised his voice a little now, as the wind had picked up. He looked around, and the trees had started swaying in the meadow. Mary was still shouting.

"I will NOT be frightened away from MY home – not by ANYONE!!" She looked around as she shouted this, just in case anyone might have been listening.

The wind had definitely picked up now, and it had started spitting…..

"Mary…!" Henry shouted. He was now getting blown about.

All of a sudden, Patsy shouted from over the wall.

"Mary…the oven…There's smoke coming out of the oven. THE BREAD…!!"

Mary had totally forgotten about the bread in the oven.

"Oh for God's sake..!" She shouted, and raced off and back to the house.

There was smoke pouring out of the oven when she eventually got back round to the cottage. She turned the oven off immediately, and flung the door open, and brought the sorry looking bread out, which was charred black. She opened all the windows and both doors, and got a tea towel out of the drawer, and was wafting the smoke away – until it eventually disappeared; but there was still a strong smell of charred bread.

"Phew….!! Good job I made two batches then isn't it..!" she said smiling, as she saw Henry, Patsy and Wilbur appear at the back window.

"I'm sure I can salvage some of this loaf and cut away the charred bits. Would you like some; I made extra….?? In fact, let's have some now, I could do with a snack and a cuppa after that…!!
Also, I just really wanted to say a big 'Thank you' to you all for looking after the garden; AND I wanted to tell you I've had a few thoughts about the Will"

They sat at the table and tucked into the fluffy, warm fresh bread, and best butter.

"Mary, I've called a meeting at lunchtime" Henry said looking at his watch. "….and I'm going to tell everyone about you, as I think they all should know. After all, this is YOUR garden, but especially as we now have a problem on our hands. I think we should all be vigilant, and come together to tackle this; we have children to consider their safety for, and I know there is going to be a lot more than meets the eye, as to what has unfolded already" He looked rather grave.

"Henry, don't worry – I'm not afraid" Mary said brightly. "…besides, now that I know I belong to a family of witches, who knows what I might be capable of doing..!!" She laughed as she poured herself more tea from the teapot.

"Mary..??" Henry kept his eyes on Mary's tea, as she poured; not really wanting to ask her the next question, but he continued.
"When you get angry, does the weather always seem to change…??"

At that point, he took his gaze from the tea, and looked up at her.

"Now I don't mean to pry, or if it's something you don't want to talk about, I understand; but with what just happened outside now, and then what you told me the other day…..it just seems to be a little strange and coincidental…."

Mary put the teapot down……

"Well, if I'm being honest, and now I know what I'm slowly remembering – looking back, yes, it does seem to happen"

"Mmmmmmm……" Henry was thinking. "It's definitely got something to do with who you are…. .Mary, what if you can CONTROL the weather..?!!!" he suddenly said.

"CONTROL the weather…??!" repeated Mary, half laughing.

"...but what if you can Mary – think about it..?!....it's possible…!!" Henry was shrugging his shoulders, and looking at Patsy and Wilbur.

"I think it's when I become emotional or angry" She replied, as she sat thinking.

"Exactly my point..!!" Henry exclaimed, as he walked backwards and forwards on the table.
"If it happens when you are angry or emotional, then you could 'potentially' make the weather change……it's because you've never tried – it's always just 'happened'….think about it…!"

"You're probably right Henry; but I can't say I really knew what was going on when I was a child. I just remember that my Mother never seemed to want to discuss anything. I mean – that day she got really angry at me when I asked her if she could hear animals talking too - like I could.
I really remember that quite vividly as a child, looking back. It was a perfectly normal question from where I was coming from, as I just thought that probably everybody could. She was furious. I don't think I've ever seen Mum get that angry before. I didn't understand because we had a budgie, and we talked to the budgie, and so did Mum. Well actually, I used to talk to the budgie quite a lot when I think about it now, and he used to answer me back, but never the words that we had taught him to say. We'd chat about all sorts. Quite funny really…..but I knew from that moment, that something was wrong – well not

wrong, but bad enough to see Mum like that; so I never spoke of it again – to anyone, apart from Jenny, my friend. She was the only one that knew"

Mary's eyes glistened over as she thought and remembered her friend.

"Poor Jenny…… I wonder what REALLY happened to her…
Now that my memories seem to be returning slowly, things are becoming so much clearer. No one spoke of her disappearance or that day, well not to me anyway. I was just whisked away to hospital, and then I went to stay in a house in the country – yeah that's it, it was rather a grand house, very big, and very quiet"

The others were listening intently.

"Can you remember what happened in the house?" Henry asked.

"Up until now, no…." Mary was slowly uncovering something that had obviously been buried deep inside her for many years.
"Let me just think a minute…… Yeah….. I was feeling a bit hazy, because this Doctor had just come into the room, and had given me an injection"

Mary had stood up now and was slowly walking around the kitchen.

"The door opened…..and….and…someone walked in…that's right…..someone big and tall, wearing black, but I didn't know who it was, I didn't see their face, as my eyes kept closing. All I remember is them whispering in my ear, and saying……saying….something like…..'It's alright Mary, don't be afraid….one day you will know why…'   Then I don't remember anything else…."

"Well, this is just becoming more curious by the day…" Henry was pondering.

"Mary…?" Patsy suddenly spoke. "Was your Mother there when the Doctor gave you the injection, and what was it for, and did anyone supervise that….??"

Henry and Wilbur were a little surprised to hear Patsy speak. She was usually quite quiet, but she was very bright and always seemed to say the right things at the right time.

"I actually don't remember my Mother being there much really. She would come and visit on days when I sat out in the chair by the big window that looked out onto the garden. She didn't really like hospitals or places like that; she said it always made her feel ill and anxious. As for anyone else being there to supervise - no, not that I can recall. I have no idea what I was being treated for come to think of it…. my memories of everything just slowly faded"

Patsy seemed a little puzzled. Then made an alarming statement…..

"So….. you said that you had lost your memory since that day at the woods ……so was the hospital and the big house you stayed in, a way of helping you try to remember, whilst resting, because maybe the trauma of it all had made you lose your memory……OR……was someone trying to make you FORGET, and that's what the injection was for…..??"

Mary slowly turned to look at Patsy.

"Oh God Patsy, you could be so right there, I haven't even had enough time to think about any of this properly yet..!"

Mary quickly sat down, her eyes were searching as her brain quickly began to process what Patsy had just said.

Henry spoke up. "Sounds to me like someone wanted you to forget EVERYTHING…!!… I think you could be onto something there Patsy…"

"….but…" Mary said …. "the question is…… 'WHY'…?"

Mary picked the Will up, and was looking at it, hoping it would suddenly reveal something to her. Then she said.

"What I wanted to tell you was, last night if you remember, you worked out that Endor and Agnes's Christian names were jumbled up to make their middle names, right..? Well, it's not only THEIR names – look"

She opened the Will out and first pointed to Magnus's name.

"See, it says there" and she read it out loud.

# "Magnus Gunsam Le Fey"

"If you swap the letters around from his name, it makes Gunsam..!.. Also, look at his son's name"

# "Samuel Elmaus Le Fey"

"Can you see – Samuel makes Elmaus, just like Endor makes Dorne and Agnes makes Sagen. Then Magnus mentions his wife's name – look!"

# "Bridget Begdirt Le Fey"

"Bridget BEGDIRT..??!" Wilbur winced as he said her name.
"Eurgh - I don't like the sound of HER!"

Henry, Patsy and Wilbur poured over the names, and slowly worked them out - and it was right..!!

"Mary, what was your Father's name, Eldon wasn't it..?? Did he have a middle name..?" Henry was most intrigued.

"Yes, he did, and I knew what it was, but I always thought my Dad came from Irish descent, so I didn't think it was a strange name"

"What was it..?!" They all asked at the same time.

"It was Donel" Mary answered. "It was spelt D, O, N, E, L. Yes…" she said quite proudly. " Eldon Donel Le Fey……."

Then Mary realised for the first time, that her Father's middle name was a scrambled version of his first name, and looked at Henry in a delayed shock.

"Mary, you know what I'm going to ask you now don't you…? Henry said.

"I do…" she said. "…and yes, I DO have a middle name; and like Dad's, I was led to believe that it was from Irish descent as well….and it's Mayr.
It's spelt M, A, Y, R, but pronounced just like May, but the letter 'r' is silent"

"Mayr…??" They all said together.

After a moment, Henry said.

"Well, Mary Mayr, it seems to me then, that you are definitely a direct descendant, and now we're positive that Samuel Elmaus Le Fey has got to be your Grandfather, because Endor and Agnes have no children…!! So….. you've found your Father's Father…!!"

"Yes, and I feel so happy about that..!" Mary said smiling. "I had a family that I never even knew about..!"

"What about your Mum, Mary, that's where I'm getting to with this..?? Your Mum seems to have been a very quiet, nervous woman. What was her name?" Henry asked.

"Well before she married Dad, her name was Sarah Jane Howe – that's it"

The three of them looked at each other like they were trying to work out a puzzle, and repeated her name.

"Sarah Jane Howe…??" They all said.

"That's odd" Henry was puzzled. "She seems to be the only one who doesn't have a middle name that has been made up from her first name"

"She could just have been an ordinary woman"

Wilbur suddenly spoke up, and then shrugged his shoulders as they all slowly tuned to look at him; so very surprised that he had spoken.

Wilbur's big eyes stared around at their gawping mouths.

"Well…well….what IF…" …there was a gap, as Wilbur continued to look at them, and then he carried on…. "…well……look, it just seems obvious to me that no one wanted Mary to know who she was, and they probably wanted her to lead a normal a life as possible – so maybe Mary's Dad was TOLD to marry an ordinary woman, or maybe he just wanted to, and not marry a Witch……. I mean, I might be wrong, I'm…I'm just saying……."

They still stared at him….

Wilbur didn't like the gap in the conversation, and hurriedly said.

."….in fact I'm probably very, very wrong, and yeah….yeah…. just forget that I said that….."

Wilbur looked decidedly awkward.

"WILBUR….!! Mary suddenly shouted…… "…of course – that makes perfect sense to me!!

"R…r…really..??!" Wilbur nervously laughed, as he realised he may have said something of importance.

"Well spotted Wilbur..!!" Henry slapped Wilbur on the back… That was the third time that day, and Wilbur rubbed the top of his shoulder as he gave Henry a sideways glance.

"Henry – the meeting..!!" Patsy suddenly cried out – looking at the clock on the wall. It was 12:25pm.

"Blazing buzzes…!! Where's the morning gone…??! Right…..err Patsy, Wilbur, you can both stand at Tree Stump Corner with me, as this meeting can't come sooner, and I may need some back up if I forget anything..!!.....but right now….. I actually think I could just do with one of Lars's wheat beers…!!!"
Wilbur was so pleased that Henry had involved him, and he felt quite important.

"Mary, if I need you to join us, would that be ok..??" Henry asked her, as they all made their way to the window.

"Of course – I can't wait to meet everyone..!"

They all flew out and over to the top of the garden. Wilbur's wings were working perfectly together. No more hopping…!!

# Chapter 17

## **<u>Introductions – Bad & Good</u>**

Henry really hadn't had much time to prepare anything at all for the meeting, and there was a lot to get through.
Everyone was waiting; there was quite a crowd..!!

Henry shushed the gathering, and began.

He told everyone about the mystery that had surrounded him, as to why all of a sudden, after all these years, that Mary and James had been able to move into the cottage, when, everyone knew the story of Endor casting the spell. He told them how he came about trying to be detective, and then discovered the old woman at the gate. When he told them all who she really was, there were a lot of shocked voices from a few in the crowd, and worried faces – some looking at each other.

"Does this mean we are safe here Henry.?!" Nancy spoke up from the front.

"Well, for now – yes. We still have Endor's spell protecting us, but for how long – we don't know. The fact that we are actually here, means that it's possible now that Endor's spell is weakening"

Nancy looked rather worryingly at her husband. She had children, like some of the others.

When he got to the part where he spoke about Mary, and the conversations they'd had, there were a lot of gasps from most of them; plus a lot of questions.

"She can hear us TALKING….how…??!" someone said.

"Maybe she has been put here to spy on us all" said another.

"Is she a Witch…??!!......and the questions continued, as concern spread throughout the crowd, and lots of conversations began between each other.

"Everyone….everybody….please, please can we keep calm here…!" Henry tried to calm everyone by putting his hands in the air.
"Ssh…please….EVERYONE…!!" Henry managed to bring the gathering to a hushed crowd again.

"Technically…" Henry carried on. "This is not 'our garden'. It belongs to Mary and James who live here". Henry was now sensing that there was a lot of disturbance in the crowd, and he was worried, but needed to instil some hope.

"We are much safer here than we were in the meadow. Come on everyone, you all know how worried we were for all those years, and our families before us – this is our future here in this garden. This is our safe haven….!! We have safe shelter – at last. We have an abundance of food….!!"

"Here, here..!!" A few shouted.

A very clear, and slow, rather snidey voice suddenly spoke up. "How do we know if we are safe, if she is a 'Le Fey'..?!"

"Who said that, can you step forward, or raise your hand..?" Henry replied, craning his neck to see who spoke.

A worm suddenly appeared at the front of the crowd – he had slid his way through, and stared up at Henry.

"Oh, I don't believe we have met, do I know you..?" Henry asked. He looked at the worm. The worm was wearing what looked like a bandana that fit tight all around his head.
Henry was trying to remember the worm, as he pretty much knew everyone that he had brought over the wall from the meadow to the garden.
The worm suddenly gave a wide grin.

"Yes, yes, I came over that day with everyone else, don't you remember..?" The worm said with a wide smile.

"..Erm...I...I... can't say I do remember you..." Henry was broke off in mid-sentence by the worm who interrupted him.

"...Well, you were so busy with your list, and getting everyone over here safely, you probably didn't really notice me... Anyway, Henry, my name is Wimble. Sorry we haven't had the chance to meet properly yet....... So, as I was saying, how do we know we are safe if this 'Mary' is a Le Fey..??"

Henry stared at the worm, and said slowly.
"I never actually said that she was...."

Wimble quickly spoke up.....

"......but let's just suppose she was then, it's very possible – how else could someone just come and walk into this cottage, and live here..?? No one has been able to do that for many years....as we all know of the curse the Witch put on the cottage and garden. That couldn't be broken by just anyone"

He looked around the crowd, and nodded to them all, trying to make everyone agree with him. Many voices answered.

"Yes, how can we trust her..?" said someone.

"If she can hear us talking, and talk back to us, then that's the sign of a Witch alright..!!" shouted another.

"Yeah, yeah...!!" a few more shouted. Wimble turned back to Henry – and smiled, and raised his eyebrows.

Oh dear, Henry wasn't expecting this kind of reaction. He actually couldn't answer the question that Wimble had posed. How DID he know if Mary could be trusted if she was a Le Fey...?? He hadn't known her long enough at all... His head was in a whirl. What should he do...? He turned to Patsy and Wilbur.

They had both seen how Henry was getting questioned.
Patsy stepped forward to speak. Everyone suddenly became quiet.

"Everybody – please, please calm down. We are holding this meeting to be truthful with you all, and to tell you what we know already. First of all, let us just remember and reflect on what our lives were like in the meadow before. We were frightened, vulnerable, scared, and very protective of our elderly and our little ones. This USED to be our home many years ago, and now we are back, back to where we belong – in a garden, where we all thrive. There is plenty to eat here, there are safe places to sleep and rest. We are so very lucky, and I for one, feel much happier here than in the meadow..!!"

There were lots of cheers..!
Patsy carried on.

"Yes, we all are aware of the story about the sisters – the Witches, but do any of you know the truth..?? Well I do…. I have had a few conversations with Mary myself…!" There were gasps, and heads turned to the person standing next to them. "..Yes, I have, and Mary is one of the nicest people you could ever wish to meet. She has built this garden with her own strength and love, not magic. She wasn't even aware that she could speak to animals until recently. An awful lot has happened to Mary, of which she is coming to terms with, and she needs our help..!! She is letting us live in her garden, and we should be grateful. She didn't know anything about the sisters either, or that she was even related to them, until we found out….!! She needs our help……!!"

"Oh so she IS a Le Fey then…?? Wimble enquired, who was now smiling - with the biggest grin on his face, and his eyes narrowing, as he waited for an answer.

Henry looked at Wimble, and his eyes lowered. He had been watching Wimble throughout Patsy's speech…….he cleared his throat behind Patsy – he didn't want her telling them anymore than she already had.

"Ahem…ahem…yes....thank you Patsy. Now what I'm going to do is invite Mary out here; and I know that she is very excited to meet with you all…." There were whispers, and some fearful chatter.

"There is nothing to fear, or be worried about whatsoever, Mary is quite lovely"

Henry turned towards Wilbur and Patsy.

"Wilbur, would you go and ask Mary to come out here please?"

Wilbur looked a little shocked that Henry had asked him to do something.

"Y...Y....yes, of course Henry".....Wilbur realised that now his wing was mended, he could be of more use, and was of course very fast. He flew away at once towards the cottage.

Henry turned to everyone, and said.

"If you have any questions when Mary comes out, please ask her. If some of you don't wish to be here, that is absolutely fine, you can make your way back to your homes"

Some of the residents of Tree Stump Corner wanted to stay and were very excited; others didn't quite know how they felt, so decided to leave. Henry turned to Patsy, and said in a low voice.

"Patsy, have you ever seen Wimble before, because I don't recall seeing him at all...??" Henry was a little curious to say the least.

"No, I can't say that I have Henry, and I was surprised when I saw him come to the front of the crowd"

"Mmmmmm.....well like I say, I don't recall, but then again, he could have been part of the journey across the meadow, and I just didn't notice him....." and he shrugged his shoulders.

Just at that moment, Mary was walking up the garden path.
Wilbur had shouted Mary from the kitchen window after flying down to the cottage. He had felt a little nervous on his own, but when he told her that Henry had asked her to come to the back garden to meet everyone, she felt nervous herself, which made Wilbur feel a little better.
"Oh really...?! Yes of course I will. Oh I'm so excited and quite nervous to meet everyone now..!"

"Well....... I'm not sure that everyone is 'completely' happy, just to let you know Mary..." Wilbur felt bad saying it, but he knew there had been worried faces.

"Oh......but why...??" Mary asked.

"Becaaaaaauuse….." Wilbur strung out the word as he looked down at his feet. "……erm…becaaaaauuse…well…some of them think that you might be related to the Le Fey sisters because you have suddenly been able to come and live in this cottage, and because you can have conversations with animals as well, that you could be bad, and maybe not to be 'trusted'…..??" His voice went up at the end.

"Oh no….well I suppose I'm just going to have to reassure them all….!" Mary felt even more nervous now.

Wilbur hopped onto the windowsill.

"We'd better go, Henry will be waiting"

Wilbur flew out of the window, and met Mary coming out of the back door.

As Mary approached Tree Stump Corner, she was struggling to see where to sit- she didn't want to sit on anyone, but Henry flew up to greet her.
"Thanks for coming Mary; if you wouldn't mind sitting on that bit of grass there" Henry pointed, and Mary sat down.

She smiled, rather nervously, and whispered.
"Henry what if they don't like me..??"

"I doubt that very much Mary, you will be fine…"
"It's alright everyone, you can come out now" Henry shouted as he flew from plant to stone to tree.

One by one, those who had wanted to meet Mary; and the ones that were just inquisitive, began to emerge rather slowly. Some were walking, and some flying. Those that weren't so sure, had all stayed in their homes and were peeping from behind doors, leaves, and blades of grass.
Henry introduced everyone including Nancy and her family. Patsy introduced Mary to her best friend, Bonny the spider, and also to Elma, the Daddy Long Legs.

"This is who I patrol the wall with every night Mary". Patsy said, beckoning towards Elma.

As Elma came over, showing his biggest smile, he tripped on a pebble, and did a bit of a roly poly, but recovered himself very quickly, and ended up on one knee, very close to Mary. Everyone laughed. Elma looked up at her with his big eyes.

"Sorry, I'm a bit clumsy, but it's so very nice to meet you Mary" and put one of his feet up. He didn't know whether to do a 'high five', shake her hand or wave, so he gave Mary a little awkward wave.

"Ahh, Patsy was telling me that she patrolled the wall with someone – it's really nice to meet you Elma – and everyone else for that matter. I can't believe you patrol the wall, but I'm very grateful…! What exactly do you do it for…??" Mary asked.

"Erm….well….." Elma took his gaze away from Mary and looked quickly at Patsy for an answer, hoping she would help him out, and then returned his gaze back to Mary.
Patsy stepped in…

"Well, like I said Mary, we just want to keep everyone safe, and it just makes us all feel better. We don't mind, do we Elma..?"
"Wow, I AM impressed". Mary said.

Elma was still staring up at Mary; he couldn't take his eyes off her. He didn't even hear what Patsy had said.

Mary was looking around at everyone, and smiling, she couldn't quite believe it.
Suddenly, someone could be heard making their way through.

"Excuse please, I am vonting to meet viz Miss Mary..!" It was Lars.

"Mary this is Lars…." Henry introduced Lars, as he stepped forward. "His job is patrolling the garden on an evening on his bike – and he does a very fine job, for which we are all very grateful for"

Mary was very impressed as Lars bowed his head as usual, and gave her a little salute. Mary had put out her hand, but seeing his salute, she quickly put it down - a little redundantly, as she thought Lars wanted to shake her hand.

Instantly, Elma quickly stepped forward to shake her hand instead – still staring at Mary.

"Oh….." Mary gasped, as Elma took her hand with two of his.

One by one, Mary was being greeted by everyone that wanted to meet her, and some of the ones who had gone back to their homes, came out and came over too.

Jeremy the Snail came forward, but he had set off a while ago, and just got to Mary as the last one to greet her. He started to tell her about the night that Lars had found him on the path, but Lars interrupted him, and told Mary the rest of the tale, much to Jeremy's disappointment, but to the amusement of everyone else, as Lars and Jeremy were both quite funny.
Henry was pleased that Mary was chatting away to everyone, and suddenly everyone wanted to ask her questions.

Jeremy slowly came up to Henry.

"Henry, I'm a little concerned about something" he said in his slow voice. "….but I think it's worth mentioning. Have you got a minute..?"
Henry thought that a minute with Jeremy would probably be 10 minutes, but Jeremy looked a little worried.

"What is it Jeremy..?" Henry asked as they walked away for some privacy.

"Well, just a little earlier, before the meeting, Jemima and I took little Ben for a walk over by the greenhouse, where there is a little compost pile, so we took Ben for a little snack, and showed him what he could eat." He said slowly, as Henry was listening intently. "….While we were there, we heard two voices whispering from behind the wall. We both listened, and told Ben to be very quiet. We couldn't make out who it was, and we couldn't make out everything they were saying, but I distinctly heard a low wicked voice saying something like …**'find out'** ….and… **'I'm almost sure she is'**……and….. **'I need to know, so do your job…!!'**  Now like I said Henry, I don't know who those voices were, but I just didn't like the sound of any of it. Jemima and I thought it best to inform you, but there is something else…"

Jeremy took a quick look round, and then said.

"I don't know everyone properly yet, but there's something about that worm, Wimble that gives me a bad feeling. Very shortly after we heard that conversation, we saw him, slowly and quietly emerging from around the back of the greenhouse – away from the wall"

At that point he looked at Henry and shrugged his shoulders and raised his eyebrows.

Henry spoke closely to Jeremy and said in a low voice.

"Thank you so much for that Jeremy, please just keep this under your hat for the time being, as I need to think about this. I don't like the sound of it either. We all have to be extra careful at the moment, and everyone's safety is important"

"You have my word Henry, and if I can be of any help, please ask; as you know, I am eternally grateful to you for giving me and my family a home here". Henry nodded as Jeremy slowly made his way back to the crowd.

Someone not that far away – was listening…..

# Chapter 18

## <u>Shocks, Fears &  A Deadly Twist</u>

As Mary walked back to the cottage, smiling, Henry flew at her side.

"Well…" she said quite brightly, as she turned to Henry. "…. that went rather well didn't it..?"

"Yes, better than I thought" Henry replied, but he was a bit distant in his thoughts.

"What's troubling you Henry…?? I haven't known you that long, but I know you have something on your mind"

Henry then proceeded to tell Mary what Jeremy's thoughts were concerning Wimble the worm, once they got inside the cottage. Henry was a little perturbed.

"We're really going to have to keep an eye on him I think" Henry said.

"So, if Jeremy's concerns are correct, and it WAS Wimble talking to someone behind the fence – who would it have been…??" Mary asked.

They both looked at each, and then all of a sudden, both their eyes grew larger.

"Agnes…!!!" They said together.

Henry was walking up and down on the windowsill that looked out onto the back garden.
"Oh no, no, no…. this won't do at all. So she's got a spy working for her, and now he's in this garden…!! I thought I hadn't seen him before…AND he was asking questions at the meeting..!!"

Mary was furious.

"If I see that horrible blasted Witch again, if she dare comes anywhere near my garden gate, I'll……."

Henry stopped Mary in her tracks.

"Please Mary, don't get angry……please…!!" Henry pleaded…… "She wants to get into this garden and cottage for reasons we don't yet know, and according to this Will that was written by the man we suspect is your Great Grandfather, HE didn't want her to have anything to do with this cottage either……so we have to find out why – and soon….!!!"

Just at that moment, Patsy and Wilbur flew in rather quickly through the back kitchen window.

"Henry, Mary, come quick, something's happened to Jeremy…!!" Patsy was out of breath and near to tears. "His wife Jemima was shouting for help at the front of their home, and Bonny ran over quickly, and found Jeremy on the floor outside. He doesn't look well at all. QUICK…!!"

Mary and Henry got to Jeremy's little home in no time at all, followed by Patsy and Wilbur.
Just at the front of the two plant pots, Jeremy was laid on one side, quite motionless, and Bonny was looking after him while his wife Jemima was behind one of the plant pots, comforting their son Ben who was crying.

"What's happened Bonny..?!" Henry asked quickly, as he flew down towards Jeremy on the path.

"Is he breathing…?!!"

"Yes, only just..!" Bonny was upset.

Mary moved in closer, and looked around the plant pots.
She suddenly scooped Jeremy up, and run over to the water butt in the garden. She held Jeremy in one hand, and with the other, she scooped water from the water butt and washed Jeremy over and over again.

"Come on Jeremy, come on, you can make it. Come on…." Mary was trying to stay calm and speak soothingly to the poor snail, who at this moment, looked like he wasn't going to make it at all..!

"Have a little drink….that's it, nice and steady. It's ok, I've got you….."
"Mary what's happened to Jeremy…?!" Patsy cried, as she quickly flew up "Jemima is so upset..!"

"Patsy, go back to Jeremy's at once, and don't let ANYONE walk around outside his house. Tell Jemima and Ben to stay indoors and not to come out until I get back. Tell everyone to move away…..quickly; I'll explain later – GO..!!!" Mary shouted.

Patsy flew off quickly, while Mary was still bathing Jeremy in lots of water. Henry joined Mary, and was quite shocked and upset to see Jeremy's condition.

"My God, what on earth has happened to Jeremy Mary – what's going on…..and what's happened to his skin, he looks like he's aged by about 30 years…?!!" Henry couldn't believe how poorly Jeremy looked.

Mary didn't answer, she gave Henry a quick, but very grave look, and kept bathing and bathing him and making him drink.

A few moments passed by, and Jeremy started to come round very slowly. He turned to look up at Mary, his eyes half opened.

"I….I…" Then his head flopped back onto Mary's open palm.

"Is he going to be alright Mary…?" Henry asked in a faint whisper.

"Yes – he's weak, but I was afraid for a few minutes then – phew…..Come on little guy, you're going to be ok – just keep taking sips of water". She turned to Henry. "He needs to keep wet for quite a while".

Mary walked off to the cottage, with Jeremy still in her hand. She returned with an empty milk bottle full of water, and a small bowl with a little bit of water in the bottom, and Jeremy was sat in the bottom of the small bowl. He was awake, but looked weak.

Lots of the others had now shown up at Jeremy's, as word had spread around the garden that he was ill, and Patsy and Bonny were keeping everyone back from the front of his home, as instructed by Mary.

As Mary brought Jeremy back, everyone was silent, waiting for news.
Mary knelt down on the ground, and put the small bowl gently down next to her. Everyone was craning to see.
Jeremy moved about slowly in the shallow water.

Mary told everyone to move away from the plant pots. She then carefully encouraged Jemima and Ben to crawl onto her hand, and she carefully and slowly put them down by the side of the bowl that Jeremy was in. Both Jemima and Ben were crying with happiness to see Jeremy who was now weakly smiling at them both, but was so glad to see them.
Mary then emptied the contents of the water from the bottle all over the ground, and in and around Jeremy's home. Everyone gasped.....What WAS she doing...?!!

Mary then went to fill a large bowl with water, came back and as she put it on the floor said.
"I want everyone to wash in this water; any one of you who has been anywhere near Jeremy's home in the last hour, especially your feet".

Everyone looked at each other, puzzled.

Mary put Jemima and Ben in the water and encouraged them to rinse themselves. Then everyone else followed suit.

"Jemima, you, Jeremy and Ben will stay at mine for the next couple of days until Jeremy feels stronger. Can everyone else please be careful around your homes, and if you see anything on the ground that looks suspicious, keep away from it, and let me know as soon as possible. Jeremy will be ok, but he has had quite a scare".

"Mary...?" Nancy the Ladybird stepped forward. "Please can you tell us what it was..?" Nancy looked very worried.

"Yes, I can – I'm afraid it was salt....." There were a few gasps. Salt...but how..??

"I've no idea how it got here, but please, everyone be careful"

Mary picked the two bowls up, and walked back to the cottage. Jemima and Ben had crawled into the one with Jeremy in, and Jemima was mopping Jeremy's head, and Ben was cuddling up to his Daddy.
Henry, Patsy and Wilbur flew back to the cottage after Mary. Once inside, Mary took the bowl into the living room, and told Jeremy and his family to rest where it was cool.

In the kitchen, the others were sat on the kitchen table and waited for Mary. She came in and sat down, and the others waited for her to speak.

"Well - that was close; I thought he wasn't going to make it for a few moments" Mary said rather wearily. "I didn't want to panic anyone, but we nearly lost him…!!"

Henry was looking very worried indeed. He sat down rather heavily, and put his head in his hands.
Wilbur and Patsy were looking a bit puzzled.
Henry looked up at Mary and said.

"Salt…..really…??!!"

"Henry, this was sabotage. Someone has deliberately put that there..!!" Mary said sternly.
"Yes – I know. That's what worries me…!!" He answered.

"As soon as you said what it was, I just knew that no amount of salt anywhere could have got there by itself…..This is all very dangerous. Someone has maliciously meant to cause harm to Jeremy, and nearly killed him in the process..!!"

"Why would salt be dangerous Henry..?" Patsy timidly enquired.

"Salt is dangerous in large quantities to anyone, but especially snails and slugs. It dehydrates them as they absorb it very quickly through their skin, that's why Mary had to keep washing it away from Jeremy, and also made him drink it, to hydrate him. It can be fatal, and Jeremy could have died…!!.....and whoever it was that did this, wanted Jeremy dead….why…??!"

Henry didn't have to think for too long, and neither did Mary.

Henry turned to Patsy and Wilbur.

"Did either of you see Wimble, that sneaky worm, when Mary came out to meet everyone..??"

They both shook their heads.

"Right, well in that case then, he must have been hiding, and i suspect that he heard Jeremy when he came over to talk to me about his concern for Wimble; and telling me about those voices he'd overheard from behind the wall. Also, I actually EXPECTED Wimble to be there to meet Mary, as he seemed very interested in her, and was VERY vocal at the meeting about her..! I reckon that after he had heard everything Jeremy was saying, he's slinked off, and then came back with some salt. Obviously because he thought Jeremy might have blown his cover..!" Henry was getting really angry.

He then had to explain to Patsy and Wilbur what Jeremy had said to him at the meeting.

"Oh no, this is just awful…!" Patsy looked very tearful.
"Poor, poor Jeremy……and that awful sneak, Wimble!"

Wilbur had put his head down, and shook it wearily……. this was all a very sad, but dangerous situation.

Mary had gone into the room to check on Jeremy. She came back, went into the fridge, took out some cucumber, and chopped it up into little pieces, and took it back into the room.

"They need to eat" she said, coming back into the kitchen. "….especially Jeremy. He's ok but still quite weak"

"I've just been thinking" Henry said. "I'm going to ask Lars if he will extend his patrol this evening. Patsy, I want you and Elma to be on alert from now on. In fact, take someone else with you; and Wilbur, I'd like you to do the same at the front, and also the back" They all nodded.

"What about me..??" Mary asked.

"You stay indoors Mary, and look around this cottage, there HAS to be something in this house that has got something to do with your past, or something of any worth or interest"

Wilbur asked, looking at the other three. "What are we going to do about Wimble…??"

Mary smiled, and spoke up.

"We do nothing about him, we ignore him. He will be expecting a reaction, so no one say anything to him. If he is working for Agnes, then any information he can give her, he will. So don't tell him anything…."

They all agreed.

Suddenly there was a little tap at the back kitchen window. Everyone looked round, and Patsy, Henry and Wilbur flew over swiftly - to see Elma standing there….
"Hi, I hope you don't mind me coming down….." Elma said, trying to squeeze his self through the gap, but there wasn't much room……

"I just wanted to know if…if….ouch…..if you wanted any help, and I wanted to know…..how Jeremy is….aaghh..!"…he said as he continually tried to get through the little gap; but because his legs were so tall, he got stuck.

"Erm…I'm stuck, can you pull me in……anyone..??"

Patsy laughed as she got hold of one of his legs, while Wilbur got hold of another leg, and they heaved, until he popped through, but he tumbled and banged his head.
.
As he sat rubbing it, Patsy said……"and why are you so dirty..?!"

"Well…erm…. I wasn't quite sure of the way in, so I got a bit muddy" He said as he looked down at himself and saw that he was filthy, so began rubbing dirt away – which he just made worse.

"…and….and…I just wondered if……if maybe Mary…erm…...w…was ok..?"

He said the last bit rather awkwardly, but then looked straight up at Mary, as she walked up to the window
Wilbur, Patsy and Henry gave each other a quick look then lowered their eyes, and Patsy put her hand up to her mouth to stop herself smiling.

Henry spoke up.

"Elma that's very kind of you, and yes, we were just discussing the security around the garden from now on, after the incident with Jeremy"

Elma looked from one to the other as he was still wiping his hands on his chest.

"Sorry about the dirt" he said with an awkward grin.
Mary stepped forward with a hanky.

"Here Elma, don't get yourself dirty, wipe your hands on this" and passed him the hanky, but he didn't look at the hanky, he just took it as he kept staring at Mary….

"Look, come in and lets all sit at the table, I could actually do with a cuppa"

As Elma made his way down the side of the kitchen cupboard, and onto the floor, the other three flew over to the table, and were already there munching on a bit of bread and honey that Mary had put out.

As Elma walked across the kitchen floor, he was looking around nosily, and not really looking where he was going. Mary got up from her chair, and began to walk towards the stove to turn the gas off, as the kettle had boiled. She didn't see Elma, as she went into the cupboard to get a tea bag from the tea caddy, but Patsy had quickly glanced over towards Mary, and out of the corner of her eye, she caught sight of Elma nonchalantly staring around as he made his way across the kitchen floor.

Mary was about to stand on him….!

"MARY…ELMA…!!" she shouted.

Elma was startled, and froze. Mary dropped the tea caddy tin, which crashed onto the floor, so all the tea bags fell out. The tin rolled quickly, and was heading straight for Elma, who managed, right at the last second, to skedaddle to the right, which in turn made him go into a spin on the kitchen floor, so he was going round and round and round in circles as he continued to head for the wall. The tea caddy just missed him, and crashed into the wall, where Mary had three copper saucepans hanging on nails. The bang made the saucepans fall to the floor, with an almighty CRASH; and they all scattered, going in different directions. One skidded quickly across the stone floor, making a terrible scraping noise, and over to the table where the others were sat, and it crashed into the table legs. The other pan bounced awkwardly towards the living room, as it landed on the carpet, then it came to a stop as it hit the door frame. The third pan had headed straight for the wall, right where Elma had finished spinning.

There was silence for a few seconds.......

# Chapter 19.

## **<u>Accidents will happen…..</u>**

"Elma……ELMA…!!" Patsy shouted as they all quickly made it over to the wall where the saucepan had ended up…..but there was no sign of him.
"Elma…??..I don't want to look..!" she cried. She had visions of Elma being crushed by the heavy saucepan.

Mary knelt down, and turned to Patsy before she lifted the saucepan away from the wall.

"Turn away Patsy…"

Patsy turned around sobbing, and Wilbur came up and put his arm around her shoulders.

Henry and Mary looked at each other, and nodded. Mary very carefully picked the pan up, half expecting poor Elma to be splattered on the wall……but in fact what had happened was…..the pan had hit the wall with the opening to the wall, and trapped Elma inside, so nothing had actually hit him…!!

Mary looked at him for a few seconds, and saw that he was breathing; then she bent down to carefully pick him up, so as not to hurt him. He looked very dazed. She stood up and walked back to the kitchen table, stepping between all the scattered tea bags. The others came over to the table, and peered over into Mary's hand.
Elma slowly started opening his eyes, as he laid in her palm, still muddy from the garden, and with the hanky still in his hand.

"Ahhh there he is…!" Henry said cheerfully.

"Elma – you're alive…!!" Patsy cried with joy.

Elma opened his eyes fully, and he was staring right up into Mary's eyes.

"I am…..are you sure??.....AM I…..alive….or…or am I…..in heaven….?" A dreamy smile appeared on his face as he continued to stare at Mary, with his eyelids blinking slowly.

"Oh Elma – really…?! Trust you…!!" Patsy started to laugh through her tears, and gave him a little nudge.

"Thought we'd lost you there buddy". Wilbur said. "Blimey, what with Jeremy and now you..!"

"Oh crikey I'd better check on Jeremy.!" Mary said quickly. "…and YOU'RE obviously ok Elma" she said with a little smile, as she put him down gently on the table.

Elma looked around at the others and said.

"I thought I wasn't going to stop spinning then…I'm a bit dizzy!"

"You can say that again..!!" Patsy said laughing; which set the others off laughing.

"What happened anyway…?" He asked, quite dazed.

The others started filling him in on what happened; and Elma particularly liked the bit when Wilbur told him that he went into a spider roll and kept spinning and spinning.

"I haven't done one like that for years..!!" he said rather proudly, as Mary came back through into the kitchen.

"Jeremy is a lot better, thank goodness, but they all heard the commotion and wondered what was going on, so I told them what had happened". She said as she stopped to pick the saucepan up that had landed outside the room door.

"What a bloody day..!!"

Mary recovered the second pan from the foot of the table, and then went over to the one that had landed against the wall – which was the biggest one of the three.

"I can't believe how lucky you were Elma…!!  There wouldn't have been anything left of you if that pan had landed the other way…!"

As she bent down to pick up the pan, she noticed that when the heavy pan had crashed so hard into the wall, it had actually made a small hole.

"Oh no, look at that…!" she said as she put the pans on the side and bent down to take a closer look.

"What's happened..?" Henry said as he came over. "Oh dear…that will need sorting" he said scratching his head.

"Wait a minute though…" Mary was puzzled. "….I thought that this wall was solid, but it looks like….." She got on her hands and knees and bent right down, and tried to look in through the hole.

"Oh my God, there's a gap at the back, but I can't really see..!.. Wilbur would you bring me the pencil that's over there on the table?" Wilbur brought the pencil over, and Mary put the flat end of the pencil through the hole. The pencil went in about 4 or 5 inches, until it touched the other side of the wall. Mary gave it a few taps; the wall appeared to be solid on the other side.

"Yes there's definitely another wall or something..! How strange. I painted this as well, thinking it was just a wall, but this hole that's been made looks like old plasterboard and layers and layers of old wallpaper, look!"

Mary started carefully pulling away at the edges, and bit by bit, began pulling off thick strips of old wallpaper that had also been painted over. It was really thick, so was quite tough.

"Mary let me go in and have a look" Henry suggested. "Do you have a torch..?"

Mary went to the kitchen drawer for the torch, and shone the light through the hole, as Henry flew in.

"Up a bit Mary.......now, now down to the right.....aaghhh I see. Ok, shine it up over to the left....!"

Henry was shouting instructions so he could get a better look between the small gap.
He came out – his eyes as big as saucers.

"Well, you're not going to believe this, but behind this wall, it looks like there is a bloody great big door..!!"

"A DOOR..?!" Mary exclaimed...."Eh…well that can't be right. This wall is the outside wall…?!"

"Could it be the cellar door Mary..?" Wilbur asked.

"No" said Mary. "The cellar door is right there Wilbur - next to it; and this part here, is definitely the outside wall. The only thing that is behind this wall - is the pathway outside that runs from the front of the cottage to the back…… So why is there a false door next to the cellar door..?" Mary was very intrigued.
"…..and why would it be boarded up..?" she asked, as she looked around at each of them.

Elma was still sat on the kitchen table, yawning…..

"Well if you ask me…" He shouted over. "That's been boarded up for a reason. Maybe whoever boarded it up didn't want anyone to know it was a door……and let's face it – all doors lead to somewhere….."…..then he yawned again.

They all looked at each other, and then looked over towards the table at Elma, who was now trying to find a comfy spot on the tea towel.

"What…??" he said, when he saw them looking at him. "What have I said now, have I said something wrong..??"
Mary suddenly turned back towards the wall, and said.

"Right, this is coming down..!... I need to know what's behind there..!"

She didn't waste any time at all, and started pulling bits of thick hardened wallpaper away from what looked like an old wooden frame, with lengths of wood nailed across, with the layers of wallpaper over the top, which were coming off quite easily in her hands. At one point, she had to go and find a knife to cut away chunks and chunks of it.

Patsy decided to go and see how Jeremy was.
He looked so much better, and much more 'plumper' than before. He had obviously hydrated enough as nearly all the water had gone from the bowl.

"Oh Jeremy you do look so much better, how are you feeling..??....and how are you Jemima, what a fright you had..?!"

"I'm feeling so much better but quite tired Patsy, thank you so much. I'm just so glad that Jemima and Ben hadn't stepped outside when we'd heard a noise – that's why I went out you see - to have a look..!"

"Oh, so you HEARD something..?!...I didn't know that, I thought you were walking INTO your home, coming back from the meeting..!" Patsy was surprised.

"No, I had only just got in, and then I heard something outside; but now when I think about it, it was obviously the salt I heard being poured onto the floor...... funny thing was though; I never heard any footsteps...."

"Don't look so puzzled Jeremy" Patsy said.

Then she explained to Jeremy who the others thought it was.
Jeremy was quite shocked to hear this, but then said.

"It doesn't surprise me actually; he's a very sneaky character. Do you know, I'm sure I've seen him somewhere before, but I just can't think where...." Jeremy was thinking really hard.

"Look, you all need some rest, and at least you can be safe here for the next couple of days; and I will keep popping back in to see you. I had better get back to the others; it's getting very noisy in there"

"What's going on in there Patsy..?" Jemima asked.

"Oh well…. When Elma and Mary nearly collided with each other….."
Then she stopped in her tracks; as she realised she had better not say any more about the hidden door. The poor Snail family had had quite enough upset for one day…… "Basically, Mary is trying to fix the hole in the wall. What's more important right now, is that you all have a good night's rest"
Patsy waved as she flew quickly back to the kitchen.

It was taking Mary some effort trying to get the old wallpaper off, that was stuck to the wooden slats, and she began to feel really frustrated, as it was only coming off in small bits. It was going to take her absolutely ages to get it all off. This was years and years, and layers upon layers of both paint and wallpaper.

"This damn wallpaper – why won't it come off….??!!" She shouted.

As she shouted the last words, she banged her fists against the wall in temper, and then kicked the bottom of it where the hole had been. Then she stood back away from it, wondering what to do next, and in her anger and frustration, she shouted, as she gestured her arms towards the wall.

"How the hell am I going to get that off……and whatever is behind this bloody wall – I want to know.…!!..NOW..!!"

In that split second, a sudden gush of energy jolted through Mary's body, her eyes flashed a crimson colour, and suddenly, sparks flew from her finger tips, and straight at the wall, which blasted a hole in it, nearly the full size of the wall..! This startled her, and in her shock at seeing sparks flying from her fingers, she staggered backwards, with her arms still in the air, but they were wavering all over the place – but the sparks were still flying out, and tearing streaks across the ceiling, as Mary had got startled.!

Suddenly, chunks of the ceiling quickly fell down, including bits of wood, and years and years of dust and cobwebs; and showered them all in what looked like white plaster…….. as Mary screamed….!

It was pouring with rain outside.

She landed on the floor on her bottom, and the blast of the sparks had jolted her backwards…

Everything went into slow motion. Henry, Patsy and Wilbur had gone flying and spinning through the air with the force of the blast, like they had been caught up in a tornado, and they turned over and over in the air, until all three of them were flung onto the sofa which was over at the other side of the kitchen. They bounced into the back of the sofa, and fell down onto the seats below; leaving white powder dust marks where they had hit the back of the sofa.

Mary's face and hair looked like she had just poured a bag of flour over her head. She sat still where she had ended up on the floor, motionless, just staring at a cloud of dust in front of her.

Elma, who was snoozing on the table on the tea towel, had also got caught in the blast, and the tea towel had flown off the table, into the air, and then onto the floor, like a magic carpet, but thankfully he too, had had a soft landing.

Eventually Mary looked round and spoke up.

"Is everyone alright…?!"

She frantically looked around.

"Henry, Patsy…..where are you….??! Wilbur….Elma..??" She couldn't see a thing. There was a fine haze of white dust in the air, which was slowly settling. Then she heard some distant coughing coming from the sofa. It was Patsy.

"Patsy, Oh my god Patsy, are you ok..?!!" Mary crawled over. Patsy's beautiful coloured wings were all white.

"Ahem…ahem….I'm....ahem…..ok Mary" as she coughed onto the back of her hand.

"Henry…??!"…Patsy looked to the side of her – Henry was motionless. He looked like a grey old bee with all the dust on him. Patsy began rubbing the dust from him and trying to rouse him.

"Henry, wake up, wake up…!!"

Henry suddenly coughed and spluttered, and slowly sat up. Wilbur was groaning from the other side of the sofa. Mary staggered over to him.

"Wilbur – are you ok, are you hurt..??"

"I'm not sure, but I think my wing might have broken again" he looked really sorrowful.

"Oh no......I can fix that for you again; as long as you're alright"

Suddenly Elma's muffled voice could be heard over on the kitchen floor. He had landed on the tea towel he had been laid on, but it had somehow fallen on top of him as well. Suddenly the tea towel moved, and Elma's head poked out from under it, but he looked like he had a hanky on his head, and he still looked as dazed as he did when he emerged from behind the pan.

"How can anyone have two accidents in one day, and be lucky enough to escape both times..?" Wilbur said, holding his broken wing.

Henry slowly turned to Mary, looking at her with wide eyes.

"Mary....what did you do...?!"

"I....I...honestly don't know, I've never seen that, or done that before – whatever 'that' is" she looked worriedly back at Henry.

"Mary, there were red sparks coming out of your fingertips.....that was magic – and YOU conjured that. Something is bringing out more and more of probably who you really are – and it's all since you came here" he said, as he patted white dust from his fur.

Mary was knelt down on the white powdery floor, and she looked down at her hands, turning them over and over again, and wondering how those sparks could have come from them. After a few moments, she said.

"I DID do that, didn't I.......What I mean is – that was me - wasn't it.??"

Then she gasped as she put her hand to her mouth.

"Oh no, I've just realised something.....I had that same feeling; like what just happened to me then, on that day I met the old woman, Agnes at the gate. Remember I told you Henry...??...Yeah, she picked my hands up and was turning them over and over again in hers, but as soon as she touched me, I got a strange like rush of air that just seemed to sear right through me, and it made me shudder….and since then, that's when I started to get my memories back…!!"

Mary had stood up now, brushing the dust from her clothes, as she faced the others.

"It's all happened since she touched my hands…!"

Patsy was gently blowing the dust from her wings and said.

"She has obviously made some kind of connection with you Mary, and it has suddenly unlocked all of your memories, and who you really are"

"I hope she didn't cast a spell on me, or anything like that" Mary said, shuddering at the thought, as she too, dusted herself down.

Wilbur spoke up.
"It sounds to me like she just wanted to know who you are, and how you suddenly came to live here, and she probably already knows now"

"Do you really think she knows…?" Patsy said, now looking down at her very pretty self again.

All this time, Henry had been quiet – he had been staring straight ahead – eyes like saucers, and motionless.

"Henry…??" Patsy looked worried. "Are you ok..? What's wrong….Did you bang your head or something...?"

With his mouth slightly open, he just pointed without saying a word – at the wall.

One by one, each of them turned around and looked over towards the wall. The dust had now completely settled, and the sight that met their eyes, made them speechless……..

# Chapter 20

# **The Wall**

Mary's anger and outburst had, indeed resulted in Mary causing devastation to the kitchen, and the majority of the downstairs. Something that had never happened to her before.......had just occurred there and then, without her even trying, or knowing what she was doing.

She had somehow been able to summon some kind of spell that she knew nothing of, causing a huge blast, which had brought most of the kitchen ceiling down, but more so, a huge hole in the wall, where chunks of plaster, wood, and wallpaper lay strewn all over the floor, and now under a mountain of dust.......but now all the dust had settled, they were all looking at what had been revealed behind all of that mess.......

They were staring at the most beautiful, ornate, and wonderfully carved old wooden door. The door was huge, with the top half of the door still hidden under broken plaster, and a large crack could be seen going up to towards the ceiling.

There was silence for just a few moments, until Mary began to slowly walk towards the door, with her hand on her chest. As she got closer, she could see that some strange but intricate carvings had been made into the wood. Mary had never seen anything like it.
She let her fingers touch the wooden door very carefully, but instantly each bit that she touched, glowed a crimson red. She gasped....

The others had joined her, and were now staring open-mouthed at the wonder that was in front of them. Wilbur had hopped over, and Elma was still staggering from side to side – he could still hear the faint hum of the copper pan in his ears.

Henry finally spoke – quietly.

"Well – I have never seen anything like this in my life…ever. It's almost mythical. Look at the carvings…!! They're very unusual, and celestial; and look at the strange moons and stars and creatures from another world…!!….This has been covered up for many, many years Mary, and has probably been here since the cottage was built. This means something incredibly important……"

Earlier on in the day, when Mary had come out into the garden to meet everyone, many of the crowd were still eager to speak to her, and ask her lots of questions. Wimble the worm however, had slid away unbeknownst to anyone, and found a spot between two stones. He squeezed himself through the gap, which gave him just enough space to watch – and listen - very carefully….

When the Jeremy, the snail wanted a quiet word with Henry, and pulled him to one side to speak, and told him of his fears about Wimble…..Wimble was close by, and had heard every word…
He quietly made his way over to the greenhouse, and disappeared behind it. In no time at all, he had crawled through a tiny gap in the stone wall, and waited patiently on the other side, looking up and down the pathway that ran alongside the cottage garden. Suddenly, Agnes Le Fey appeared from nowhere.
She bent down to speak to Wimble.

"Well – what is there to tell me, what have you uncovered my sly friend..?" she asked.

"Well I think you might be right Mistress Le Fey" Wimble answered in his snidey wicked voice.
"I believe that Mary may be related to you"

"Really, HOW SO…?!!" Agnes retorted back angrily.

"She has found out by some means, to which I do not know the answer……"

Agnes interrupted sharply.

"Find out..!! I need to know, so do your job…!!"

"…… but…..let me tell you this, Oh Great One….there has been a meeting between all the dwellers of the garden……AND Mary. She is able to speak with them…..and hear them….!!"

Agnes's eyes grew wider as she heard this information.
"She speaks with, and hears creatures…?! What else have you found out…??" she asked.

"The Snail – Jeremy; he knows about me. His suspicions have been brought to the one who runs the garden – a Bee called Henry. I don't like the snail – there's something about him I'm not sure about, but he's one to watch"

"You must eliminate him, he could be dangerous..!! I want to know as much about this Mary as possible – and whose child she really is, and where she's come from. I felt something when I met her at the gate, like nothing I have felt in a long, long time. Collect as much information as you can, and get rid of the Snail, with this…..".…and produced a bag of salt with her wand.

She then waited, as she looked at Wimble. "Is there anything else..?!!" she barked at him.

Wimble looked a little uneasy, and lowered his head.

"What is it…?!!.......tell me now, or I'll have your head..!!!"

Wimble began to speak, this time, a little uncertainly…

"…well…well my Mistress….I…I….overheard a…a…."

Agnes got hold of Wimble by the throat…..her eye twitching; which was the same side as her scar. The deep jagged line, now more wrinkly with age, ran all the way down to under her chin.

"…Get…. On…. With…. It……." She whispered through gritted teeth, as she held Wimble up, and he slowly left the ground. She was angry and losing patience.
Wimble choked as she dropped him to the ground. He carried on.

"…well…they, they…..know that someone was at the foot of the wall the other night, which is when we were there – because Mary has two of them patrolling the wall….."

"AND…??!" Agnes was getting angry.

"…so Mary came out to have a look around the back of the wall, that's when they knew someone had been there…and then that's when……when….."
"…When WHAT…..??!!" Agnes shouted….."If YOU don't hurry up you snivelling little wretch, you will be boiled, bit by bit – very SLOWLY…now TELL ME…!!!"

Wimble quickly hurried the last bit….

"…..well that's when she got really angry, because she thought it might be you again, trying to get in, but she got angrier and angrier, and then that's when…when….the weather suddenly changed, and the thunder clouds gathered, and it started raining….!!!...I saw it all with my own eyes….!! She……she……she can…c….control…the…weather…!!" Wimble looked up so fearfully at Agnes, he was quivering.

As those last words came out of Wimbles mouth, he cowered back against the wall with wide eyes, breathing heavily, half expecting to be turned into something nasty. Instead, Agnes quickly lowered her head, and looked up and around her, as if she was expecting someone to drop something heavy on her at any moment. She was afraid. It was the first time Wimble had seen his Mistress look so frightened.

"This won't do…. So…….she can control the weather….??! How do you know this…?!"

"…because I stayed to watch and listen; and the Bee – Henry - he knows as well, as he was telling her to calm down – so she didn't get any angrier…!!"

"Mmmmm……I don't like this at all - this is worse than I thought…… much worse..!! Keep your eyes peeled…!!" She looked around again, nervously, and up to the sky once more….then vanished…….

In the kitchen of number 24 Copley Lane Meadow, Mary, Henry, Wilbur, Patsy and Elma were still staring at the huge wooden door. What they didn't know, was that Jeremy, after hearing the blast - had slowly made his way into the kitchen from the bowl on the windowsill of the living room. He had crossed the kitchen floor, and up onto the windowsill at the back kitchen window, and was sat there, keeping very still…….He was watching…..but he was watching someone else……..who was ALSO watching…

Wimble the worm, was at the back kitchen window. After speaking with Agnes, he wanted to please his mistress as much as he could, but he also didn't want to lose his head in the process if he dis-pleased her. So, he made it his mission to find out as much as he possibly could, and listen in on every possible conversation.
What he didn't expect, was to witness everything that had just happened……

He had a wild excited look on his sly face. Wait until he told Agnes – she would be so proud of him for finding out what he had just seen with his own eyes. He couldn't believe it himself.
He watched as the reflection of the crimson colour from the wooden door reflected in his huge eyes, as they widened, as Mary kept running her hands over the wooden carvings.

Jeremy had been watching Wimble the whole time. What Jeremy did next, was unbelievable…..

Jeremy raised himself up slowly from his shell, until he became much taller; he lowered his head towards Wimble, and white flashes of light discharged from his eyes – straight at Wimble..!! As Wimble slowly turned at that moment, in slow motion – he saw his perpetrator – before he took his last shocked intake of breath……

He suddenly disintegrated……

Everyone had turned around, just in time to see the final moment before Wimble met his fate.

"JEREMY…!!" Henry shouted. "What in the name…...?!!"

Jeremy dropped back down to his usual size, and spoke in a voice that was calm, well spoken, and not in his usual 'slow' voice.

"Henry, it's ok, he's gone now…"

"..but….but you've….you've just killed him…..and…..WHY…??!! Who are you….??!!"

# Chapter 21

# **<u>The Old Man</u>**

Everyone stood still where they were…… not wanting to go any further. They were stunned; what on earth had just happened..??!!

"Jeremy…?!!" Patsy blurted out, and wanting an answer…
But before Jeremy could answer Patsy, there was an unexpected knock at the back door, which made everyone jump. Elma clutched his chest. He couldn't take any more excitement.

Mary cautiously unlocked the door, and opened it just a little, with her foot at the back of it, just in case she had to shut it quick.
There, stood smiling, was an old man, with a long greyish brown beard, a big old floppy hat, a shabby looking floor length mole skin coat, big muddy boots, and two bags, one slung over each shoulder. He was holding a big wooden stick, and looked decidedly wet from the quick down pour of rain.

"Hello Mary, it's so wonderful to meet you - at last…!! Please - may I come in…?" he said brightly. But before Mary could answer, he barged through the door, and walked into the kitchen.
"I suppose that sudden rainfall we've just had was down to you..?" he said nonchalantly, as he patted the rain from his coat.

"Oh – I see you have found the door….about time too" He said smiling, as he pointed towards the big oak door. "We'll come back to that in a while, but in the meantime…."

He made a 'tutting' sound as he looked around at the mess.

"…..Tsk, tsk, tsk….. I think we need a bit of a tidy up, seems like you haven't mastered your strike yet Mary" he said looking around at the total devastation and the big lightning bolt across the ceiling.

"M...my...my...what...??!" she stuttered, as she stood rigid to the spot – covered in dust.

"Your strike...?? your hex.....??" The old man answered, gesturing his hands, as if Mary knew what he was saying – but she didn't. Mary still shook her head.

"Your 'hocus pocus' then..." he said laughing. "Not to worry Mary, we'll get around to that as well".......and with a wave of his hand, he muttered a string of words no one could understand, and in a flash, the kitchen was clean, tidy and free of all dust. All the chunks of plaster, wood and wallpaper had gone, and the full ceiling repaired....Even the remaining dust from everybody was gone. Wilbur looked down at his feet, Patsy checked her wings, and Mary's jumper looked and smelled like it had just come out of the wash..!! They were all stunned. Not only were they shocked at the quick 'clean-up', but the arrival and presence of an old man.

"....Aaghhh, just in time I believe..!!" said the old man, as he looked towards the window, where Wimble had stood. Then looked across, and saw Jeremy.

"Jeremy, my good fellow, there you are!"...and he promptly walked over to the windowsill. How is Jemima, and young Ben...??" Before Jeremy had the chance to answer, Mary walked up to the old man, and said, rather stiffly.

"Erm...excuse me, but would you mind telling me who the hell you are, and what on earth is going on around here...?!!!"

"Mary, forgive me, I do apologise" The old man turned around, and greeted Mary with both his hands held out to clasp hers. Mary withdrew her hands immediately – not feeling overly comfortable with THAT gesture again.

"Oh don't worry, I'm not Agnes Le Fey, or anybody like her. My name – is Ooshiya-Lion, and this...." and held up his long wooden staff.... "...is Bam Bam..!" The stick gave a little wiggle, and the top of it bowed before Mary.
"He is very honoured to meet you at last – as am I" The old man bowed his head too.

"What....? .....but.... I don't understand....." Mary's head was in a bit of a spin. Only moments ago, the whole kitchen had been covered in white dust, there had been a terrific blast, and Jeremy had just killed Wimble..!!... Plus the events of the day were now just beginning to take effect. She put her hand to her head.

"Please Mary, you must sit, there is a lot to explain, and not much time" He ushered her towards the table.

"Come along everyone, this involves all of you. You too Jeremy…"

Henry felt it was time to speak up.

"Now look here Mrrr… er…er…Lion…." The old Man put his hand up and spoke immediately.

"Henry, dear, dear Henry, please - let me explain" Then he put his finger out to shake Henry's hand.

"I knew your Great Great Grandfather very well indeed actually. Splendid chap Herbert Bee" He winked at Henry.

"You…you did…? You knew my Great Great Grandfather..?!"
The old Man laughed and nodded as Henry's chest puffed out. He was very proud of his ancestors.

"Now, now everybody, gather round. Mary, please can you shut the curtains at the front. We don't want the likes of Agnes Le Fey poking her nose in. She's not one to mess with is that one, but she has her weaknesses…" and he winked as he tapped the side of his nose with his finger.

"Oh, before we begin….." he said, as he stood up, and went over to the back window. He brought out from his inside coat pocket, a tiny glass bottle and a little brush, and swept up what was left of Wimble into the tiny bottle. He popped the cork in and put it away, back in his inside coat pocket.

"Nasty little fellow that – one of Agnes Le Fey's little helpers, should I say"

Everyone gasped.

"Yes, yes, it's true; and we have Jeremy to thank for that; and it looks like he had got himself there just in the nick of time by the looks of it. What Wimble had just witnessed in this kitchen would have got back to Agnes this very night, and that would have been a very grave situation indeed. So our chap Jeremy here – is our hero. He's one of our best men….. 'one of ours' shall i say"….and the old man began clapping, which made everyone else clap in turn.

"He was sent to keep an eye on things, and intervene when necessary; although the incident with the salt was most unfortunate, but we have Mary's quick thinking to thank for that"

Elma suddenly spotted a lamp slung over the back of Ooshiya-Lion's shoulder. Then, after a few moments of thought, he burst out with.

"Was that you by any chance with the lamp..? The night that Patsy and I were patrolling the wall, we saw a lamp swaying backwards and forwards in the distance"

"Yes Elma, it was me. I was slowly making my way towards the cottage, and just made a few stops along the way…."

He then looked over at Wilbur.

"Oh dear, I see your wing has been damaged again Wilbur. That won't do……" Ooshiya-Lion waved his fingers towards Wilbur's broken wing and muttered.."…cornu instaurabo…"

A little magical flash and a sprinkling of what looked like fairy dust, fell onto Wilbur's wing. Instantly, a brand new wing had appeared instead of the broken one, and back to how it was before it got broken all those years ago. Wilbur gasped.

"My wing..!!" he said looking down at his brand new wing, as he flapped it up and down.
"Thank you" Wilbur said to the old man.

"You're very welcome" he smiled back at Wilbur.

Mary was very quiet, sitting there, and propping her chin up with her hand. The old man looked across at her.

"You my dear, have had such a lot of information to take on board since you found out who you are, and not forgetting about all your memories that have returned to you; and there is still so much you don't yet know, but that is why I am here. I will do my best to explain everything to you all, but in the meantime, I think that you should all resume your duties for the rest of the day. Patsy and Elma are to resume patrolling the wall as usual. In fact, no – looking at Elma, maybe walking across the high wall tonight won't be a good idea. I wouldn't want you to fall again Elma - you've had enough accidents today young man. You should rest. Wilbur, you should go with Patsy to do this. Henry, you need to resume order in the garden with everyone. You have been missing for quite some time, and today has been a very long day – a lot has happened. Call a quick meeting. Maybe get Lars to help you with that. I will stay here with Jeremy and Mary"

"How do you know everyone's name Ooshiya-Lion..?" Patsy asked.

"I know most things my dear" He smiled. "We will resume matters tomorrow"

Henry stepped forward.

"What should I tell everyone..? They will have all been so worried, especially with Jeremy's accident with the salt"

"Tell them the truth" The old man smiled at Henry. "You do a very good job Henry; I don't know what anyone would do without you"

With that said, Henry, Wilbur and Patsy left the kitchen, and flew out across the garden. The old man went over to Elma, and picked him up gently.

"I think a good rest is in order for you Elma, I suggest you have a little sleep"….and with that, he opened the back door, and put Elma on the ground.

"Go steady now" and waved at Elma, who slowly waved back, still in a bit of a dizzy state, and walked up the garden path, but not in a straight line. He kept going from one side of the path to the other.

Ooshiya-Lion returned to the kitchen, patting his tummy.

"Do you know what, I'm so hungry, I could eat a full turnip…all to myself…!!. What shall we have…??

 Mary was about to open her mouth to speak, then she scraped her chair back to get up, when the old man quickly put his hand on her shoulder.

"No, no, no Mary, you stay right there". He looked into her eyes and said.

"Leave this to me"

He suddenly produced a tiny little bottle from his coat pocket, and Mary could see what looked like little white cotton pom pom balls inside it. She stared - bemused.

"I know just the thing…." He said, as he looked at her and winked. He unscrewed the lid, and threw the contents of the bottle up into the air. Mary let out a shriek. As the cotton pom poms fell, and were just about to go bouncing about all over the table; Ooshiya-Lion waved his hand, muttered something inaudible, and in front of them - a fine feast appeared. When Mary looked down at the table, she quickly realised what it was; she looked at the old man.

"How did you know…??" she asked.

 "I know more about you than you think I know; and actually Mary, it's one of my favourites too" he said smiling, as he said the last bit behind his hand, and almost in a whisper.

In front of them, on Mary's own plates, on top of the old lace tablecloth that her Mother had made many years ago, were lots of Mary's favourite things to eat. Baked beans on slices of thick, hot buttered toast, with a jar of peanut butter at the side. Ooshiya-Lion had the same. In the middle of the table, there was a plate full of Viennese Whirls, and a dish of Mary's favourite chocolate digestive biscuits. There were chocolate peanuts, Turkish delights and custard creams. There was even a plate of jam and bread. Mary hadn't realised how hungry she was. There was also a hot mug of Yorkshire tea each.

Jeremy had a small plate of fresh salad. He was starving too, and had only munched on a bit of cucumber all day. He also had some water, which he gulped down immediately.

"Yes you need to keep topping up my friend" The old man said to Jeremy with a knowing look.

Mary looked at Ooshiya-Lion.

"This is just lovely, and brings back such a lot of memories for me as a child – thank you"

"Tuck in" he said heartily.

They ate and chatted about Mary's garden, and then she talked about her life in the city, which seemed like a life time ago now.

"What am I going to say to James..??" Mary asked hopelessly after they had eaten.
"I miss him so much, but I just don't know what I'm going to say to him – where do I even start..?!"

"Don't you worry about James Mary; everything is taken care of. He will ring you tomorrow to tell you that he can't come home as there is a lot more he has to do with his work, and he may be some time. Tell him that everything is fine, and not to worry. He cannot possibly come home yet"

Mary thought it best to try and not think about James, and changed the subject.

"I wonder how Henry has got on with telling everyone..?" Mary asked.

"Oh don't worry yourself Mary, Henry is very good; he comes from a very good strong family of bees that have tended this garden for many years"

The old man sat back in his chair, and pulled from his pocket, a long thin knobbly looking smoking pipe. It just looked like a piece of twisted willow branch. He lit the pipe with the end of his finger, and soon, the kitchen was filled with a strong sweet, woody cherry tobacco smell.

"I always find that smoking a pipe makes everything seem better, would you like some..?" he offered the pipe to Mary.

Mary shook her head.

As he took a long draw of the pipe he said.

"Tomorrow is a busy day, and there may be many more after that; but for now, we can rest a while"

He hiccupped, and then burped.

"I do love beans on toast, but they don't love me..!" He laughed as he took another long draw of his pipe, and blew the willowy smoke out. As Mary sat back in her chair, she watched the smoke rising and twirling around. The smoke began to make shapes, and Mary watched it, completely mesmerised. Ooshiya-Lion began humming a tune. It sounded like an old Nordic folk song, and Mary thought she could hear faraway music; really soft and faint, like fairies singing. The smoke from the old man's pipe had now taken the shape of lots of figures and animals dancing. There were fairies, nymphs, centaurs, elves and dwarves – all making merriment. Eating, and drinking mugs of wine and mead. There were foxes and hares jumping about. It was so hypnotizing to see. Jeremy had fallen asleep in his salad, and was snoring quietly.

Mary's eyes were getting heavy.

A mug of hot milk materialized on the table, sweetened with honey – another of Mary's favourites. She smiled, as she picked up the mug, and cupped it, as she slowly took little sips – closing her eyes every time. It was so creamy with a hint of malt. She had never tasted anything like it before……..

# Chapter 22

# **<u>Dreams</u>**

Mary slept well that night, but she also dreamt a lot. She saw her Fathers face really clearly for the first time, and he was smiling at her, as if he was really pleased to see her. She saw Bruce the dog, running away into the distance. She saw her Mothers sweet smile, looking at her with her apron on, whilst she was baking in the kitchen…and then turning away to cry. Mary couldn't help her; why was she crying..??

Then she was running through the fields when she was a little girl, when she stopped to look across at a big dark cloud in the distance, which made her frown. She saw James, but not his face. She then saw her reflection in the mirror, but didn't recognise herself.... Then the wooden door came into her mind, and she saw all the markings glowing red……..and her Mother's voice came through to her from the day she passed away… '…find your Father…'

She woke - her heart beating…..

She never knew what her Mother had meant by that, but just put it down to her losing consciousness and being so ill at the time. Mary wearily got up, and put her dressing gown and slippers on over her pyjamas. She walked down the stairs, not remembering how she got to bed really. As she walked from the room into the kitchen, the first thing she saw - was the huge wooden door – and she stopped abruptly. She stared at it for a few moments, then made her way over to it slowly, and felt a great urge to open it, like it was calling her to do that.

As Mary got to it, suddenly all the beautiful carvings started shining the iridescent crimson colour that she had seen the day before. She touched the door, and let her hands wander over the intricate markings. What was behind there, and why had it been covered up all these years….??? As she stood, admiring the beautiful carvings, she thought she could hear faint whispers coming from behind the door. She moved forward and pressed her ear gently to the door to listen. In that instance, a strong force, like a magnet, drew her whole body forward to the door, and she was stuck to it, unable to move.

"Ow…!" she yelped, as the side of her face pressed hard into the door.

She then felt that strange feeling, similar to when Agnes had touched her hands, like a rush of air had taken her breath. She immediately broke free from the door, like the magnet feeling had let her go. She staggered backwards a few paces, rubbing the side of her face, wondering what magic the door held. She wanted to open the door, but there was no handle…. She needed to talk to Ooshiya-Lion.

At that moment, as she turned to walk away from the door – Mary stopped in her tracks. Her kitchen suddenly wasn't her kitchen anymore. Nothing in it belonged to her; it was all set out very differently. It looked almost like it was set in the 1960's. It was all very clean and tidy, and nothing was out of place; same stone floor, and walls, but the table and chairs were different to the ones that she had. Then she noticed that the table was set for 1, and next to that, there was a baby's high chair. There was no sofa at the back of the kitchen either. She turned around and instead of her big oven, there was a little old gas oven and next to it, an old combustion stove, that was used to heat the house, and a bucket of coal at the side of it.
Where were her things..?! Mary started panicking. She looked around and wondered where everyone was. What had happened – had she gone back in time..?? She looked back towards the big wooden door – and it had vanished; only a plain plastered wall that was there before.

She looked out of the back kitchen window at her lovely garden, but it wasn't 'her' garden anymore. It was wilder; still lots of flowers, but completely different. What was going on..??
Then she remembered that Jeremy, Jemima and Ben would still be in the room on the windowsill. She ran in; but there was no sign of them, not even the bowl of water that she put Jeremy in. Everything in the room was different as well. There was a little neat pile of toys which belonged to a young child, stacked in one corner.

'…this is so strange...' she thought.

She went back into the kitchen, and unlocked the back door, and went out into the garden, looking round. It was around midday.
"Henry…? Patsy….?" She shouted. She carried on walking up to where Tree Stump Corner was.
"Hello….anyone…? Wilbur….Elma..?"

Nothing……Tree Stump Corner wasn't even there.

Then, a slight breeze came and went, and it became apparent to her that it was now early evening, and the sun had shifted in the sky.
She looked on the ground, and someone had been digging, as there was now a small fir tree that looked like it had just been planted, as there was fresh soil around it. There was a spade laid on the ground next to it, with some soil still on the end of the spade. It looked like it had been dropped quickly, as some of the soil had scattered – like someone had left in a hurry…….and that's when she heard some commotion coming from the front of the cottage; and heard raised voices.

Mary ran in her dressing gown and slippers, and as she got to the front of the cottage, she almost skidded in slow motion. For there, at the garden gate, in the same spot as before, was Agnes Le Fey…!! She somehow looked younger, and the hideous scar on her face wasn't there, and her back didn't seem as stooped.

There was another woman on the inside of the garden, facing Agnes, so Mary could only see the back of her, and she was holding a small child, maybe about 18 months old. The woman was of slim build and had her light brown mousey coloured hair, in a low messy bun at the back of her neck. She was wearing a calf length cotton dress with small printed rosebuds on, and had a soft pale cream knitted shawl around her shoulders.

Mary plucked up her courage, and strode straight out, rather defiantly, and shouted, as she reached the two women.

"What the hell is going on here…?!!" Mary pointed her finger straight at Agnes.

"YOU…!! Keep away from my house, and don't you EVER come back here again, do you hear me…!!

The two women ignored Mary, and carried on arguing.

"I SAID…!" Mary got closer. "KEEP AWAY FROM MY HOUSE..!!"

The two women still took no notice of Mary.

"…and excuse me, but who are you, and what are you doing in my garden..?!"

Mary turned to the woman holding the child. The woman was younger than Agnes, and had a nice kind face, but she was obviously fraught with anger, as she kept exchanging angry words with Agnes; and all the while, the woman held the child closer to her. The child was crying, and Mary's heart lurched.

Upon speaking to the woman, and getting no reply, Mary touched the woman's shoulder to get her attention– but her hand went straight through her..!

"WHAT THE HELL'S GOING ON HERE…??!!"….she shouted in frustration…but then Mary realised that neither of them could hear her….or even SEE her….!!

"AAGH….!!" Mary screamed in her rage and frustration as she waved her arms about frantically.

The skies suddenly darkened and spots of rain began to drop…
Mary looked down at the child; it was a little boy, and as he continued to cry, tears pearled down his little round, rosy cheeks, and for a split second, she thought that he had seen her, for he looked right at Mary, and he had the most beautiful turquoise eyes, and a wisp of red hair.
The woman holding the child was vengeful but hysterical, and shouting….

"WHAT HAVE YOU DONE TO HIM….??!!..she screamed as she looked down at the boy, whilst still holding him, and then she looked back up at Agnes.

Mary looked over towards Agnes – she knew she was witnessing a serious argument. Agnes was now laughing and Mary wondered what she could have done…!
The woman looked down at the little boy she was holding. His eyes had shut, and the colour of his cheeks seemed paler.

"Edward..!!" cried the woman…. "EDWARD…?!!!"

The little boy showed no signs of life. Mary was distraught, but could do nothing to help. She put her hands to her mouth in shock, and cried "NO…!!"

The wind started blowing, and the rain was now coming down fast.
Mary turned towards Agnes, her eyes full of hated for this woman, and was just about to curse her, when the other woman shouted.

"I HOPE YOU BURN IN HELL FOR THIS..!! You have committed the most heinous of crimes, and killed a child for your own GREED..!!….How COULD you…?!...May the forces of evil be upon you forevermore; and I hope you rot in hell…!!…YOU'RE NO SISTER OF MINE….!!!

In that smallest of moments, time slowed down, and Mary felt that she was locked in slow motion. She looked at the woman, with her mouth open in horror at what she had just witnessed and heard.

"SISTER…?!!" Mary spoke out.

The woman holding the child – was Endor Le Fey.
Mary realised that she was witnessing the fight between the two sisters that they'd had all those years ago.

As Mary slowly turned back to look at Agnes, Mary's hair whipped in slow motion around her face, which was soaking wet with the rain. Agnes looked afraid as she kept looking around her, and up to the sky. It became obvious to Mary that Agnes was clearly afraid of the pending storm…..
At that moment in time, everything happened all at once.

Endor lowered her head; her eyes slowly turning a dark emerald green, as she fixed her stare at Agnes. Her obvious hatred for her was prominent, as her anger rose within her.
She began muttering magic under her breath, as she continued to glare at Agnes. Mary turned to Agnes and lurched out at her, but her hands went straight through her.
Everything was going too slow….!!
Mary's anger too, was rising very quickly; there was nothing she could do to help, as no one could see her, or hear her. She cried out in frustration.

Agnes raised her wand; and flashes of silver flew from the tip towards Endor. Immediately, Endor raised her hand and stopped the flow from Agnes's wand, as she turned her head to shield her face away from the bright flash of light, and the collision.

The weather had quickly worsened; now with clashes of thunder rolling across the sky, and lightening which came immediately after, which meant that the storm was directly above them. The wind had joined forces, and was blowing everything into a rage. The surrounding trees had their heads bent so low, that they looked like their backs would break; and leaves, debris and twigs were swirling around above them....!! Mary's gaze, still  in the frustrating slow motion, turned back to Endor, who was clutching the seemingly lifeless body of little Edward in one arm, and her other arm had now risen up above her head - her fingers outstretched towards Agnes. She was shouting incantations....!!

Mary's mixed emotions of anger, frustration, horror, and now grief for this poor child, had made her sob, after witnessing this awful scene. As she wiped the rain and her tears away from her face with the back of her sleeve, she looked over briefly at Agnes, and saw on the ugly old woman's face, that her eyes were bulging with excitement, as if she knew that she had got the better of Endor.
Mary's emotions changed suddenly in that split second to such a deep rage. She took a deep breath in, and with fists clenched in frustration, she SCREAMED all her anger, at the top of her voice at Agnes's face...!!.........

At exactly that same moment, a bolt of lightning came, so quickly from the raging stormy skies, and struck Agnes. The bolt cut deep into Agnes's skin on the left side of her face, which caused a huge burn. She let out a scream, took her hand from the gate post which she was holding onto in the wind, and put her hand up to her face.... As quick as a flash, Agnes's feet left the ground, and she hung in mid-air for a second, the wind blowing her about; when all of a sudden, she was sucked backwards, away from the cottage. Her arms outstretched and her feet in front of her, as if she was being pulled away by some strong magnet. She got smaller and smaller as she went further into the distance, and then suddenly and quickly, she was sucked away into nothingness, like a vortex which had suddenly appeared behind her.  She had completely vanished within a second – her screams fading into the distance.

Mary – shocked at Agnes's quick departure, turned back around to the woman.

Everything was still going slow. Endor plucked a wand from her coat pocket. The wand looked like a small ornate piece of glass. She waved the wand around Edward's head in small circles, whilst gently speaking soft words, as she cried silent tears. Small silver and blue wisps, like a thin streak of smoke circled from the end of the wand, and onto the little boys head. She then aimed her wand at the cottage, and all around the garden, murmuring and reciting spells over and over again, with sparks and flashes emitting from her wand, like hundreds of fireworks. All of this seemed to take such a long time, but it was seconds…..Mary was witnessing Endor casting her spells over the garden and the cottage…

The early evening sky which had, just moments before, turned dark, was becoming lighter. The rain had stopped now, and the wind had calmed down, but the thunder was still rumbling in the sky. Endor looked so tired and distressed, and Mary felt for her. She continued to watch the whole scene unfold, and it felt strange that she was invisible, but she could see clearly, everything that was going on.
After she had finished casting spells over the cottage and the garden, Endor conjured a piece of white paper, and in mid-air, she wrote a letter with the tip of her wand. Mary saw that she was sobbing whilst doing this…. The letter folded itself up, and flew towards the cottage and through the letterbox.

She eventually put the tip of the wand to the top of the child's head, and then to her own head, and recited more magic as she closed her eyes. She quickly put the wand back in her pocket, and wrapped her shawl around the little boy. Suddenly, a white fog appeared around them both, and lots of tiny white feathers swirled around and around. As the white fog swirled and spun quicker and quicker, the woman and the child began to spin with the fog, going faster and faster, as they disappeared down, down, down and into the ground……and then, they were gone…..

"No….no…..don't go…!!" Mary shouted - her hands on her head. Suddenly there was silence, and Mary was left in the front of her garden, alone.
Just at that moment, before Mary had to time to even think, she got a strange feeling in her stomach. Instantly, she felt like she was being pulled backwards. Her feet left the floor, and she vanished…..

Mary staggered a few paces, as she looked around bewilderingly, wondering where she was. She soon realised she was now on a hospital corridor, outside a ward. The sound of people's shoes running could be heard in the distance, coming closer and closer down the corridor, and a trolley which was rattling as it was being pushed quickly. Two Nurses and a Doctor came into view. The Nurses were wearing long white starched pinafore dresses, with a white bib at the front, and a fob watch on the bib, white tights and shoes, and a white cap. The Doctor had a long white starched coat on, white shirt, black tie, and black trousers. As they were running, one of the Nurses turned to the other one and said.

"She's early – don't know why, but we'd better get in there quick…!"

As they quickly ran towards a very dazed Mary, it was obvious they couldn't see her. They passed by, only inches away from her, and quickly turned right into the ward. Mary followed. As she entered the ward, the Nurses and the Doctor had rushed up to a bed. A woman was screaming. The curtain was pulled round the bed very quickly, and lots of hurried chatter was heard.

"Get her on the trolley quickly, I doubt if we'll make it to the labour ward..!" said one Nurse.

The next moment, the curtains flew back, and a woman with a sheet over her, half sat up, with her knees up to her chest, was being wheeled, very swiftly out of the ward. She was still crying out in pain, and rolling around on the trolley.

"Eldon….Eldon…!" The woman cried, as her outstretched arm brushed past a man's coat, as she was quickly wheeled away. The man had just walked out from behind the curtain. Their fingertips quickly touched for the briefest of moments. The man, a very tall dark haired smart gentleman was ushered out of the way to one side.
Mary stared after the trolley, as it was quickly wheeled past her, out of sight.

"You'll have to stay there Mr Le Fey, you can't come..!!. Sit outside the Nurse's Station, and we'll get word to you once it's born…!!" shouted one of the Nurses, as all three of them ran out pushing the trolley….

Mary suddenly realised at that moment, that the woman who was about to give birth…..was her own Mother..!!....and the baby she was about to give birth to – was Mary…!!

Mary immediately rushed up to the man, and stood in front of him to take a closer look.
Instantly, her hands flew up to her mouth, and tears sprung into her eyes.

"Dad……Dad…??!" she whispered through her fingers. "Dad it's me – M…Mary"…and pointed her fingers to her chest.

The man was obviously very worried, and looking rather lost; and of course he couldn't hear or see Mary.

In the distance, the woman on the trolley could be heard shouting, as she was wheeled quickly away down the corridor.

"Eldon…..Eldon….!"

Mary's face had crumbled, as she took a long look at a very handsome younger version of her Father. She just stood staring at him, as she was drinking in every inch of his face that she once knew, and his handsome good looks.
His eyes had filled up, and he was running his fingers through his hair. Obviously his wife was about to give birth, and he was naturally nervous. He glanced out of the window, and the weather had suddenly changed. It had been fine a while ago, a lovely sunny August day, but now it was raining really hard, and dark clouds had filled the sky. He looked slightly concerned as he continued to stare out of the window. He then run his hand down his face, and stopped at his chin, then rubbed the back of his neck.

Mary was still looking up at her Father- she couldn't take her eyes off him. She hadn't seen him since she was a little girl, and her memories were faded, but here he was, standing right in front of her. She reached up to put her arms around his neck, but her arms went straight through him.

"Dad……I miss you……" she wept as she whispered to him.

For a fleeting moment, Mary thought that he might have heard her, as he put his head onto one side, as if to listen more intently to something. Mary's mouth opened to speak, but just then, a woman's voice made Mary and her Father jump. It was the Matron.

"Come along now Mr Le Fey, don't be standing here doing nuthin'. You need to go and wait at the Nurse's Station. Chop, chop..!! You're neither use nor ornament stood there. Come along..!" she urged him in her thick Yorkshire accent.

"S..s..sorry, I…I…" he began.

"Yes, yes, I know, now hurry along..!"

The Matron ushered him out of the ward – Mary followed.
They arrived at the Nurse's Station, and Mary's Father had no sooner sat down, when a Nurse came half trotting down the corridor.

"Mr Le Fey..??" she enquired.

"Yes…?!." He said and stood up straight away.

"Congratulations – you have a fine healthy baby….."

The look of relief on his face was over-whelming for Mary to see.

"Already….?? …. Oh, thank you, thank you…so much…I…I…"…and he shook the Nurse's hand vigorously. "Oh…sorry, I….I'm sorry…..I'm just so happy, glad in fact, yes, really happy…! Is….is my wife alright, is she ok..??!!"

The Nurse was smiling as she looked at the happy, but very nervous man.

"Yes, yes…she's resting" she said smiling. Then paused and said.
"Do you want to know what you have….??" The Nurse asked, still smiling, with her head on one side.

"Yes sorry…yes….of course…!! I DO…..what is it…? I mean…
I mean….what….." He put his hand on his head.

"You have a very healthy, and very beautiful little girl Mr. Le Fey…..and might I say, she's a strong 'un. She didn't need much help at all…….going to be quite an independent young lady that one..!!"

"A girl…a GIRL…??!..Oh really…??!" He was smiling, very broadly.

Mary watched with tears in her eyes.

"I've been so nervous, I thought there might be complications, you know…..I….I'm so happy..!!"

The Nurse put her hand on his arm.

"There's nothing to worry about; Mother and baby are doing just fine.
You know……you're not doing too bad at all for a first time Dad. I've had some faint before now….!"

"Oh it's….it's ….er… it's not our first child – I have a son at home - Edward" he said brightly.

The Nurse smiled as she walked away.

"Oh how lovely, one of each. Would you like to see her..?" She enquired.

"Yes, yes, of course..!" he said happily.

"It's this way, and just five minutes mind, your wife's very tired and needs her rest"

Mary's face suddenly stopped smiling. She looked around her searchingly; looked back at the Nurse who was now half way down the corridor, and then back to her Father - with wide eyes.

"….a son….??" She whispered…. "….but…."

Suddenly Mary didn't feel too good, she felt a wrench in her stomach, and everything around her started fading…. She looked down at her hands - they were disappearing in front of her.

"Dad…Dad…..!!!" she cried out, but her Father couldn't hear her – he had started to walk away after the nurse down the corridor.

"DAD…!! She cried out, as she clutched her stomach, and stumbled with weakness. She grabbed at the chair to stop herself falling – but her hand went straight through it.
Mr Le Fey stopped, and turned around…….shook his head, turned back around, and carried on walking.

Mary was sobbing. She could hear people calling her name over and over again. She collapsed to the floor in the hospital corridor, her face hitting the cold tiled floor, and as her eyes slowly closed, the last thing she saw, was her Dad - walking away………

# Chapter 23

# **The Couch Conversations…and Arguments**

"Mary…..Mary….!!... Wake up….Mary..!!"

"Give her some time - she'll be ok" An old man's voice said soothingly.

A few moments passed by as everyone waited patiently for Mary to wake up.

"Ah….!" The old man said brightly, as Mary slowly opened her eyes.
"Well, well young Mary, we didn't know where you had gone for a time then, but you're here now"

Ooshiya-Lion was sat on the edge of the sofa at the back of the kitchen, smiling down broadly at Mary, who was laid down on the sofa with a blanket over her.

"We were so worried about you, I'm so happy you're alright!" Patsy had obviously been upset, as she was carrying a small handkerchief.

"Mary what happened…?? Henry asked. "We came in from the garden to find you on the floor!"

"Yeah, you gave us a bit of a fright. It's good to see you" Wilbur walked forwards onto the sofa, he was smiling at her.

Mary struggled to speak, but her voice was hoarse. She put her hand to her throat, and tried to clear it.

"No, no, don't try just yet Mary; but now that you're awake - I can give you this" Ooshiya-Lion said as he produced a tiny earthenware cup.
"….calor.." he muttered, and the liquid in the little mug began to steam.
"Here, sip this very slowly, it will do you the world of good" he said with a knowing nod and a wink. He looked at Mary for a few seconds as if he knew something.

"Wh…What…..?" she pointed to the mug as she tried to ask what was in it.

"It's one of my finest blends of 'pick-me-up' Honey-Lavender elixirs" He said proudly.

"Mmmmm…would I like that..??" Henry enquired, as he sniffed the air. He loved a nice brew of Honey tea.

"I've no doubt that you would my furry little friend"

Mary took a few sips. It was so rich and sweet and just the right temperature. She passed her tea to the old man as she tried to sit up.

"Now  now - not too quickly. Be very careful my dear" Ooshiya-Lion steadied Mary, as she felt a little woozy on sitting up.

"Mary….!!" Elma shouted, as he was trying his best to walk quickly across the floor on 6 of his legs, as he was carrying 3 daisies with his front two legs. He had a big grin on his face.

"He's been so worried about you Mary". Patsy said smiling.

Elma quickly climbed up the sofa with his long legs and onto the blanket that was covering Mary, but in true Elma style, he tripped up and the daisies nearly ended up in Mary's Honey-Lavender Elixir…!!
Mary smiled…..

"Oh….ahem…ahem…" She coughed. "…El….Elma, that's so sweet…ahem …of you"

Mary choked a little, but the elixir was working. She picked him up and gave him a little kiss…!! His face was a picture. His eyes opened so wide, and the look of …. 'did that just really happen…??!' was funny to see; but he was so shocked he fell backwards, and went into a spider roll. He'd only got to the bottom of the blanket near Mary's feet, but got up really quickly, and lightly touched the side of his cheek.

"I'm not washing that – ever…!!"
There were groans of 'oh Elma, really' as Elma grinned through his blushes.

Mary's smile faded, and she looked up at the old man.

"I've got so much to tell you, and lots of questions I need answering" her eyes misted over, and she lowered her gaze. Ooshiya-Lion looked at her.

"I know….I know…it can't have been easy – whatever it was…" He answered, and put his hand on her shoulder.

"I'm so grateful for you……. all of you...." Mary said to the rest of them that were stood around, looking up at her.
"I really don't know what I would do without you all…"
She managed a weak smile, and they each smiled back at her in turn.

"Drink as much of that as you can manage Mary, it will definitely make you feel better" The old man urged. His special elixir was full of natural uplifting herbs, and Mary was already feeling much better.

"I'm not leaving a drop. It's – just what I needed after……after all that"

"You were screaming REALLY loud and.…….." Elma started to say, but Henry gave him the elbow and a stern look.

"It's alright Henry, I can remember everything; and Elma, don't look so worried, I'm ok, really"
"I need to talk about it all anyway, as I need some gaps filling in"…..she looked up again at the old man.

"You know - don't you..?" she asked him, as she looked directly at Ooshiya-Lion. He frowned a little, but said nothing.

"It's alright". Mary said looking away. "At least it will help me understand more if you can help me. The thing is, I thought I was dreaming at first – but I wasn't dreaming at all – I was THERE..!!"

Everyone looked a little puzzled, as they exchanged glances.

"What do you mean…? Are you saying you WEREN'T dreaming..?" Henry asked.

"Yes Henry, that's exactly what I'm saying – I didn't dream any of it.......I went back in time – I know that for sure" Mary answered.

Nobody said anything, but they just kept looking at her, and they too, had lots of questions....

Ooshiya-Lion stepped back from everyone, turned around and looked at the wooden door. He had a very concerned look on his face. He called to his trusty staff.

"Bam Bam....here" The staff came straight over to his side. He bent down to his staff and spoke to it in a whisper. Suddenly Bam Bam vanished.....

Mary had already begun telling them all exactly what had happened after getting up and coming downstairs in her pyjamas, and about the wooden door, but before she told them about seeing the argument between the two Witches, she turned to Ooshiya-Lion.

"Is it true - did I have a Brother..??"

Henry quickly intervened.

"A BROTHER...?? No Mary that can't be right – you must be wrong there, you would have known...surely?"

"Henry......I saw him" Then she looked back at the old man, hoping for an answer.

He waited a few moments before he answered.

"Yes. It IS true. He was your parents first born child, and his name was...."

"Edward...." Mary butted in. His name......was Edward....... I know"

The old man carried on.

"His full name was Edward Drewad Le Fey, and he was born on 5$^{th}$ October 1962"

Mary was shocked at the old man's knowledge.

"His parting from this world came as a great shock to us all"

Ooshiya-Lion and Mary exchanged long looks, and Mary's face crumpled as she remembered the look on little Edward's face.

After that was said, they all pleaded for Mary to tell them what had happened, but the old man continued to look worriedly at Mary. Patsy cried when Mary told them that she looked straight into her Brother's eyes and they were the most beautiful turquoise blue.

Mary then asked Ooshiya-Lion why she had been sent back to that moment, when the two sisters were fighting. The old man seemed to be very careful how he answered Mary.

"That – I'm……not quite sure about Mary; there must be consequences and/or reasons. Was there anything that you saw that was strange, different maybe…….anything at all…?" he queried.

"Well everything was strange and different because it was the 1960's" she answered.

Then, as she sat, she thought about every little snippet from the first part of her dream-like time travel. Then she began to recall….

"When I went into the back garden, I walked up towards the top of the garden, what would be Tree Stump Corner now, to see if I could see any of you, but strangely enough, I just knew that none of you were there….now I know that you wouldn't have even seen me or heard me anyway.
The garden was so different to what it is now; but when I looked around - it seemed like someone had been digging – right where the fir tree is now. The spade looked like it had been abandoned, as it was on the ground, like it had been thrown, and there was mud scattered. Then I noticed there was a little green fir tree that had just been freshly dug into the soil, and an empty plant pot on its side.
I realised then, that it was the same fir tree that I saw when we first moved in. Obviously it was much bigger, and it looked like it had died because most of the branches had gone brown. That's the reason I called it Tree Stump Corner,

because of that fir tree. James was going to dig it up, but I just couldn't let him. I felt something strange that I couldn't explain, so instead, I had him cut it down to a small enough stump, just in case one day, it may start to grow again. Anyway – it's strange, but i think it was Endor who planted that tree, that very day, but something distracted her, and that's why she dropped the spade…….. So really….."

Mary stopped to think for a moment. Everyone was silent and listening intently to Mary's 'dream'. ……She carried on……

"…..yeah….so really……the date that I went back to - was the day I was born, which is the date that the tree was planted…… but also the same day my Brother died…..Oh my God, I didn't actually realise that..!!" Mary sat up a bit more as she realised what she had just said.

Everyone gasped.

The old man spoke up.

"I knew Edward's parting was your day of birth – that, I do know. Maybe the fir tree is of significance" He pondered.

Mary felt very sad. "All this time, and I never knew I had a brother – I wonder why my parents never spoke of it..?"

"Mary, that would have been because it must have been very painful for them" Henry said gently.

Everyone else agreed as they nodded.

"I'm starting to realise now why my Mum was a very nervous and sometimes, sad woman. She was obviously carrying a lot of grief; now that I know there was a child before me. That's probably why she was so protective of me; and yet she KNEW I had a gift, or was special in some way, and was just frightened that if I knew too much about it, I might not know what to do with it, or how to use it. It's still very confusing, but a lot of it is making much more sense to me now, but I just feel so sad"

Wilbur had been thinking, and didn't understand something….

"Mary…?" he asked. "How did you know that it was your Birthday – that very day of the tree being planted and the argument with the Witches……how would you know…??" he looked puzzled.

Mary answered instantly. "Well that's because I nearly saw myself being born…!!"

"What….?!!" Henry exclaimed.

Then everyone spoke at the same time. "Mary, you haven't told us the rest of your story yet..!"
"So what happened, and how did you nearly see yourself being born…??!"

Ooshiya-Lion quickly called Henry over to speak with him for a few seconds.

Mary yawned. "Oh I'm so sorry everyone - I'm really tired – what time is it..? I don't even feel like I've slept – well I guess I haven't really have I…??"

"It's half past 11, and a lovely morning out there" Wilbur answered.

"Half past 11 – really..?! I can't believe I've been in bed all that time after that lovely supper last night!"

"Ooh lovely; if it's 11:30 – it's  nearly lunchtime then!" Elma sat up eagerly. Eating was one of his favourite things.

"I quite agree Elma, I'm quite peckish myself..!" Ooshiya-Lion said happily; although he was very concerned after listening to what Mary had just said. "Let's have an early lunch..!"

Soon enough, the table was a fine feast for all. Mary had specifically asked for a chip butty with a gravy dipping bowl. Ooshiya-Lion had never heard of that combination before, but it quickly became his favourite.

Whilst everyone was chattering at the table, about what was going to happen next, Ooshiya-Lion nodded to Henry. Henry excused himself from the table as soon as he had finished his bit of lunch, and said that he needed to check on everyone, and make sure the garden was ok. He gave a little nod to the others, who quickly made their excuses to leave as well. Henry knew that the old man wanted to chat with Mary privately. He had noticed the way the old man had been concernedly looking at Mary.

Mary still felt very emotional. She didn't want to say anything, but seeing Endor crying as she cared for her baby brother, then looking straight into her Fathers eyes were images that she couldn't shake from her mind. Then her thoughts went back to the argument between the two sisters. Mary was picturing Agnes's face laughing. She hated that woman more than ever now. Her evil horrible face…her face…….that awful face…. with that scar….the SCAR….?!

"Mary……..what is it….?"

The old man calmly asked her. They exchanged looks, and then Ooshiya-Lion averted his stare to the fork in Mary's hand. Mary hadn't realised it, but she had dug the fork into the table. Mary looked down.

"I was just thinking about Agnes laughing whilst poor Endor was trying to protect my brother; but I've just realised something. When I first saw her when I encountered the argument, I first thought how much younger she looked, and how she didn't have the stoop, but I saw her face – that face I now hate so much…. and thought to myself…'where's her scar' It wasn't there…!"

The old man instantly stopped eating….wiped his mouth with his napkin, pushed his plate away, and looked directly at Mary…. then said…

"Are you saying her scar wasn't on her face when you saw her..??"

"Yes…..that's EXACTLY what I'm saying…… it wasn't there……...but now I know that it was ME who caused it…!"

"How so…what do you mean YOU caused it…?!" he said slowly.

"Well, because I…well…I…"

"Mary, this is very, very important, and I want you to tell me EXACTLY what happened!"

Mary blurted it out…..

"Well….. I saw them arguing horribly. When I realised that they couldn't see, or hear me, I got so angry, because it was so frustrating and upsetting watching all of this. Endor was distraught, and I felt so much anger. A storm came from nowhere, and it got worse. Endor was trying to cast a spell on Agnes, whilst holding the baby so closely; and I couldn't do anything to help, and I just lunged towards Agnes, but my hands went straight through her, so in my anger – all I could do was scream at her at the top of my voice – out of sheer frustration! At that moment, a bolt of lightning came out of nowhere, and struck her on the side of her face. She screamed, took her hand from the gate post, put it up towards her face, and that's when she got sucked backwards – and disappeared…!"

Ooshiya-Lion scraped his chair from beneath him, stood up quickly, and paced the floor - wringing his hands. Mary watched him closely. She felt a little worried – up until now, she hadn't seen the old man get uptight about anything.

"Wh…..what's happened, what's wrong, have I said something…??! Tell me…!"

Mary was feeling nervous.

The old man spun around his eyes looking darker.

"Mary, I have been watching and listening to you telling us all about your dreams from last night; and I must say - they were very accurate…."

Mary, at that point cut in.

"They weren't dreams Ooshiya-Lion – I……I….WAS…..THERE…!!"

"That's my fear Mary – how COULD you have been there, it's not possible..!"

"Well I was….and I'm NOT going mad..!! I looked directly into the eyes of my brother AND my Father; and when I collapsed on the hospital corridor, I shouted for my Dad, and he turned around, and I KNOW he heard me…!!" Mary was now crying.

The old man looked out of the window, and the skies above had darkened.

"Keep calm Mary – you are going to have to control this"

"…..but you don't believe me..!!" she shouted.

Outside in the garden, a few drops of rain had started to fall and a slight breeze had lifted and was bending the heads of the flowers.
Henry was in the garden, and stopped and looked up and around him, and then back at the cottage.

"Oh no Patsy – I hope that's not Mary….."

Back in the kitchen the old man walked over to the table, and put both his hands down hard on the table, which made the crockery jump - he bent close to Mary. Mary drew her head back a little. He spoke to her in a low voice.

"It's not that I don't believe you Mary – I DO, but what I need to make clear to you right now, is that IF……. and it's a big 'IF '…. you are telling me exactly what happened and how you saw it all, and it most definitely was NOT dreams that you had, then we have a bigger problem than I ever thought…..
Let me tell you now – there are very, very few Witches who can time travel. What you have just told me about not seeing Agnes's scar on her face when you first saw her, and yet…… in your anger and frustration at seeing this whole ugly scene play out in front of you, and then your outburst of anger, by screaming so fiercely, that it caused that bolt of lightning to happen, that struck her face…it…..it means………"…and he paused, as if he didn't want to utter his own words. "…….it means Mary; that you caused that IN YOUR TIME TRAVEL PHASE…!!! Do you even understand what this means….?!!

Mary glared at Ooshiya-Lion.

"Look – just a minute here….!!…I didn't ask for ANY of this to happen…!! All that I've done - is buy a cottage in the countryside with James – that's it; and now all THIS…!! I just feel like selling up, and getting out of here…!!

Ooshiya-Lion looked at Mary…. "I'm afraid that's not possible…." He said very solemnly.

Mary looked hopelessly around her, trying to find an answer, or something to say.

"Mary, I know how very hard this must be for you……Mary – look at me…"

"You have absolutely NO idea how I'm feeling right now…!"

Ooshiya-Lion sighed – and continued.

"You caused Agnes to disappear with the force of your scream. Endor was trying to KILL her – and rightfully so…!!...and that's why she's still alive…!! Endor must have thought that she HAD killed her, by using all of her powers to do so, but your intervention must have pushed her back into another vortex, or time or something, before Endor had time to finish her off..!. She must have thought it was because she was exhausted, and she knew she had to protect the cottage and the gardens, so she saved all that she had, to be able to do that, and used up all of her strength trying to protect it all, and of course little Edward. That goddamn woman just won't die – that's twice she's escaped death..!!"

Ooshiya-Lion was more or less talking to himself towards the end.

"What do you mean by that…?!" Mary quizzed.

"Oh….." he said rather unruffled. "There is so much you still don't know."

"Well isn't it about time you told me…?!!" Mary asked as she looked at him, sternly.
"There's a bloody great big door over there that I have accidently uncovered….How and why, I don't know..!! I don't know WHY it's there, I don't know where it goes to, or anything…!! I have a weird, nasty Great Aunt that I knew nothing about, who is hanging about outside my house, and who just so happens to be a Witch, and has cheated death twice apparently…..and I'M experiencing things from my past that I knew nothing about..!!! I NEED answers…!!

# Chapter 24

# **Scrolls**

The old man came back to the table, sat down and looked at her.

"Yes, you are quite right Mary" He said, rather calmly.

Mary was still talking….."I mean, where on earth have YOU come from, who ARE you, what are you doing here…and who the bloody hell am I…?!" She put her arms on the table and buried her head, and started crying….Then she brought her head back up….

"…and another thing…." she said through her tears. "Why did Agnes murder my little brother…..WHY….??!....why would she do such a thing…??!.. I HATE HER……and one of these days, she's going to pay for what she's done…. !!"

It was now pouring with rain.

"Tell me what you heard Mary when you went back in time, tell me…." The old man was trying to sympathise with her, and calm her down. She had been through such an emotional ordeal, whilst uncovering yet more things about her past that she didn't know a thing about.

Mary told him what she had heard, and seen in detail, and also about the moment she saw her Father, and how it made her feel. Ooshiya-Lion knew it was more about Mary seeing her Father that had made her feel so upset. She calmed down as she continued to speak, which helped her – and the weather outside had also calmed down….

Ooshiya-Lion presently got up from the table and walked to retrieve his bags from the kitchen floor, and said.

"Now Mary, I'd say more than ever - you need some answers, plus, it's important that you know as much as possible, especially after what you have just told me. We have to work quickly. Agnes will now know that something has happened to Wimble, so there may be more from her, and we need to keep our eyes peeled. I have already spoken in length to Henry and the others whilst you were sleeping, and explained that things could get bad; but we're all in this together. The reasons why Agnes Le Fey wants to get into this cottage and garden are very essential to her. Have you ever wondered why this cottage is so important..??"

Mary looked at him with her tear-stained face, and nodded.

"Well yes, of course I have, but everything seems to be shrouded in mystery, and I don't have a clue..!"

From his bag, he brought out some old looking scrolls, and put them down on the table.

"What are these..?" She asked.

"These – Mary, are what you have been looking for, and contain a lot of answers about your family. Now come on…. There-there, no more tears, dry your eyes" ….and gave her a hanky.

"Here" He said, passing her one of the scrolls. "Start from here"

He passed her the scroll, which Mary took very gently as she looked at him. As she opened it carefully, he looked at her, and felt her anguish and pain.

"…but it's blank" Mary said, looking up at the old man.

"Ah…." Ooshiya-Lion said, producing his wand.
"I am only letting you see the obvious at the moment Mary, as this could all become rather confusing. For now, I just need you to know who we are talking about, and where people fit in. Some of the names that will appear on these are not significant at the moment either, so I will simplify it for you, for better reading"

He put the tip of his wand to each of the parchment scrolls, closed his eyes, and quietly said…

"Manifesto"

The most beautiful pen script began to appear onto each of the scrolls, like an invisible ink pen; and Mary could hear the noise of the pen nib scratching onto the dry parchment. The writing was incredibly flourished, as it moved quickly.

Suddenly the writing stopped, as Mary had been looking down in astonishment.

There in front of her, were names that she had never seen or heard of before.

"Don't worry" He said, reassuringly…..."By the way, this cottage was always meant to be yours Mary" He said, resting his hand on her shoulder. "…. it always was. The lengths that your ancestors have gone to, to protect this cottage has been nothing but formidable…you should be proud…"

"Will you stay while I read these – I think I might need some help..?"

"Of course – that's why I am here" He said encouragingly.

Mary looked up at him and said with a smile….

"Don't you EVER take that hat off….??" …and nodded towards his head and his big floppy hat.

He smiled back at her and said. "Well…….if you insist…..and don't be too shocked….."

With that, he removed his big floppy hat, and shook his head, and to Mary's complete surprise – well, shock really, Ooshiya-Lion had the biggest Lions mane she had ever seen…!! It had a shimmery fine golden-green colour running through it, which shone in the sunlight

"What the….oh my God…..HOW…??!!" ..as she began to laugh.

"Mmmm - I know" He said nodding. "…feels good though….and yes I know what you're thinking. It's a long story – one for another day perhaps. Anyway there is a lot to read, so let's get on with it"

"By the way" Mary suddenly said. "I've seen the Last Will & Testament from my…..well….who I 'believe' to be my Great Grandfather, Magnus Le Fey. It's over here"

"You have…??! Where did you find it..?? Do you know; that was the only small detail that we were missing..!. Ooh yes please, let me see…..and yes Mary, he IS your Great Grandfather, and all these people on these scrolls here, are you ancestors"

Mary gave the Will to Ooshiya-Lion, and said.

"The Will was inside an old earthenware pot that Henry actually found by accident just recently. The pot was here when we first moved in and I really quite liked it, so I cleaned it up a bit, but I couldn't get the lid off, it was stuck. Then Wilbur accidentally smashed it, otherwise I would never have found it..!" she said.

"I wonder why it was in an old pot..??" Ooshiya-Lion enquired. "…odd…."

The old man poured over the details.
"Aahhh yes, this is perfect….and very, very well written I'd say"

As he read through it, he reflected.

"….Yes, he was a lovely fellow was Magnus – your Great Grandfather; very soft though, and a quiet man, but annoyingly headstrong. Unfortunately, he was over-ruled by his evil wife. She was the most horrible woman"

His face winced like he had just had something sour to eat.

"Bridget" he said. "**Bridget Begdirt Bishop** was her name, before she married your Great Grandfather Magnus. Now, I can understand why your Great Grandfather fell in love with Bridget; she was definitely a beauty. Long dark wavy hair, pale skin, ruby red lips, very alluring – but she was a nasty, mean and hateful Witch. Unfortunately – this is your Great Grandmother I'm talking about here…!!"

"Now, let me tell you a little story about The Bishop's, as I would rather like to get them out of the way first. So this one here…" (and referred to one of the scrolls) "…is where the Bishop family come into the story, and the one you have in your hand, is more about the Le Fey's"

Ooshiya-Lion passed Mary the scroll.

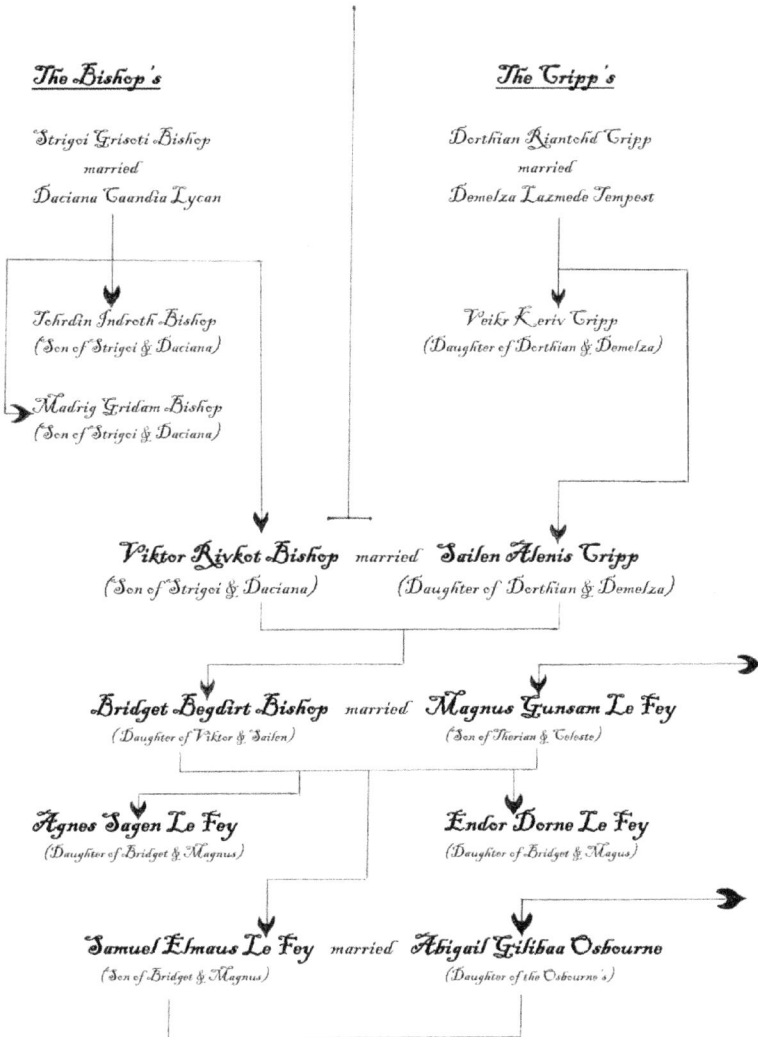

The Bishop's

Strigoi Grisoti Bishop
married
Daciana Caandia Lycan

The Cripp's

Dorthian Riantchd Cripp
married
Demelza Lazmede Tempost

Tohrdin Indroth Bishop
(Son of Strigoi & Daciana)

Madrig Gridam Bishop
(Son of Strigoi & Daciana)

Veikr Keriv Cripp
(Daughter of Dorthian & Demelza)

Viktor Rivkot Bishop   married   Sailen Alenis Cripp
(Son of Strigoi & Daciana)      (Daughter of Dorthian & Demelza)

Bridget Begdirt Bishop   married   Magnus Gunsam Le Fey
(Daughter of Viktor & Sailen)      (Son of Thorian & Coleste)

Agnes Sagen Le Fey
(Daughter of Bridget & Magnus)

Endor Dorne Le Fey
(Daughter of Bridget & Magus)

Samuel Elmaus Le Fey   married   Abigail Gilibaa Osbourne
(Son of Bridget & Magnus)      (Daughter of the Osbourne's)

A chapter within a chapter.......

# **<u>The Story of The Bishops....</u>**

Ooshiya-Lion began to tell the story of the Bishops......

"The Bishops were a nasty, nasty family. They had come from a line of Warlocks – part demon and part human......
Bridget's Father, Viktor was one of three brothers, and their parent's names are on here, but they are of no significance just now.
The Bishop's knew that there was something very special about number 24 Copley Lane Meadow, and they wanted to find a way in, and were hell bent – literally, on finding it's secret. It almost consumed them, and they would do ANYTHING to get into this cottage"

"Their names were Viktor Rivkot Bishop, and his wife, Sailen Alenis Cripp. See here" and pointed to the top of the page of the first scroll.

"Sailen's family, the Cripps were a nasty bunch as well. It was a great concern that Magnus was intending to marry into such a hateful, disorganised evil bunch of people"

"Magnus's Father tried very hard to warn him about the union, but his attempts were in vain. He didn't want his son to marry into the Bishops; they were not of good stock at all. Their family name had been frowned upon from many centuries past; but the Le Fey's on the other hand, had a very important family legacy – this cottage. The Bishops, of course, pushed their daughter Bridget forward to ensnare the young Magnus, and make him fall in love with her - obviously for her to get nearer to the secret of the cottage, and of course to become part of the Le Fey family"

"Magnus's Father tried to make his son realise the greed of this awful family, and tried to tell him the REAL reason why the Bishops wanted their daughter to marry him; but even though Magnus knew the importance of the family secret of keeping the cottage safe - he was blinded. He was foolish, and stupidly fell in love with her"

"So the story goes - Bridget was supposed to have said that she wasn't really that keen on Magnus anyway – and that he wasn't her type…...but she had to do, what she had to do…… It was the only way to marry into the Le Fey family"

"Much to his Father's dismay, AND against his wishes; Magnus and Bridget were married. In fact, the marriage was rushed on much sooner, because Bridget was pregnant by 4 months. This was a deliberate ploy"

"Their first born child, a daughter – Agnes Sagen Le Fey was born - just 5 months after their wedding.
Bridget's parents were ecstatic. Bridget had succeeded. Very soon after Agnes was born, Bridget's parents urged her to have more children straight away.
Very soon after Agnes was born, Bridget became pregnant again…….this time, with Samuel – your Grandfather"

"By the time Samuel had arrived, Magnus had become very wary, and very tired of Bridget. He had come to realise what she was really like, and what she was capable of. He knew that she didn't love him; but he couldn't escape. Magnus had great powers, but always seemed weak in his wife's company…..."

"Bridget didn't get pregnant then for quite a while, much to the Bishop's annoyance. Magnus had had enough of her, AND her interfering family, and he didn't want any more children. Agnes had already began to show signs of being quite a nasty and downright evil child, even at only 3 years old; she was indeed, just like her Mother, as young as she was"

"Well, Bridget DID become pregnant again, and Endor was born….. Love Potions had most definitely played a part…….and when Endor came along, Magnus loved her so much.
Bridget was completely uncaring for her new born baby girl, but at that particular time – she was a much needed child to Magnus, for reasons I will

explain later. She was a breath of fresh air. She was such a different little girl to Agnes. She was kind, happy, pretty, and had a lovely, caring way about her. She would happily play with butterflies in the summer months, and the fireflies on an evening; and she loved her big brother Samuel, but neither of them liked Agnes – at all…..”

“So, Bridget had succeeded in bearing 3 children with Magnus”

“At the time of Magnus writing this Will that you found; which waaaaas…let me see….yes, the year of 1936 – Bridget was already dead. She died quite young, at the age of 46”

Mary, at this point, having been hanging on to every word of the story of the Bishops, suddenly asked.

“What happened to her, why did she die so young…?!”

“He killed her….mmmmm…..and about time it was too…”

“He did WHAT…??!! Why did he kill his own wife…??!!”

“Well…” Ooshiya-Lion said, very nonchalantly, and carried on with the story.

“Magnus’s Father was dying, and whilst on his death bed, he told Magnus something really bad, that angered Magnus SO much, that one night, when he knew his wife Bridget had gone out in the car with their daughter Agnes, he conjured a really bad storm…..and it WAS a bad storm. Magnus was so enraged…!”

“The car they were in; was found. It had run off the road, and a huge tree had fallen due to the storm, right on top of the car, and killed Bridget instantly. It should have killed Agnes as well, but it didn’t – she was literally inches away, and was only knocked unconscious due to the crash. That – my dear, is why I said to you earlier, that Agnes has cheated death twice”

“So, that was Bridget gone; the Bishops only child. The Bishops had their suspicions that Magnus may have had something to do with their daughter’s death, but they couldn’t prove a thing……. Thankfully though - Bridget was out of the way.

The Bishop's only connection to this cottage – had gone……apart from their oldest grandchild – Agnes…!!"

"The death of Bridget was very good news indeed - Magnus did the right thing! He knew that if he didn't kill her – she would have killed him, in time, and then Bridget and her parents would have moved in, and taken over the ownership of this cottage, and God only knows what would have happened…! It doesn't bear thinking about"

Mary thought for a few moments, and then said.

"…but surely, going by 'the rules' - isn't the cottage supposed to be passed down to the next child in line – which should have been Agnes……"

Then the penny had dropped with Mary….. "Oh…….!!!"

"Exactly…!" Ooshiya-Lion said. "Yes, you're correct in saying that Agnes WAS their first born child, but she was more of a Bishop than a Le Fey, and this cottage was not intended for anyone else, apart from a 'true' Le Fey to live here, who had good intentions and a kind heart – and let's face it, Agnes didn't have either of those. So that part of the ruling where the eldest child takes over the cottage was changed. THAT is why Magnus wrote this Will; just after Bridget had died…..good job he did really….and made his statement very clear – so Agnes was NOT allowed to live here or have anything to do with this cottage. This is why it is so important that she doesn't get through that door…..!"

"Thank you" Mary said. "The Will actually makes more sense to me now than it did when I first read it….but there's something that's puzzling me…"

"What's that..??" the old man asked.

"What did Magnus's dying Father, actually say to Magnus on his deathbed, that made him so angry, that he had to kill his own wife…..?!"

Ooshiya-Lion got out his pipe and lit it.

Suddenly, the phone rang, which made Mary jump.

"Oh that will be the phone call from James I told you about yesterday. He's ringing you to tell you that he has to work away from home a bit longer. Assure him you are just fine"

Mary answered the phone – it was James. They chatted for a little while.

Whilst Mary was distracted with her phone call, Ooshiya-Lion spoke to Bam Bam.

"Bam Bam, did you deliver my message to the Elder…..and what was the outcome…..?"
The old man's trusty staff relayed information to him, which he listened to, intently.

Mary put the phone down.

"Everything ok..?" he asked.

"Yeah" Mary said, rather heavily. "He said that he had a very interesting, but top secret job that he was working on, but felt terrible that I was on my own, but I told him that I was keeping really busy, and he was ok with that"

Mary sat down, and Ooshiya-Lion carried on.
"So, in answer to your question Mary – the reason why Magnus was so angry; is this……"

"Magnus's Father had kept some information from Magnus for many years. The reason he didn't tell him sooner, was the simple fact that he didn't want to hurt him"

"God, it must have been bad..!"

"It was……."

"What was Magnus's Father's name..??" Mary eagerly asked.

Well his name – was Therian Rathnie Le Fey – which was your Great Great Grandfather. Look, there he is….." as he pointed him out to Mary from the scroll.

Mary suddenly felt proud.

"Therian Rathnie Le Fey…??" she repeated. "What a rather majestic sounding name!"

"Yes….now he WAS a good man, I have to say……well all the Le Fey's were good people – apart from Agnes, as you know"

He continued.

"So if you look on this scroll here, you will see that Therian married a lovely, lovely lady called Celeste Selcete Fallswood – your Great Great Grandmother"

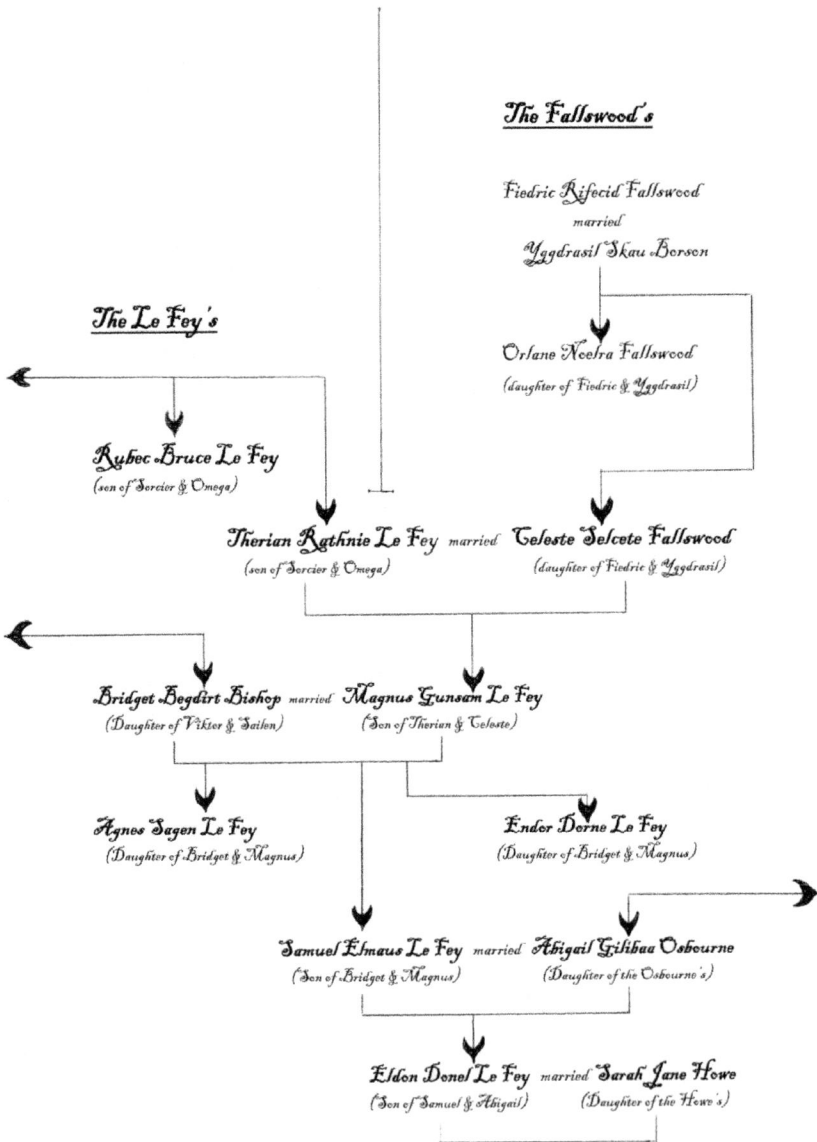

The Fallswood's

Fiedric Rifecid Fallswood
married
Yggdrasil Skau Borson

Orlane Neelra Fallswood
(daughter of Fiedric & Yggdrasil)

The Le Fey's

Rubec Bruce Le Fey
(son of Sorcier & Omega)

Therian Rathnie Le Fey   married   Celeste Selcete Fallswood
(son of Sorcier & Omega)                (daughter of Fiedric & Yggdrasil)

Bridget Begdirt Bishop   married   Magnus Gunsam Le Fey
(Daughter of Vikter & Sailen)            (Son of Therian & Celeste)

Agnes Sagen Le Fey
(Daughter of Bridget & Magnus)

Endor Dorne Le Fey
(Daughter of Bridget & Magnus)

Samuel Elmaus Le Fey   married   Abigail Gilibaa Osbourne
(Son of Bridget & Magnus)            (Daughter of the Osbourne's)

Eldon Donel Le Fey   married   Sarah Jane Howe
(Son of Samuel & Abigail)          (Daughter of the Howe's)

Mary looked at the scroll.

"Fallswood....Fallswood..? That's the name of the woods I used to play in when I was a little girl, called Fallswood Woods. It's not far from here. That's a coincidence.......or is it...?!" Mary looked at the old man, knowing that anything could be possible.

"That's another story" He said, smiling.

"So…" Mary said…... "Getting back to the story; what was the information that Therian had kept from his son Magnus for all these years...?!"

"Therian had an older brother called Rubec Bruce Le Fey…..but they weren't just brothers – they were very close and the best of friends. They grew up together, and had a really special bond – although they were both very different. Rubec, being the older one, was not one to be messed with"

"Ooh, I like the sound of him already…!" Mary laughed.

"All these names will mean something to you eventually Mary, just concentrate on the story for now"
"So, when Magnus was born, his Uncle Rubec loved his nephew so much. As he got older, he would take Magnus out on lots of walks, showed him everything there was to know about the outdoors, and all the caves, dwellings, and the fields; and taught him about all the animals. Therian loved the fact that his brother Rubec was so close to his son"

"…..Rubec was a wonderful young Wizard, very, very strong, and he was quite a stocky chap too. He loved animals, and they loved him. Wherever he went, there were always some animals on his heels, and on his shoulders, or in his pockets. He was surrounded by them - wherever he went. He used to go off walking, sometimes for days, sometimes for weeks – but he was never alone. He also had a very special 'talent' I shall call it"

"A talent – like what..??" Mary eagerly enquired.

"Well he had traits of being a Morphic and a Therianthrope"

The look on Mary's face - needed no questioning.

"…so, that means that he was able to take on a specified shape or form, or shape-shift into animals, but not just one particular kind, but anything. He was an exceptionally talented Wizard – a bit of a loner, but a lovely, kind and caring man"

Then Ooshiya-Lion stopped talking for a few moments, and sat staring ahead.

"Are you ok..?" Mary asked.

"Oh…y…yes….yes…" Ooshiya-Lion was distracted by his thoughts.

"There's one other thing I need to tell you about your Great Great Uncle Rubec" He looked at Mary, as her eyes widened – waiting.

"I almost forgot until now – but he was the only Wizard I know….that could Time Travel – like you did…….and like I said earlier, there are very, very few who can do this; but Rubec was the only one I knew about…..until now…...."

Mary, completely fascinated by all of this, was speechless for a moment; then she asked.

"So, did Rubec have anything to do with what Therian told his son Magnus on his deathbed..?"

Ooshiya-Lion sighed, and said gravely.

"I'm afraid he did. You see Rubec had unfortunately died many years before. What Therian told Magnus on his deathbed was…….. When Rubec had died – he had, in fact…….been murdered….."
Mary put both of her hands to her mouth, and gasped inwardly. She wasn't expecting to hear that. Before she had time to ask anything else, the old man carried on with his tale.

"What happened - was very unfortunate and very sad. Rubec had died three years after Magnus and Bridget had married. Apparently, Rubec had gone out on one of his long treks – but he never returned, and was never seen again! His rucksack was found at the top of a huge ravine, and it is believed that he lost his footing, took a tumble and fell over the edge and down into the ravine. His body was never found"

"Magnus was completely distraught on hearing that his Uncle Rubec had gone missing – presumed dead. Obviously at the time, Magnus had two young children, Agnes and Samuel. His wife Bridget was very uncaring. She thought he was weak, she didn't support him, didn't care, and actually left him, and stayed at her parents, and took Agnes with her, and left Samuel, who was only 2 with Magnus. Magnus's parents had to help with baby Samuel at that time"

"Magnus would go out walking many, many times, just endlessly searching for him for miles upon miles, and going over the same routes that they had walked – but to no avail. Unfortunately, Magnus fell into a deep depression"

"Bridget eventually 'won' her way back into the cottage, as her parents urged her to return, to keep up the façade, as she was already pregnant with Endor. So she DID return, but Magnus wasn't bothered, and didn't care. He was still very much grieving for his Uncle"

"Rubec's death was indeed a shock – he was only 52 ….. He was such a well-loved man, but there were SOME that didn't like him at all - and THEY….were the Bishops…."

Mary looked puzzled. "….but why……why didn't the Bishops like Rubec??" she asked.

"Rubec had (in the Bishops eyes) become too 'vocal', shall we say at his disdain regarding the forthcoming marriage between his nephew Magnus, and their daughter Bridget. He wasn't happy about the marriage at all, and he didn't hide the fact that he wasn't happy either.
The Bishops were furious that Rubec was trying to intervene, and I think there were clashes and arguments. Magnus naturally felt caught between his Uncle and his Fiancée, and of course, his Father; but the marriage went ahead anyway. Even after the marriage, Rubec still tried to tell Magnus that this was a dangerous liaison, but Agnes had been born, and your Grandfather Samuel was on the way. Magnus kept assuring his Uncle that he was alright, and not to worry, but Rubec would not let it lay. The Bishops obviously became more irritated with Rubec's interference, but headstrong Rubec knew that the legacy of this cottage had to be protected at all times – no matter the cost"

"Let's not forget of course – this cottage was Rubec's home"

Mary looked a little confused.

"So if Rubec lived here alone, being the eldest where did his younger brother Therian and his wife Celeste live, and their son Magnus of course…??"

"Well, as the rules went, as far as this cottage goes, the oldest or first born lives in the cottage, and Therian, being the younger brother of Rubec, lived in the barn of course, with his wife and their son Magnus, in answer to your question – as any other member of the family lived, until it was their time to move into the cottage"

"The barn……what barn…?? Mary asked.

"The barn which belongs to this cottage….you didn't know about that….??" Ooshiya-Lion was surprised. "It's just over the road, and up the lane…..mmmmm…?"

"No I didn't know……unless James knew about it, but he would have told me"

The old man carried on.

"Well anyway, the Bishops had been scheming and plotting for some time, about how they would gain access to the cottage; but they knew that Rubec – being the older brother, would live in the cottage predominantly, and was not about to leave anytime soon. BUT….if Rubec was 'out of the way' so to speak – the Bishops knew that Therian (Rubec's younger brother) would 'OBVIOUSLY' move in with his wife Celeste, and their son Magnus – and that would be perfect…….for THEM!!"

"Aaaghh – I understand now" Mary said. "Blimey, they really DID go out of their way didn't they…?!"

"Rubec wasn't married you see, and didn't have children, so it wasn't as if the cottage would then be passed down to HIS children, because he didn't have any. The Bishops knew that, which they were very happy about; and also knew, that in time, the cottage would be passed to his younger brother Therian, and then it would be passed to Therian's son Magnus – who just so happened to be marrying their daughter Bridget……but they couldn't wait… What if Rubec lived to a ripe old age..??…..which would mean, he would NEVER leave here. That was a big stumbling block for the Bishop's; knowing that it would be years and years before they could get into this cottage, and Bridget certainly didn't intend being married to Magnus any longer than she had to"

"The Bishops would have no doubt got rid of Magnus anyway, and then they would have swooped on the cottage like a swarm of flies – and the legacy would have gone forever…....BUT, there was still a chance that Rubec COULD find someone, and get married and have children; and then the Bishops plan would have been completely thwarted, and they would be pushed right back out of the picture altogether…..and they weren't going to let THAT happen…!"

"Like I said, they were horrible people, and would do ANYTHING to get into this cottage…..
Sounds very complicated, I know, and quite sinister, but that's what they had planned…..but Rubec knew all of this. He had them sussed out……"

"Do you know (the cheek of them) -The Bishops even went as far as wanting more of an alliance with Therian and his wife, and tried to be-friend them, seeing as their daughter had married their son; but this was only for their own greed. Obviously Therian wanted no such thing. He had his wits about him, and knew exactly what was going on.
The Bishops were never invited to the cottage, much to their anger. They were never going to step foot inside the door. Bridget would often ask Magnus why his parents didn't invite her parents around for tea"

"Anyway, as I said earlier, Rubec was in the Bishops' way, but he just wouldn't back down"

Mary interrupted.

"…but surely, Rubec couldn't have been on his own with all of this – did anyone help him, or try…….to keep this horrible family away from trying to get near this cottage, and whatever it was that they wanted…?!" She was suddenly feeling fiercely protective of her home, and the legacy – the more she heard.

"Rubec didn't need any help, he was a strong enough character on his own – he wasn't afeard by the likes of the Bishops. He was just doing his duty as head of the family…..but very sadly….so the story goes – the Bishops had Rubec killed……"

Mary, again, shocked at what she was hearing, couldn't speak….

"The funny thing was, Rubec was never found – he just disappeared. The Bishops never admitted or denied having anything to do with Rubec's disappearance, but they were very, very happy because he was out of the picture, and out of their way. Therian, on the other hand, was beside himself with grief. He had lost his only brother and best friend. He couldn't bring himself to tell his son Magnus how his favourite Uncle had come to die, as this would have had so many complications, and Magnus was grieving enough at his Uncles' disappearance. So Magnus was led to believe that his Uncle had died whilst out on one of his treks, and fell from a ravine"

"Therian eventually DID tell his son the truth when he knew he was dying – that the Bishops had plotted to kill his Uncle Rubec. On hearing the truth from his Father; that his Uncle had died at the hands of his in-laws, whilst he was trying to protect this cottage, enraged Magnus very much. He realised he should have listened to his Father, and his Uncle, about the dangers of marrying into the Bishop family, but he was too over-ruled by his evil wife – of which he had no time for now. Magnus knew that the only thing he had to do – was to get rid of his wife. If he didn't kill her – she would most definitely have killed him, AND their two youngest children, Samuel and Endor. Magnus didn't have any use or time for Bridget anymore"

"The whole Bishop family would have descended on the cottage and taken it for themselves, and
Magnus didn't want to be the only one from his whole family line, that didn't adhere to the rule that the cottage had to be protected and looked after by the Le Fey family, going down the generations. He had been too fool-hardy in the past, and felt that it was his own fault that his Uncle Rubec had died because of his foolish heart…….. He knew what he had to do……."

"He had no relationship with his oldest daughter Agnes. She was very much a Bishop, and spent all of her time with her Grandparents, Viktor and Sailen"

"When only a couple of months or so had gone by since the eventual passing of his Father Therian – Magnus caused the storm that night, which killed his wife, which was a blessing I might add; but Agnes survived as I said. Then straight after Bridget's funeral, Magnus sat down and wrote this Will, that you have here. That is why he specifically states that under no circumstances, could Agnes enter the cottage……and the reason why Endor was such a breath of fresh air to Magnus when she was born, was that she helped ease Magnus's grieving over losing his beloved Uncle……"

"Such a sad story……but THAT, my dear Mary………. is why Magnus killed his own wife….!!"

On hearing all of this, Mary sat back in her chair. She had been completely dumbfounded, but enthralled at everything that Ooshiya-Lion had told her. From thinking that she was completely on her own, to finding out that she had relatives she knew nothing about. She somehow felt stronger and more responsible for knowing all of this.

"There is more to tell you Mary, but I think that is enough for one day, but…..."

The old man hadn't quite finished his sentence, when - out of nowhere, there was a loud bang on the back kitchen window. They both jumped with fright and looked, to see a black crow, flapping about and pecking vigorously at the window pane. It was huge…!! Then it began squawking. Suddenly there was another bang, and it was joined by another, and then another, and then another. In a matter of seconds, there were several crows banging and pecking at the window.
Mary screamed at the noise. Straight away, the old man outstretched his right hand towards the back window, and shouted 'Mori' at the top of his voice..!!
The black crows suddenly fell from the window and thuds could be heard on the ground below.

"THAT….is Agnes getting closer…!" The old man spoke loudly. "She'll get a shock when they don't return with information..!"

Mary's adrenaline was racing…..

"What do you mean Agnes – was that HER doing…?!!"

"I'm afraid so; she has sent them to spy on you, and then send word back to her on what they can see….!! Her spells are working slowly……mmmmm….what's todays date….?? Mary, how long is it to your Birthday…..??!"

Mary turned to Ooshiya-Lion, and looked upon him like he had completely lost his mind….

"What on earth has that got to do……"
MARY….it's important…!!"

"W…well it's a week on Monday…...what do you want to know that for…..??! Oh I'm just going to stop asking questions….?!!" She said exasperatedly, and flung her arms up into the air.

Suddenly Henry flew in.

"Mary, Ooshiya-Lion are you ok..??!!" Henry shouted as he made his way quickly to the table, but then stopped in his tracks at the sight of the old man's huge mane of hair!
He was soon followed by Patsy, and Wilbur, who nearly bumped into each other in mid-air. They had heard the squawking, and then seen the dead crows on the ground below the window, and then too, stopped sharp as they saw Ooshiya-Lion's hair.
They just stared…….

"Yes, thank you, we are both ok"… the old man answered.

Mary pointed to Ooshiya-Lion's mane of hair, which had obviously caught the others' attention and said "It's a long story….."

They nodded in silence, as they kept on staring, when suddenly Elma appeared at the back window. He had run down the garden as fast as he could, following the others who had flown in quickly. As he got to the window, he remembered that the last time he tried to get through – he'd got stuck. Then he shouted out loud…

"….Oh I can get through, I can get through….!! Ha haaaa - I must have lost a bit of weight….!!." He was laughing, as he began to run across the unit top, then looked up and suddenly skidded to a stop and shouted.

"W O A H…!!! ….check the mane out Lion Man, you look like one of the Hair Bear Bunch….....!!!!"
"What….?…what did I say…?!" he said as they all looked at him.

 Wilbur was waving his hand underneath his chin, trying to make sign languages to him to tell him to shut up…

Henry interrupted.

"We were just talking in the garden with a few of the others, when we heard the noise on the window, and saw the crows flapping about, and then all the squawking…..What do you think is happening….?!!"

Wilbur said. "Well, I guess that was no accident, or a 'one off'…??"

"No…" Mary answered. "It was Agnes up to her tricks..!! Sending spies now she is..!!"

"Spies…??" Henry repeated, looking from one to the other.

The old man looked like he was quietly calculating, and then said.

"I really could do with putting a spell all around the garden wall to stop her from letting any more of her allies into this garden, as I've got a feeling that the spells could be weakening, but I don't want her to know that I'm here….but it's possible that I may have some help….."

Mary suddenly scraped the back of her chair back, stood up sharply, and said.

"Well I'll tell you what I'M going to do…!!"

She went to the drawer, took out a large garden waste sack, and strode defiantly out of the back door, slammed it, and went round to the back of the house. She picked the dead crows up, one by one, put them into the black bin liner, and threw them over the wall, and shouted…

"There AGNES…… take back your motley crew, they didn't quite manage to do whatever it was you wanted them to ….I SAW TO THAT….!!!"…and with that, she strode back into the house, and slammed the door.

"There – that's what you do with people like that, you show them who's BOSS….!!"

Everybody looked at her with open mouths.

Ooshiya-Lion burst into laughter…..

"Well, that's certainly made my day…!" Everybody else joined in laughing. Then Mary started laughing…..

While everyone was still laughing, and talking about Mary throwing the crows over the wall, Ooshiya-Lion quietly called Bam Bam over to him.

"I need you to do me a favour my trusted friend….." and he whispered to his trusty staff………… Bam Bam disappeared.

Outside, an old woman with a big scar down her face, scowled, as her eyes grew darker with anger and hatred.

"Nobody mocks me…..…." She whispered to herself, and clenched her teeth as she heard faint laughter coming from inside the cottage.

# Chapter 25

## **<u>A Dragon & some Stew</u>**

Agnes slipped away from the outside of the cottage as dusk was approaching.

Her greed was consuming her. All of those many, many years that she had waited, when SHE - Agnes Sagen Le Fey should be the rightful heir and owner, and yet here she was, still trying to get into that cottage. The spell that her sister Endor had cast all those years ago – was soon to run out, and then everything would rightfully, and finally belong to her - at last.......once she got rid of the current occupant…..

She smiled as she walked quietly away from the cottage, and up and along the road a little.

'Not long now' she whispered to herself, as she shuffled along with her thoughts.

She took a small left turning in the road; walked along a narrow lane, and came upon a very old barn that was practically in ruins. She went inside and closed the door. The inside of the barn was much bigger than it appeared to be on the outside, and didn't look so ramshackle.

"Too long I have been away, but soon everything will be mine…." She laughed as she lit the fire and one by one, lit several candles around the small barn.

"……and don't forget – it will also….. be mine….." a voice breathed heavily from the darkness at the back of the barn, as a large pair of green eyes emerged firstly, followed by a large scaly head.

A Dragon walked slowly from the dark into the candlelight.

Agnes took a sharp intake of breath.

"Beruc…??!!" she spoke the Dragon's name.

"Did you forget about me, and the wager we had…??" the Dragon said, as he stepped further into the light, looking straight at Agnes.

"N….no..no – Beruc, how could I. You saved me after all" Agnes hesitated as she spoke.

"Goooood…" the Dragon drawled.

Agnes scowled at the Dragon. "How long have you been here..?!" she asked nastily.

"Oh…..long enough to see, and hear…." The Dragon smiled, showing lots of teeth. "How long will it be before we have full ownership of the cottage, and it's secret…??"

"Anytime soon". Agnes answered.

"Aaaghh……it could be the child's Birthday" Beruc smiled knowingly.

"Who's Birthday..??!" Agnes snapped.

Beruc leaned in even more, making Agnes lean back away from him.

"The one who dwells in the cottage as we speak….." he said, slowly.

"B…B…..But what do you mean. How do you know this..?!!"

"There's a lot of things I know – I've been around much longer than you……anyway, I for one, cannot wait to meet her; but unfortunately, it will be only a short meeting, as I tend to get a little over-excited when I meet people for the first time, and things may start to get a little 'heated'….ha ha haaaaa..!" Beruc laughed as smoke swirled from his mouth and surrounded Agnes. "Any word from the worm you sent in, by any chance..?" Beruc asked.

"No – something must have happened to him..!" Agnes said – furious that Beruc had just turned up from nowhere.

The Dragon sniggered to himself.

"What's so funny..?!" Agnes snapped.

"Well, I mean – 'a worm'….really…??" Beruc was being sarcastic.

"He did his job and I got the information I needed..!" Agnes answered back – now smiling to herself.

"WHAT information did you receive…?! The Dragon shot Agnes a look with narrowed eyes.

"Well, she definitely has something about her – there's some strong magic, although how, I don't know; and yet she can…..can….somehow…." Agnes broke off as Beruc sharply interrupted.

"What….??! What can she 'somehow'…..??? Tell me…!!" he bellowed.

Agnes trembled a little.

"She can control…..c…control the weather…." She quickly said.

The Dragon burst into laughter…….

"What's so funny..??!!" Agnes burst out, snarling at the Dragon.

The Dragon was still laughing.

"Oh….oh….oh….I haven't had a laugh like that for centuries…!!"

Agnes didn't ask him anymore, as he continued to laugh. She walked over to the little stove and poured some meat stew that had been slowly cooking, into a bowl, and sat by the fire, on the edge of her chair, with her back to the Dragon.
Presently, Beruc asked.

"Anything else you need to tell me…??"

Agnes didn't look round, she just sat hunched over, eating her stew, then said…

"She definitely has some help…… I'm quite sure that she doesn't really know who she is, or where she is from, and therefore can't perform any magic…. I feel it…. I have to find out more about her, but I can't get into that wretched garden….. Who could possibly be helping her…..??" Agnes took a long gaze towards the fire, which was now burning steadily. The flames reflected in her eyes as she stared…..

"Not long now…." She said quietly. "Not long now….. It's been too long…"

The Dragon slumped onto the floor, and grunted as he got comfortable.

"That day……" He said slowly. "…..the day you and your sister Endor fought"

"What of it…?!" Agnes snapped as she half looked over her shoulder.

"She must have got very, very angry to push you into another timeline….." He carried on as Agnes didn't answer. "Did you know that your sister had the power to do that…you know, push you into another timeline…?? That's some powerful Witch……" He was looking at Agnes all the time.

"NO…!!…I didn't know her powers were so strong…." Agnes answered as she stopped slurping her stew, and raised her head from the bowl, as if she was thinking….

"So, your purpose being…." He continued… "…was to 'eliminate' the next heir to the cottage, which was the baby boy, Edward, who was your nephew – Eldon's child – correct…?"

Agnes just grunted.

"You tried to kill that child – the boy Edward, didn't you…??"

The Dragon looked at the back of Agnes's head. She could feel the weight of his stare.

"I DID….and I succeeded…!!" Agnes blurted out, she was sick of Beruc's questioning. " I saw him close his eyes as she cradled him, as his little face turned pale…."…she laughed softly whilst slurping on her stew, and it dripped down her chin, as she continued to stare at the flames….

Beruc carried on.

"…So……your sister Endor didn't have any children, and neither did you…. Why DIDN'T your younger……PRETTIER……sister, have children….?" He smiled sarcastically, as he felt Agnes prickle with hatred and envy.

Agnes shifted about in her chair, still staring at the fire….

"…Because the stupid, honourable, 'goody-two-shoes' Witch that she was……betrothed her LIFE to looking after children..!!. Firstly, looking after our Brother Samuel's little runt of a boy, Eldon from the age of 3….after Samuel and his silly wife died…" She gave a little laugh….. " ..and THEN, years later, she's looking after Eldon's only child, the baby, Edward..! …..Anyway, why do you want to know all of this, I thought you knew the whole story…?!" she snapped as she fully turned around, to see Beruc, looking down at his claws nonchalantly.

"…because I had forgotten some of the details, and I wanted to hear it all again…" he said, slowly, whilst shining his claws. "…..besides, I'm bored – and there's nothing else to talk about…!!"

"So, tell me…" he carried on. "Why DID she betroth her life to looking after the boy – Eldon, when he was only 3…??" He then looked over at Agnes.

"Is it because he was orphaned, because his parents had died…??"

"Yes"……She answered stiffly.
"Mmmmmm….your Brother and his wife died..?? They must have been very young to leave a child of 3….what did they die of again….?"

Agnes got up, wiped her mouth, and chin on the back of her sleeve, and gave Beruc a quick sideways glance, went over to the stove, and poured another ladle of stew into her bowl.

"What's the matter – cat got your tongue…??!" Beruc laughed at her.

She swung around and banged the bowl of stew down so heavily, that it made some of the contents spill over onto the table. Beruc had obviously made her angry.

"Look, you heavy lump of 'good for nothing fireball'….YES..!!...They were both killed when their car crashed, and do you know what…??...... I killed them both…!! Yes – ME…!!" and prodded her finger hard on her chest, as she stared around the cottage in a glorified manner.

The Dragon's eyes lit up as she spat out the horrible truth.

"Tell me again…!!" he grinned

"My Father, Magnus killed my own Mother – my beautiful, beautiful Mother Bridget – his own wife…!!! Can you believe that…?!!!... I was in the car with my Mother that night - and he meant for me to die too….his own daughter…… but I DIDN'T…!!!" Agnes was now walking around the room and feeling her anger rising.   "…So…… I eventually got my own revenge on that horrible man, who was my Father - who I hated……and I killed his son - my brother….YES, I killed my own brother Samuel and his silly little wife Abigail……in exactly the same way he killed my Mother, in a car accident…...but their young son Eldon didn't die did he…?! So my stupid sister Endor, looked after him…..because he was the next heir …!!"

"Rather childish, don't you think…?" Beruc asked.

"What was childish, what are you saying….?!" Agnes snapped.

"Well….killing your brother and his wife in a car accident, exactly like your Mother and you – couldn't you think of anything else…..??"

Agnes scowled at Beruc.

"My Grandmother Sailen wanted revenge, just as I did, so giving my Father a 'taste of his own medicine' was the best thing….!!"

"Like I said – very childish….. I mean 'an eye for an eye'…….really…??!......and – what's very interesting Agnes, is that you never told me before that your Grandmother was an accomplice in this 'charade'. Soooo….. You didn't work alone...?? Mmmmmm…."

Agnes looked shifty.

"I don't remember saying that my Grandmother Sailen was involved….. I just said that she wanted revenge, because my Father had killed her daughter Bridget – my Mother..!"

"Yes, yes, yes……so you keep saying… " Beruc answered sarcastically; but he had noted the new information…..

"Anyway, why didn't YOU go and live in the cottage after your Brother died…. I mean….was KILLED…….. You were the oldest, and doesn't the cottage automatically go to the next in line…??"

Beruc was playing with Agnes, and loved watching her squirm.

"I…I…I couldn't …..get…in..in the cottage……"

"Speak up, speak up, I can't hear you…!!" Beruc interrupted, and was smiling at Agnes, waiting for her to explode.

She cleared her throat…. "Ahem….I said…."

"Yes, yes, you couldn't get in…….WHY…?!!"

"BECAUSE I WASN'T IN THE WILL…!!" Agnes finally exploded.

Beruc repeated her words, and gasped sarcastically. "You weren't in the Will…??!"....Do you realise how much of an outcast that makes you – Agnes Sagen Le Fey…..?! You're the only one in the history of that cottage that isn't in the Will…….Well that's definitely nothing to be proud of; and what makes you think you're EVER going to be able to own that cottage……?!....well, well, well…. More for me then….!!" He laughed heartily.

Agnes swung around to face him, her hatred and anger building up inside her. "Don't think for one single moment, you are getting ANYTHING from that cottage...!!! She shouted.

"Oh but we have a deal my dear Agnes, have you forgotten...?? If I'd have known who you REALLY were that day that I found you, I would have left you to die.....!! In fact, now I know that you weren't even in that Will at all, at least I have more of a chance than... YOU...!! Oh this is so much fun...!"

Beruc watched Agnes as she was now walking around the room, wringing her hands as she recalled her vengeance.
The Dragon was enjoying seeing Agnes getting angry. He then butted in, and watched for Agnes's reaction, but didn't let her speak.

".....so, listening to all of that, it sounds like history repeating itself, doesn't it......?? Your Father kills his own wife – (your Mother) - but didn't manage to kill his daughter – YOU...!"...and pointed at her with one of his long talons...... "And then YOU decide to kill your brother and his wife; for revenge.......and just to get them out of the way – but YOU didn't manage to kill their son...Eldon...I mean...??" ....he then gestured.... "It's such a coincidence – isn't it...??

Beruc was being especially sarcastic.
Agnes knew what he was doing, and refused to let him see that she was now seething with rage, but her mind was racing. As her back was turned to Beruc, she spoke, half to herself, and half aloud ...

"......I could never get near that boy Eldon for love, nor money. Endor protected him soooo much. Then apparently, he grew up and married that non witch woman – Sarah what's-her-face...!! I mean, why....??! Why marry a non-witch, it's never been heard of before...?!! Then they went and had that little boy – Edward; and I got to him that day, whilst Endor was digging away in the garden – and I poisoned him with some blackberries......ha ha haaa....!!" Agnes laughed and laughed as she walked around the room.

Beruc watched carefully as Agnes began to tell him the tale of her greed and want for the cottage.

"How do you know that your sister looked after Eldon from the age of 3, for years, until he married the 'non-witch' woman Sarah, you speak of….?? You told me that you went to Transylvania with your Grandparents…..very soon after you killed your brother and his wife?? You seem to know an awful lot……I heard that you had to flee - for fear of the wrath of your Father….!!"

"We went to Transylvania to see some of my Grandparents relatives" Agnes couldn't look Beruc in the eye.

"Mmmm….same thing as fleeing if you ask me"

"Well I'm not asking you – AM  I…?!!"

He slowly asked….

"Did you ever see Eldon much and his 'non-witch wife – Sarah'…?"
"No, strangely enough, they never left that cottage, or went out. Very odd behaviour; no one ever saw them" Agnes said, thinking back.

"Mmmmmm……..well that's because they had moved out, a long time ago - away from the cottage – did you know that…?" he asked casually; then carried on. "They didn't really live there at all……Endor, your sister – lived there……alone. You were obviously not in the Will, your brother wasn't around anymore – YOU saw to that, so your sister lived there by herself"

Agnes slowly turned around and stared at the Dragon.

"What do you mean…..exactly….Are you saying that Eldon didn't stay in the cottage once he married??" Agnes stood her ground as she challenged Beruc.

"Well – after you poisoned their baby, that poor little boy - with blackberries, who knows what would have happened next….Endor cast the spell over the cottage and gardens, you ended up travelling back in time, which is when I came upon your sorry little self……and Eldon and his 'non-witch wife' Sarah could easily have moved back into the cottage – especially with you out of the way, but they decided never to go back again. They were too distraught having lost their baby at the hands of YOU. It has stood empty all these years. Yes, nice little quiet life they led……bringing up….. their…..daughter….."

As he said this, he quickly looked sideways at Agnes, and smiled as he looked with much contempt at Agnes, who was now boiling with rage…..

"DAUGHTER….??!! What do you mean – 'daughter'…?? They didn't have another child, only the baby, Edward….!! What do you know….Another child – a daughter you say…?!!.Tell me……NOW…?!!"

"Haven't you worked it out already…?? tsk tsk….Agnes, you ARE getting slow, but there again, you HAVE been away, haven't you….??"
Agnes held onto to the side of the kitchen work top with both of her hands, and turned around in the room, staring searchingly… How could this be..? How did she not know…?

Beruc laughed heartily. "You mean you didn't know…??!... So, the child, the 'daughter'…… Mary, who turns 30 very soon, is the daughter of Eldon & Sarah, and the natural heir to that cottage – so - she's in her rightful place if you ask me…!!" he laughed and laughed.

"How do you know all of this…??!! It can't be true…..!! …….
I knew there was something about that girl, and that it could be possible that she was a Le Fey; but thought it could have been a mistake; or she was a distant relative…..but I just KNEW she was…!! When I touched her hands at the garden gate when we first met, I felt something…yes, yes I felt something…. I felt more than just some power – I felt anger and aggression…"
She was now half smiling, realising that Mary would have Bishop blood running through her veins. "I could get her on my side…. yes…that would be good…."

She walked around the barn half talking to herself, and half out loud….. Then she swung around.

"Anyway – why are YOU so happy that she is the heir to the cottage..?? I thought you wanted some of that for yourself…?!" She said this as she walked slowly towards Beruc, looking at him and wondering.

Beruc rose up, tall, lowered his head, narrowed his eyes, and said in a hoarse whisper….

"My needs for that cottage don't concern YOU….and if you ever call me a 'good for nothing fireball' again…..I will tear shreds of skin from you bit by bit, with my claws, and then watch you slowly scorch to a cinder…… I remember the day when you came hurtling back in time onto that meadow, many, many years ago, with your face cut to ribbons. I watched from the hills, and then came down and tended to your wound. You would have died that day. Do you remember….??!!" Beruc now had his claw around Agnes and was squeezing her slowly as she left the floor.
Suddenly, there was a knock at the door. Beruc dropped Agnes to the ground.

"Say nothing of my being here…." He warned, and disappeared back, into the darkness of the room.

Agnes opened the door cautiously…….there was no one there…..

Back at the cottage, as they all sat down to a hearty meal, and still discussing the crows that Agnes had sent, Mary said to Ooshiya-Lion.

"It calls to me you know – the door…."

"Well that's good…..and it doesn't surprise me…" He answered, smiling.

Nobody said anything.

Mary looked over towards the door. "Why was the door covered up, and where does it lead to..?? I can't just ignore it Ooshiya-Lion. I'm thinking that it was meant to be found by me, and I have some significance…"

"Well, Mary this is your home now; and everything in it and around it belongs to you – so if you want to open it - go and open it….." The old man said.

"….but I can't…..there's no door handle, no lock, and no key…..I've tried…!!." She answered, exasperatingly. Then she remembered the wooden key that she had got through the post……

"Mmmmmm…...well you need to work that one out for yourself – and soon"

"Who are you, Ooshiya-Lion, and what are you really here for...??" Mary asked him.

He paused for a moment, and then took a deep breath in, and said.

"I was called upon by The Magisters; and before you ask, they are a group of extremely powerful Wizards, Mages, Beings etc, with exceptional high ruling. Some of them dwell among the high cities, and conduct matters of great importance, steer lost souls, and are the most intelligent of people"

"Oh...ok...... I wasn't expecting any of that....!!." Mary was shocked.... "...but why are YOU here..?"

"I'm here because you need my help and guidance, and this timeline we are in at the present moment is of great significance. I'm glad you're all here actually, because now – it's about time I told you all a story...."

Ooshiya-Lion sat back in his chair, got out his pipe from his inside pocket, and filled it with tobacco from the old leather pouch, and lit the thin pipe with the click of his fingers. Mesmerising smoke swirled through the air, and danced around, filling the kitchen with another beautiful smell – this time is was rosemary, lavender and lemon balm. He began to speak......and here is the story.....

# Chapter 26

## **The Story**

Many, many years ago.
**Monday 1st August, 1864......**

Far away on a mountain top – three people stood in a line.... A mighty Wizard, an Enchantress, and a powerful Mage.

The Wizard, whose name was Sorcier, turned to his right, and gravely asked a question.
"Are you ready..?!"

As he looked at his pregnant wife, he put his hand on her shoulder for reassurance.
She looked back at him, not answering his question.

"Drink this Omega" he said; and from his cloak, he produced a phial – which he offered to her.

In the phial, she could see a gold swirling liquid. She stared at it for a few moments, as it held her gaze. She briefly looked at Sorcier, then back at the mesmerising liquid, and then back at her husband. Without taking her eyes from his, she took the phial from his hand, put it to her lips, and tipped the contents into her mouth, then threw the phial behind her, wiping her lips with the back of her long cloaked sleeve.

The moment the golden liquid entered her mouth, it lit up her entire body, and from within, she glowed a beautiful rich gold and green.

Besides Sorcier and his wife Omega, on the mountain top that night - was also Omega's younger sister, Kairos. The three of them had waited for this moment for some time now.

"Omega — now, are you ready..?!"

Her husband repeated his question. Omega was stood in between her husband and her sister
His eyes were searching hers wildly for an answer, but his eyes were fiery and a little afraid; but they seemed to be asking her, reassuringly.
She slowly turned her head away from him, to her right, where her sister Kairos stood; and their eyes met.

"I am ready..!!" Kairos shouted loudly and boldly.
Omega turned back to her husband, and nodded.

"Yes. We are ready.....!"

Sorcier turned his head up to the night sky, and bellowed...

"Then let us begin......!!"

From the mountain top, on this dark night, all the three slowly closed their eyes, and tilted their heads back. They took a breath in, and slowly breathed out, repeating this, three times. On the last breath out, their arms reached up towards the dark night, and in turn, they began mumbling incantations and reciting magic.

After a few moments, the rich gold colour which was shining through Omega's body, had now travelled down her arms and to her fingers. Golden sparks suddenly left her fingertips, and flew out and up towards the black sky.
She slowly and carefully lowered her arms down, until they were stretched out in front of her. Her husband and her sister also repeated this.
Omega opened her eyes, and they flashed the same beautiful golden and green swirling colour that was in the phial of liquid. The reflection of light that came from her fingertips lit up her eyes even more.

A faint roll of thunder was heard in the distance, the wind started to pick up, and small drops of rain started to fall, as Kairos began to conjure.

Kairos Soriak Gata was a member of one of the most powerful astrological families; and as an Enchantress, amongst many other things, she could conjure and control the weather — and tonight, was the most important night of her life, along with her sister and brother-in-law.

On this very night, she was conjuring a huge storm for the assignment, which was given to the three, by the ever powerful, Magisters — the most senior of the magical world.

The Magisters had chosen carefully, the three most powerful people to wield the Eldritch Power, and to summon what was called 'The Happening'. This had been decided after fears of losing the earth to other worldly beings, which was foreseen in the future by the Magisters themselves...and this was to happen — this very night — Monday 1st August 1864 - as this would have great relevance in the future.

Sorcier Resoric Le Fey, was one of the most important and prolific young Wizards of his time. Along with his wife Omega, who was a famous Mage and Sorceror, and her sister Kairos; were the only people who, collectively, could do this.

With all her strength that she had - Omega imposed all her will upon the task in hand, along with her sister, and husband to bring about 'The Happening'.

Kairos closed her eyes tightly, and swayed from side to side in her long dark mauve and black dress, as she muttered and conjured. Her hands waved in time to her movements, and then they began to make shapes.

The wind was now blowing strong, and as she opened her eyes wildly and looked towards the sky, she raised her right arm and slammed it down.......! Immediately, a lightning bolt suddenly appeared and crashed down to the earth below. Her eyes turned violet as she watched, excitedly laughing.

Then, she raised her arms to the sky again, repeating her magic incantations; and thunder roared across the night sky, as torrents of rain now lashed down, as the wind picked up even more, which blew her long black hair wildly; and she danced to the storm. With her arms still in the air, she then suddenly slammed them both down; and another thunderbolt of lightning broke from the thunder, and lit up the earth below once more.

Sorcier was continually supporting his wife and sister-in-law by muttering magic over and over and over.

As Kairos held the weather, Omega summoned the Eldritch Power. Bright orange and yellow colours had formed in the sky from the golden sparks that had emanated from her fingers, as she searched the night sky. All the while, she had been conjuring – her husband Sorcier kept looking at his wife. He knew that this was an exhausting task for her, especially in her condition. She was only 4 weeks away from giving birth, but there was no other time for 'the happening' to occur.

She stole him a quick look, and shouted over the storm, as the wind whipped her auburn hair.

"I'll be fine Sorcier — we HAVE to do this..!!"

"Omega, quickly, I can't hold it much longer...!!" Shouted Kairos.

The rain had completely soaked them through, but the wind was now raging so bad, it was hard to keep their footing, as they stood on the mountain top.

"Omega...!!" Kairos shouted again.

Sorcier held his wife, to help steady her, while she closed her eyes and muttered under her breath. Then, opened her eyes wide, flung out her arms to the sky and an array of the most enchanting colours left her fingertips. Suddenly the Orionids Meteor Shower could now be seen over a large area of the sky. At the point at which the showers emanate from - called The Radiant.....this lies in the constellation of Orion; and could now be seen so clearly.

Suddenly, a bright ball of orange/yellow light started to form in the night sky. It grew bigger and bigger as it swirled round and round, collecting all the colours which had emanated from Omega's fingertips, and was now hurtling straight towards them.

"It's here...!!" Shouted Sorcier. "Quickly Kairos, the wind.....I will give it the co-ordinates..!!"

Sorcier began chanting.

Kairos lowered her head, clenched her teeth and glared at the fiery ball, her long dark hair blowing uncontrollably, as her eyes flashed the beautiful violet they had now changed to. The ball which was now making much headway, was only seconds away from colliding with the mountain.

"Kairos......NOW...!!" Sorcier roared.

Kairos then took a deep breath in, and blew out - and a huge gust of wind headed towards the beautiful coloured ball to stop it. The ball quickly slowed down, and eventually stopped as the gust of wind held it - right in front of them.

As it stopped it in its tracks, they all stared, bewildered at the most beautiful of colours, swirling in front of them; and the light from the huge ball reflected in their eyes.

Kairos then waved her right arm, round and round and round in circles, getting faster and faster, as she held the ball in mid-air with her left outstretched arm. Then, propelled all the energy she had spun, towards the ball and a huge blast of white light appeared. A large cyclone of wind completely circled the huge ball, keeping it safe for those few moments. At exactly the same time as Kairos held the cyclone, Sorcier closed his eyes, and opened his arms wide.

Suddenly, from behind him, a noise could be heard, like hundreds of high pitched screams. In a flash, a swarm of bats flew directly over the top of them, and straight to the ball of light. As they approached the bright light, they naturally turned away from it and veered to the left, and flew off, away from the mountain.
The coloured ball of light swiftly turned to follow the bats, and headed after them in the same direction.

So, with the bats guiding the coloured ball, and the wind keeping it on course — it was on its way — at last....

As the brightly coloured ball could be seen slowly fading away to the west, the orange-yellowy colour began to fade to a deeper darker aubergine colour, and then eventually = black. The large dark sphere, was now completely disguised, as it had travelled further into the distance towards the earth below.

The weather suddenly began to ease; and calm returned on the mountain top. The night sky had turned back to the beautiful starry sky it was, before the storm....

The storm that Kairos had conjured, had disguised the beginning of 'The Happening' and had steered the ball towards a quiet pretty meadow, at the other side of the stream, in an old Yorkshire farming village, completely un-noticed........
The Farmers and folk of the village, never knew of 'The Happening'. It was never seen or heard that night, because there was a huge summer storm that washed over the villages, the meadow, and the surrounding fields; that lasted all of a few minutes. No one would have seen or heard a dark shaped ball fall from the night sky, with a faint orange tail behind it. It fell so quickly, but so strangely silent,

that it landed on the ground very softly, making no noise at all.

When it got to the exact spot it was supposed to fall, the ball began to emit the most radiant colours, like hundreds of rainbows swirling around together. As the colours swirled around faster and faster, the ball began to burrow into the ground, making no sound. Down and down, and round and round it went, whirling faster and faster, with crimson sparks flying out of the ground. As the ball went deeper and deeper into the earth, the colours eventually faded, and the sparks became faint – until it had completely disappeared beneath the wet ground. Suddenly, the earth began closing up around the hole, and the ground was as it was before, like nothing had touched it.

The thunder and lightning had stopped, the wind had died down, and there was just a gentle breeze. Everything was just as it had been before – a calm, warm summers' night.

The time.......was 11:08pm.

Monday 1<sup>st</sup> August 1864 was the day the most powerful wizards came together and produced 'The Happening', thus creating a new world – a safe world, where only the great and good, and other kindly beings would live. The Magisters also foretold that exactly 100 years from that very date, a powerful one would be born to eventually stand tall amongst the new world.

However, if the entrance or doorway to the new world was found and entered by anyone who was of bitter heart, an evil being, a demon, or a Warlock; the world could collapse, and the safe haven would be gone.

This task had been carried out by the most powerful collective family, the Gata/Le fey family.
Sorcier Resoric Le Fey was a prominent young Wizard with great powers, who knew that his wife to be, Omega Mogea Gata was also a successful and prominent Mage and Sorceror. When they had married some years before, everyone rejoiced. Omega's younger sister Kairos Soriak Gata was a very beautiful Enchantress, who was admired by everyone, and was Omega's chosen Bridesmaid. Everyone came from far and wide to celebrate the union of the two most powerful families.

Shortly after the Eldritch Power was wielded, and the bright ball fell to earth that night; Omega went into early labour. There were doubts initially that she would not be able to follow the task in hand, but this she did, with great conviction. Sorcier had feared silently for his wife's health before the task, so had made her a powerful potion, to give his wife the strength she needed to help her wield the Eldritch Power that night, on the mountain top.

Her son, a second child for the couple, was born that very night, a month early, but he was a strong healthy boy. His name - was Therian Rathnie Le Fey. His older brother Rubec Bruce  Le Fey was to become his best friend, and ally, and they would grow up together, by each other's side.

# Chapter 27

# **<u>Families….</u>**

Ooshiya-Lion finished telling his story, and lit his pipe once more as he sat back in the chair.
A warm, sweet pear and cinnamon smell soon filled the room.

The story he had just told, had left everyone…Completely. Dumbstruck….!!!

They each in turn, looked at one another's faces, unable to speak. Then they turned to look at Mary, to see what she would say.

Mary scraped her chair back, stood up silently, and walked over to the window at the front of the cottage, and stared out of it for a few moments, with her arms folded around her sides, looking around. She couldn't really see much of the front garden that well, as it was getting very dark outside.

"I really need to get this front garden into some kind of order, it's getting so over-grown again" Mary suddenly spoke as she continued to stare.

Henry, Patsy, Wilbur and Elma, all looked at Ooshiya-Lion – waiting, with their mouths slightly open. Henry took a breath in, and was just about to speak, when he looked over at the old man, who shook his head slightly from side to side.

Ooshiya-Lion got up from his chair, and walked over to the window to join Mary.

"Mmmm….. Yes, I see what you mean – rather messy isn't it..?" he said, with one hand behind his back, with his fingers crossed, so the others could see, and the other hand holding his pipe to his mouth, as he rocked from heel to toe.

Mary slowly turned to him.

"Is that all you can say..?" she asked.

The old man looked quickly sideways at her, and then back out onto the garden, then said.

"Well, I completely agree with you. There's quite a lot that still needs doing; although we can achieve this much quicker – you and I together. We'll have it done in a flash..." he smiled as he looked out.

"It's me isn't it...?!!" Mary asked defiantly. "The story you've just told.....I'M the one who was born one hundred years from the storm that was created that night – wasn't I ...it's me – isn't it..??!!" She pointed to her chest, and then her face crumbled as she started to cry.

Ooshiya-Lion put his arm around her. "There, there..." he said soothingly.

Mary sobbed into the old man's coat.

"Why me...?!...why..?!.....what the hell can I do – I don't know ANYTHING...??!!" she cried as she drew her head away from Ooshiya-Lion's coat.

"Mary..." The old man put his hands on both her shoulders and turned her around to face him, and continued.

"Since Agnes touched your hands when you met her at the garden gate, she connected with you, and somehow that connection has made you remember everything from your past. But what it also did was – it brought your powers - your TRUE powers; back to you, but you obviously weren't aware of who you were then. Look at what's happened since then. The weather changes every time you become emotional – EVERY time. You blasted a hole in the wall without any force, and that was just your own anger. You travelled back in time, and saw things from your past that you didn't even know about; and you also – IN your time travel, pushed Agnes back into another timeline, and caused the lightning bolt which struck her face. I'm sure there have been other little things that you haven't even mentioned. These things have happened without any conjuring, any force; none at all. You Mary - are more powerful than you know. Please, come back and sit at the table, there's something else I need to tell you"

They walked back to the table, and sat down. Everyone else just stared and listened without saying a word.

Ooshiya-Lion continued, as he put his hand on top of Mary's on the table, and held it.

"Endor was asked by her Father - Magnus, to care for your Father when he was just 3 years old.
Your Father's parents – your Grandparents were….were killed, which left your Father an orphan…"

Mary gasped, as did the others….

"WHY….I mean…. how…….what happened…??! Oh my poor Dad…..!!"

 Mary trailed off as the old man continued speaking.

"I will explain what happened, but listen Mary. Your Father was an only child, and he HAD to be protected. He was left so vulnerable when his parents, Samuel and Abigail had died – at the hands of someone else, and he had no siblings. He would probably have had more sisters and brothers, if your Grandparents had lived, as they would have had more children no doubt; but it was so important for him to be protected, and there was no one else but Endor, who could do this"

"Magnus was distraught at losing his only son, Samuel – your Grandfather, AND of course, your Grandmother, Abigail; so Endor pledged her life to raising your Father until he was of an age to marry. Agnes and HER Grandparents, the Bishops, moved to Transylvania to flee"

"It was then that it was decided, by word of The Magisters, that when Eldon grew up, he would lead a normal life as possible, and to be kept away from Agnes and her family, and from them ever knowing anything about his whereabouts, but the cottage still had to be protected. There was great danger to your Father and this house. Also….." Ooshiya-Lion stood up at this point, and re-lit his pipe, and continued as he walked around the table.

"....when The Magisters foretold everything that was to happen - and the date in question in the future...which was the 1<sup>st</sup> August 1964 – your Birth date.....they knew that this would be the date that a powerful one would be born – you....Yes, Mary, it IS you...." ...and he looked at her and nodded.

"...they also knew that powerful families would marry into the Le Fey's, like the Bishops, and like the Fallswood's etc. All of these people Mary - your ancestors, going back in time, would eventually, down the ancestral line, culminate to a point, in the future, and bring forth such a strong, but extremely powerful individual being born, that could potentially have become SO strong, and maybe even indestructible, and more powerful than any other Witch, Sorcerer, Mage, Enchantress etc., that The Magisters chose for your Father to meet your Mother – Sarah. A normal, and non-magical, pretty young woman. This union between your Mother and Father would dispel any of the fear of a 'too' powerful one being born, and would bring about a calmer, less challenging, but still a very strong individual within the magical world. They would be strong, fair, kind, caring, funny, not afraid, and brave of heart, but would still have many traits of their ancestors, but with a small interjection of a non-witch parent. This is what was decided Mary; and these are all the qualities that you possess......"

He stopped talking for a moment, to allow Mary to absorb everything he had said.

"It was all meant to happen, albeit a few things on the way which weren't expected...."

"Which was what...??" Mary asked.

"Well, you going back in time in your sleep/dream state, and pushing Agnes into another timeline, and also causing the storm when Endor and Agnes were fighting at the gate, which in turn caused Agnes's scar. It was thought that Endor had either killed her or made her vanish somewhere"

"So where did Agnes 'go'...??" Mary asked, rather quizzically.

"That, we are not quite sure of. She was missing – presumed dead for 30 years, by some; but some of us believed her to be very much alive, and so have been waiting for her return. She disappeared on the night you were born, and has recently turned up since you arrived…!!"

Suddenly, Ooshiya-Lion's faithful staff Bam Bam materialized.

"Ah, my trusted friend, what have you found…??" the old man asked.

As the two seemed to be having a conversation, Mary, for the first time looked at her friends, who had all stayed quiet, until Elma, stepped forward and spoke.

"Mary…" he said, rather sheepishly. "Whatever happens, whatever you have to do, or wherever you have to go – and…..and I….I know I can speak for all of us" and he turned around to look at the rest of them…… "We will go with you, help you – anything. If you need us, we'll be here…."

He walked over to Mary, and she put her hand out. Elma climbed onto her hand, and she brought him up to her face. With tears in her eyes, she said.

"You know Elma, out there somewhere, there is one lady Daddy Long Legs, who doesn't know it yet, but she is going to become one lucky spider, when she meets you. You are so funny, caring, and very charming, and you have just made me smile" and she kissed him lightly on his cheek.

It took Elma all of 3 seconds before he did a back flip from her hand, and went into a perfect spider roll onto the table, whilst shouting "Yessss…!!" and punched his fist in the air.

It certainly broke the silence as everyone laughed at him, as usual.

Then they all started talking at once about the story the old man had just told, as Henry came up to Mary and said.

"Mary, please try not to worry. Now you know - more than ever who you are, you have nothing to fear - really. You have Ooshiya-Lion by your side to guide you; and like Elma's just said, all of us will be here to help and support you, no matter what it is"

Mary was just about to talk back to Henry, when
Ooshiya-Lion suddenly spoke up.

"Apologies for interrupting, but I have just been made aware of a little something to which I have to attend to, with Bam Bam. So, for the time being, I have to bid you all farewell – I need to go out for a while"

With that, he picked up Bam Bam, covered his mane with his hat, slung his bags over his shoulders and headed for the door, then stopped, and turned around.

"Oh…. Mary…. by the way; while I'm gone, you HAVE to try and open that door – somehow……you'll be fine. Got to dash…."

……and with that, he was gone……

# Chapter 28

## **<u>In the Meadow</u>**

Mary went to bed that night, with her head full of fear, shock, and a feeling of complete bewilderment. The stories that Ooshiya-Lion had told, were still sinking in. She had learnt even more about her distant relatives, and the sacrifices they had given, and it completely over-whelmed her with the courage they had displayed, and the lengths they had gone to.

She felt very vulnerable and alone all of a sudden.

She wondered that if she had just stayed in the city, would any of this have happened..?...but she knew somewhere deep down inside - that this was all meant to be.

Imagine – her whole life mapped out for her, and she never even knew….but did she…? Her Father had protected her so well. Everything was making sense now – everything; but what about Jenny….?? What happened to Jenny, and why did she disappear..?? Tears came to her eyes. She missed James – so much. What was HE going to think about all of this…? He might not even want her anymore…!

So many questions….

She cried and cried, as she turned over in her bed.

"Oh Dad, Mum, please just try and help me, and guide me - anything, I just need some help. I don't know what to do…!!"

Mary cried herself to sleep eventually – and she dreamt an awful lot…..or did she…?

Saturday August 1st 1834

A crow flew into a nearby copse of trees, and squawked loudly, as the leaves above rustled. Then, after a few moments, the crow flew out of the tree, and down onto the ground below – possibly looking for worms, and insects.

Suddenly from the behind the small group of trees, a large Dragon walked forward. He was a thick set Dragon, about 10 feet tall, and had reddish/purplish scales, with a tiny hint of gold, and indigo coloured eyes.
As the dappled sunlight hit his face, he stopped, tilted his head up towards the sun, and closed his eyes, feeling the warmth on his scales. He slowly walked out of the small copse and into the bright sunshine, and then he lay down on the grass. He heaved a big sigh, smiled slightly, and seemed very peaceful.

After a long rest, he opened his eyes, and looked around at the fields and meadows in the sunshine. He looked behind him at the small thicket of trees, and felt like he was been watched.

A squirrel darted up a nearby tree.

The Dragon realised he was quite hungry. He flew off into the distance, towards an area of high ground, where there were fells, and a group of very tall hills that were quite rocky. He found a very big opening in-between two large rocks; and climbed inside.

It was a small cave. He explored the dwelling and thought it perfect for him. He then flew out over the hills and all around a huge meadow down below, looking for food. He came back to his cave with lots of apples, corn and grass. After his feast, he lay down on a bed of hay that he had also collected whilst out, and slept again.

It was late afternoon, early evening when he awoke, and looked down from his cave at the beautiful landscape. As he scoured the land, he suddenly saw something bright, like a large flash appear on the grass way, way down, not far from the little copse of trees. He set off and flew down towards the spot to find out what it was. When he got there, he saw that there was a person on the grass, right where he had seen the flash of light. An older woman lay with her eyes shut, but there was a huge, fresh cut down her face, which was bleeding.

The Dragon pulled the woman towards the trees, to take a closer look. The old woman began to mutter, as she was trying to get up, as she started to slowly open her eyes.

"Be still woman" the Dragon said. "Who are you, and what is your name..??" he asked, as her eyes opened fully and she saw the Dragon standing right over her.

She shielded her face with her arm in fright, as if blocking out a bright light. The woman was clearly in shock, and completely bewildered. Blood was now oozing from the large wound on her face. The Dragon raised his right fore-claw, and pointed one of his talons so close to the woman's face, that she fainted. The Dragon muttered some words, and suddenly the wound on the woman's face slowly began to close and threads began to stitch the wound up.

The Dragon sat looking at the woman and was wondering.

"Mmmmmmm...." He said to himself.

Presently, the woman 'came to' and looked straight at the Dragon.

"Tell me your name and who you are, or I will open that wound back up on your face..!" The Dragon said without any care.

The woman sat up, feeling much better, and touched her face.

"You have magic..?" she said.

"Your Name...!!" the Dragon said, now much louder.

The woman looked away, as if thinking; then turned back to the Dragon and said.

"I...I..don't....I don't know. I don't know who I am..."

She got to her feet, and held herself steady as she leaned against a tree.

"Where are you from...??" He asked her, giving her a sly look.

"From...?? Well I'm from here aren't I..? Yes, yes I think I am....." she answered as she looked around.

The Dragon was getting a little bored.

"Who are your family, your parents, siblings, anything..?!" he asked.

Slow realisation began to tell on the woman's face, as her eyes widened, and then looked at the Dragon. He slowly rose, keeping his eyes on her, as he knew she had just remembered something.

"Well...?" he asked impatiently, as he then looked more closely at the clothes she was wearing. His eyes narrowed a little.

"Bishop...!" she said loudly. "At least I THINK that's my name....or is it...??

The Dragon looked at her contemptuously.
"Your parents....are they called Bishop, or is that YOUR name...?

The woman thought....

"Yes..!!... I mean no..! Oh why can't I remember..?!" she answered frustratingly.

"Who gave you that wound on your face...?" He asked slowly. "That was no accident..." He stared at her reaction.

The woman touched her face and winced at the pain.
Then, her eyes opened wide, and she shot a quick look towards the Dragon.

"I...I...I don't know.....I can't remember anything" she answered. "Anyway, who are you, great beast, who has tended to my wound..?"

"My name...is Beruc" he answered, abruptly.

Beruc rose.

"It is dusk, you must rest here. I will be back in the morning".

Without another moment, he flew off towards the high hills, and back to his cave.

# Chapter 29

# <u>Magic, and......The Meet</u>

The next morning, Mary woke with a headache. The dream she had the night before about Agnes and a Dragon felt so, so real – as if she had been there, witnessing the whole thing...!!

As she made some toast and tea, she looked over at the door, wondering how she was going to open it. The wooden key she had been sent was of no use, as there wasn't even a lock, or a handle. Her thoughts went straight back to the dream. If the dream was real, then Agnes had travelled back in time after the argument with Endor - and she had encountered a Dragon. 'A Dragon..?' Mary whispered to herself.

Then, the year that the dream happened suddenly popped into her head. She said the year out loud to herself.

"1834.......1834..??! Why so far back..?!" She closed her eyes momentarily, as if trying to re-live the dream again. She couldn't remember seeing the cottage – nothing, just the meadow and hills and a small group of trees.

She walked over to the door.

"Why won't you open...? What do I have to do...?!" She said out loud.

Maybe it was a certain word or a special name that she had to say, or did she have to press something on the door.
She just stood, staring at it. It was so beautiful. She laid both her hands upon it, and instantly, it began to glow the same red colour as before, like it was coming to life again.

"Open" Mary said. Nothing happened.
"Open PLEASE....?" Still - nothing.

She then thought that if she was a Witch, then maybe she should try and do 'some magic'

"O P E N  S E S A M E..!" and she waved her hands in a funny kind of way that really looked like she didn't know what she was doing. Some faint sparks came from Mary's fingers, but just fizzled out, and dropped onto the floor. She was shocked, but quite happy that she produced a hint of sparks at least.
She then began to say names of the people who had lived there, even saying her own name. She pushed and pulled and nudged the door, and pressed lots of the knobbly carved wood, waved her hands about – but nothing.

There was a little tap at the back door. Mary walked over and opened it, and there was Ooshiya-Lion.

"Ah, I smell toast…!! He said brightly, and he walked through into the kitchen, smiling.
He saw Mary's tired face.

"Any luck…??" he asked, and nodded towards the door.

"Nope……" Mary answered flatly. "Nothing works, I've tried everything"

"Well, you have to make this your priority. Keep thinking. We only have until your Birthday Mary"

Mary looked up at the old man as if to ask why, but didn't open her mouth to speak. She was just too tired.

Ooshiya-Lion took a long look at Mary.

"Just to remind you of the importance of this – as soon as you turn 30 Mary, the protection that was created all those years ago, and put over this cottage will be no more. All of Endor's spells will be gone. The sacrifices that your ancestors made - will be in vain. Agnes will be able to freely walk into this cottage, take over the ownership, probably kill you, and find a way behind that door. Then lord knows what will happen…"

As Mary was listening to Ooshiya-Lion, something inside her – a feeling, a very strong feeling, began to surge through her body. As he spoke, she began to think about all of her family members and what they had gone through to protect the legacy that was bestowed upon them, to save this cottage; what they had sacrificed, what they had gone through. Some of them had died through the greed of others – just because they were protecting this cottage, which was now Mary's. She was the last in line, and all hope was pinned on HER…!! This was her home, and she wasn't about to let anyone take it from underneath her – especially Agnes Le Fey….!!!

She felt her anger rising; and a very strong power surge seared through her whole body. She looked at her hands and they were trembling.

"What's happening to me….??!!!!" She shouted.

"Mary…?!!" Ooshiya-Lion raised his voice.
"You can control this…!!"

"How…??!!" Mary's hair raised up like it was caught in a strong gust of wind. Her eyes went completely white, as did her face.

Outside, a huge storm had erupted overhead, with lashing rain against the windows, black clouds filled the sky, and then a flash of light lit up the sky, which was immediately followed by a crash of thunder right overhead..
All the teacups and tea plates in the cupboards, and every bit of cutlery in the drawers were rattling loudly. The back windows flew open, and a huge gust of wind blew in.

Ooshiya-Lion had to hold onto the table as the force of the wind would have hurled him to the back of the wall. Mary kept her footing with her arms by her side, and her palms upturned.
"Mary, try and keep your anger contained…!!!" Ooshiya-Lion shouted loudly over the sound of the wind and the storm, as he shielded himself.

Vases and pots were now lifting in the air, and swirling around the room. The drawers had opened, and all the knives, forks and spoons lifted in the air, and were now going round and around with the rest of the pots and pans that had now joined them. Ooshiya-Lion had to keep ducking out of the way.

Mary took a deep breath in, as she closed her eyes. When she opened them again, her eyes had turned from being completely white, to the green/hazel colour they were before; and now to a pale yellow green. Her dark mousy brown hair colour had changed to nearly black. She suddenly started laughing, as she threw her head back, like she was enjoying the madness. She was laughing and laughing wildly….!!

"MARY….!!! Think about your Mother and Father. Think about James….!!! The old man shouted.

He was just about to intervene, when Mary looked down at her hands. She realised swiftly that all the energy that was emitting from her finger tips could be used……on HER….!! She curled her fingers up towards her, and then with a force like she was resisting a magnet, she plunged her hands towards her stomach. All the energy was released back into her body. She started jolting like she was having an electric shock. Just at that moment Ooshiya-Lion took his wand from his coat, and against the swirling storm in the house, he pointed his wand at Mary and shouted.

"PROHIBERE…!!"

Mary fell to the floor, but as she was falling, Bam Bam flew towards her in a flash, and broke her fall as she suddenly went into slow motion. He laid her gently on the stone floor. All the swirling pots, pans, cups, saucers and the cutlery, all went into a suspended animation. They were all hovering in the air.

The storm immediately died down, and went as quickly as it came, and everything turned back to how it was before. Mary was motionless on the stone floor still in her pyjamas.

"Bam Bam – the house..!" Ooshiya-Lion gestured to his friend, to put everything back in its place, to which he did, immediately.

Ooshiya-Lion looked quickly over at Bam Bam. He had never ever seen his trusty staff do anything like that before, without a command. He had never seen it save a human before, or go to the need of another. This was truly something that Ooshiya-Lion knew was very special. Thankfully, because of Bam Bam's actions, Mary had landed as gently as a feather. She was breathing at least – and just stunned.

What the old man had just witnessed, he had never seen before.

Mary had become so angry and resentful of Agnes, but yet so emotional for her family, and what they had put themselves through – people that she had never known about before, and didn't know any of them had ever existed, but had only recently become aware of. Along with a show of love, devotion and a sense of loyalty, and a mixture of anger and resentment and fright, she had caused such a powerful surge of great strength.

Ooshiya-Lion was quite over-whelmed.

"Mary – you're alright" he said gently, as Mary opened her eyes.

Bam Bam swiftly came over to her side, and bent over her. The old man realised that his trusty staff knew that he was in the presence of someone very powerful, and he knew that Bam Bam would always protect her….always.

"Well done my friend…." Ooshiya-Lion spoke softly as he patted Bam Bam.

Not too far away, in a barn, an old woman was sat on the floor, underneath the kitchen table - shaking.

"Remind you of anything…??" Beruc asked sarcastically, as he dipped his head down to look at Agnes sat on the floor, clutching her knees up to her chest. He was grinning.

As he lifted his head back up, he continued…

"I wonder why we have had a sudden storm in the middle of summer Agnes – why do YOU think….mmmmm……any ideas…??"
Without waiting for Agnes to reply, he carried on.

"Well - let me tell you what I think. I think…..that…..let me see….. I think that Mary seems to be gaining her 'wings' so to speak; but it seems to me that she is getting stronger and stronger, day by day. Oh Agnes, if I were you, I would watch my back…." Then he lowered his voice as he bent his head back down, where his eyes met Agnes's frightened ones. "I mean, you never know who is behind you…

B O O…!!!" Agnes jumped and hit her head on the underside of the table, as Beruc laughed and laughed.

With that, she scrambled out from under the table and confronted the Dragon.

"I'm NOT afraid of a child…!! How dare you – do you know who you're even talking to…??!!"

"Unfortunately – yes…I do; but she's not a child is she. She's a fine young Witch, even a Mage, probably a Sorceror, maybe even all 3…or MORE, who knows..?!! One thing's for certain……she's not afraid of YOU…!!"

Agnes turned to Beruc, and said, rather confidently.

"Have you forgotten? It's her Birthday soon; and I know that my sister put a spell on that cottage to protect it for many years. Well now I know it was 30 years, because you told me…HA..!! So when that time comes, the spells will be gone, and I can just walk into that cottage, and everything…..everything will be MINE…!! She is no match for me…!!"

"You're not who you used to be Agnes. You have spent all these years living in another time – your strength has waned…be very, very careful"

Agnes snarled at Beruc.
Beruc moved a little closer to Agnes and said.

"The only reason you're here, is because I was the only one who was able to bring you back, and the only reason I brought you back is that….and again – let me remind you of our wager….is because I want my share as well. THAT was the deal…. 50/50….that was what you said, remember…?? We wait, and we do this together…"

Back at the cottage, Ooshiya-Lion had got Mary over to the table and she was sat, looking bewildered.

"What just happened..??" she asked.

"What I have just witnessed Mary, I can't say that I have ever seen before, but what I know - is that you are ready"

"Ready....?? I don't quite understand, but I do 'feel' different"

"Well you 'look' different as well – here" and he passed Mary a mirror.

As she held the mirror, she saw her own face, but she looked somehow stronger, bolder even; and her black hair, her dark eyebrows and her paler coloured eyes shocked her.

"Mary, I believe that you could do most anything now. The power that you emitted from your emotions, and then somehow in that moment, you gave that energy back to yourself....well, it could have killed you, but it didn't, it has definitely made you very powerful. I was becoming a little worried, that with only a short time until the spells were lifted, that you would not be quite ready. Now I know that this was meant to happen. It all makes sense to me now. I am honoured to be in your presence" and Ooshiya-Lion bowed his head.

"What are you doing, why are you bowing...??" At that moment, Bam Bam slid across the floor silently. His crooked wooden frame was old and gnarled, but he stood up as straight as he could, and then bowed the top of his head to Mary. He then spoke.

"I am also very honoured to be in your presence, and I will serve you and be your trusted servant as long as you need me"

"You talk...??!"

"Mary, he has always spoken, but you could never hear him. Now you can. We are both very privileged to be serving you" and he lowered his gaze to the ground.

Mary didn't know what to say, and felt a little awkward, so she ended up saying...

"Look, I…I'm really hungry. I know I had toast and tea a bit ago, but I could really eat a bowl of porridge with some treacle and cream. I feel like I need some sugar…"
She got up to go to the cupboard, but felt a bit of a rush to her head.

The old man urged her to sit down.

"You don't have to make it yourself you know"

"Well I want to, and I don't want you to be my servant either Ooshiya-Lion"
She said defiantly.

"What I mean is……just 'make it happen'. If you want something – think of it, and with a swish of your hand, it will be there – try it"
He said, smiling.
Mary did exactly that, (a little bit theatrically though)……..and hey presto – there it was…!!

"That looks exceedingly delicious..!" the old man said sniffing the air.

"Would you like some..??" Mary asked – laughing, as she gestured towards the table, and conjured another bowl of hot, creamy porridge, with a sticky swirl of treacle.

"Don't mind if I do..!" he said.

They both laughed as they heartily tucked into their porridge.


## 24 hours earlier.

When Bam Bam had left the cottage that late afternoon on the old man's instructions, Ooshiya-Lion had sent him on a small mission.

As the old man's trusty staff materialized on a quiet country lane, he silently hovered a few inches from the ground and glided along, until he reached a barn.

He could hear voices coming from inside the barn, and they were raised voices. One was a man's deep voice and the other was an older woman's.

As Bam Bam listened, he picked up the conversation. When he had heard enough, he used the top of his head and tapped on the door. Then he made himself invisible; so when the woman opened the door, he could not be seen by her, but he could see right into the barn.
As the woman quickly looked around outside before closing the door, this had given the Dragon enough time to bring his head forward from the darkness of the barn into the light, so that Bam Bam could see him. The Dragon looked straight ahead to where Bam Bam was standing....and nodded his head. Bam Bam returned with a quick nod, and then the Dragon drew back against the wall.

On his return to the cottage, he relayed the information to Ooshiya-Lion. The old man, put his coat and hat on immediately, picked up his bags, took Bam Bam – and left, telling Mary and the others he had to go somewhere, and urged Mary to try and open the door somehow.

After Agnes had opened the door cautiously, then realised there was no one there, she quickly closed the door behind her, and then looked over her shoulder as she walked back into the room, seeming to be worried.

"Well...??" Beruc asked, as he stepped forward into the light.

"There was no one there" Agnes answered quickly.

"But SOME one....or some THING knocked, we both heard it..... Who knows of you being here..?!" quizzed the Dragon.

"No one knows I am here, do you think I'm stupid...?!!" she snapped.

Beruc began to make his way towards the door.

"I'm going outside to have a look around - stay here. Do not open the door again, and do not look out of the windows"

"How long will you be..??"Agnes asked, seeming a little unsettled.

"Do I detect a little fear in you Agnes..?" Beruc teased.

"Don't be an idiot…!! I'm not frightened of anyone…..!"

Beruc had vanished before Agnes could say anymore.

Further on past the barn, and going towards the other side of the meadow, Beruc lay low….and waited….
Presently an old man could be seen walking down the lane. He passed the barn on his left, and looked as he saw low candle light flickering from inside. He carried on for a while, until he came upon a clearing. The moon was out now and casting some light, so he could see. He stopped at a large rock formation, and waited a few moments. The large rock formation began to move. It was Beruc.

The Dragon uncurled himself, and stood up to his full height. The old man was startled and put his hand on his chest.

The Dragon spoke.

"So – you came…??"

The old man answered with a question.

"What is your name…??" he asked, as he looked closely into the Dragon's eyes.

"Beruc" the Dragon answered.

After a few seconds and with a hearty laugh, the old man patted the Dragon's side, laughed and said.

"Of course it is....!"

"What is YOUR name..?" Beruc returned the question.

"Ooshiya-Lion....as if you didn't know...!!"

Beruc laughed. "It's good to see you my old friend – formalities over"

"Yes, it's been a long time" Ooshiya-Lion said.
"A long time...."

"How are you Beruc, how are you feeling...?" the old man asked, after a few moments.

The Dragon shifted about, grunted, and said.

"I've had better days...... You..??"

"Oh I'm quite well – thank you...."

They both looked around in the moonlight.

"How is Agnes...?" Ooshiya-Lion asked.

"She's slow. She's lost so much being away for all this time; which has been a good thing, but she's determined, so we'll see" Beruc said.

"Bam Bam tells me that Agnes didn't know Mary was a Le Fey, and she was shocked to hear that she was the daughter of Eldon & Sarah"

"She had no idea at all – she was VERY shocked" Beruc answered; then continued.

"She feels there is anger in Mary, and wants an alliance"

"She does…?? What about what YOU want from the cottage..?" Ooshiya-Lion asked, as he looked upon Beruc's scaly head.

"Mmmmmm…." The Dragon smiled, and then said.

"….So - the storm earlier, obviously that was Mary…? She's becoming stronger"

"Yes….. I have a few concerns…." Ooshiya-Lion said, rather sceptically.

"Oh…?? Like what – anything I need to know..??"

He turned to look at Beruc. "She's a time traveller…"

The Dragon showed great interest.
"A time traveller….?? Ha ha ha….. I have some competition!"

"Call it what you will, but she shows great strength – she's stronger than she knows; and I have witnessed things I haven't seen in a long time – or ever…"

"Really…..?? Now I AM intrigued. I cannot wait to meet her…… 'properly' of course"

Ooshiya-Lion changed the subject.
"What of Agnes..??"

"Well, I am keeping her where she needs to be – for now"

"Good" said the old man. "I trust your judgement my old friend. It's good to see you"

The old man started to walk away.
"I must leave now; there is still a lot to do. We will speak soon – very soon" and Ooshiya-Lion put his hand up to wave.

"Why are you walking, why not just 'get to where you're going'..??" Beruc said.

"I LIKE walking" and with that, Ooshiya-Lion disappeared into the darkness, as Beruc heard his fading footsteps.

# Chapter 30

## **<u>Trust in me</u>**

Back at the cottage, whilst eating their porridge, Mary told Ooshiya-Lion that she'd had another 'dream' the night before. The old man looked concerned, and said.

"Do you think it WAS a dream Mary, or do you think you were 'there'..?"

"I'm not really sure" she answered… "....but I saw everything - VERY clearly; and do you know what the year was…? It was 1834…."

"1834…??" he repeated.

"Yes, and don't ask me how I know, I just do – AND I know that's where Agnes went. She went back in time to 1834"

Ooshiya-Lion put his spoon down.
"Tell me what you know" he asked gravely.

Mary told him about the whole dream, and how Agnes had landed on the meadow in a flash of light, with the open wound on her face. Then she told him she saw a Dragon, flying down from the hills in the distance, and who tended to Agnes's wound. Ooshiya-Lion asked her to tell him what the Dragon looked like, and Mary gave the old man the exact description - of Beruc.

"….and what happened after that..?" he asked.

"Agnes couldn't remember her name, well not at first anyway. Then he asked her lots of questions, and wanted to know who had caused the wound to her face, but she couldn't remember"

"This is so very interesting Mary….Tell me more"

Well, it was really strange because as soon as she told him what she thought her surname was, he left her, and said he would be back in the morning........and then I woke up"

Ooshiya-Lion was left wondering..... The next minute, Henry and Patsy flew in through the window.

The storm that had happened from Mary's emotional outburst, had caused such a mess in the garden; that a lot of the soil had become misplaced, some of the flowers had been washed away, and there were huge puddles. Even some of their homes had been ruined. Mary was distraught on hearing this. Henry told her that Wilbur and Patsy had to 'air lift' some of the others to safety. Mary asked how the children were, and everyone else. All were safe, he said, but there was such a lot to do. They both looked exhausted.

"Ok, I'll get ready, and come out as soon as I can..!"

"....But...but Mary, we simply must...." The old man started to say, but Mary rushed off upstairs to get changed, shouting.

"I won't be long...!"

When she came downstairs, Ooshiya-Lion told her that this was a perfect opportunity to use her magic to put the garden back to what it was like before the storm, without picking up a spade, just to get her used to it. He also said that they could tackle the front garden as well; it was important that she learn as much as she can.

"Oh yes, I never thought of that..! Yes, let's do that, but first – I must just go and see everyone, and make sure they're all ok. Won't be long...!"

Mary met Henry, Patsy and Wilbur in the back garden, over by Tree Stump Corner.

"Mary, your hair, and your eyes, you look different" Patsy said.

Henry asked.
"What happened in there...?? He looked really concerned.

Mary told them everything. When she finished, she looked at them, and said.

"What's wrong…?? I'm sensing that something is wrong. What's happened…..and where's Elma..?"

All three of them looked at each other, and then Henry spoke.

"Mary, we wanted to speak to you on your own. The garden isn't too bad actually after the storm; we elaborated a bit, just to get you out here. There's something we need to tell you"

"What is it….tell me…?!"

"Well, it's Elma that needs to tell you. He's just sleeping at the minute; he had a very….erm…long night last night. Wilbur, go and fetch Elma"

Wilbur flew off, and Henry and Patsy looked down at their feet, and looked a little awkward, which left Mary feeling really concerned. Wilbur came back, he was carrying Elma.

"Elma, what's happened, are you alright..?!" Mary waited for him to reply.

Elma looked very, very tired…

"…Erm, well…." He looked at Henry, and Henry nodded. Elma continued. "…well last night, when we were all in the kitchen; I noticed that Ooshiya-Lion whispered to Bam Bam, and then he disappeared" Mary nodded, and agreed.
"….then, when Bam Bam came back, they spoke together for a little while, and I was watching them, closely, and Ooshiya-Lion looked concerned. Then, he suddenly got up, do you remember…??...and he said he had to go….."

"Yeah….I remember – why…??" she said.
"You tell her Henry, I can't…." Elma was visibly upset.

Henry stepped forward and cleared his throat.

"…Ahem…. Mary……erm… Elma followed Ooshiya-Lion last night when he left the cottage. He stayed in the shadows, as he followed the old man up the lane, and then he turned off onto a small lane, and walked past a barn, which he noticed had candlelight on inside. He then... erm....stopped; as if waiting for someone. What Elma witnessed next has really frightened and worried him - and us"

Mary didn't like Henry's grave face.

"Just say it Henry" Then she looked at Elma. "Elma what did you see....?!"

Elma again looked at Henry, and lowered his head.
Henry took a deep breath, and spoke.

"Mary, Ooshiya-Lion isn't who you think he is"

Mary looked at first one, then the other, completely puzzled. Patsy started to cry.

Henry continued.

"He...err.... He....was meeting with.....with....someone.
.....erm...well....someTHING....It was....a...err...a Dragon..."

Mary's hand came up to her mouth, in shock. She was looking wildly around her. The she looked at Elma.

"Elma, did the Dragon have reddish/purplish scales with a hint of gold, and indigo coloured eyes...??!"

"...Errrrm..." Elma looked away briefly, as he thought back. ".....well it was getting quite dark by then, but yes, I got a pretty good look at him. Yeah, I'd say that's right...!"

Mary, how do you know this..?!" Henry asked.

"I had a dream last night, and that very same Dragon was in my dream...but I'm more concerned that the Dragon is HERE...... because my dream was in 1834...!!.....and why is Ooshiya-Lion talking to him...??!! ...and when he came back from this visit with the Dragon, why didn't he tell me about him, and why is it a secret....???"

"Are you going to ask him…??" Henry asked.

"Mmmmmm…. No. Not yet. Elma, did you say you saw lights on in the barn that you passed..?? That must be the barn that belongs to this cottage that Ooshiya-Lion was telling me about. I had no idea of that at all….but who could possibly be staying there, if there are lights on….??" Mary looked at her friends.

"AGNES…!!" they all said together.

"How dare she…?!!" Mary felt so angry, very quickly. "This is MY house, and that is MY barn…!! No, no, I'm not going to get angry, I HAVE to learn to control this…calm down Mary" she said to herself as she closed her eyes and took a few deep breaths in and out.

"Right, leave this with me. Elma, thank you so much for trying to be vigilant, and following Ooshiya-Lion all that way, you must be so tired"

The next few days were spent mainly with Ooshiya-Lion, and learning how to cast spells properly, perform magic, conjure, do disappearing spells, the art of cosmology and astronomy etc. he wanted her to know the basics, and as much as he could possibly teach her. Mary learnt fast – it was in her blood after all – and she was becoming a very established Witch. There was still an awful lot for her to learn, but Ooshiya-Lion was more than impressed.
Mary watched him closely. Sometimes he would go out for a walk on the meadow with Bam Bam, and she wondered.

The old man never mentioned the Dragon at all….but, Mary did.

"So, who do you think the Dragon was in my dream the other night …?? You haven't mentioned him at all. I find that odd"

"The main thing Mary, is that Agnes went to another time line, and there she stayed until recently. The Dragon is of no consequence. Whether she came upon him by accident, or not – who knows…?? She was stuck there for a reason, and that reason was to stop her meddling here for all those years. Out of sight is out of mind. Everything will become clear, once we safely get passed that door"

"WE…??" questioned Mary. "I thought I was the one that was supposed to be opening the door, and finding out what was behind it; and possibly venturing to somewhere that's supposed to be my 'destiny'…"

"I am here to make sure you do that at the right time. Something could get in the way, and prevent you from opening that door. With Agnes being back, who knows who she may have helping her"

"Mmmm….." Mary answered.

Over the next few days that Mary had to herself, she would walk over to the door many times, and stand and stare at it, and thinking, what could it possibly be that would make the door open. She stared at its beauty, and all the intricate carvings – wondering, feeling nervous, but much bolder than before, and not as frightened.

She knew the door seemed to sense her feelings as she spoke out loud. She knew it was listening to her. She even tried some of the magic Ooshiya-Lion had shown her – but still, nothing.

Then, one morning, two days before Mary's Birthday; which was a particularly hot one already; she was stood in front of the door, staring. As she continued to stare, her mouth opened, and she suddenly spoke words out loud, without even thinking.

"Oh great and beautiful door that you are,
Do tell me your secret, so intriguing and bizarre.
Why you stood shrouded for many a year,
…and your beauty, it does beguile me, but makes me shed a tear.

For I struggle to work the magic, that you so secretly hide,
…and time is running out, and I cannot abide;
To fall by the wayside, and feel so bereft,

…and not be fitting enough, to carry my quest.

Is it a name I have to give you, or a song you wish me to sing?
If it's a task - then I will do it, or is it a gift you wish me to bring?

Time is nearly nigh, and I implore you with my heart,
For I truly need your help, as there is no one — and I stand apart.

I ask you, and I beseech you, as I beg on bended knee.
Oh great and beautiful door that you are — please, can you hear my plea…..??"

As the words left Mary's mouth, she was astonished. She was always very articulate and had written lots of poetry, but these words just came out of nowhere, without even knowing that she was even going to speak…!

She gasped, as she stepped back, for suddenly, the door began to glow the vibrant red that ran through all the wooded grain; but this time, the colour gold appeared, and shone so brightly - and the carved wooded figures started to move and began to dance around with much gaiety, to a tiny flute that she could hear somewhere in the distance.

Then, Mary heard a voice — a young woman's voice, a voice she thought sounded familiar, but somehow not. It was very echoey, but very clear…..
It said…..

"I hear you and I see you, as I have done all the while.
I know of you, and I befriend you, and I watch you, as I smile.

Your resilience and your strength; have shown who you are to me;
…and I am humbled, as are you, dear Mary — and I have listened to your plea.

In answer to your question; I am crafted from a Fallswood tree.

A fine old oak, that grew amongst, your kin-folk – and without a key.

A door that has never been opened – but has stood; and waited for you....
....and only you can open this door..... a 'Le Fey' whose heart is so true.

Do not cry, you are not alone, and you have never stood apart.
For you have been watched and loved by those, who hold you dearest in their hearts.

You are ready dear Mary, to open this door, but the timing has to be right;
...and it will always be here for you to open many times, for shelter, and for flight.

I do not need much, or any of those things that you ask,
...my request is very small, so I'll not encumber.

The artefact you need to open this door....
......takes no thinking, and is simply – a number......


Mary's shock at hearing the woman's voice, and especially the last line, sent her head into a spin.
"A number, what number...where do I even start..??" Immediately, she thought of her birth date, the 1st August. She thought of her parents birth dates, the date she got the keys to the cottage, her age....was it one of those..??


Mary's shock was suddenly broken by Wilbur shouting her name, as he nearly fell through the window.

"Mary, Mary, quick.... Henry has sent me to get you – it's the tree...!!

Mary was still in a bit of a daze.

"Wilbur...?!! You made me jump out of my skin then...! What's going on...?!"

"Sorry, but you have to come quick…!"
Mary hurriedly went out of the back door and quickly followed Wilbur as he flew quite fast to the back of the garden. Henry had sent Wilbur, as now his wing was completely back to normal; he was much faster than Henry.

When they got to Tree Stump Corner, there was quite a gathering. As Mary approached, her pace slowed down, as she looked at what was in front of her.

The fir tree that Mary had asked James to save, and cut down to a small tree stump, hadn't really done anything by way of growing…….. but - stood in front of her, was a tall, very green, and quite beautiful fir tree, that looked about 6ft tall….!

"Oh…my…goodness…me……" Mary said very slowly, as she walked right up to the tree, which was standing rather proud, as it once probably had done years before.

"It's obviously happened over night Mary!" Henry said to her.

Mary was aghast. She walked around it, and bent down to the foot of the tree, just to make sure that it wasn't a completely new one that someone might have just 'put there'; but there she could see the old stumpy bit that James had cut. A new trunk had grown from it, and then lots of new branches, and she could smell the fresh scent of the pine.
Mary gently touched the tree branches - and immediately she felt a sudden connection, as a strong breeze blew up in front of her face, making her hair lift up, which made her step back.

A voice suddenly spoke up, and broke the silence.

"Ah, what a fine specimen…. I wondered if anything may happen with this little tree. I'm so glad you chose to save it Mary" Ooshiya-Lion had stepped forward. No one had seen him arrive, as they were all looking at the tree.

"Why has it grown so big overnight..? I don't understand…" Mary asked him.

"Well" he said gratifyingly. "I'm very glad indeed that it has; although I don't quite know for sure, but I have a good idea"

The old man smiled as he turned around and started walking back down the path.

Mary looked at Henry, bemused, and then, along with everyone else, watched Ooshiya-Lion as he walked back down towards the cottage.

Then he stopped, turned around and said.

"Oh Mary, I almost forgot, I have something to show you" and he beckoned her.

Without saying a word, and still exchanging looks between everyone, Mary shrugged her shoulders, shook her head, and walked back to the cottage. When she caught up with him, she asked him.

"Ooshiya-Lion, can you please explain to me what you mean. If there is anything to tell me about the tree, if you know- that is, please could you enlighten me..??"

"I'm hoping that you may find that out very soon" and winked.
"….but for now, I want to show you this. I do hope that you like it…..and please – if there is anything you want me to change, I will. I have done my research, so fingers crossed"

"…but….where are we going….??" Mary asked.

He walked slightly in front, as they made their way down the side of the cottage towards the front garden; then he stopped.

"Now, close your eyes, and take my arm"

Mary did as she was bade; and gave Ooshiya-Lion her hand, and put her other hand over her eyes, and shut them. As she took teetering steps, the old man led her very carefully to the front garden. Then they stopped. Mary could instantly smell a sweet aroma.

"Now Mary – open your eyes"

As Mary slowly took her hand away from her face - she opened her eyes, and immediately put her hand straight to her mouth, and gasped. Her eyes couldn't quite take in what was in front of her, as they quickly searched the whole of the garden.

The garden had been completely transformed, into what Mary could only describe as her absolute perfect garden. There were hanging baskets with an abundance of different flowers hanging at either side of the little porch at the front door. The pale cream rose bushes were still there but now, it was in full bloom. She noticed big plant pots all over the garden with lots of different flowering bushes.

There was a new winding path that went from the front door down to the gate, and another pathway going to the side of the cottage, and a fresh green lawn on either side. She noticed two baby fir trees in pots in front of the room window.

 Just past the room window, and tucked nicely in the corner, was a large, beautifully built wooden pergola, with seating underneath. Growing up either side were lots of scented white jasmine, which met at the top. Thick green hedging was now going down towards the front of the garden, and in the corner at the bottom, was a pond. Large ferns were standing tall around the pond; and in and around the many old stones, ivy and poppies were growing wild.

Mary caught sight of a dark pink Peony bush, which made tears well in her eyes. Her Mother had planted exactly the same in the garden of their home when Mary was little; and she fondly remembers picking up the huge flower head in her hands, and bending it towards her to smell.
Mary walked over to the peony bush, and did just that. She closed her eyes, and she smelt the familiar scent.
Mary turned around to Ooshiya-Lion with tears still in her eyes.

"How did you know..?!"

Then before the old man could speak, Mary let out a big gasp, as she looked up over his shoulder to the front of the cottage. There was the biggest Wisteria she had ever seen, with its familiar twisted and gnarled-looking trunk and branches climbing up the front of the cottage, and along the top of the room window. She recognised the green leaves, and knew that come spring next year, there would be an abundance of the biggest lilac coloured scented plumes on display.

This was just wonderful and so very nostalgic of her home with her Mother and Father.

A breeze gently blew and she looked over towards the other corner of the garden, and as she walked over, and in the midst of all these beautiful scented flowers, Mary could see a well - a very old fashioned looking well.

Mary walked over to it.

"Does it work…?!"

"I believe it used to do many years ago, but I'm not sure that it does now. This was actually under all the over-grown bushes, and couldn't be seen. I'm assuming you like everything..?" he asked, searching her face.

"LIKE everything….?! I absolutely LOVE it…it's all just absolutely perfect..! Thank you so much…."

"Well, call it an early Birthday present. I know how much you love your garden" he said smiling, as he watched her.

"Even the hedges are much taller..!" she exclaimed. "…..and I see I have a big new wooden front gate..!" I'm just hoping we won't be getting any 'nosey parkers' anytime soon" and gave Ooshiya-Lion a knowing look, as she was most definitely referring to Agnes Le Fey.

At that moment, Henry, Patsy and Wilbur arrived from the back garden. Patsy and Wilbur were carrying Elma, who had asked for a 'lift' as he was still a bit tired from his long journey.
They almost skidded in mid-air, and Patsy accidently let go of one of Elma's legs. (They were carrying two each). She quickly picked the leg back up, and they flew him to the front door, and carefully sat him down gently on the ground at the front porch, and then they flew around the garden, inspecting absolutely everything. In and out of the flowers they went. Wilbur especially liked the pond, and went straight over to it, and skimmed across it.

Elma was looking up at Ooshiya-Lion behind his back, and scowling. He hadn't spoken to him since he saw him with the Dragon the other night.

Whilst the others were showing their delight at the garden, Mary walked up to Elma, and bent down and whispered.

"Are you ok Elma..? Stop scowling, I can see you..!"

Elma quickly walked up the side of the porch, in and out of the rose blooms until he got to Mary's level.

"Have you asked him about the other night yet..??!" he whispered back.

"No, I'm biding my time; and I can't very well ask him now, when he has just done all this for me" and waved her hand towards the garden.

"He's been tactical if you ask me....." Elma answered with a disgruntled look on his face.

"Everything ok..?" Ooshiya-Lion suddenly asked over Mary's shoulder.

"Oh...oh yes, I'm just asking Elma how he is. He wasn't feeling too well" she quickly answered.

"Oh really – anything I can do..?" The old man turned to Elma, while Mary stepped back away from the old man's view, shrugging her shoulders, and grimacing, and miming the word 'sorry' to Elma.

"I can mix you up a fine cocktail Elma, for your 'spider belly'..."

"For my WHAT....?!" Elma asked disgustingly.

"Your 'spider belly'.... Spiders get it quite often you know, as they hang upside down an awful lot, and fall very quickly from such a height. It's quite common..."

"There's nothing wrong with my belly....thank you very much...!!" Elma answered quite indignantly.

Mary looked at Elma and opened her eyes really wide, as if to tell him to shut up. Elma saw her face, then looked back at the old man and gave him a weak smile, which looked like a sarcastic grin.

"Well, you know where to find me if you change your mind; and stay off the rotting fruit and the mushrooms for a day or two if you can, they can play havoc with your……"

"….yes, yes…. thank you, I will keep that in mind….." Elma answered quickly, to avoid any embarrassment, and still with the sarcastic grin on his face, as Ooshiya-Lion nodded his head and walked away over to the others.

"MARY, you need to speak to him soon…!!" Elma whispered back through gritted teeth.

"I know – I promise – I will find the right time" she said.

Elma gave her a sideways glance, shook his head, and then climbed back down through the pale cream roses, as Mary watched him.

As Mary stared around the front porch, she brought her gaze up, and looked up at the front door of the cottage. She smiled as she looked at it, and the surrounding roses……. and wished James was here.

Her smile quickly faded, and she sighed as she bent her head a little….She missed him so, so much…...

She recovered herself quickly, as the sound of laughter and voices could be heard, which broke her thoughts. Patsy was shouting over to Wilbur to take a look at Henry, who had suddenly decided to take a short nap in a Blue Lobelia……Mary looked over her shoulder at the garden and smiled, and then averted her gaze back to looking at the beautiful front door. She then noticed that it had been given a few fresh coats of paint, in the same Periwinkle Blue that it once had before. As she continued to look, she also noticed that two new gold numbers had replaced the old ones, and were near the top of the door. The brass numbers looked very ornate, quite antique, she thought. As she continued to stare and smile, she realised - that she was looking…….. at the number 24 on her door……….

# Chapter 31

## **The Darkness & The Light**

As the evening drew in, long after tea that night, Mary was practising spells in her bedroom with the windows open – waiting for it to get dark. She had a plan, but hadn't told anyone about it.

As dusk drew in; Mary looked outside – it was a very warm evening, and very still.
All of a sudden, she heard a faint noise, like something flapping in the wind; but there was no wind that night.

There it was again.

She followed the sound to the hallway, and looked up to where the attic was. The noise could be heard every few seconds, and it was definitely coming from the attic. She put the step ladders up to the loft hatch, climbed up, and lifted the hatch up, slowly. As her head came up into the darkness of the loft, it took her eyes a few seconds to adjust. She didn't want to put the light on, as she wanted to know what the noise was. It was like a scuffling sound.

"Damn it, why can't I bloody well see..?! I wish I had some light" She whispered under her breath.

As soon as the words left her mouth, a firefly appeared out of nowhere, and made Mary jump, but it danced about quickly, as if beckoning her to follow it. As she stood up in the attic, the heat hit her. Obviously with the weather being warm, it was like opening an oven door..!!

The Firefly danced further away towards the front of the cottage, as Mary kept following. Then she heard the noise again, and it was much nearer now. The firefly was taking her to where it was coming from. Then it stopped. Mary couldn't see anything. She looked at the firefly, and immediately shielded her eyes, as the bright glow seemed even brighter in the total darkness.

"What is it..?? I can't see anything..!" she said in a hushed whisper.

The firefly darted forwards a few inches and back again. Mary looked into the blackness, and this time she heard the noise much louder. Something was fluttering, like it was trapped. She bent down towards the wooden floor, and began feeling around, and tapping the floor.

"Firefly – here, shine your light here..!" she whispered.

The firefly flew down to where Mary was on the floor. Mary was now, right at the front of the cottage, where the roof came down to meet the front of the house. She got down on her tummy, and slid forwards. She could just make out a gap in the wooden floor, and it was obvious to her that there was something trapped. She remembered her magic.

"Leva…!" Mary said as she waved her hand towards the wooden floorboards.

Suddenly, two of the floorboards, began to lift up. As soon as there was a big enough gap where the wood had left the floor, something very small, and very quick, flew out with such speed, Mary shrieked…!

Whatever it was, was flapping around; and moving past Mary's head really quickly, and kept knocking her hair. It was obviously frightened. The firefly had gone into a bit of a shock, and between them both, they kept knocking into each other. Mary found it in herself to speak.

"It's ok, it's ok….calm down, I know you're afraid. Please…."

A high pitched voice suddenly spoke up.

"It's the light, it's the light, it blinds me…!"

Mary quickly realised that the firefly was making the whole situation worse.

"Firefly – be still. Turn off your light..!"

The firefly flew into the darkness, towards the other side of the attic, until its light was only a tiny speck.

"Thank you" Mary said. "…..and who do I have here in my attic…??" she asked into the darkness, as she knelt down.

A tiny voice spoke up.

"My name is Tufri, and I'm a fruit bat…..and I….I…I am so, so honoured to meet with you - at last…."

"…but I can't see you…!" Mary answered.

"I don't mind a little light, if the firefly wished to lend just a small amount of light this way…" said Tufri, from the darkness.

"Firefly, please can you emit just a small amount of your light over here please..?" Mary asked.

The firefly quickly emerged……

"Yes Mary, of course….." the firefly answered.

"Oh I keep forgetting that everyone can speak…." Mary said desperately…."…and what is YOUR name..?"

"My name is Luci…" the firefly answered.

"Thank you Luci, and thank you for coming to help me when I needed you"

"….but you called me." Luci said.

"I didn't…did I….?"
"Yes – you did, you wanted light, and here I am…!" she said, with a little chuckle.

Luci turned around with her back to Mary, and shone a very dim light onto the floorboard, and Tufri walked into the small spot of light, like he was walking onto a spotlight on a stage. He looked up at Mary with big brown eyes, and then bowed his head.

"I was sent to watch over you, but I'm afraid I got stuck in the eaves of your cottage Mary" Tufri said, looking a little forlorn.

"I just hope that I haven't dismayed my Master. I don't know what I would have done if you hadn't come to help me, so thank you for saving me"

"Dismayed your Master...??" Mary questioned "...but you haven't done anything wrong.....and why would he be dismayed at you...? You couldn't help getting stuck..!! Goodness me, what kind of a Master is he..??"

"Oh a very powerful one Mary" Tufri was looking quite tearful, and sat with his head hunched over.

"Was it your Master that sent you here, and why do you have to watch over me anyway..??"

"Yes, he did send me. There are many watching over you Mary. I am sure Luci here might be one of them too" and looked to the firefly.

"You too...?" Mary asked Luci.

"Well, anytime you need help....whenever....at any time, just say the words in your head, and help is always at hand" Luci answered as she turned her head around to face Mary.

Mary turned back to Tufri. It was the first time she had been so close to a Bat, and she quickly remembered sitting on the back step of her house when she was a child, and her father telling her to keep quiet, and suddenly, lots of bats would all come out and fly around, and she would squeal with delight.

"Well your Master should be ashamed of himself..! You can tell him from me. You could have died in this heat getting trapped like that..!" Mary hated injustices. "Who is he anyway...?!"

"Oh......well you will probably meet him yourself Mary, but please, please don't speak badly to him. He is the greatest and the wisest of all creatures..."

"Mmmm....well I don't tolerate bad behaviour. Anyway, seeing as you're both here, I have somewhere to go tonight, and you may as well come along, because I'm gathering you will follow me anyway. I'm slowly getting used to strange things happening to me" She half said to herself with a wry smile.

She shuffled forward on her hands and knees, until she could gain some height, and eventually stood up. Again, her head was in the heat.

"Blimey, we need to get out of this attic…it's swelteringly hot up here…!" Mary said, as she got to the hatch, and lifted it.

"Mary, please could you shield my eyes with something and carry me. I can see the shaft of light coming up through the loft hatch?" Tufri asked.

"Oh I almost forgot; here you can go in my pocket – you too Luci"

Outside in the front garden, Mary welcomed the cool air on her face, and she could still smell the heavenly scent of flowers from her garden on the summer nights' breeze.
Mary walked over to the seated area under the pergola, sat down and brought Tufri and Luci out of her pocket. Luci hovered in front of Mary, and Tufri sat at the side of Mary on the seated bench.

Mary spoke in a whisper. "Do either of you know anything about me, and what the situation is here..?"

They both nodded silently.

"Where are you planning to go so late Mary; I have to ask..?" Tufri looked up at her.

"I'm paying a visit to someone – we'll talk on the way; but we have to be quiet" she answered.

Mary was planning to go and visit Agnes – but what she didn't know, was that Agnes had planned on doing the same thing.

Agnes knew that the spells surrounding the cottage were beginning to weaken, so she had planned to visit the cottage in the middle of the night, and try and get in once more.
She wanted to surprise Mary whilst she was sleeping, cast a spell on her, and bring her to the barn and hold her captive – question her, and get to know her

in the little time that was left. Since she had come to know that Mary was a Le Fey, she was planning – not to kill her, but to side with her, make her an ally. After all, Mary was pretty much all that Agnes had left. She had distant relatives on the Bishop side, but if she befriended Mary, then the cottage, the secret, the power – all of it would be 'theirs'. Agnes would do this, just to get her way. If she didn't need Mary afterwards, then she would just get rid of her.

She had waited for the Dragon to fall asleep. She had laced his drinking water with a potion she had made, to make him sleepy. She didn't want Beruc to have anything to do with 'her' cottage, and 'her' destiny – not anything. She had let him believe that they could share everything, but that was never going to happen. He had nothing to do with the family, or the history. Yes, he had tended to her wounds and helped care for her all those years ago, but that was then, and this was now.

She was consumed – and ready.

She stole quietly through the shadows down the lane, and onto the country road, that would eventually lead past the cottage, thinking and scheming as she walked.
Mary was walking up the road – towards Agnes.

Tufri had flown ahead, but quickly turned around, and flew straight back to Mary.

"Someone is coming further up the road, I can hear them..!" he said in a hushed whisper. "You need to hide Mary..!"

Tufri's impeccable hearing had warned Mary and Luci soon enough. Mary climbed over the small wall to her left, and made for a nearby tree, where she stood up against it. Luci turned off her light, and Tufri followed – silently.

None of them knew that it was Agnes who was making her way down the road, as they had got hidden in enough time for them not to be seen by her, and for her, not to be seen by them.
Tufri gave the 'all clear' and they carried on up the road, and towards the left turn off.

Beruc had not drunk his water. He knew Agnes, and didn't trust one move she made. By Agnes bringing him water; only made him more suspicious of her. She never did anything for anyone but herself. He was much wiser than she even cared to know.

She was up to something – that, he DID know, but he had to keep tabs on her, as it was important he knew where she was at all times. He left the cottage, and sniffed the night air. He knew which direction Agnes was going, and smiled to himself.

In the distance, Beruc could hear someone walking up the lane. He lay still, not moving a muscle. He then saw a tiny hovering light getting closer and closer. He was well-hidden near a small copse of trees. Presently, a young woman came into view.

"Looks like we are here" Mary whispered, as they came upon the barn. There was faint candlelight on inside.

"What are you going to do..?!" A very worried Tufri asked. "I can't allow you to put yourself in any danger Mary, not at this stage..!" He flapped about nervously.

"Luci, have a look in the window, tell me what you see" Mary whispered.

Luci lowered her light, and flew to the window. After a few seconds had passed, she came back to Mary.

"There's no one in there at all; but someone has been in there. What will you do now?" Luci said.

Mary felt angry. She really, really wanted to confront Agnes. She wasn't afraid of her; but now she wasn't there. Where could she have gone at this hour?
Mary boldly walked up to the barn, and banged on the door. Nothing. She banged again, even louder.

"I think we should go" Tufri said. "She's not there Mary"

A voice spoke up from behind them.

"I think you should take your friends' advice"

Mary swung around with a jolt.

"Who's there...?!!"

Tufri was overhead and Luci was darting about trying to find where the voice was coming from.

A fox stepped forward, very cautiously.

"Like I said – I think you should take your friends' advice"

The fox looked at Mary, like he was looking at someone he recognised, and hadn't seen in a long, long time. Mary was surprised.

"Why would you say that, and who are you..?" She asked of the fox.

"....because...if you are wanting to speak with the woman who has been living in this barn for some time, then she left, just a little before you got here... I saw her go – she went that way" and nodded towards the lane that they had just walked up.

Mary thought for a few seconds, and then said loudly...

"I bet that was her on the road...!!. What is she doing going out at this time of the night...?!"

"I might ask you the same question – it's very late M...M..Miss..." the fox stuttered.

He then quickly recovered himself.... "I mean, it's very late and dark around here, and it's no place to get lost. Please, keep to the path..." With that, the Fox turned around and ran off into the night before Mary could ask him anymore.

"She's going to the cottage, I know it..!! We have to get there, and quick...!"

Mary stumbled off in a quickened haste, with Tufri flying overhead, and Luci leading the way. Tufri looked back as he flew away; he could have sworn he heard something…

Beruc slowly emerged from the shadows, and grinned.

"This, I have to see…."

# Chapter 32

## <u>A Fox, some Visitors, and……</u>

Meanwhile back at Copley Lane Meadow, Agnes had approached the cottage –
which was in complete darkness. She carefully and quietly walked around
outside at the front, but couldn't see over the gate, as there was a new, higher
gate in place of the old one.

"Damn that girl…!!" She snarled under her breath.

She walked around to the side of the cottage, and slowly made her way along
the stone wall. She produced her wand from her cloak, and ran the tip of it
lightly along the old stone, as she slowly walked along. All the stones lit up
around the edges, as the tip of the wand lightly touched each one. Agnes's face
lit up, and she grinned broadly.

"Yes…!!" she whispered to herself. Her eyes grew larger, as the silvery light
reflected in her old eyes.

"The spells are weakening..!"

<u>Ten minutes earlier</u>

Lars the Beetle had taken it upon himself to be of service a little more in the
garden, thinking that his evening patrol should go on a little longer, seeing as
the summer nights were quite warm, and much lighter for longer. He knew that
Patsy and Wilbur had been patrolling the wall, and letting Elma rest a little, and
he knew Henry did such a great job with everything else, like the meetings, and
just being around for everyone, that he felt it was the least he could do.

As always, he felt very important, and took his job very seriously. He had been riding his bright orange, slightly rickety bicycle up and down the little pathways, and in and out of small flowering herbs, which had the most calming aroma in the summer evenings; and he was quite enjoying the silence. He suddenly came upon Jeremy the Snail, who was on the pathway. Lars shone his torch from his bike at Jeremy.

"Ah… Mr Jeremy!" He spoke in a low tone, as he got closer to Jeremy.
"Za last time I encountered you on zis path, you vere trespassing….ha ha  ha … Are you alvight, and vot are you doing out so late?"

"Ah…. Good evening Lars. Well it's so uncomfortably hot this evening, that I find it most relaxing to take an evening stroll; it's so much cooler for me than in the day time. The sun isn't always my 'best friend' during the day. I need to take shade – as you are quite aware I'm sure"

Hearing Jeremy talk quite posh and much quicker than he did before, took a bit of getting used to, since everyone found out that Jeremy was one of Ooshiya-Lion's great old friends.

Lars answered back in a hushed voice, and tapped the side of his nose.

"Ah yes, yes, I am knowing vot it is you are saying Mr Jeremy. Za incident wiz za salt voz a very bad thing. Yes, you must be very careful, and enjoy your night stroll"

Lars cycled on, and Jeremy continued to stroll.

Jeremy suddenly started to feel uneasy, but didn't know why. He stopped, and looked around in the dark. It wasn't a good feeling he was getting either. He wondered for a moment; then, in a very quickened pace, which wasn't his usual slow pace - he made his way towards where Ooshiya-Lion was sleeping. The old man usually made a bed behind the shed, under a large tree, or sometimes he would sleep IN the shed, depending how the mood took him. When he approached him, he was under the tree, and found that Ooshiya-Lion was already awake.

"I feel it too my friend" he whispered to Jeremy. "I think this is the start of it. Agnes WILL – depending on how much the spells weaken, more than likely be able to get in, and we have to be extra vigilant. The next 24 hours are vital to this cottage. As soon as the clock strikes midnight tomorrow, it will be the end, if we don't stop her from getting in, as she may well regain some of her powers that she has lost, once she steps inside that cottage. I do hope Mary finds a way to open that door…!!"

As soon as he had said those words, he heard a strange sound like sand falling softly. His hearing was exceptional. He was very bemused, and went closer to the hedging.
Behind the hedging was the long stone wall that ran the full length of the garden, from the front to the back.

When Ooshiya-Lion got closer, he found out what the noise was. It was the sand and cement between each stone of the wall, that was crumbling, and it was pouring out very slowly from between each stone. Soon enough, all the stones would collapse, and the wall would be down, which would only leave the hedge. Ooshiya-Lion knew that Agnes was outside. He put his fingers to his lips to Jeremy, and pointed with his other hand to over the wall. Jeremy knew what he meant straightaway.

Ooshiya-Lion had to wake Mary, but also had to protect her at the same time from Agnes. Without a sound, Ooshiya-Lion made his way towards the back of the cottage. When he reached Mary's bedroom door, he tapped lightly on it, and called her name. There was no answer. He slowly opened Mary's bedroom door, and knocked again softly.

"Mary…." He whispered. "Mary, wake up….. Mary.!"

As he opened the door cautiously, and looked over towards the bed, he could see by the moonlight; that Mary's bed had not been slept in…..and she was nowhere to be seen.

A quick panic set in.

"Bam Bam – find Mary - and quickly..!"

 Bam Bam disappeared, as the old man ran down the stairs. He was met at the back door by Jeremy, who had hurriedly come to tell him that the wall had started coming down.

"Ooshiya-Lion, you're going to have to do something…!!" he urged. The old man knew what Jeremy meant.

The old man got out his wand, pointed the tip of it at his watch, and said. "Prohibere tergum in tempus" Jeremy knew that Ooshiya-Lion had no choice but to do this, and would only be done in extreme circumstances.

Suddenly, everything started going back in time, including everyone. Everything that had just happened began to go in reverse. Ooshiya-Lion watched as he was in the middle of all this chaos.
He had to find Mary..!! It was important..!! He wandered around the cottage calling Mary while everything was going in reverse. Then he went out onto the lane, and looked up and down. Where was Bam Bam..?

Suddenly he arrived at the old man's side.

"She's on the lane Master, and is heading this way. She has a bat and a firefly with her..!"

"Is she safe..?" he asked. Bam Bam nodded.

Ooshiya-Lion put the tip of his wand to his watch once more.

"Prohibere Suspenditur animationem"

Everything suddenly stopped. He had put everything into a suspended animation. He walked quickly to the side of the cottage, and there was Agnes.
As Ooshiya-Lion had put everything back in time by 10 minutes, she was just about to turn left to walk down the side of the cottage.

"Good…now I'm going to have to call for a favour"

He raised his wand in the air towards the back of the cottage, beyond the meadow. He spoke in a different language this time, and as the words left his mouth, they turned to white smoke. The smoke quickly travelled away into the distance, beyond the meadow, and towards the large hills.

He turned to his right, and pointed his wand down the lane, and towards the village and beyond to the forests. He then repeated the same words; but this time as the words left his mouth, they turned to a brown/chestnut coloured smoke, which blew away quickly towards the forest.

In the far distance from beyond the meadow, Ooshiya-Lion looked up, and in the night sky, he could see that the wisps of white smoke that had carried his words...... were now bringing Oreads of all shapes and sizes. The Oreads were the Mountain Nymphs. They flew swiftly on the white smoke. Some were wearing white, almost ethereal long dresses and robes, and veils of white daisies. They were tall with pale shining skin, and long silvery white hair. Others were shorter in stature, with a rocky, craggy appearance. Others had crystals in their hair, but they were all surrounded by a fine wispy, silvery light. Ooshiya-Lion counted, and there were 20 of them altogether. They all landed on their feet very softly on the ground, and waited for instructions. Ooshiya-Lion directed them to stand guard all the way down the long stone wall, with their backs to the wall, and all holding hands. They bowed their heads gracefully, nodded in turn, and floated right past the suspended Agnes, and to their posts.

Suddenly, coming up the lane from the village and the forest beyond was a rumbling noise, which sounded like a herd of cattle. Within seconds, a herd of Satyrs were running, but in mid-air. The Satyrs were the male Nymphs of the forest, and ran on two legs with hooved feet. They were strong, and the upper part of their body was that of a man, and the lower part was that of a horse, with a horse's tail. Some were carrying bows and arrows slung over their backs. Some carried sling shots in a pouch over their shoulders. Six of them had two short horns coming out of their heads, and had beards, and the others had curly horns at the side of their ears. There were 12 of them altogether.
As they came to a halt on the ground, a small cloud of brown dust swirled around them. One of them stepped forward. He was a very tall, strong, and young Satyr, and was wearing a red waistcoat. He bowed in front of Ooshiya-Lion

"I am Taurus Saturu Fallswood, and I am the descendant of the great Fiedric Rifecid Fallswood. I am honoured you have called upon me and my fellow men. We understand and know the urgency of your request. How can we be of service to you..?" and once again, bowed his head.

"Taurus – thank you for answering my call; I knew your ancestor Fiedric very well. A fine fellow - and a very honourable and noble one too" Ooshiya-Lion said.

As Ooshiya-Lion stepped forward to give the orders for six of them to stand at the front of the cottage, and six to the rear, beyond the wall, looking out over the meadow, a voice suddenly spoke from behind him.

"A word, if I may…?"

Ooshiya-Lion turned around, and there was the fox. He had taken a short cut across the field swiftly.

"And you are…??" Ooshiya-Lion looked at the fox.

The fox stared at the old man, and said nothing for a few seconds, then spoke.

"Mary is making her way here, as we speak" The fox said.

"Yes…I am aware of this; but she will be suspended in time too, so I wouldn't worry; she'll be quite safe……but who are YOU..?" Ooshiya-Lion stepped forward towards the fox, and the fox took a few steps back, and into the moonlight.

"I am Uber-C" said the fox, as he continued to look at the old man. A smile broke from Ooshiya-Lion's face.

"Ahhh….I see….yes…yes, of course" Ooshiya-Lion said.

"My name is Uber-C" said the fox. "Like I said…." he continued. "I need a word…?"

As six of the Satyrs took their positions at the front of the cottage, the remaining six went around to the back of the cottage, and stood guard; Ooshiya-Lion took the fox to one side.

"What is it..?" he asked of the fox.

"Mary is not frozen in time – she is walking......By the way, is all of this necessary..?" said the fox.

.

"Goodness me, that girl continues to surprise me; but you DO know what's at stake here, surely..?" Ooshiya-Lion answered.

"Of course I do, but I need to tell you about Agnes"

"Which is what? Quickly, we don't have much time..!"

"She isn't who she thinks she is" The fox said earnestly.

Ooshiya-Lion waited for the fox to continue.

"When she was gone for all those years, her witchcraft slowly began to diminish. What she didn't realise.....was....was that the...the....'Dragon' - was cursing her, and was taking away her powers. This had to be done very, very slowly over many years, so she didn't realise. She still does, however, have SOME powers, but nothing like what she had before. I just don't think all of this is necessary" and he nodded his head towards the army of guards around the cottage.

"Well....that may be so, and I'm pleased to hear this, but I would rather air on the side of caution, seeing what is at stake here" Ooshiya-Lion said.

 "Besides...." He said, looking over towards Agnes's suspended stature. "I'd quite like her to think that she still has what it takes......mmmm.....this could be interesting...." And he smiled. He turned back to the fox.

"I could have been told this earlier by the way, but anyway, I can't see what difference it would make now. Also, why have you......." Before Ooshiya-Lion could finish his sentence, the fox interrupted.

"Well I couldn't exactly.....you know...."

"Ahhhh.....of course....yes of course...." And he nodded.

At that moment, Mary had turned up, having made it down the lane. As she slowly stepped forward, she looked at Ooshiya-Lion.

"What's happened….and what the hell is going on here….and who are these….these people…??!!"

"I had to call in a favour Mary" the old man, very casually said.

"Agnes was about to enter the garden, and had so far begun to take down the wall, so I had to step in, turn back time a little, which I didn't really want to do, because it DOES play havoc……."

"Ooshiya-Lion…??.!!! Mary shouted, and indicated towards the Oreads and the Satyrs.

"Ah well, now these here are the Oreads Mary…..do please come and meet them." And he began to walk forward.

Mary slowly followed, looking completely astounded. Tufri the bat flew right overhead, and Luci flew at her side.

"Oh I see you have encountered some new friends. Hello…" and he tilted his hat towards Tufri and Luci.

Suddenly Mary saw Agnes, and stopped in her tracks.

"It's alright Mary, she is suspended in time – well for now anyway – but not for too long, going by my watch…." He said as he quickly looked at his wrist.

Mary had to stop and take a long and somewhat, cold hard look at Agnes. She hated every single thing about her - EVERYTHING...!! She couldn't believe that she was even related to her..!
Mary's eyes shone bright in the darkness, as her loathness for the witch stood in front of her, grew.

"Mary……Mary..!" Ooshiya-Lion shouted, as he looked back over his shoulder, and saw Mary stood in front of Agnes. A faint breeze had picked up, which was quickly getting stronger.

As Mary continued to lock eyes with Agnes, wisps of Agnes's steel grey hair began to blow across her ugly old face. Mary saw the scar, and began to laugh.

She threw back her head and laughed, as if suddenly possessed. Somehow it looked like Agnes was afraid inside her motionless body.

"MARY…!" bellowed Ooshiya-Lion. He put his hand on her shoulder and quickly turned her around.

As her gaze left Agnes's, and she looked upon the old man's face, the wind died down, and everyone seemed to heave a small sigh of relief.
"Enough..!" he said to her.

Mary composed herself, as if she had no recollection.
The fox followed behind Mary, with his head lowered, and looking rather skittishly, as he looked back at Agnes, and then at Mary. A smile appeared on his face.

The Oreads were indeed beautiful to look at. Their ethereal presence was very calming. Mary had never seen anything like them before, and stood in wonder. They each looked at Mary, and slightly bowed their heads. Luci the firefly was indeed very excited, and danced about in the air, for she knew the Oreads, and they exchanged smiles.

Of course, all the commotion would have woken the rest of the garden up at the cottage, but everyone was just as they were, before Ooshiya-Lion had changed the time and frozen everyone in that moment.

As the six Satyrs had appeared at the back wall, Patsy and Wilbur had been walking along the top of the wall, chatting whilst patrolling, but of course, they had frozen in time. Lars was still on his orange rickety bicycle and had just ridden away from Jeremy, after having spoken to him, but Jeremy had already gotten to Ooshiya-Lion to tell him about the 'funny feeling' he had, and had followed him to the front of the cottage.

Ooshiya-Lion was now introducing Mary to the Satyrs, who were lined up, with their backs to the front of the cottage. Mary looked up at the tall, fine looking beasts, with complete astonishment. Taurus broke his place in the line, and stepped forward, and bowed low to Mary with one of his knees bent right down to the floor, so he was Mary's height.

"I am honoured to meet with you Mary Le Fey, of the Le Fey dynasty. Your ancestors gave my ancestors a home many, many years ago; and much shelter. We have grown into a small community within the forest of Fallswood, and I….WE…. are eternally grateful. I am Taurus Saturu Fallswood, of the Fallswood Folk, and I am most happy to be meeting with you. We hold great respect for you, and we are very privileged to be called upon, and to help you protect your home"

He bowed his head, and put his hand up to Mary's. Mary quickly looked up at Ooshiya-Lion. The old man nodded, and Mary took the large, very gnarled hand in both of hers, and said.

"I am also honoured to have you here – Taurus, you are more than welcome, and I am eternally grateful to you also." She looked up at the old man, and he nodded respectfully. She suddenly felt a sense of familiarity, as she held his hand; and Taurus lifted his head.

"You have a strong, kind heart Mary Le Fey, with great boldness, and many gifts……some, you still know nothing of. I, we, pledge to serve you as you need us"

With that, he stood up, stepped backwards into line, and smiled down at her. Mary suddenly felt very safe and protected.

Immediately and unexpectedly a voice broke that moment.

"What is THIS…?!!" It was Agnes. The timing was up, and she was suddenly staring at the Oreads that were all still standing in their positions along the side of the cottage.
The look on her face was indeed, one of fright and surprise. She deftly produced her wand from her cloak, and stood her ground. Ooshiya-Lion put his finger to his lips for Mary to see, to tell her to be quiet, and ushered her over to the Satyrs, out of sight. Mary wasn't too keen on hiding; she wanted to face Agnes full on and challenge her; but Taurus put his hand on her shoulder and shook his head
.

Ooshiya-Lion suddenly made himself disappear. Agnes was afraid, and stood her guard, wand in hand, as if ready for an attack.

"Who ARE you, and what are you doing outside my home..?!! Leave at once white spirits, and never return...!! Where is she, where is Mary....??!!"

The Oreads said nothing, and their silvery white sheen that surrounded them, swirled in and out and around them as they stood still. She lifted her wand, and began reciting some incantation, as she pointed it at the Oreads, but the Oreads were protected by the white silvery aura that surrounded them, so Agnes's magic did nothing. The Mountain Nymphs continued to stand, surrounded by the ethereal light. Shocked at her failing spell, she thrust her wand forward and angrily shouted.

"Flailing spirits from whence you came,
Leave this wall...... and your duties – refrain.
Take to heel and make your path....
...and return to your dwelling, with a defeated task..!"


She waved her wand up and around her head, and then unleashed her anger towards the Oreads. Again, her magic did nothing, and fell before the Mountain Nymphs feet.

"What is this trickery....??!! I demand you to GO – NOW..!!

Agnes tried and tried again to wave her wand, but nothing worked, only a few sparks lit up the floor. She looked around wildly, as if fearing she was being watched, and looked up towards the sky. She scurried quickly to the front of the cottage........and that's when she saw Mary – stood between the line of Satyrs. Mary was smiling.

"There you are, you little WRETCH....!!! What have you done....??!! Who are these spirits and these woodland folk, and where have you sourced your help...??! WHO IS ADVISING YOU...??!!"

Agnes shouted towards Mary. She was obviously afraid, and very, very angry.

There she was, stood in the lane, and looking up at the cottage......and Mary's anger slowly started to rise, as she saw the Witch in front of her - that same horrible Witch who had killed her ancestors. Mary's eyes glowed brightly, as a strong breeze had started up, and blew the warm summer night's air around.

"I've been waiting to see you again – Agnes…."

Agnes looked around her, as the breeze got a little stronger, and blew the dry dusty earth. Mary continued to stare at her, as a strong wind followed, and the old woman staggered, as she tried to keep her footing.

"Feeling afraid yet Agnes……Remind you of anything….?!!" Mary shouted, as she watched the old woman's face looking up and around her.

Agnes's face suddenly changed, as she looked back at Mary, and a dark scowl appeared. She began to advance towards Mary in the wind, but Mary outstretched her arm, and the old woman stopped in her tracks, unable to walk any further forward. Agnes shouted back from her stilted position.

"…and I have been waiting to see YOU….!! Since we first met, I knew there was something different about you Mary – I felt it…..!!" Agnes's eyes widened as she stared at Mary excitedly, as the wind blew Agnes's grey hair.

"You're getting very angry……ha ha ha ha….goooood, very good Mary. You're a BISHOP, and you know it…!! Take those angry feelings you have, and you can make them do the most incredible things – think about it….!!!"

As Agnes shouted these words, she held both her hands in the air and looked up. "Look what you can create Mary – look what you have become…!! You are more powerful than you know….!!!

"I'll NEVER be a BISHOP, you stupid old crow…!! You have bad blood running through those ugly veins of yours... I am a LE FEY….!! ….and yes, you're right – there is something different about me….something you should be very afraid of; but you're never going to get the chance to find out…..because this is where I reap MY revenge on YOU….!!!"

"You don't frighten me, you silly girl, standing there with your army of spirits…. and…and…goats, and no wand….!! Can't you fight me on your own…..?! Do you even know who I AM….??!!"

Taurus glowered at Agnes, when she referred to him and his fellow men, as 'goats'. Mary felt Taurus's hand lay heavy on her shoulder, and tapped it, then took his hand away, as if giving her permission for Mary to leave his side. Mary didn't hesitate, and slowly stepped forward – and very calmly she said.

"Have you ever wondered……who REALLY gave you that scar on your face Agnes…? Who do you think it was..? Could it have been Endor, your beautiful, younger, caring sister..?? Possibly, as she was the last person you saw that day. Do you remember, you fought with her before you suddenly disappeared..?! So it could have been Endor….or could it…. Oh that's right, you don't remember do you…??!!"

Mary made a few more steps towards Agnes. Agnes's worn and angry face suddenly looked confused, as if trying to think back to that moment in time. Mary was revelling in this moment, and tilted her head back, and laughed…..

"Oh this feels soooo good…!"

The strong wind was now blowing Mary's hair wildly. Her eyes had turned white, and she looked directly at Agnes, and bent her head quickly to one side, and then the other. Strong gusts of wind began to knock Agnes from side to side, as she shifted from her position quickly from left to right…..Mary was controlling the wind which was knocking Agnes over.

Agnes managed to raise her arm towards Mary, as she was being thrown from side to side and shouted something that Mary couldn't understand. It sounded like old magic. Suddenly a large fireball appeared from nowhere, and was making its way straight for Mary……. There were a few shocked looks on the line of the Satyrs faces, but they stood their ground. As quick as a flash, Mary threw her arm out in front of her, directly at the fireball, and stopped it in its tracks. She held it there, as the two women stared at each other. Before Agnes could make a move, Mary had looked up at the night sky at the storm above them, and in a second - a sheet of rain, like a huge monsoon came down with such force, it completely knocked Agnes to the floor, as it fell straight on top of her; and the huge ball of flame vanished under the sheet of water, and drenching Agnes in the process.

"I can do this all night Agnes – you've met your match with me….!!! Give up while you can, and walk away….you're too old…!!"

"As if I would give up my family home, to the likes of YOU…!!"

"You have no right to even call it your home…!! You had your chance, years ago – but you failed because of your greed….because you took the wrong side. The Bishops were never going to have this cottage!!........Still thinking about who gave you that scar….??! Think about it again Agnes….yes….you think back Agnes to that time when you were in MY garden, yes MY GARDEN..!! It wasn't Endor who gave you that scar – IT WAS ME….!!!

Mary was now enjoying telling Agnes, as she moved even further towards her, as the Witch took a few steps back.

"You lie - that's not possible – that was 30 years ago……you weren't even born….!!!" The old witch spat out, as she looked at Mary with disdain.

"Oh, but I WAS there – and I saw everything that happened..!!"

"How…?? How could you..?? I don't believe you – you're LYING…!!!"

"You just keep thinking back Agnes….." and as she said those words, Mary raised her right arm, and shut one eye, as she focused with the other, and aimed her finger, like a pointed gun at Agnes. She slowly drew a line over Agnes' scar; from the top of it, going down to under her chin. The scar slowly began to open up as the woman screamed, and put her hand up to her face, as fresh blood began to pour from the open wound.

As Agnes clutched her face; and with blood running through her fingers, Mary shouted…..

"Now do you remember…?!!

Then Agnes suddenly stopped looking afraid, and remembered back to that evening, and began to smile, as blood ran into her mouth, and coated her teeth. She snarled at Mary, dipped her head, narrowed her eyes, and looked directly into Mary's eyes, and said, spitefully.

"Oh….so if you were really there, as you claim to be, you should also recall then, that that was the night that I killed your BROTHER….!!!" She spat out those last few words, as spots of blood sprayed from her mouth.

Mary began to shake from a mixture of anger, hatred and grief. She glared so hard at Agnes, that Agnes took a step back. All of Mary's pent up emotions that she had been harbouring for years; the loss of her beloved Father, the disappearance of Jenny, and then the death of her Mother, finally reached its peak, as she let out the biggest scream as she thrust both her arms forward towards Agnes, as she continued to glare. It was as if all of her emotions could be seen leaving her body, as a cascading river of red fiery sparks flew towards Agnes. The decibels of sound from Mary's scream were so intense; they could be seen leaving Mary's mouth. The Oreads and the Satyrs all held their ears….. Agnes brought her hands to her ears and screamed in pain, as her feet left the ground.

Mary had brought both her hands up as she was controlling Agnes in mid-air. Then she slammed the woman to the ground. Agnes turned around quickly as she fell and conjured another ball of fire that came hurtling towards Mary. Mary quickly re-directed the ball of fire into the sky, and it quickly faded. Mary swiftly brought Agnes back up from the ground, and held her there, suspended. Before Agnes could cast anymore spells, Mary had conjured lots of pieces of rope, which quickly flew to Agnes's hands, and bound them tight behind her back. Mary then began swirling her right hand round and round in circles, which made the old Witch spin round and round, going faster and faster in the air. Mary was playing with her, and was enjoying the game. Agnes was screaming out as she went faster and faster.

Mary shouted at Agnes.

"MY VOICE IS THE LAST VOICE YOU WILL EVER HEAR…..!! GO LIVE IN ETERNAL HELL, WHERE YOU BELONG…!!"

With one last push of anger that had built up inside her; Mary quickly looked up at the sky, and a loud rumble of thunder crashed and banged overhead, and a huge black storm cloud came out of the sky, and raced down towards Agnes, who was now unconscious, as she continued to spin. The storm cloud enveloped Agnes like a cloaked demon completely, until she no longer could be seen. Then the black cloud raced off into the night sky, taking Agnes with it.

As the black storm cloud raced away, a huge bolt of lightning careered jaggedly out of the sky, and made its way straight to the black cloud. There was an almighty crash and bang, as they both collided with each other, followed by an explosion that was so loud, it reverberated all around, and then it slowly faded away into the distance, until there was nothing left....

Mary fell to the floor............

# Chapter 33

# **<u>The Wand</u>**

It must have been in the early hours of the morning when Mary awoke to find herself on the top of her bed, fully clothed. As she swung her legs around slowly, she sat momentarily on the edge of the bed, with her head bent. She cupped her hands over her face, and thought about the long, long day from yesterday, and the events from the night before.

She got up and went over to the front window, and peered outside from behind the curtain. The Satyrs were still stood there, guarding the front of the cottage. She looked out from the back bedroom window, and could just see the faint white silvery light coming from the presence of the Oreads. Mary felt a sense of guilt – they were all out there, guarding her home. She wearily wandered back to her bedside, and just stood still on the spot, feeling so tired. She decided to go back to bed…..She lay down, pulled the duvet up around her, and she fell asleep straight away.

Mary suddenly woke up, and she was in the kitchen; but she was back in the year she was born – 1964. She knew it was that year, because she remembered the kitchen in the cottage from her previous dream. She saw the old gas stove, the bucket of coal next to the old combustion stove, and the kitchen table with the table set for one person, and a baby chair next to it. Mary knew that this was the day that Endor and Agnes had fought outside. She walked over to the front kitchen window, and peered through some net curtains onto the front garden of the cottage. There was no one outside. She looked up at the sky, and realised it was morning. The two sisters had argued later on that afternoon. She wondered why she was there. She walked over to the back of the kitchen and looked out over onto the back garden.
There, in the garden, sat on the grass, was Endor, and next to her, was her baby Brother – Edward….

Mary laid her hand on her chest, and drew a little breath in. She stood and watched for a few minutes, which seemed like such a long time, but she was trying to take in as much as she could – knowing of course, what would happen later on that afternoon.

Tears pricked in her eyes, and she felt angry because she didn't know why she was back here, on 'that' day. She watched as Edward played in the morning sun, trying to catch a bumble bee, and then fell abruptly on his bottom, and then laughed.

Mary longed to go outside.

Suddenly…..from the garden, Endor turned around, and looked directly into the kitchen window. Mary bobbed her head down, wondering if Endor could see her; but how could she..?? Mary decided to go outside. She ventured into the back garden with such trepidation, and nerves, but as she tentatively took small steps, and became closer and closer, she realised that Endor couldn't hear or see her. In a way, she was glad, and sighed.

Endor looked around again, as if she had heard something. Mary stopped in her tracks, and then she heard Endor say to Edward.

"We keep hearing things don't we Edward..? Yes, we do…" and tickled the child, who giggled so infectiously, that Mary's heart lurched.

"It must be just the wind eh..? Yes…. Yes… just the wind, playing tricks on us" and she laughed as she tickled him again.

Mary looked at Endor, and wished she knew her. What a wonderful, brave and courageous woman she was, to have looked after, and cared for Mary's Father Eldon; and here she was, looking after Edward, Eldon's son. She carried on witnessing the special bond between them both. Endor had put a little old blanket on the ground, and they were both sat down on it and Endor was making pretend tea, with a blue painted teapot – the very same teapot that Mary had found in the undergrowth of the bushes when she had first cleared up the garden.

Edward got up onto to his feet, and started walking, and then within a second, he was at the back of the garden. Mary was shocked; how could he move so fast?! Endor quickly went to retrieve him; but he kept doing it. Endor was laughing, and then said.

"I'm going to have to keep an eye on you, young Edward; you're picking things up so quickly..! Yes you are; you're just like your Great Great Grandma Celeste – she was exceptionally quick as well. She could get anywhere within seconds. Goodness me, you're keeping me on my toes young man..!" ......and she laughed again, as she swung Edward up in the air and round in a circle, and then back down, and the little boy giggled with glee.

Mary then realised how Edward had got himself to the front of the cottage so quickly, later on that afternoon, and had encountered Agnes, without Endor even noticing that he had gone. He obviously had a gift of moving swiftly. Endor hadn't realised that he wasn't there next to her while she was digging away; and that's why she had left the spade - still with soil on it, as she had hurried to the front of the cottage; but Agnes had got to him already.

Mary's anger suddenly grew again at the thought of Agnes, and how she had mercilessly killed her Brother. Why oh why couldn't she have gone back in time to just before it had happened, then she might have been able to save him…?!!
A cool breeze blew through the garden, and turned a little stronger, as Endor looked up and around her, as she held onto Edward. Mary realised that she herself was causing the wind, so she quickly breathed in slowly as she closed her eyes, and within seconds, the warm, calm sunny morning had resumed. Endor looked a little puzzled; but her thoughts were interrupted by Edward chattering.

"Doe, Doe…."

"Yes, my precious child, that's me, your Auntie 'Doe'…"
Mary smiled, as it was obviously Endor that Mary's mother was referring to all those years ago, when she used to say to her …'you're just like your Auntie Doe'…

Mary wished that she could just stay in that moment. Endor had started chattering to Edward again.

"So, Edward, look what we have here. This is a little baby fir tree. Do you want to help Auntie Doe plant it this afternoon..??" she asked the boy.

"Yes, yes....tree" he answered, whilst clapping his little hands together. Mary's eyes filled with tears once again. This was so lovely to see, but so heart breaking at the same time.

"Ok, well let's have some milk and cheese and biscuits first, then we can play, and then we can plant it afterwards. It's a very, very special little tree you know. It was given to me by the tree folk..!" she smiled broadly as Edward looked at the little tree in a pot on the ground, and looked back at Endor with wide eyes.

Mary watched as Endor walked back to the cottage, carrying Edward on her hip, and then looked down at the tree. How wonderful that the tree folk had given it to her. Mary then realised the importance of the little tree, because of where it had come from, and knew how important the tree was to her as well. She bent down, to touch the tiny tree branches, but her hand went straight through it. She had forgotten that she was in a dream.
She knelt down on the ground, then turned around and looked back at the kitchen window of the cottage. She could see Endor still carrying Edward, and talking to him as she was walking around in the kitchen, and getting milk from the fridge.

Mary looked back at the tree – closed her eyes, and for a few moments, she 'wished' she could touch it, and how the branches would feel in her hands. She opened her eyes, and put her hand forward towards the branches. She could feel it..!! Her hand didn't go through it..!! Mary gasped. She rubbed the greenery between her fingers and put her hand to her nose; she could smell the pine..!! How..?!

She remembered what Luci the firefly had said to her – that if she thought about wanting something, she just had to think about it.....but that was in real time, not in her dream. She suddenly wondered if it was possible that she could maybe just touch her baby brother's little hand, just once. She got up quickly, brushed the soil from her knees, and made her way to the back door, which was open. She could hear Endor singing to Edward.

"Incy Wincy Spider – climbed up the spout.
Down came the raindrops, and washed poor Incy out..!
Up came the sunshine, and dried it all away.....
......and Incy Wincy Spider, climbed the spout again"

Edward clapped his hands with glee, and was shouting 'again, again'…
Endor began to sing 'Humpty Dumpty' this time, as Mary walked into the kitchen.

Edward was sat at the table in his high chair, banging the table with his hands. Mary walked in cautiously, and Edward looked up, and looked straight at Mary, and a broad smile appeared on his face. He could see her…!! Mary smiled back and waved at him. Edward lifted one hand up and waved it up and down.

"Mare-yee, (*Mary) Mare-yee…"he said.

Endor stopped singing, and said.

"What are you saying Edward..? Are you learning new words?!"

Endor still had her back to him, as she cut up some pieces of cheese.

"You ARE a clever boy…! Are you singing, 'Mary, Mary, quite contrary, how does your garden grow… ??"

"Mare-yee, Mare-yee…!" he shouted again, excitedly as he looked at Mary. Mary realised that he was trying to say her name…!

Endor turned around. Mary had just gone over to her brother, and he was smiling up at her and now banging his hands on the table with excitement. His skin looked so soft, and she longed to pick him up. As Endor had turned around, she could see Edward looking up into thin air, and laughing.

"Yady, Yady (*Lady)…." He said, as he looked over at Endor; but was pointing at Mary.

Endor, very carefully put the cheese down on the table, and looked around, and also at a blank space where Mary was stood.

Endor carefully picked Edward up from his high chair, as she continued to look around. Edward's arm stretched back to try and touch Mary's hand. Mary gave him her hand, and he clasped hold of her fingers. Mary's other hand went to her mouth, as she began to cry.

"No kyi,….(*cry)……no kyi yady……. (*Lady)…" he said. Mary burst into tears.

"Doe, Doe… yady kyi"….(*Lady cry)…..he said to Endor, and pointed to where Mary was stood.

Mary now had both of her hands over her mouth, and was sobbing…..
Endor slowly reached for her wand. Mary was shocked.

"It's ok Edward, they won't hurt you, Doe's here…" she said soothingly as she jogged him up and down on her hip whilst still looking round.

"I would never hurt my brother, never…!" Mary said out loud.

Endor suddenly stopped rocking Edward.

"Who's there…? What did you say…?"

"I'm not here to hurt you, or my brother, please - believe me…!" Mary wailed.

Endor spoke.

"I was told I may encounter a visitor today, in a dream that I had last night, but I was not to be afraid, as this was of great importance. I would know when that would be, so I gather this is now....... I have a message for you. The message is this...." Endor thought for a few moments, then said:

**"Do not fear – stand tall amongst people.**
**Those that love you are listening.**
**Craft your wand from the tree"**

"I hope that I have been of help to you; and that this makes some sense"

Mary realised it was time to go. She saw a piece of paper and a pen on the side. She walked over, and stood. Then she willed herself to pick the pen up, which she did, and she managed to write:

### Thank you so much.......Mary...

Endor was surprised to see the pen move on its own, and when the pen went down, and she read it, she said:

"You are very welcome...I am happy to help"

"Bye yady…..(*Lady)….." Edward waved as Mary walked out of the door. She turned around, just one more time to see those turquoise blue eyes for the last time, and waved back. She walked out of the door, and to the back garden, sobbing…...

Mary suddenly woke up in her bed. Her pillow was wet with tears. She laid there, and just cried and cried until she could cry no more. She looked at the time, and it was very late in the morning. Her clock on her bedside cabinet said 11:30am.

"Come on Mary Mayr Le Fey, pull yourself together" she said to herself. "It's your Birthday tomorrow – so today is going to be a good day…!"

She had a shower, and just stood there, letting the water keep splashing on her face, until she felt much calmer. She couldn't get little Edward's face out of her mind.

Then her mind went back to last night, and the confrontation with Agnes. She needed to speak with Ooshiya-Lion….

Everyone was outside in the garden; it was such a warm day again. Mary blinked in the bright sunlight, and shaded her eyes. Ooshiya-Lion was up at the top of the garden, and sat in the shade of the tree, with his mane out. It was too hot for him to have his hat on, or be in the sun.

"Ah there you are sleepy head" he beckoned to Mary. "Are you alright Mary, and do you remember anything from last night..?"

Mary sat down on the grass at the side of the old man under the shade of the tree. She picked at the grass nonchalantly.

"Yes, I do remember Ooshiya-Lion, of course I do"

"So how do you feel about Agnes then..? You do know that she's gone don't you..??" he asked her, as if she wasn't taking anything in.

"Yes……I don't know where though. All I know is that, again, I was SO angry with her for what she's done….. and….well, my temper just gets the better of me" She shrugged her shoulders, as if she didn't care less.

"But Mary, she's gone…" Ooshiya-Lion said earnestly. "….and the way you handled yourself was quite remarkable, I have to say…"

"Well she went before and came back didn't she – so who knows…?! I wasn't afraid of her anyway. She's nothing but an old woman, whose spells don't seem to work anymore, and she's weak. Something happened to Agnes when she went back in time – I know it. It's like half of her has been taken away, like someone taking away someone's memory, where you can only remember a little bit"

"What's REALLY on your mind Mary..?" the old man asked.

Mary hesitated.

"I don't know what tomorrow will bring. I don't have a clue what's going to happen. I don't know how I feel about it all really......
I always thought my 30th Birthday would be a big celebration with family, friends, maybe a husband....and children....." she trailed off as she quickly looked away, not wanting Ooshiya-Lion to see tears in her eyes.

The old man lowered his head – he really felt for Mary. Without looking at him, she said.

"I had another 'dream' last night...."

"Where did you go...??" he asked.

Just at that moment, Mary quickly jumped up.

"I know what I have to do, I nearly forgot...!!"

She made her way quickly to the shed, and came out brandishing a saw and a small axe. She strode straight over to the fir tree, which was so tall and green now, and she began looking through the branches. Ooshiya-Lion rushed over to her.

"What are you doing...?!" he asked, worryingly.

Mary ignored him, and bent down on her knees. Henry, Patsy, Wilbur and Elma all turned up, as they had suddenly seen Mary get up quickly from talking to Ooshiya-Lion, go to the shed and come out with some tools.

"Mary....what are you going to do...?!" Henry shouted. "Are you alright..?? Is she alright..?" and turned to the old man, who just shrugged his shoulders and shook his head, and had a blank look on his face, the same as the others.

Mary bent down closer, and suddenly began whispering to the tree.


**"Oh tree of wonder, which I have come to know.**
**I've seen you, and loved you, and watched you grow.**

I am bound to ask of you, a question with much guilt;
A branch I must cut, so re-grow, don't wilt.
A wand to be made from a tree so young;
and forever in your debt, until thy day is done.
This purpose it serves me, and will remain with me evermore.
Please help me to choose one, for it will open the door....."

Again, Mary didn't quite know where the words came from. The tree suddenly began moving and rustling. Mary stepped back a little, as did the others, and watched the fir tree move and shake. Then a faint voice was heard, which seemed to be coming from the roots of the tree.

*"Waited, I have waited, for this day to pass*
*For the honour is mine, you see.*
*The finest branches I have grown,*
*And I fear not, that a branch to be mown*
*My choosing, is the finest one from me.*

*So I choose this one for you, for its strength and its shape*
*Use it well, and it will never let you down.*
*Let it be by your side, and be your friend and your guide*
*And together, you will both be renowned."*

Immediately after the voice stopped, a loud crack could be heard, and then the branches parted, and there in the undergrowth, a single branch lay. Mary stooped forward to retrieve the branch, and slowly picked it out, and into the sunlight. It was slightly thick at one end, and the other end went into a finer point. As soon as Mary held it, a huge sense of strength surged through her. In an instant, her pale yellow/green eyes shone so brightly, that the light from them, lit the tip of the branch. The light surged straight through the branch and into the whole body of it, right to the thicker part that Mary was holding. A sudden gush of wind blew past Mary from nowhere, then circled around her completely, and lifted her from the ground, as it continued to hold both her, and the branch. She looked down and around her at the others who were now looking up at her. Then after a few more seconds the wind cyclone brought her back down very slowly and gently, and onto the grass, then it was gone.

Ooshiya-Lion eventually spoke. "That's a bonding I haven't seen in a very long time. How did you know….??"
"My dream…." She answered.

"Oh, I see….well that was quite spectacular Mary. You and the tree have had a very special affinity since the day you saw it, when you first came here. Now you have your very own wand. Keep it safe, and use it wisely"
He got up to walk away, and then turned around and said.

"I feel like celebrating, and I'd love a chip butty, anyone care to join me..?! Mary I want you to tell me all about your dream. Let's eat..!"

As they walked back down the garden, Henry, Patsy and Wilbur 'flew' Elma, and they were all chatting excitedly. A Robin had been watching from the tall tree that Ooshiya-Lion had been sat under, not a few minutes before. It flew down the garden after the others, and perched on a bird table not far from the back kitchen window. It started to sing a very chirpy song in the midday sun.

During lunch, which Mary had 'arranged', they all chatted about the fir tree giving up one of its branches to Mary, which led Ooshiya-Lion to say.

"What was your 'dream' Mary. Did it have anything to do with the fir tree..?"

"Yes, it did" And so she proceeded to tell everyone about the dream that she had, and how lovely it was to see Edward again.

Ooshiya-Lion was most intrigued to hear that Endor could feel her presence, and almost hear her. When she told them about picking the pen up, and writing a 'thank you' to Endor, the old man nearly fell off his chair.

"This is fascinating that this could happen….!!…. but more so, that Edward could see you; but then again, children are very susceptible to seeing 'things' apparitions and spirits etc"

Elma was still not totally happy with Ooshiya-Lion. He looked at him whilst he was talking, with a furrowed brow.

Ooshiya-Lion realised that Mary was quite down, and knew that it was because she had seen Edward, and not really looking forward to her Birthday, and whatever else may happen tomorrow.

After lunch was over, Mary went to the shed, and sought some fine grain sanding paper, and began to sand down the branch, and pull away bits of old bark - not too much, as she quite liked the gnarled looking branch. It did feel indeed like she had suddenly got herself a new friend; she felt a really strong bond with the wand so much already.

Ooshiya-Lion talked quietly with the others in the kitchen

"What's going to happen after today..? I'm quite worried" Henry asked the old man.

"I haven't the faintest idea, but I think we are in quite safe hands if you ask me" and smiled as he looked out of the window towards Mary in the garden. The Robin was still hopping about outside. Ooshiya-Lion looked straight at it, got up off his seat, and went to the window.

"I still don't trust him" Elma said in a low voice.

"Oh Elma..!" Patsy said.

"He HAS got a point" Henry said whispering. "He still hasn't explained about the conversation with the Dragon yet...!"

"Well, he's a Wizard, and I think they do and say strange things all the time" Wilbur said, and shrugged his shoulders. "We'll just have to see what happens tomorrow"

Ooshiya-Lion came back from the window, and said brightly.

"What about having a party for Mary tonight for her Birthday..?!
I think she needs it, and we could all do with letting our hair down, and have a bit of a boogie. I'll sort everything out, if you go and tell everyone that they are all invited. I think it will make her very happy, she's had it tough; and let's have a big cake and candles..!!"

All the others agreed that it was a good idea.

"See" said Patsy, giving Elma a nudge. Elma shook his head.
Patsy then said to him "I know what you should do" she said. "Think of a really nice Birthday present you can get for Mary..!"

# Chapter 34

# **The Party**

After Mary had spent quite a bit of time in the garden, sanding down her wand, she felt really tired all of a sudden.
She told the others that she was going for a lie down and not to disturb her.
Ooshiya-Lion went outside to the front of the cottage, and spoke with Taurus, but Taurus was troubled.

"Ooshiya-Lion; I feel something. There is unrest somewhere. The wind blows differently through the trees – I hear it, and I feel it"

"Mmmmm…. I do too. I cannot tell this to Mary, she is not herself lately. She is resting again, and she needs her strength. I need to take a walk. Be vigilant Taurus"

They parted company as the old man began to walk up the lane. After a little way, he turned left into the small lane and walked along, until presently, he came upon the barn. Ooshiya-Lion stopped at the door, and tapped lightly with the foot of his staff. There was nothing. The old man tapped again, a little louder this time.

"One thing I am NOT – is deaf..!" a man's voice said from inside the barn "Give me one minute..!"
After what seemed like a long time, the door finally swung open.

"Well, are you going to stand out there, or are you coming in – you've been waiting long enough..?"

"I thought you might be sleeping" Ooshiya-Lion said brightly.

"I was…." Beruc stepped forward. The Dragon did look quite tired.

Ooshiya-Lion walked in through the door, closed it behind him, and took a chair by the little window.

"Well, I'm not surprised you're tired, you've been quite busy lately, haven't you..?" the old man said, looking at Beruc with raised eyebrows.

Beruc looked at the old man.

"Well I could say the same to you. Anyway, as I'm sure you are quite aware; it's very difficult for me sometimes to......."

"Yes, yes, I know. Well I won't stay long, so you may as well try and get some sleep. I just wanted to tell you that there is a party tonight – and you're invited...!"

The Dragon looked straight at the old man.

"Why didn't you tell me this before when...."

"....because it wasn't sorted out then". Ooshiya-Lion hurriedly said.

"What's the reason for the party? Obviously Mary's Birthday .....anything else?"

"Well, the other obvious reason being Agnes's departure..."

"Mmmmmm...." Beruc pondered.

"The other reason..." said the old man. "..... is that Mary is very quiet, and not her usual self, she's very tired, and a little down, so a gathering of fun should raise the spirits..!!"

"I would be careful how you phrase that" Beruc said. "Anyway, I thought last night's 'performance' went quite well I'd say. I was chuckling to myself, I can't lie" Beruc showed lots of teeth, as he laughed softly.

Ooshiya-Lion looked sideways at Beruc, and with a wry smile said.

"How will this affect you, now that Agnes has gone..?"

"That, I do not know – it all depends how tomorrow goes"

"So….." the old man said, as he stood to his feet. "…should we be expecting you at what time tonight..?

"Well…..that depends on what time I get up. I need more sleep"

"Well I dare say that I need you there my old friend – don't let me down, and when you get there, keep your eyes peeled"

Ooshiya-Lion left the barn, and the Dragon settled down on the floor. He thought for a moment, then closed his eyes, and settled down to sleep.

"See, I told you..!!" Elma whispered to Patsy, Henry and Wilbur.

They had followed Ooshiya-Lion to the barn, and had heard every word of the conversation.

Henry looked very concerned, Wilbur was scratching his head, and Patsy was nearly in tears.

"Henry, I can't believe that Ooshiya-Lion has invited this Dragon to the party, what are we going to do…??!" Patsy asked, feeling rather upset.

Henry was deep in thought.

"Right, this is what we're going to do……..nothing..!" he said.

"NOTHING..??!!" they all said at once.

"Yes - and the reason for that is…… if something bad is going to happen tonight, we all need to be on our guard. Mary has all the Oreads, and the Satyrs - and she has us; even though we aren't big in size, we can make up in bravery. She has Tufri and Luci as well now, AND she just fought Agnes Le Fey off, and can quite look after herself"

"…but he's just invited a bloody great big Dragon Henry…!!" Elma said in a hushed exasperation.

"Look…" Henry said. "We have to be practical – there is nothing we can do. We just act normal at this party tonight. Be vigilant, ok..?? ….and let's keep off the alcohol; I know it's a party, but we need to keep focused. Now that Agnes has gone, the pressure is off somewhat, but we potentially have a Dragon at the party. Agreed….??"

"Agreed" they all said at once.

From inside the barn, Beruc had been listening…he could, after all, hear anything. He laughed to himself, as he curled up in the corner of the barn, as little swirls of smoke unfurled from his nostrils.

Back at the cottage, Ooshiya-Lion had started to decorate the whole of the kitchen in a great big party theme. There were multi-coloured tissue garlands strung from one end of the room to the other. There were balloons of every colour and shape. He had conjured all of Mary's favourite foods. There were bottles of Mead, Honey Wine, Blackberry, Lime and Pear Wine. There was some Wheat Beer for Lars, and Barley & Maple Beer for the Satyrs. There was something for everyone – even lemon flavoured rain drops for the Oreads.

Everyone had dressed smart. Patsy looked extremely pretty in a dress that Bonny the spider, had helped her with. Bonny had spun lots of webs, rolled them all up, and both of them had spent ages combing the web out with old twigs. Red rose petals had been soaked in water, which had turned the water a pale pink; and this was then dabbed on the webbing with some garden moss. Bonny attached the rose pink webbing under Patsy's wings with some more fine spun webbing to keep it in place. It was beautiful. Henry had combed his hair down and put his favourite waistcoat on which had belonged to his Grandfather, and had been made by his Grandmother out of dried dandelion leaves. He had a gold watch hanging from his pocket by a chain over to his other pocket.

Wilbur was stuck for something to wear, so had asked Ooshiya-Lion for some help. Next minute, he was stood in a cowboy hat, and 3 pairs of cowboy boots…but he couldn't walk in them, so he just wore the hat.

Elma was wearing a black dickie bow with red and white spots on it. He wanted to look exceptionally smart, so had asked Nancy the Ladybird to help him make him one out of old sweet wrappers. He had slicked his hair down and had a side parting, but it kept springing up, so he had to keep wetting his hand and 'combing' it down. He had picked a tiny rose for Mary from her garden, and he had made her a card from an old bit of paper he had found in the shed, and stuck a few pebbles and bits of twigs and leaves, and an old bird's feather on it, using some glue that Patsy and Wilbur had to fly up to the top shelf in the shed to get it down for him.

Lars was looking dapper in his favourite waistcoat and black jacket, and obviously was wearing his very shiny boots.

Everyone was ready - and waiting for Mary.

Elma had a sneaky taste of the Blackberry, Lime & Pear Wine when nobody was looking, which, after taking quite a gulp, was alarmed to find out that it was quite strong. This in turn made him cough into his fist, and turned his face slightly purple, as he tried to hide his cough, and also made his eyes go really big.

'Blimey, that's good stuff….' He said to himself.

After he had recovered himself and stopped coughing, he turned round and got himself another glass. The thing was; with the Blackberry, Lime & Pear Wine, it DID make your lips and mouth turn purple. So after two glasses, Elma looked like he was wearing a nice shade of pale cherry coloured lipstick…!
Mary eventually woke up. She had slept soundly, without even moving in her bed at all. She was really disorientated, having already got up that day from her bed. She focused on the bedroom clock, and it said 7:30pm.

"Oh my God, I've been asleep for three and half hours..!! I won't sleep tonight now..!"

She got out of bed, and made her way into the bathroom and had a shower to wake herself up. Tufri had been keeping a look out whilst hiding behind the bedroom curtain. He quickly flew downstairs to tell the others that Mary had just woken up.

Mary got dressed into some slouchy but clean, and very comfortable cream coloured lounging pants, and a white t–shirt, and felt so much more refreshed. Her wand was laid at the side of her bed on the bedside cabinet. She walked around to pick it up, and turned it over and over in her hands. It was such an unusual shaped branch; and the gnarled grain stood out – it was beautiful. Mary smiled, and said to herself
'I knew there was something special about you the moment I saw you. Thank you'

The wand shook a little in her hand.

"What is it…?!" she asked.

A slightly worried look appeared on Mary's face, as she heard a faint voice say.

"Beware Mary, but be ready……"

Mary seemed to understand, and with that, she slipped the wand into her right pocket. She was just about to make her way downstairs, when she stopped, turned around, and walked back over to her dressing table. On the dressing table stood the little old box which she had received through the post with the old wooden key inside. She opened the box, took the key out and put it in her pocket. Then, she made her way downstairs.

As she went down the stairs, she could smell food cooking. Who was in her kitchen cooking..??

As she walked into the kitchen, she was loudly greeted with a host of voices shouting a big 'SURPRISE'..!! She stopped still. Suddenly lots of loud cracks could be heard, as everyone let their popping confetti off into the air; and the whole kitchen was covered in millions of bits of coloured paper. Then Ooshiya-Lion produced lots of whirling, sparkling Catherine Wheels, which were whizzing around the kitchen. Everybody was cheering and clapping, and shouting 'Happy Birthday…!'

There were paper lanterns in every colour just hanging in the air; and paper butterflies were darting about here and there. There was a huge Birthday cake in the middle of the kitchen table, which had three tiers, and was draped in gold and green icing, and there was so much food – all Mary's favourites. There were scones with cream and jam, sausage sandwiches, jelly and cream, jam butties, jacket potatoes and beans with peanut butter, and more.

Everything was all higgledy piggledy….just like Mary loved…and the kitchen was full..! Ooshiya-Lion was there, with Henry, Patsy, Wilbur and Elma - who looked like he was going to burst, he was that excited..! Everyone from the garden was present; and Nancy the Ladybird's children were running in and around the jam butties, and squealing with delight. Bonny the spider was there; she was chatting away to Patsy. Even Taurus had left his post outside the front of the cottage, and drinking some of Henry's Honey Tea. Three other Satyrs had come in to enjoy the fun, as had six of the Oreads. Luci and Tufri were on top of the kitchen cupboards, away from the light, but cheering and clapping, Jeremy the snail, with Jemima and Ben, who were already munching on cucumber from their own bowl. Everyone was smiling, and shouting Mary over. Mary felt completely over-whelmed. She had never before, had so many people gather at a party for her.

Bam Bam raced over to Mary, bowed his head, and said.

"With the utmost respect, please - take my arm, I would gladly walk you to your party table"

Bam Bam raised himself up to Mary's height, instantly grew another nobbly, woody arm from his thick body of wood, and guided her. Mary looked to her right, and took his arm. Ooshiya-Lion was looking at Bam Bam's incredible show of subservience towards Mary.

"If I'd have known there was a party, I would have dressed for the occasion..!" Mary said, feeling very 'un-party like'.

"Welcome to your party Mary..!!" Ooshiya-Lion shouted, then went into a resounding 'Three cheers for Mary, and 'Hip Hip, Hooray' three times. Everyone cheered and clapped.

Mary felt over-whelmed and tearful.

As she got to the table, Elma ran up, a bit wonky, with some hair stuck up that he couldn't flatten down, and very, very purple lips; and in a slightly drunken voice said.

"Mary, I have a preshjent for you..!" he said in a slurred voice.

"Elma..!" Shouted Patsy. " Have you been on the Blackberry, Lime & Pear Wine..?!"

"No....I have mosht shertainly not – nope, not me....I wasshjn't even there....Nope, it washz them over there..!" and pointed over his shoulder, at no one, and then looked up at Mary.

"Here Mary, I made you thisssh" and promptly shoved his card in her hand with all the twigs and leaves and the birds feather on it, and he had signed it with each of his legs, which he had dipped in mud. Then he produced the tiny rose from behind his back. Mary took it from him, and laughed.

"Oh Elma, you are so sweet. This is the loveliest present I have ever had. You do make me smile…and….I DO love you..!"

His face was a picture….

"I DO…??!....and, and DO you..????!....becosshz I do" Everyone laughed, which made him laugh, and he showed lots of purple stained teeth…!!
Mary then began looking around at all the decorations, which were like nothing she had ever seen before. Her kitchen table was decorated with many exquisite crystals, which adorned her Mothers vintage table cloth.

"These are just so elegant and so beautiful – I'm lost for words..!" Mary exclaimed, as she picked a few up in her fingers, and turned them over, examining them. "They are just absolutely beautiful..!"

"These are a small gift from the Oreads Mary – from beneath the mountain" Ooshiya-Lion explained. "They are 'Protecting Crystals'. So you only need to carry a few in your pocket, and they will always be of assistance should you need it"

Mary looked at the leader of the Oreads, who had stepped forward.

"Thank you – very, very much, it's so kind of you"

"It is with our pleasure. We are most grateful to you Mary, descendant of Omega and Sorcier" she answered in a very faint but breathy voice. She bowed her head. Her long thin silvery hair was like a sheet of the finest spun silk, which fell to her knees, and the crystals which adorned it, shone; and each had their own pale hazy orb surrounding them. Mary was completely mesmerised. The white floaty dress she wore, seemed to be covered in a white hazy fog, which gave the illusion that she was floating.

Mary put the crystals she had in her hand, into her pocket.

Taurus stepped forward. He bowed his head, and handed Mary a wooden gift box.

"Our gift to you, Mary - we hope you like it"

He stepped back as Mary looked down at the box. It was about the size of her hand, and she could see that it had been hand crafted with the smallest of tools; and the details and craftsmanship were unique. There were moons and stars, strange looking flying objects, shooting stars with green sparkly tails. There were hares, foxes, owls, bats and trees with faces. It was exquisite. Mary opened the box slowly, and inside, and lain on a bed of soft feathery down - was a necklace. The chain was made of the tiniest rings of wood, and on the end of the chain, was a tiny crafted oak tree. Mary picked out the necklace, and carefully placed the box on the table. She turned the necklace over and over in her fingers. Again, it had been crafted with the smallest of detail. It had Mary's name, and her birth date carved on the back of the tree.

"Oh…. I'm completely speechless, this is just…..so…..beautiful.
In fact….I can't even find the words…. Thank you so much…."

Taurus proudly explained.

"The necklace has been carved from the oldest oak tree in the forest Mary. In fact, the oak himself was more than happy for us to take some of his wood. The fairies, the nymphs and the wood speckled butterflies have contributed to the carvings. When worn, this will protect you, should you ever need to hide. Just hold the tree in your hand, and close your eyes; and you will go un-seen, as you blend into the object to which you stand closest to"

Mary gasped at the information, as she slowly put the necklace over her head. Everyone came to look and marvel at it.

"It's not my Birthday until tomorrow, why the celebrations today..?" Mary looked at Ooshiya-Lion.

"Well, a little 'un-Birthday' celebration never hurt anyone – besides, this is also a 'happy' party, seeing as Agnes has gone..!"

Mary walked to the front kitchen window, and Ooshiya-Lion followed her. She was looking at the back of the remaining Satyrs still standing there outside the cottage.

"They don't have to be there really, do they…?!" she asked.

"Well, one never knows…... They are more than happy to help Mary…"

Mary looked up at the old man….

"Why did you disappear last night…? You vanished – why..?" Mary looked at him quizzically.

"I didn't want her to see me. She knew that you had help from somewhere, and it would have only made it worse. You had plenty of help around you, should anything have happened – but you didn't need any……..did you…??" he looked down at Mary and raised his eyebrows, then smiled.

"Come on, back to the party. Tomorrow is indeed your Birthday Mary, but today we celebrate, for we know not of what will happen tomorrow, and we have to be prepared…"

Patsy shouted Mary over.

"Mary, come and light the candles on your Birthday cake..!!"

Mary returned to the party, whilst Ooshiya-Lion went over to speak with Taurus.

"Go on Mary, light your cake..!" Wilbur shouted.

Mary braced herself, held her right hand up, and clicked her fingers, and whispered.

"Ignis"

A small flame appeared on the index finger on Mary's right hand. She walked to her cake and lit all 30 of her candles.
There were lots of clapping and cheers. The candles weren't just ordinary candles though; they were ornately shaped green and gold candles, each of them on gold spikes. As soon as they were lit, all the icing on the cake came to life, and began swirling and moving around on the cake.

Taurus took a tiny flute from his waistcoat, and began to play. Everyone began jumping up and down, and doing little jigs along to the merry pipe tune. Ooshiya-Lion lit his pipe, and soon there was a mesmerising smell in the room, like chocolate and wood bark, with a small hint of herbs. There was so much laughter. Mary hadn't had as much fun in a long time.

Bam Bam started to 'do-si-do' with Mary, and then everyone joined in. Elma, Wilbur, Patsy and Bonny were doing the 'do-is-do' on the tablecloth. Jeremy, Jemima and Ben also did the dance around the salad bowl. Nancy and her children were dancing to it, in and amongst the crystals on the tablecloth. Ooshiya-Lion put his hand out to the Oread to dance, until everyone was doing the 'do-si-do'…. The paper butterflies were doing it in the air, the plates were spinning around, and everyone was clapping and dancing. The music seemed to be getting louder and louder, and the clapping and 'whoops' of laughter continued through the evening…..It was the best party Mary had ever had.

The party went on for hours. There was not a moment that wasn't filled with something funny or happy. Mary loved every minute of it.

Henry, Wilbur and Patsy, had been keeping a sharp eye out for the Dragon…… but he never came.

# Chapter 35

# **The Coming Dawn…..**

Ooshiya-Lion looked at the time, and it was fifteen minutes to midnight. He clapped his hands a few times, and shouted.

"Can I have everybody's attention please…?!" Nobody really heard him, as they were all in the throng of the party and it was difficult to get them all to be quiet.

Ooshiya-Lion nodded to Taurus, who took his horn from his waistcoat, and blew really loudly, which certainly caught everyone's attention straight away.

"Thank you everyone. Thank you so much for attending tonight, but before we say farewell and good night, the time is approaching midnight, and we have a very special song to sing to a very special person" He looked at Mary.

Then, he led everybody into a resounding 'Happy Birthday'. When they finished singing, they all cheered and clapped!! More party poppers were popped, and lots of laughter rang out.

Suddenly, out of the blue, a huge bang, like the loudest clap of thunder rocked the cottage. The merriment ceased immediately as Ooshiya-Lion shot a look at Taurus, who quickly ran outside with his fellow men. The rest of the Satyrs had been startled, as had the Oreads.
Henry, Wilbur and Patsy looked at one another.

"He's here…!" Wilbur said.

"Take cover - EVERYONE…!" Ooshiya-Lion shouted, as he produced his wand from his inside coat pocket, and dimmed the lights. He looked at Mary, and nodded, as if asking her if she was ready. She responded by nodding back at him.

From outside, a loud and most wicked voice broke the silence. It was a man's voice.

"Where are you.....the one who resides in this property…?!! Come outside, and meet your fate…!!

Mary looked horrified at Ooshiya-Lion. Who WAS that…?! The old man put his finger to his lips, and without a sound, he made his way over to the back kitchen window, and peered outside into the back garden.

The voice rang out again.

"It's YOU we want, nobody else…!!"

It was a voice nobody had heard before.

Mary stood up to go to the back door. Ooshiya-Lion grabbed her arm.

"No Mary….!" He said in a hushed whisper.

"It's me they want….!! If I don't go out to them – whoever they are, God only knows what they might do to this cottage….I HAVE to protect it….!!"

She broke free from his grip, and slipped passed the old man. He tried to grab her leg, but missed.
She got to the back door, but stopped, just before she went outside. She quickly looked to her left, and saw that the huge oak door was now glowing, a bright fiery red.

Mary, with her hand tightly holding her wand in her pocket, shouted out, as she slowly made her way out of the cottage.

"How DARE you come into my garden – show your face, and tell me who you are…!!"

There was silence for a few moments, and then the voice said.

"So…….we meet at last…!! Supposedly the last remaining Le Fey family member I presume..?! Although there IS Agnes, but she is more of a Bishop; and I suppose she will be here any time soon, as she wouldn't have wanted to miss this for the world….!!"

The voice was coming from up above.

As Mary had stepped outside into the darkness of the back garden, the heads of the tall Oreads' could just be seen on the other side of the wall; their ethereal glow shining. Mary looked up into the dark sky, and she could just make out several black silhouettes, that were all hovering on broomsticks……

"Who ARE you….??!! Mary shouted. "How dare you come to my home and invade my garden, demanding time with me….show your faces – all of you…??!!!

"You speak with such bravery - Miss Le Fey….but this is NOT your home…!!

"Yet I am the one who dwells here…." Mary answered - flatly "….and if this is NOT 'supposed' to be my home – then who does it belong to….??!"

The voice shouted back, but a slight breeze had suddenly picked up, and Mary could now see the cloaks of the intruders billowing in the wind.

"It belongs to US…!! The Bishops…!!"


Inside the cottage, Ooshiya-Lion put his head in his hands. Henry, Patsy and Wilbur had flown to the back kitchen window, and were looking up into the dark sky.
Ooshiya-Lion was suddenly startled by someone coming through the back door, which Mary had left ajar. It was the fox…..

"Why are YOU here…?!!" Ooshiya-Lion asked sharply in a hushed voice.

"….because I am a creature of 'stealth'….??.....anyway, I thought you might need some help. Who's outside…??"

"Worse than I thought – it's The Bishops…" the old man answered.

"….but how….??!" said the fox. "The Bishops…??.. I don't understand..!!"

"Me neither – they must have been waiting a long time for this moment. Mary is outside, but she is stronger than I ever thought she would be, but at least we are all here together. Tonight is the night I have been dreading for some time….."

"What's the plan…??" The fox asked.

"There isn't one……." The old man answered. "I need to speak with Taurus, so keep an eye on Mary. I cannot show my face to whoever is out there, but I need to know exactly who it is – although I have my suspicions….."

Ooshiya-Lion quickly vanished.

Outside, Mary stood her ground. She spoke up.

"So…… are you going to introduce yourselves, instead of hiding up there in the shadows…?? …..and why HAVE you waited until now…?!"

"We have indeed been waiting a long, long time, and tonight, at any moment soon, when the clock strikes midnight, on this day 1st August 1994, is when the spells from dear, dear Endor….are no more…and in a few moments, you too will be…. no more"

"So what's you plan….??" Mary defiantly asked.

The voice laughed, and so did a few others.

"You might be a Le Fey, but you are nobody to us, and you are no match for us either – and there is no competition – believe me…!! Here you stand with your flimsy mountain ghosts on the other side of the wall, and a bunch of misfits from the forest – and you think they can PROTECT you…??!!"

Mary laughed. "You too speak with bravery – oh great shadow of the night…."

Her anger was rising, and she wasn't about to try and keep calm. She knew that this moment was of great importance.

The wind blew a little stronger, and the trees in the garden and in the meadow beyond, could be heard rustling in the warm summers evening. Mary felt a tingling in her fingers. She quickly looked towards the back of the kitchen window, and through into the dimly lit kitchen, to the clock on the wall. The time – was 11:55pm……

In her pocket, her wand began to move slightly. Mary grasped it tightly. She remembered the crystals in her other pocket, and the necklace around her neck. From the pit of her stomach, she could feel a strong surge, as if her adrenalin was ready to burst out of her.

The man's voice spoke up again.

"I would have been the one standing just where you are, if my ancestor wasn't KILLED by your delusional and foolish Great Grandfather….!!"

A breeze encircled Mary, and blew her dark hair up, as she glared up at the figure.

"There was nothing delusional about Magnus Gunsam Le Fey…!! All he did was protect what was, AND still is, rightly, a Le Fey property, and YOU have no say…!!!...and I'm so very GLAD Magnus killed Bridget….She was no Le Fey; only by marriage, to get her greedy hands on this cottage, along with her equally greedy parents. She was nothing but a poisonous, evil, hard and cruel witch, who deserved to die…!! Oh – and by the way, Agnes won't be attending your little soiree…..because she's DEAD….!!!"

"You FOOL – Agnes has been waiting for this day for as long as we have…!! You lie…..what of her death…??!"

"I killed her….last night actually….about time too, she was really getting on my bloody nerves….!!!"

There was murmuring between the others. The speaker put his hand up for them to stop, but one of them spoke.

"I will go fetch Moroi…." and disappeared.

The speaker slowly descended onto the ground, and left his broomstick hanging in mid-air, until he was stood facing Mary.

He stepped forward slightly from the darkness, just so his face could be seen by the light of the moon. He had very black wavy shoulder length hair, and a neatly groomed black moustache and a beard, which came to a sharp point. His eyes were dark. He wore a high necked black shirt with small gold buttons, and a long black cape, and his face was worn and lined, but quite distinguished. There was something about his face that wasn't quite as menacing as Mary had thought.

He then spoke.

"In answer to your earlier question, my name is Vagust Tusgav Bishop"

At that moment Vagust did a strange thing, and seemed to be looking at Mary, as if he wanted to tell her something – but couldn't. As he stood looking at her, he quickly shifted his eyes to the left, and then to the right, and then looked back at Mary pleadingly….which Mary thought was very odd.
She held onto her wand tightly in her pocket. Vagust suddenly composed himself, and then said, almost like he was acting….

"So…..you say you have killed Agnes…How…?? He asked flatly. "She was a distant cousin to me…"

Mary answered him, rather sarcastically. "Well, she was my Great Auntie, but she meant absolutely nothing to ME!"

A few minutes before, as Ooshiya-Lion had gone to speak urgently with Taurus at the front of the cottage. The old man quickly relayed to Taurus what he had heard the voice outside say. Taurus immediately spoke words, softly into his large hands. He then blew onto them as he flung out his arms. As his words were released, they were carried by his breath, towards the forest. A reply came back quickly, to which the old man looked slightly relieved. Ooshiya-Lion crept back to the cottage, and sent the fox to the side of the wall where the Oreads stood, to tell them not to attack until he gave the signal. He had also sent Tufri to the back of the garden wall to relate the same message to the Satyrs – who were ready, and waiting.

Ooshiya-Lion looked at his watch, and tapped it with the tip of his wand, and began murmuring a spell. Suddenly, time stopped, and so did everyone else, apart from himself, Taurus, Mary……and Vagust.

Ooshiya-Lion appeared beside Mary, along with Taurus.

"What have you done, and why have you stopped time..?!" Mary asked, as she had realised what had happened.

"We have to go…!!" he urged quickly.

"GO…?!! What do you mean…? Go where…and why…?!"

Ooshiya-Lion looked at Vagust and raised his eyebrows. The look on Vagust's face, suddenly changed, and he looked helplessly at Mary. Then to her utmost surprise, he knelt before her; and looked up at her, pleadingly, with that same look in his eyes from only moments before.

Ooshiya-Lion looked down at the man kneeling before Mary.

"We don't have much time – QUICKLY…!!" Ooshiya-Lion urged.

Mary was looking from one to the other, hopelessly.

"Mary" Vagust caught her attention, and spoke in a softer tone than before.

"My deep apologies for the intrusion and my anger towards you, but you must listen carefully. Yes, I am a descendent of the Bishops, but I am not like the rest of them, but I live under a lie. My cousin Moroi will be here any minute, and he will NOT spare you. His Mother is a vampire, and he is merciless. My Father and his Father were brothers, but we have led different paths. I have waited for many years, and lived for this moment, as I knew it was coming to pass. My wife Dreegar and my young son are taking shelter not too far away. I cannot go back to the ways of the Bishops, but please, if you spare me and my family, I will serve you and be your personal protector, always…. Please Mary…!!"

He caught hold of both of Mary's hands, but Mary withdrew them immediately. He looked up at her and then across at Ooshiya-Lion, hopefully.

The old man stepped forward.

"Vagust, you have been brave for many a year. I was not aware of your existence, but I have had word back from the tree folk and the wise men of the forest that your word is honourable"

Ooshiya-Lion turned to Mary and said.

"This fight is not yours Mary, leave it to us – it is dangerous"

"Oh yes it IS my fight, and I will NOT..!" she said defiantly.

"You MUST…! THERE IS NO TIME TO ARGUE WITH ME…!!" he bellowed. Mary had not seen him this angry before.
"My job, as everyone else's – is to 'protect' YOU Mary..!! YOUR job is to get us through that door…!! There will be many situations that you have still yet to handle – but THIS is not one of them…!! Vagust, your family are been brought to you as we speak. The fox is taking care of that. Now GO, and take Mary with you, into the cottage – and be ready…!!!"

"…b….but Ooshiya-Lion…..no….I can't do this, I HAVE to help…!!" Mary said in exasperation.

"GO…!!" he shouted. Vagust took Mary's arm and quickly led her into the cottage.

Ooshiya-Lion stood outside, his cloak blowing in the wind which Mary had summoned through her anger. He tapped his watch, and time resumed. He had needed those few precious moments to address Vagust. Mary watched hopelessly from the kitchen window; as her bewilderment, frustration and anger worsened. Vagust stood behind her, looking equally as worried. Suddenly, the Fox appeared in the kitchen, along with a woman, who was holding the hand of a small child.

"Dreegar, my love….!!" Vagust ran to his wife, and held them both close.

"Papa…!" cried the little boy.

"It's alright Ivan, you are safe..!"

Henry, Patsy, Wilbur and Elma stood trembling in the corner on the window ledge.
Mary looked over at them and said.

"Henry, it's all going to be ok, but we need everybody here from the garden, and I want you all to stand over there by the wooden door..!"

"Leave that to me Mary…!" the fox interrupted.

Henry spoke up.

"They don't know who you are. I will have to go with you". He said, as he flew over to the fox.

The fox nodded in agreement, looked at Vagust and said.

"Vagust, you stay here with Mary and your family, and don't leave this room, and keep away from the window..!!"

The fox vanished with Henry. The others made their way to the wooden door, which was still glowing red.

Outside, Ooshiya-Lion was stood – waiting, then looked down at his watch – it was 12am.

Immediately after Ooshiya-Lion had resumed time, one of the dark figures on the broomsticks spoke out.

"Where is Vagust…?!!"

There was another loud bang – similar to before.

Something large and dark had appeared at the side of the three remaining warlocks on their broomsticks, who had now suddenly began to move once more, hovering, with their cloaks blowing in the strong wind.

A huge winged creature that looked like a Dragon, but had only two legs, landed on the ground. It had a long serpent's tail. Ooshiya-Lion knew straight away that this was a Wyvern, a creature whose tail held venomous poison. Someone was sat on the Wyvern's back, holding its reins

"Where is my cousin Vagust…?!!" the voice from the Wyvern shouted. He had a Transylvanian accent. It was Moroi.

"He is gone, never to return. LEAVE – NOW…!!" Ooshiya-Lion shouted.

"Where is he…??!!" Moroi shouted. "I have come to claim what is rightfully mine Wizard; now get out of my way…!! ….and where is 'she', where is the Le Fey girl. I want to see her, just once, before I kill her..!!"

Mary, without thinking, ran for the door, but was suddenly held back by a strong force. Vagust had put her in a holding spell. She tried to struggle against the resistance, but she couldn't move. Her anger and frustration rose to the surface like boiling water. She screamed and broke free from the invisible resistance spell.
Shocked - Vagust tried once again as he held his arm out towards Mary, but in that split second, she had reached for her wand, and pointed it straight at him.

"Duratus..!" she shouted. Vagust had frozen to the spot.

Dreegar and her son ran to him, crying.

"Why..?!" she cried. "He's trying to help you..!!"

Mary ran outside. The fox had come back with everyone, and they were all stood by the big oak door – trembling. The fox then followed Mary, but stayed in the shadows.

"GET BACK INSIDE…!!" Ooshiya-Lion shouted when he saw Mary.

"Ahhh…there you are….!!" Shouted Moroi.

Suddenly Ooshiya-Lion whistled very faintly and a shrill sound left his lips. The tall Oreads quickly rose above the fence and hovered, all with swords and shields. Some of the Satyrs jumped over from the back wall, and stood guard, armed. In the same moment, more hooded figures on broomsticks, and small winged creatures materialized in the air.

"Kill them all....!!" Moroi shouted, laughing wildly, as he raised his arm, and slammed it down, as he looked directly at Mary. His eyes seemed to glow a strange yellow as he held her stare.

A battle began as they all came together. Some of the Satyrs had left their posts from the front of the cottage, and had now arrived at the back, as the fight broke out. Mary had her wand at the ready, but Moroi had his sights firmly set on Mary. In an instance, he had slithered very quickly, and was at Mary's side within a split second, but she had already put her hand into her pocket and held the crystals. A white glow suddenly encased her, like a swirling fog. She saw Moroi close up as he stood inches from her face. This gave Mary enough time to look at him closely.

His eyes were indeed evil, and a strange yellow. He had short black hair, which was sleeked back, and very pale skin. His lips were dark and there was a faint colour of red around his eyes, and she noticed his fangs, as he smiled sarcastically. Mary felt totally protected by the crystals, but she didn't want to hide behind them, she wanted to fight.

Ooshiya-Lion in that moment had come to Mary's aid, but Moroi, in a split second, and without even looking sideways, put his arm out, and had grabbed Ooshiya-Lion around the neck. He was holding the old man in a choke hold, as he continued to grin at Mary, tilting his head to one side. His strength was one of ten men, as he picked him up with his gnarled white hand, which had incredibly long talon-like fingernails. Ooshiya-Lion was already struggling to breathe as he tried to free himself from Moroi's clutches; but before he had time to reach for his wand - his arms fell limp at his side.

Mary's anger rose quickly, as she looked sideways at Ooshiya-Lion suspended in mid-air, with his head flopped forward. Her eyes came back to Moroi's stare, and she too glared at him. The weather had now turned stormy, the rain was lashing down, and the wind was forceful; but as the weather worsened, the more stronger and confident Mary became. The weather was her strength, as was the love she had for her family, her home, and her loved ones. Mary's eyes bore into his, as her hair whipped up and blew wildly.

"THIS IS MY HOME….!!" she shouted at Moroi, who was still staring back at her, looking quite impressed.

Taurus, at that moment, had lunged forward at Moroi with his horns, which made Moroi lose his grip on Ooshiya-Lion's neck. The old man fell to the ground. Taurus had sunk his horns into Moroi's side. Moroi turned around quickly and slashed Taurus with his talons, gouging and tearing his flesh on his abdomen. Taurus fell clutching his side.

Mary, seeing the old man on the floor, and now Taurus, both hurt and wounded, she dropped the crystals into her pocket, and the encasing protecting fog left her. She glared at Moroi.

With all her anger, she opened her mouth and screamed. The blast of the noise made those who were battling; drop their weapons and clutch their ears. Moroi, who wasn't expecting this, was suddenly catapulted backwards, right across the garden. His back slammed into the hedging, and through to the garden wall, and he dropped down, stunned, momentarily.

Mary bent down to Ooshiya-Lion.

"Are you alright….?! Speak to me…!!" then turned to Taurus. "Taurus…??!"

In a flash, Moroi had recovered himself, and he flew directly over to Mary, obviously enraged, and his mouth wide open, showing his fangs, and his hands held out to strangle her. Mary, remembering her necklace, grasped hold of it, and immediately vanished. She had blended into the tree she was stood next to and Moroi couldn't see her. He almost collided with the tree, and she could see that he had just been about to sink his fangs into her…!!

Mary could see from her hidden shelter that the Oreads and the Satyrs were fighting the onslaught of many ugly looking demons and strange looking creatures. The Wyvern was thrashing its poisonous tail about, and Mary realised that this battle could go on for hours, and there could be many casualties, but thankfully back up had arrived from the forest. Many of the tree folk, like the wood nymphs, dryads, more satyrs, fairies, foxes, hares and owls had descended into the garden.

As Moroi was trying to find Mary, he suddenly caught sight of the back door of the cottage, and casually started to walk towards it, head down, and his evil eyes fixated on the door, and grinning. Mary saw him. She knew she had to stop him from being able to just walk straight in.

"NOOOO…!!" she shouted, as she ran quickly away from the tree, to run towards Moroi. She wasn't going to let him get into that cottage if it was the last thing that she did. She stopped and outstretched her arm. Moroi left the ground, and she had him suspended in the air. He laughed down at her, as she turned him around to face her.

"AAH…!!" he shouted "So there you are….!! Now what are you going to do…??!!" He laughed wickedly as he looked down upon her.

Suddenly, loud screeching noises could be heard above the rain and wind.
In the night sky, hundreds of winged creatures were flying towards the cottage……

Mary looked wildly over her shoulder as she held Moroi suspended; at the swarm of creatures in the distance, getting nearer and nearer.

"Ah, just in time….!!" Moroi shouted. He was thoroughly enjoying this.

The fox had been skulking in the shadows all of the time, watching the whole fight. He had run along the side wall, towards the cottage door, when he had seen Moroi striding towards it.

As Mary swung around to face Moroi, her temper and frustration had got the better of her. A surge in the pit of her stomach got stronger and stronger, and she couldn't control it…..

In that split second, a huge gust of wind and a flapping noise could be heard above. Mary looked up, and there - was Beruc the Dragon. In-between each of his scales and around his entire body; a glowing fiery red colour could be seen. His head was arched forward, and he was looking straight down at Mary. Both Moroi and Mary froze. Beruc opened his mouth, and Mary put her arm up to shield the heat coming from the Dragon. If Mary was going to die – it would be now. She was just about to reach into her pocket for her wand, when a huge blast of fire came hurtling from his mouth – and right over the top of Mary's head. Like a hosepipe full of water, Beruc reigned torrents of fire onto the demons and creatures below him, and even onto the surprised Wyvern. Mary was motionless and shocked in that split second. She looked down to the ground and saw that Taurus was helping Ooshiya-Lion to his feet, who thankfully had come round, and was now breathing.

The Dragon stopped hurtling fire towards the enemy for a moment, looked down at Mary and shouted

"Just KILL him Mary…do what you have to do….!!!" and looked at Moroi.

Just then, the winged beasts had arrived.

"NOW…!!" ordered Beruc. He turned back to the creatures that had just landed in the garden, and the ones which were still in the air, and resumed his fire breathing, and scorching everything in sight.

Mary, shocked at the arrival of a Dragon, looked at Moroi, who had also been shocked by Beruc's appearance. She looked down at her wand, and knew instinctively what she had to do. She looked back up at him, as he was still suspended in the air, and a smile suddenly appeared on her face. The surge of power she had just felt was still there – she just needed to channel it…!

As Moroi saw her face, he got out his wand, and glared at her, grinning.

He flung his arm out to one side, and the spell knocked Mary over onto the ground, which made her lose her concentration, and Moroi slowly came to land on the ground. He strode over to her, as Mary was trying to recover herself from the floor, but had dropped her wand. Moroi's foot stamped on Marys arm, stopping her from recovering her wand. He bent down to pick it up.

"Strange design, and well-crafted…." No sooner had the words left his mouth; the wand in his hand began to glow a bright golden yellow, and began to burn into Moroi's hand. As he screamed out and tried to drop the wand, it didn't leave his hand, and continued burning into it, which was now oozing with blood.

Suddenly, out of nowhere, Bam Bam appeared.

"Mary, use me to strike him…..you know where the weakness of a Vampires is…. DO IT NOW…!!" Bam Bam shouted.

He wanted Mary to plunge the end of his stick into Moroi's chest. Mary somehow knew that if she did this, Bam Bam would most certainly die……but her own wand already had the blood of Moroi on it.

Moroi's mad laughter rang out loud, as his hand was being scorched by Mary's wand.

As Mary quickly looked around her, everything went into slow motion, and she was able to capture every ugly scene that was evolving in front of her. Ooshiya-Lion had recovered himself, and was helping Beruc fight all the winged serpents that had descended, flashing his wand time and time again as spells tore out and blasted the creatures which were materializing every few seconds. Taurus had got up and was holding his side and slaying as many as he could.

The Oreads and the Satyrs who were still standing guard, as they tried to protect any entry in through the wall and the hedges, as they fought off dozens of small ugly creatures who were trying to get in. There were Trows, Hobgoblins and Lizard-Folk trying to fight their way through the white ethereal fog that surrounded the Oreads. The Satyrs, with heads down, were bulldozing their horns and gouging anything that came near, while some were using their sling shots and firing arrows from their bows, at the many ugly creatures that had come flying through the air, and descended on the ground, and who were all instructed to get into the cottage at any cost.

In the cottage, Vagust's frozen state had only lasted a few moments, and he was guarding the back door to the cottage after telling his wife and son to hide under the table. Tufri the bat had placed an invisible spell on the chimneys to stop any creature flying down and into the loft. The Satyrs at the front of the cottage were putting up a fight with all the creatures that were just appearing out of nowhere.

The battle was raging on and on around them, as Mary had to make her decision, and fast.

Moroi's hand was badly burnt from Mary's wand. This wand had strong magic indeed. His hand had turned black, which was now rising up his arm slowly. The wand suddenly released itself from Moroi's hand, and Mary picked it up, and stood her ground.

Her anger had now got the better of her, after witnessing the carnage going on around the cottage, which had once, only hours before, been a beautiful happy and sunny day. The storm was now at its peak as thunder and lightning raged above them as Mary gained more strength. A thick swirl of dark angry clouds began to form above her, like a cyclone, picking up rain and lightning, and growing in strength, like a black hole.

Moroi held his arm tightly with his other hand, trying to stop the blackness travelling up any further, but the badness was rising. He suddenly let go, and outstretched his hand with his talons pointing at Mary, laughing wildly, like he had gone mad.

Mary's eyes changed to white, as she dipped them down, and then back up to glare at Moroi.
A fleeting panic came over Moroi's face, as he watched the change in Mary.

"WELL…??!!" Mary shouted at Moroi - her voice suddenly sounding thunderous. "WHAT ARE YOU WAITING FOR…??!!"

As Mary waited for Moroi; an image of her little baby brother, Edward, came into her head. She channelled her thoughts, and before Moroi could do anything, Mary had transported herself forward towards Moroi in a split second; and as she got to him, in a flash, she plunged her wand right through his heart…..

Like all vampires, that was the only way to kill him….as she let out an almighty scream. Her face turned pale, and you could see every blood vessel as her skin became translucent.

Momentarily, everyone felt immense pain in their ears as the decibels rang out. Moroi fell backwards onto the ground. His skin started peeling back from his face, and he looked up at her with a frightened stare. She glared down at him with such anger and venom.

He took one last look at Mary, with those evil yellow eyes, as Mary pushed her wand a little deeper into Moroi's chest until she could feel the ground beneath.

As the light from his eyes slowly faded, the wind above began to die down, his body quickly turned black, and then to dust. A quick breeze appeared and whipped the dust up into a small ball, and carried it away. Mary's wand was left stuck in the ground. She bent down to pick it up.

Some of the creatures, on seeing Moroi fall, began to flee or vanish. Others, including the winged creatures were still fighting on.

Then she heard Henry's voice from the kitchen window.

"Mary, the door...!! The red light is fading – hurry...!!"

Beruc turned to Mary from the air and shouted.

"Mary, the door, you must go NOW...!! Otherwise, before we know it, there will be a lot more creatures and winged beasts on their way...!! NOW HURRY...!!

Taurus had taken Ooshiya-Lion inside the cottage. Mary could see flashing red lights flickering on and off from the kitchen. She looked back at the Satyrs and the Oreads.

"I can't thank you enough.....all of you..!!" she shouted.

"Mary, the door.....NOW..!!" Beruc bellowed.

Mary ran inside, and said to Vagust as she quickly brushed past him.
"I'm so sorry, I know you were trying to help...!!"

She turned to face the door, and walked up to it. It looked like the light was finally going out. She put both her hands onto the door, and felt the familiar surge she got from it. She closed her eyes fleetingly, got out her wand, and put the tip of the wand onto the door. Suddenly, it felt like the wand and the door connected.

Everyone was stood around – watching; with their tired tear stained bloody faces.

"Hurry Mary…." A weak Ooshiya-Lion said, as Taurus held him.

She opened her eyes, and tears streamed down her face. Not knowing what was going to happen next, or from thereon in, Mary spoke to the door, through her tears…


The time is here……and now here I stand,
Where  you, have stood waiting…….for me.

I thank you for your loyalty, as I call upon you now.
Oh listen and hear me, great Oak tree.

If the one that I have chosen, is the one that you need,
Then let us all pass through - with wonder.

The one that comes to mind, I have treasured all my life,
And more than ever…….is my favourite number….


Mary took a deep breath in, and then said….


"Please open your door…………. **Number 24**….."


There were suddenly lots of noises, like bolts being pulled back, and keys unlocking in key holes.
All the wooden figures on the door were dancing. The Hares were jumping about, the Owls and Bats where flying and fluttering around. The moons and the stars were all twinkling. The red light was starting to flicker, as if it was

going to go out, but then a shaft of white light shone out so brightly around the edge of the door, that everyone shielded their eyes. Mary stood back. Everyone seemed like they were holding their breath, as they all stood, and waited.

Then with a loud creaky whine, the door opened, but outwards. All that could be seen was the bright white light. Mary didn't move, she just stared and looked forward.

Ooshiya-Lion slowly walked up to her....

"You did it Mary" he said as he put his hand on her shoulder.
 Then he whispered in her ear.

"You need to walk through first – go...." as he gave her a little nudge to start walking.

Mary looked back at everyone, then turned to the white light, and began to slowly walk through. The white light dazzled around her as she stepped further into it. She turned around, and beckoned to the rest of them. Each of them in turn, all slowly made their way through into the bright light.....

The loud creak of the door could be heard, and it banged shut.


They were plunged into darkness........

.

Printed in Great Britain
by Amazon

63320623R00231